TO THUNDEROUS APPLAUSE

Also by Keith C. Blackmore

Mountain Man
Mountain Man
Safari
Hellifax
Well Fed
Make Me King
Mindless
Skull Road
Mountain Man Prequel
Mountain Man 2nd Prequel: Them Early Days
The Hospital: A Mountain Man Story
Mountain Man Omnibus: Books 1–3

131 Days
131 Days
House of Pain
Spikes and Edges
About the Blood
To Thunderous Applause
131 Days Omnibus: Books 1–3

Breeds
Breeds
Breeds 2
Breeds 3
Breeds: The Complete Trilogy

Isosceles Moon
Isosceles Moon
Isosceles Moon 2

The Bear That Fell from the Stars
Bones and Needles
Cauldron Gristle
Flight of the Cookie Dough Mansion
The Majestic 311
The Missing Boatman
Private Property
The Troll Hunter
White Sands, Red Steel

131 DAYS

BOOK 5

TO THUNDEROUS APPLAUSE

KEITH C. BLACKMORE

Podium

All rights reserved. No part of this publication may be reproduced, stored in a retrieval system, or transmitted in any form or by any means electronic, mechanical, photocopying, recording, or otherwise without prior written permission from Podium Publishing.

This is a work of fiction. Names, characters, places, and incidents are either products of the author's imagination or used fictitiously. Any resemblance to actual events, locales, or persons, living, dead, or undead, is entirely coincidental.

Copyright © 2018 by Keith C. Blackmore

Cover design by Karri Klawiter

ISBN: 978-1-0394-8354-5

Published in 2024 by Podium Publishing
www.podiumentertainment.com

TO
THUNDEROUS
APPLAUSE

1

Nordish Front

The Second Klaw moved.

    The army group, composed of Sujins, Lancers, regular horsemen, spearmen, and archers, marched southwest, traversing the moist evergreen tangles of the lower Hrand. The sun cracked the towering forest heights and stabbed the earth with dreamy tethers. The woodland brimmed with humidity thick enough to chew. Every now and again, a breeze, carrying the smell of hidden brooks, would pass through those cluttered emerald halls of light and shadow. That scent tantalized a fortunate few, giving them a moment's respite from the surrounding morass of sweating, unwashed bodies and animal offal clinging to the armed force. Mud and soft earth squished underfoot, slowing the army five thousand strong. The tradespeople and wagons containing supplies necessary for maintaining that sizeable force lagged behind, their progress hindered by dips and ruts in the earth, natural pitfalls that attempted to swallow feet, hooves, and wheels whole. The creaking of timbers and leather, the trudging of boots, the labored breathing of horses, and the low noise of armored bodies pressing forward drowned out all other sound, except for the odd shout and curse that cut through the forest.

Those occasional notes worried Lancer Right Koor Tubrius. The Klaw was moving at best speed, resulting in a racket anyway, but it was also war time. The Nordish would hear them long before they saw them.

So he grimaced at the mouthy, two-legged ass whistles as they squealed in rage farther down the line, secretly hoping an enemy arrow might find its mark. Tubrius rode a large brown gelding of some fifteen hands, and his animal sank and righted itself as it struggled along the uneven forest floor. Even with a good saddle, the lurching and dipping was unpleasant for the officer, and several times he leaned back sharply to prevent himself from falling forward. He hoped his animal didn't come up lame from the treacherous ground. Thoughts of his mother and aunt back in the city of Sunja flittered across his mind then. No doubt they were in their shared kitchen, window open, baking fresh bread while the smell of it filled the house. They would not be impressed with him in the least if they knew the hardships his horse had to endure. Truth be known, if he'd understood the reality of war on the front, Tubrius would not have answered the call but remained home with those two dear ladies.

He peered ahead, seeing nothing more than the backs of a broad procession of Lancers. His own command of fifty riders rode in a ragged formation around and behind him. The column worked its way through the wooded depths, at times flowing around huge trees. The Second Klaw followed a flattened path left by the Third, but Tubrius didn't think the army had traveled it for a good long time. Every now and then, he looked around, over the shoulders of his Lancers, eyeing the dense underbrush.

His frame tingled, gently alerting him of danger.

It was a feeling Tubrius had grown to trust.

A yellow flag from the column's head signaled a halt. A thousand-plus horses slowed to a stop, and the trailing foot divisions followed. Tubrius reined in his animal, glancing around yet again at the surrounding foliage. The Hrand was an old forest. Ancient. Back when the world was young, Paw Savages were said to have once populated the woodland, before the Sunjan clans beat them back into what was currently known as Paw Savage territory, far to the west. The Nords, in their relentless onslaught, had pushed past that place and advanced well into Sunjan lands, cutting off all access to those wild tribes.

That was, perhaps, the one good thing about the Nords being so deep in Sunjan territory. The Paw Savages could strike at *their* lines for a change.

But the untamed tribes of the Paw weren't the only danger of the Hrand. Plenty of people had disappeared within the woods. The most recent story came from the king's palace itself, where an armed force of Sujins, Lancers, and even fabled Axemen had vanished somewhere up north, devoured by spectres, it was whispered.

Spectres.

The notion brought a frown to Tubrius's unshaven face.

No ghosts inhabited these woods. *Trolls* perhaps. Even ogres. But nothing that might challenge and dispose of a group composed of seasoned officers and battle-tested Sujins. Tubrius didn't remember the exact purpose of the missing force, but rumors were spread of vast sums of gold and jewelry being transported abroad, to sway Marrn into sending aid to Sunja. The entire expedition was even led by a pair of Cavaliers, one of them a right and proper hellion called Bloor.

Tubrius and a few other officers believed the Jackals had stumbled upon the escort and killed the entire lot, probably while they were sleeping. The very thought turned his guts.

A second flag rose, a blue one, or so Tubrius assumed, as the riders ahead of him began dismounting.

He did not.

"Malos," he said, eyeing the bright streamers of light all the way back to the forest ceiling.

"Sar?" asked the nearby Koor serving under him.

"Keep the lads in line, will you?"

"Sar."

With that, the Right Koor urged his horse to the column's edge and then rode toward the front.

There the commander waited.

Tubrius trotted past the hundreds of Lancers and regular horsemen, noting their lowered visors and sheathed weapons. In the spotty light, mail shirts and barding gleamed. Shadow dappled metal scales. Some men turned their backs and checked their horses while others faced the forest, watching the hollows with wary eyes. Tubrius rode by them all.

The smell of water hooked his attention as he drew closer to the column's head.

The trees pulled back, and the foliage overhead thinned, brightening the land. Mosquitos and other bugs drizzled the air in hateful clouds. A river came into view, the surface gilded by the sun. Speckled rock of various sizes and slabs filled the lower section. The current wasn't strong, but a soft rush of moving water was pleasing to the ears. Horses lowered their heads, their tails swishing, while their riders let them drink. A good many had access to the river, but another good many were left waiting. Tubrius's gelding snorted, well aware of the water and the possibility of a drink, but the Right Koor didn't stop just yet. The soft ground receded underfoot, becoming white rock. On the other side of the river, forward Lancers patrolled.

Tubrius located Jusek, Commander of the Second Klaw, farther up the shore. Jusek stood and conversed with other officers while their warhorses drank. The officer was an older man, perhaps in his fifties, with a narrow, clean-shaven chin and pale, wispy hair. His complexion and eyes were both a haunting gray, as if he'd witnessed a truly terrifying spectacle. The man's armor shone like wet stone, and a huge broadsword hung from his side.

As Tubrius drew closer, the clicking of hooves on rock distracted the commander and the gathered Koors.

"Lord Jusek," Tubrius said, remaining on his horse.

"Tubrius," Jusek said in a calming, gravelly voice.

The others acknowledged the Right Koor with respectful nods.

"Pretty place for a rest," Tubrius commented.

"I thought so," the commander agreed. "Glad you approve. Won't you join us?"

Tubrius dismounted and let his horse wander to the water. A mosquito hovered before his face before he waved it away.

"Just telling the lads here," Jusek said, "there's trolls in these parts."

Tubrius winced inwardly. All he needed was the commander telling stories of monsters.

"Huge things," Jusek continued. "Eight feet tall or more."

"They wouldn't come at us, would they?" asked a bearded Koor called Saros.

"They might. There isn't much they're afraid of. Especially when they're hungry. Though, truth be known, I'd be surprised if they did try and take a bite from all of this."

"I haven't heard tell of a troll in years."

"They're about," the commander assured his Koor. "I've seen two in my lifetime. Actually smelled them. Well before my father and I spotted the monsters. Still as stone. A man could walk right by them in the forest and not even know it. Not until they grabbed you. Be too late then, of course. Not nearly as numerous now compared to back then, but . . . they're about."

The assembled officers glanced about uneasily.

Satisfied that he'd unnerved his subordinates, Jusek fixed his attention on Tubrius. "You didn't see Bovello back there?"

"No, I did not, sar."

"And you didn't wait for him." It wasn't a question.

"I did not," Tubrius answered. He didn't like the Sujin Right Koor, and the man didn't like him. Bovello didn't like any of the Lancers, in fact. The other infantry officers were decent enough fellows, professional enough to put aside pride when it mattered, but not Bovello. The lad could be a sore and bleeding dog blossom on the best of days.

Jusek stroked his chin, warning Tubrius with a look to watch his tongue when the Sujin arrived. Tubrius looked down the line of Lancers and regular horsemen waiting for their turn at the river, but he couldn't see the Koor.

"Cavaliers are gone on ahead," the commander said, gesturing to the river. "See if they can spot any sign. Scouts say the area's clear, but Pakal is careful. Prefers to do the work himself. As he should be."

No one said anything to that.

"I fished streams like this when I was a boy," Jusek revealed, changing the subject. "Fish to here"—he placed a hand midway up his outstretched arm. "Monsters themselves. Pink to the bone and a pleasure to eat. A shame we don't have more time."

It is a shame, Tubrius thought, glancing at the nearby shallows.

"That was a long time ago," Jusek said. "And the Nords were much farther north. No chance of an ambush then."

That drew the attention of the gathered officers.

"They're close," Jusek stated grimly. "You know that. We wouldn't be moving to reinforce the Third if they weren't. Just keep doing what you're doing. Stay vigilant. Assume they're watching us this very instant, figuring on the best place to strike. Just a nibble, mind you, but enough to let us know they're about. I wonder just how many. A pack of Jackals or a small army. I think they're getting ready to face the Third. Or whatever's left of it."

Not two weeks earlier, while guarding the Hrand's western front against Nordish incursions, the Third Klaw had been struck at night—struck very hard, indeed.

Five days later, a single messenger, the lone survivor of five, arrived at the more northwesterly encampment of the Second Klaw, expressing the Third's request for reinforcements. The word had been grim. A sizeable force of Jackals had attacked and inflicted considerable casualties before being driven off. Commander Ronus suspected that the Jackals might have belonged to the Nordish Ikull. He believed the enemy army could very well be lurking nearby, perhaps only days away from the Third's encampment, heralding a considerable confrontation—one that required the Second to attend.

After dispatching messengers informing King Juhn of his intention to travel to the aid of the Third, Jusek mobilized the entire Second and marched hard to the southwest. That decision wasn't easy, as doing so would leave the northwestern front undefended all the way to Sunja's walls.

But leaving the Third to the mercy of the Nords was unthinkable.

"These trails are old," one of the Lancer Koors said.

"These trails," Jusek explained, "were marked by our own engineers. A map is flat. The land isn't. Regardless, they marked the quickest path to each front just in case a Klaw had to do what we're doing right now. Just be thankful we're not marching up the side of a mountain somewhere or having to cross a much wider river. Or worse."

Tubrius was thankful. These trails, such as they were, were laid out like a web ruined by a windstorm, far and away from the more populated routes used by traders and travelers. The Klaws facing Nordun were spaced apart by days, but if needed, one could march to the other's aid by these very paths.

One of Jusek's aides handed him a water bag. The commander drank, and when he finished, he handed the bag back and looked around. "Speed. Stealth. That was the thinking behind all of this. To travel over great distances in the fastest time possible. Arriving relatively fresh and ready to fight."

No one commented.

"That was the thinking, anyway," Jusek said, distracted by other thoughts.

"How far away are we from the Third, sar?" asked a tall, bearded Lancer Koor.

"Five days."

The frowns deepened at that, and gazes flicked about.

"We'll do it in three," the commander said with grim assurance. "If Ronus is right, and the Nordish Ikull is facing them, then we'll make our own history. Our own Field of Skulls. Have no doubt the Nords are every bit as tired of this war as we are. Time to finish it."

Just then, a man approached, encased in gloomy mail with slabs of iron strapped to his torso. He was tall, just a few fingers higher than Tubrius, and broad across the shoulders. An impressive broadsword hung from the man's waist. Somehow, the Sujin Right Koor managed to keep most of his face shaved except for a thin tail hanging off his chin.

Tubrius thought the style looked ridiculous.

"Bovello," Jusek greeted the arriving Right Koor.

The officer dipped his head in greeting. "Thought I smelled water," Bovello remarked and glanced at the horses. "Loading them up so they can piss it all out later?"

Jusek frowned at the jab. The Sujin was starting early.

"Apologies, sar," Bovello said. "It's the heat. Makes me brazen."

"How're the lads?" the commander asked.

"In better shape than what I saw walking here," Bovello answered and looked at the Lancers. "You ladies don't even have to walk, and you still look like the shite clankers hanging off a sheep's blossom. Apologies again, sar," he directed at Jusek. "Heat and all."

"Enough of that gurry, Bovello," Jusek warned, with just enough edge to his tone to remind the Koor he was one of those ladies himself.

"Water looks lovely," the Sujin muttered. "Don't suppose my lads will get a sip?"

"That's enough, Koor," Jusek ordered.

"Apologies, sar, apologies. As I mentioned . . ." *The heat*, he left unsaid.

Jusek changed the subject. "Your lads are keeping up?"

"Keeping up, sar. Keeping up. No worries there."

"Good. Now that you're here, I'll get on with it. We'll rest for a short time. Move along the river's edge, and cross over a little further up. Keep moving until sundown, whereupon we'll sleep wherever we are. Understood?"

Everyone nodded even though no one wanted to sleep on unfamiliar ground with the danger of Nords running about.

"We'll rise before dawn," the commander continued, "eat, squat, march, and do it all again. Understood?"

More nods.

"Good."

"Ah," Bovello started, drawing attention, "forgive me, sar. But as much as I have faith in the Third, aren't we making a mistake here?"

Jusek's expression didn't change. "Go on."

"Only saying my mind, sar."

"Say it then."

"Well . . ." Bovello glanced at Tubrius. "I've been talking to my lads, sar. We discussed things. The potential for things. This. All this. Could all very well be a trap. A very well thought out trap. With the Second down here, there's nothing stopping the Ikull from pushing straight for Sunja."

Jusek stared at the Sujin Koor.

"Just speaking my mind, sar," Bovello said with a roll of his shoulders.

For a while, the commander said nothing. Then, "Bovello. You're something of an unfit ass packer. One that's exceptionally brutal and effective, but an ass packer—common knowledge and nothing you don't already know. My officers generally dislike you simply because you jab their profession. I tolerate you myself because you've managed to stay alive to this point, even with that unfit mouth of yours. You're a fighter—there's no doubt of that. You're Sujin. And I'm thankful you're behind me. But truly, have I failed you yet?"

Bovello's lips twisted before answering. "No sar."

"Your thought about it being a trap has crossed my mind," Jusek allowed. "I believe that this is a gamble we're taking, but the Third's called for us. They believe the Ikull is coming at them, and for that fight, they'll need our support. We've left behind enough scouts to track any Nordish movement from the northwest. If the Nords try and slip by us, we'll hear of it. Then we'll have a footrace. All the way back to Sunja's walls."

That didn't lift the officers' spirits.

"What I want from you, Right Koor," Jusek said to Bovello, "is to ready our *own* packs. Light armor and weapons. Fast runners. Dogs that will pick up a Jackal's scent, track them down, and kill them. Expertly. Quietly. Our Lancers can't leave the paths. The underbrush will hamper the horses. You, however, will be able to get into places where only Jackals go. Understood?"

"Understood, sar." Bovello nodded. The officer glowered at the others and eventually lowered his eyes.

"I've gone over every scenario there is to go over," the commander explained further. "And the course of action is still the same. We were called upon to help. We go to help."

Bovello nodded again and studied his boots.

"Lancers might still be of help, sar," one of the officers offered.

"Not here," Jusek said. "The Jackals would lead them into places where they'd cut them up. They might very well lead our Sujins into those same places, but I'll place coin on our lads every time."

A Lancer rode his horse through the river's lazy flow. A veil of insects clouded the man's features. The Lancer approached the officers and quickly dismounted before Jusek.

"What is it?" the commander asked.

Tubrius looked upriver upon hearing the report.

As he operated far ahead of the Second, where stealth was necessary, the Cavalier called Pakal was outfitted accordingly rather than in full battle armor. A leather cuirass protected his frame, while bracers and greaves covered his limbs. A tight cap of black cloth failed to soak up his sweat, and his cheeks and neck glistened in the undimmed sunlight. There was no shade on this part of the river, just a wide expanse from one verdant shoreline to the other, choked with rocks of varying sizes.

The Cavalier stood upon one of the larger rocks, next to a messenger's dead body, not far from where the Second had stopped. The butchered man lay splayed over a slanted white rock, his bare feet dangling about four fingers from the river's surface. Maroon blots and speckles spattered the stone, as if the messenger had been slammed against it, but that wasn't the case. Blood had flowed like a horrible syrup from the corpse's grisly apertures, all the way to the rock's edge, where it had dripped into the water. Dried gore crusted the chopped sections of the dead man's leather armor. Flies darkened the air, darting around the gray-white carcass.

The officers of the Second arrived at the scene along with twenty Lancers. Jusek dismounted and waded through the shallows, the water churning about his knees. When he reached the corpse, he stopped and frowned at Pakal before bending over and inspecting the dead man.

The head had been cleft down the middle, skewing the nose to one side. The eyes were opened, the whites shriveled. The armor was Sunjan, and Jusek motioned for two of his escort to pull the body up onto his side. They did so, the leather crackling as the blood bonding the corpse to the stone broke. They turned the carcass over. One scout pried back the armor covering a shoulder, revealing three talons etched into pallid flesh.

Jusek gazed upon that marking. After a moment, he nodded at the two men, and they lowered the body back onto the stone mantle.

"One of the Third's messengers," the commander muttered and studied the green shoreline. "One that didn't reach us."

"We haven't found anything else," Pakal reported, his swarthy face shining. "But scouts are still searching farther up the river."

"Keep them in sight," Jusek said and shook his head. "I'm glad I didn't dispatch messengers to the Third. No doubt we'll find others along the way, squeezed for information before being butchered."

"He's been here for days," Pakal said.

"Waiting for someone to find him," Jusek stated and looked at his officers. "Unfortunate bastard. Right. We knew the Jackals were about. Keep the lads in their lines. Open eyes and ears. Steel ready. Pakal?"

"Sar?"

"Get your scouts out there and make certain that these bastards aren't nipping at our flanks."

The Cavalier nodded.

"And have a few push farther ahead," Jusek added. "Daresay it'll be dangerous, so make sure they're vigilant. I want to know the Third is still there. We'll push on at a slower pace until I know what's waiting for us."

"Sar."

"This was meant to frighten us," Jusek said of the dead man decorating the river rock. "The Jackals are farther along than we thought. Or at least they want us to think that."

Tubrius believed. The dead man at his feet convinced him.

"Saros," Jusek said to a nearby koor. "Send word to Sunja. Tell them what we've found. We'll either find the rest along the way or worse, find what's left of the Third. If we're fortunate, we'll find them ready for a war or running for Sunja's walls. If we're unfortunate, they're all dead."

Tubrius studied the trees along the riverbanks. The tops swayed in a warm breeze, and he wondered who might be hiding in the nearby foliage.

And who might be watching.

2

A mop splashed down into a bucket, causing Halm to flinch in his chair. That movement alone caused him a sharp, reprimanding twinge of discomfort. His ribs would take a long time to heal.

"A big man like you afraid of water?" Miji asked the Zhiberian.

Keeping his yellow overlapping shards of teeth tucked away, Halm smiled back, a touch uncertain. His bright blue eyes narrowed in doubt, but the left one, still swollen to epic proportions, became more of a slit. His face hurt when he moved it, sending a warning.

He righted himself on his chair. He looked at the lady of the little alehouse, then the mop bucket, then her again.

"Ah," he said. "But you wiped these floors yesterday."

"So I did," Miji affirmed.

"Sooo . . ." he drew out, eyeing her for understanding.

She waited, not understanding in the least.

"You're going to do it again?" he asked.

"I am."

Halm glanced around the alehouse's sleepy interior, with its rustic log walls, four tables, and an assortment of worn chairs, one of which he currently occupied near the bar. The main door was wide open, as well as every window in the place, allowing daylight to glare through. Thin sheets of netting covered each opening, keeping the bugs out while coloring the world beyond into a gauzy gray. A nice breeze blew off the nearby lake and flowed through, filling the place with fresh air. It was barely midmorning, but Miji wasn't one to wait around for work.

After only a few days in the village, Halm was just starting to realize that.

"But . . ." He indicated the empty room with a tentative hand. "There's no one here."

Miji's thick eyebrows scrunched together in mild puzzlement. "So?"

"There were only two people here last night. They sat over there."

"I remember."

"Two." He held up a pair of fingers—one of which was heavily stitched. "And they only drank a mug each."

"I remember you drank two pitchers."

"To entice them. To drink more. To buy *more*. For you."

"It didn't work."

"Which means there wasn't much to clean last night when we closed the door, good Miji," Halm stressed softly, one hand straying to the bandages looped around his midsection. "There wasn't much to clean yesterday, but we cleaned."

"*I* cleaned," Miji said. "You mostly sat and watched."

"I wiped off the bar. And the mantel."

"That you did. Apologies. And?"

Halm waited, sensing sarcasm now but continuing anyway. "It doesn't need to be cleaned now. It's not dirty."

"My dear Zhiberian," said the woman who'd taken him into her arms and house, the words pleasing to the ears. "This is what I do. Every day. Everything gets cleaned. Everything."

"Even me?" Halm asked, self-consciously keeping his mouth closed.

"If you need to be."

"I need to be. Very much so."

She gave him a saucy frown. "You'd like that."

"I most certainly would. Because I'm a man."

"You're a man held together with a lot of string. And bandages."

"But I'm still a man."

"I like the way you talk."

"So you've said. Many times. Just wait until my face returns."

Miji smiled. Though she was missing her right incisor, her teeth were much better than his own chipped and discolored fangs. He had never been so aware of their poor condition until Miji. And despite the punishment he'd endured at the hands of some exceptionally brutal pit fighters, his teeth somehow remained intact. He supposed he should be thankful.

She indicated the mop's handle. "If you remember, I said there was plenty to do while we were eating breakfast."

The breakfast of bread, cheese, and honey was modest, but it was one that she freely provided and he tentatively enjoyed. The grand swelling on the left side of his face had started to subside, but the deep cuts carved into his chin caused him some discomfort when chewing and even talking.

"You did," he admitted.

"There's always plenty to do around here. Every day, we clean. If we don't clean, the dust will gather. The mice will find their way in and eat the crumbs."

"Then there's less to clean," Halm pointed out.

She chuckled, a sound that pleased him.

"I clean," she said. "You don't need to help me. You're still healing."

"I'm well enough to do something."

"You sure you won't bleed over anything?"

Halm smiled that time, putting pressure on his healing nose, which had been smashed and broken by a savage from the Iron Games, the one called Sibo. Sibo had imparted several reminders of their brief but brutal encounter.

"You shouldn't smile," she pointed out. "It hurts you when you smile."

"Only a little."

"Just watch me if you must. Let me know if anyone enters the alehouse."

That deflated Halm's otherwise good cheer.

Miji sensed it. "All right, if you feel you can do something, take a cloth and wipe down the tables and the chairs. Even the tankards. I think I have to replace one. Oh yes, and the bar. You can shake out the nettings, and if you're still in one piece, replace them with clean ones. Then wash the dirty ones. Slowly."

"You have a sharp wit," he observed.

"I know. There's some supplies I'll need. If you don't mind the walk, maybe I'll send you off with a list. Can you read?"

A twinge of fear lanced him through the chest but didn't reach his face. Even if it had, his features had been bashed about so badly that such emotion would've been difficult to see.

"Can you?" Miji repeated.

Halm didn't answer.

"All right, you can't," she said, guessing the truth. "Perhaps I'll teach you."

His unease became surprise. "You'll teach me how to read?"

"If you're willing. How did you learn the Sunjan language?"

"That's a long story."

"Don't worry, then. I'll teach you. During the day, while we're waiting for customers."

"Ah, I'd prefer your house."

"Here is fine," she said.

The fear returned. He was more self-conscious about his inability to read than his teeth.

"That's later," she said and dropped a hand cloth into the bucket at her feet. She wrung the material out and handed it to Halm. "Now, you clean. And clean it right, or I'll have you do it again."

She headed for the bar. Halm watched her go, admiring how her plain red dress and brown vest matched. He then studied the cloth and the task set before him. With a groan, he got to his feet and lumbered to the nearest table. He wiped down everything Miji had asked him to, resting when needed. His breathing remained shallow, and he wondered if that hellish dew Shan had given him to rub into his hurts was doing anything at all. Still, he finished his chores and felt good about it. The chairs he took particular pride in as he carefully placed them around each table. He chuckled to himself, and his ribs reminded him not to overdo things, but if Pig Knot could see him now, cleaning alehouse tables . . .

Well, jabs would fly like arrows.

Once he was done, taking care not to slip, Halm swapped out the netting hanging around the interior with fresh sheets taken from a wooden box behind the counter. Not a drop of blood seeped from his person, much to his relief, nor did he fall apart. The breeze blowing through the alehouse diminished while the heat increased. By the time he finished with the netting, sweat glazed his hairy hide. That surprised him, but not for long. Miji directed him to take a bucket down to the water's edge, fill it halfway, and bring it back. Then she would show him exactly how to clean the sheer material . . . if he was able.

Halm scoffed. Oh, he was able. Right and proper able. But . . . *Clean the netting? Who cleans their netting?* he puzzled as he labored with the bucket toward the lakeshore. *Do all Sunjans do such a thing?*

At the end of the only wharf, two men prepared one of the three small boats moored there. They lifted wooden boxes into the hold and mulled over smaller items that Halm couldn't quite see. They eventually noticed him watching.

"Lovely day," one of them called out, waving.

"Lovely day," Halm said, beaming, his face locked in a half squint. "What are you doing?"

"Fishing. Lake trout. The size of your forearm."

Halm considered his forearm. *Big fish, indeed.* "Good fortune to you then," he called back and finished his task. He'd only been in the village for a short time, but the people remembered him and had taken a liking to him. They even, dare he say it, *marveled* at the sight of him. They remembered how he'd killed mad Thaimondus and his sons. He recalled how the people had burned the old trainer's residence to the ground, cursing and spitting on the name. They had greeted him with open smiles and approving nods, and Halm found himself enjoying the fame.

When he returned to the alehouse, Miji was waiting. She showed him how to wash the netting, then she showed how to hang it just so, from a line outside, hitched from one corner of the building to a pole some twenty strides away. Once that was done to her satisfaction, she took him back inside and directed him to clean the fireplace mantel with a wet cloth. Wood would be needed for the night, but she'd have to do that task herself.

"I can lift a junk or two of wood." Halm said.

"You'll burst at the seams if you bend over," she warned him. "Remind me to check those bandages after your reading lesson."

Reading lesson. That made him smile again, and *that* made his face throb.

"What are you going to do?" he asked her. "While I'm cleaning."

"Cleaning," she said.

That surprised him. "Cleaning *what*? What's left?"

She didn't answer.

Just after noon, well after Halm had done everything Miji had asked him to do, he sat and waited at a table. Miji had disappeared inside the kitchen, which he'd glimpsed but not fully explored.

She returned a short time later with a cold roast on a platter, along with some neatly sliced fruit. A pitcher and a pair of knives lay beside the food.

Halm reached for the pitcher.

"This is water," he discovered with a sour note.

"Aye that."

"No beer?"

"It's too early for beer," Miji said and sliced the roast.

"Too early for . . ." He sputtered, not bothering to hide his teeth. He placed a hand to his ribs.

Miji offered a slice of beef, balanced on the knife and kept in place by a thumb. He took it and ate. She ate the next one. The wind from the lake blew through the open door, and what looked to be a flying finger buzzed around outside, unable to pass the netting. At times, voices from beyond could be heard, some laughing, some conversational.

"It's quiet here," Halm said upon finishing his food.

"That's the way of it. Ever since you."

"Me?"

"Well, you put down Thaimondus and his brood."

"I did, didn't I?"

There was no more talk about it.

"Are you done?" Miji asked, fixing her hazel eyes upon him.

"I am. That was good. Was that from last night?"

"It was. We have to eat it. I'll cook another tonight, just in case someone wants it."

The wind picked up, blowing hair across her face. She flicked a few strands away. Then she stood and stepped over to his side. She leaned in close and kissed him, lightly, on one corner of the mouth, before finding the rest. That gentle connection sent a lovely shock throughout his person, one that melted all thoughts from the Zhiberian.

"Evil woman," he muttered when she broke away, careful not to reveal how much he enjoyed the kiss. He noticed half a smile before she walked away.

She knew.

Lords above. She had him fish hooked right and proper.

And he liked it.

Much later in the afternoon, well after Halm had finished his chores, he was sitting and waiting, bare chested and brazen, at the same table as before. Miji wandered in from the kitchen and stopped in her tracks.

"I've been wanting to ask," she said. "Where's your shirt?"

"I don't have one," he replied.

"A tunic?"

"Too tight."

Miji placed her back against the bar and studied him. "You go around with one pair of pants, and that's all?"

"I have a second pair. At your house."

She remembered. "Just the two, then."

"Aye that."

"What about in winter?"

"Winter?"

"Yes, winter. When it's cold."

"Oh, I'll buy something then to cover my hide," Halm said. "And throw it away at first sign of spring."

"You throw it away?"

"At first sign of spring."

Miji winced. "Because it's worn out?"

"Aye that. Usually worn out. Or torn. Or something." He lowered his eyes and self-consciously cleared his throat. He picked at a knot in the wood.

"What do you buy? Usually."

"A shirt and coat."

"Each winter."

He nodded.

"And you don't have that now?"

Halm didn't like where this questioning was leading. "Not yet."

That got a chuckle from the woman. "Go to my house and clean yourself, Halm of Zhiberia. I can see I have more work on my hands."

Halm watched her for a dubious moment, not exactly sure what that work was, and wondering if it included him.

So he left her and returned to her house. He cleaned himself in the wash barrel, dipping at the knees when he scrubbed his manly bits and ample crevices. His pants were off, and he felt their dampness from the day's work. He supposed he was due for a bath of sorts, and no public bathhouses were about Karashipa, just water barrels and cleaning cloths. He changed his bandages and checked the stitches where he could, dabbing ointment across the pinched skin. Miji would help him with some of the more serious wrapping. He left his pants in a wash bucket and donned his other pair, which didn't smell fresh in the least. Not dwelling on it, Halm went back to the alehouse, where the lovely scent of roasting meat tantalized him upon entering. Village life had its advantages, he thought, sitting at a table already set with knives, wooden plates, and cups.

Miji stuck her head out the kitchen door and saw him. "That's better," she said.

Halm hoped so. He looked around the empty setting and frowned. Not a living soul. The distinct lack of people visiting the alehouse concerned him.

Miji appeared in the doorway.

She carried supper to their table and loaded up his plate with steaming potatoes, carrots and beans, a gob of what looked to be sweet jelly, and an ample portion of chicken covered in a brown crust and oozing gravy.

"Seddon above," Halm whispered. "How much will this cost me?"

"Nothing." She poured water from a pitcher into his cup. "Except your chores. You like mead?"

He nodded, his attention fixed on the food.

Miji brought another pitcher to the table. "A cup each, but nothing more. Good for the healing."

Halm understood that. She'd explained to him earlier that she couldn't have him guzzling her complete stock as it was for customers, such as it was. She could be generous from time to time, however.

She sat down beside him, and they ate. The woman knew how to prepare a meal, that much he knew. He would've had to pay good coin back in the city or anywhere for such fare. When he finished, she offered him seconds, and he accepted. For the healing, of course.

Once they were done, he leaned back and looked around again. Wood smoke drifted through the place, coming from the nearby houses. Hardly any voices could be heard outside, however, as most people were no doubt eating their own suppers. Halm studied the darkening interior and knew that the fireplace and oil lamps would eventually be lit.

"It's quiet here," he said simply, conscious of his own voice.

"It is," she agreed.

Halm grunted softly.

"You don't like the quiet?" she asked.

"No. No, I like it. Truly." He gripped his cup. "It's just that I'm not used to it. There was always, ah, *noise* in the city. All the time. Well, most of the time. And then there were the smells."

"The smells?"

"City smells. Not always pleasant. Not like here."

"I've been there. Three times. I know the smells you're talking about. This place is better."

"I think so."

Miji smiled. "You think so?"

Halm didn't mean to offend her. "It's just that I'm used to . . . much more."

"Do you think you could get used to it here?" she asked, watching him carefully.

"I think so."

She frowned, but in a playful fashion. "Did you speak to anyone today?"

"A few men at the wharf. No one else."

Miji leaned forward, placing her elbows on the table. "It's a different place here, Halm of Zhiberia. Even more different now that Thaimondus and his sons are gone. I rarely see anyone outside the people of my own village, and when I do see travelers, I listen to their stories of life beyond the trees and the great plains. My parents lived and died here. I'll do the same. Contentedly."

"You don't have any trouble here?"

"Trouble?"

"Bandits? Dezer? Troublesome ass lickers?"

That last one summoned a smile to Miji's face. "No. None except Thaimondus and his sons. And the cutthroats with them. And if there was any trouble—say, the Nords finally got through to us—then we'd run inside the palisade surrounding that old bastard's house. Or where his house once stood."

"Thieves?" Halm asked.

"Thieves?" Miji's smile widened. "There's barely a hundred people in this village. My home is across the way, and I can see my front door from the kitchen window here. If I was outside, all I need do is look around a corner, and I can see my house. There're no thieves here. Not anymore. You and your lot killed them."

"And if the Nords did come here? And you were all forced inside that palisade?"

"We have a small armory," she assured him.

"Oh, you do?" he asked, keeping his face neutral.

"Yes. Spears and bows mostly, but they'll do well enough, I expect."

Halm kept his mouth shut.

"Some of the menfolk are quite good with a bow. They're not champion archers now, but they can bring down birds and deer well enough."

"That's all you need, then."

She looked squarely at him. "Was that a jab?"

"No. Yes . . . Perhaps."

"The people here would fight the Nords. Or anyone else for that matter."

"Like they did with Thaimondus?"

Miji's face froze. "That was different."

Halm frowned. "Apologies. I've upset you."

She remained silent for a bit, then she stood up and walked over to the bar. She reached behind it and brought out a piece of parchment, which she brought back to the table.

"What's this?" Halm asked as she sat.

"Your first lesson."

"Reading?" he squawked.

"Hold on now," she warned and gripped his hand, keeping him in place. "Now, wait," she stressed, smoothing out the parchment. "These are all the Sunjan characters, and see these?"

Halm leaned in. "Pictures."

"To help you remember the sound of each. Say the picture's name, and that first sound's the one you'll need to read. After that, it's just putting them together into complete words."

"You have a bird here," Halm pointed out.

"Yes."

"That's a terrible picture of a bird."

She pinched his hand. "Let's get to work."

"Why are the characters like this?"

"This is the way I had to learn."

"Oh." Halm squinted at the lines and curls and oddly shaped circles. It wasn't his own language, but he couldn't read that one either.

"A mystery," he said, studying the parchment.

"Are you ready?"

He nodded.

So they read, going through the thirty characters belonging to the Sunjan alphabet. It was difficult for him, breaking down the sounds and then remembering, but Miji was patient, focused. She guided him through the scrawls and their sounds, and despite his initial reluctance, Halm found himself actually enjoying the lesson.

And sometime into the evening, when the growing shadows forced Miji to start lighting lamps, he stopped and smelled the air.

Rain.

He shared a look with Miji.

"Rain's coming," she said. "Tonight."

Halm looked toward the door and heard a distant rumble rolling over the waters.

3

The air cooled, breaking the viselike heat clamped about the city of Sunja. Thunderheads crept across the sky, flaring every so often with crackling traceries of light. A godlike thrashing of boulders followed shortly after, causing the populace to stop and gaze fearfully at the angry heavens. The rooftops should have been shining with a glorious evening light, but the black clouds cast a miserable shadow over the streets. Sentries posted along the battlement heights shifted uncomfortably as they eyed a gray wall pouring from the storm clouds' underbelly, a shimmering screen that drifted over the landscape below and erased the world. Hills and forests easily seen on a clear evening disappeared beneath that violent curtain. Lightning flashed deep within the billowing clouds, briefly illuminating the dismal, churning guts of the storm.

That awesome veil of rain and fury crept over the surrounding plains, swallowing the land whole. A darkness that wasn't quite night drew over Sunja. The sky grumbled even more loudly, and the Skarrs flinched behind their tall battlements at both the sound and the drop in temperature. Moisture thickened the air, aching to be released. The smell of rain became stronger as that wall of mist bore down upon the city. A light drizzle soon fell across the visors of the sentries, beading on metal, batting at eyes.

The storm front slunk over the plains, devouring the few twisting roads that led to the city, until the first stinging beads exploded against armor.

City guards and civilians cringed when a sound like a mountain having its spine broken boomed directly overhead.

Heartbeats later, an angry drizzle thickened into an almighty downpour that swept over the ramparts. The Skarrs patrolling there vanished from sight.

"Sweet Seddon above," muttered Salwark of the Stable of Slavol as he looked at his study's ceiling, fearful that the timbers above would collapse at any moment.

The closed shutters rattled from the impact of the storm. Such summer tempests weren't unusual, but that unexpected explosion damn near made him piss his leisure robes, adding yet another embarrassment to the day. He tensed, waiting for another blast and listening to the rain pound the roof. Fresh torches were fixed in their sconces, but the hour seemed far too early to light them even though the chamber had darkened considerably. Concern marred his handsome face, and he laid a hand upon his sandy-blond hair, searching for any dampness. Finding none and sniffing his palm, he lifted a silver goblet, the third drink poured from a decent bottle of wine, and smoothed down the front of his robes.

"Seddon above," the owner's son repeated. He supposed he should check on his ailing father. He'd need more wine for that. He'd need a *lot* more wine for that . . . and perhaps a stab of firewater or two though he didn't really enjoy the drink. He shivered like a wet bird trying to choke down that particular evilness, but he would need more of something to face his father this night.

And tell him that Sorban the Balgothan had perished in the arena, killed by the Free Trained upstart known as Goll.

Salwark sighed, took in the scrolls and bookshelves of his deceased mother's study chamber, and gripped a nearby chair as if steadying himself. In truth, he was fortifying his senses, drinking himself along that narrow precipice of functional fearlessness and being too unfit to speak.

Sorban wasn't the first gladiator to have died under the stable's name, but it was the most unexpected . . . and disappointing. Sorban wanted revenge over the Kree called Goll, who was responsible for killing Baylus the Butcher, another Balgothan and friend to Sorban. Salwark shook his head. Damn them for that. Gladiators befriending each other at any time was a bad idea. He should enact a law to stop such foolishness. What made it worse was Sorban having been so damn promising. The man had been *good*. Worse still was that he was respected and well thought of among this current collection of bone breakers and life takers, and even as the fire pit consumed the Balgothan's remains, Salwark detected a solemnness much greater than usual from the few pit fighters who had accompanied him to the funeral burning.

Even on the trip back to the family grounds, they were quiet.

Salwark finished his drink and poured himself another. News of Sorban's death and defeat had no doubt already circulated throughout the stable, except to his father. That one meeting Salwark wished to delay just a bottle longer.

A knocking on the door interrupted his thoughts.

"Yes, who is it?" he called.

"Master Salwark," a servant said through the wood, obeying the son's wishes that the door not be opened until *he* opened it.

Salwark dipped his head and shook it. "What is it? Didn't I say I didn't want to be disturbed? Didn't I say that no one was to disturb me? Didn't I say that?"

Silence from beyond the door.

"You did, Master Salwark," the man finally answered.

"Then unless it's news about the passing of my father, *leave me alone.*"

More silence.

"Wait!" Salwark yelled in frustration. "Wait. My father's not dead, is he?"

A pause. "Not since I last checked, Master Salwark."

"And he hasn't asked for me?"

"No, Master Salwark."

The owner's son sighed with relief. "Check on him, then. Make sure he's comfortable. Give him anything he wants. Including wine. *Suggest* wine, even. No, wait... Don't even ask. Just bring a bottle to his bedside and leave it there. Understood?"

The drink would help when he finally did confront his father with the unfortunate news.

Sorban, you unfit tit, Salwark fumed, angry at the gladiator for dying so damn *easily*.

"But, Master Salwark—"

"*Go!*" he shrieked. "And don't come back unless my father truly is right and proper gone! Don't come back!"

Silence fell again beyond the door, filled by the torrential rain pummeling the roof and shutters. Salwark calmed himself and returned to drinking. Lords above, how he hated shouting like that. It hurt his throat, not to mention damaging his image of being gentle nobility—or what he thought gentle nobility should be.

He drained his goblet and went for more. He drank half of that and pulled a chair out from the grand table taking up the center of the chamber. Then he plopped down and grimaced at the much-too-solid landing. Cushions had been there at one point in time, but they were presently gone. He snarled at discovering he'd also spilled wine and the only bottle with him was nearly done.

Salwark planted his elbows on the table and covered his face. A deeply troubled sigh warmed his cheeks. Again, he swore on Sorban. The season was ruined. No one in the current roster could replace him. Blacktooth was finished, his ankle smashed. They had Punder, but Salwark doubted the man could defeat the kog who had so easily killed Sorban. Aidas, perhaps, but again Salwark doubted it. Then there was the Marrnite called Zillari. Salwark didn't think he could do it either, but Zillari would certainly give it a go. That one thought he could twist the unsavory bells off Saimon himself and get away with it.

He couldn't think of anyone else who might remotely stand a chance against the Kree.

One good thing, Salwark supposed, peeling his hands away from his face, was that no shortage of gladiators would be willing to avenge Sorban. The problem would be choosing who would go after the Kree without insulting the rest. Then there was the question of whether or not the chosen one could actually *kill* Goll.

The study doors flew open then, startling Salwark. He half rose in reflex, only to feel his knees go weak.

"*Slavol,*" a woman spat at him with unchecked fury.

His expression drooped with surprise.

She was short, shapely, and dressed in fine robes of berry red and black. A wide belt of leather accentuated her curves, giving her a dangerous air of nobility. Blond hair was tied in a serpent's tail at the back of her head so that her piercing blue gaze could unnerve anyone in her way. And that gaze was presently fixed upon Salwark.

It wasn't just any woman. It was Sorban's wife—his *angry* wife.

"You unfit bastard," she charged behind a raised and pointing spear of a finger. "You ripe slick of gurry clinging to a cow's hot hole. My husband's dead. *Dead*, you miserable pisser. And how did I find out? How did I find out? I found out only from my *neighbors*, who finally got up the courage to come knock on my door well past the death of the afternoon. 'I'm truly sorry for your loss,' they said. 'Well and truly sorry for your loss.' 'What loss?' I asked, the horror only then clawing at my heart, and then I hear that my husband had been cut down on the arena floor. Dead and gone, and *no one saw fit to let his wife know!*"

Salwark flinched, keeping the woman in sight, but hazarded yet another quick peek at the roof. A jarring rumble overhead, powerful enough to split the ceiling, drowned out the last blast of words.

The moment he took his eyes off her, Zelia rushed around the table.

Salwark matched her, keeping that large slab of wood between them. A manservant cringed just outside the study door, the same servant who had spoken earlier—who had attempted to warn him sooner.

"Look at me!" Zelia screamed, both her hands slamming into the table.

Salwark looked. He looked as if his life depended on it, and no doubt it did.

"I couldn't believe what I'd heard, so I marched to the Pit itself. I hate that place, you pretty bastard. I hate it with all my being. But I went into those stone bowels, where the smell of shite and piss and blood and other filth I have no knowledge of clings to the walls and fouls your skin like the licks from a half-dead cat. I went straight to your private chambers only to find you'd gone."

Salwark swallowed and licked his lips. He blinked as if a wagon carrying wine barrels had just rolled over the back of his neck.

"Right then," Zelia spat, "right then, I knew you'd gone to my door. What owner of a gladiator house wouldn't, of course? What decent person wouldn't?"

That stung, and Salwark flinched again.

"So I hurried back to my residence," Zelia continued, "enduring all those looks of pity. And I shut myself in just to escape those looks. And I waited. I *waited*, you unfit punce. I waited for you to knock on my door, to bring me my husband's body and an explanation of what happened. I waited. And waited. And *waited*. And when I could wait no longer, I came here, through that unfit piss storm."

Salwark swallowed until it hurt, his face hot enough to slide off his skull.

"And when I entered your hallowed training grounds," she went on, "*more* looks, from my husband's fellow pit fighters, except they were even more miserable. But by that time, my horror, my *sorrow* had been replaced by something greater—and my *anger* knows no bounds. So here I am, Salwark, son of that diseased husk whose name I don't care to remember. What happened? Tell me. And then explain why I had to come *here* instead of you coming to me?"

Salwark could answer the first question easily enough—it was the second question that frightened him. He'd blatantly *forgotten* Sorban had a wife, even though he'd arranged for the gladiator to meet with her just the other day.

"There was a fight," he started.

"I know there was a fight, you idiot. Against a Kree called Goll."

"There was—there was that. Yes. It was a good fight. A very good fight, except . . . except in the end, Goll cut Sorban down and . . . and killed him. The shock is still a blinding thing. A bewildering thing. I . . . I couldn't face you this evening. See this?" He held up the goblet. "I needed this to comfort myself, to reinforce my nerves. It's . . . it's the first time I've had to give such unfortunate news to a gladiator's family. And face his wife."

Zelia's scalding glare didn't waver, but a few heartbeats later, she did squeeze her eyes shut. Her lips moved as if chewing on a particularly sharp retort, and Salwark could not blame her for it at all. He braced for another round of cursing then remembered his manners.

"Would you like some?" he asked meekly, indicating the bottle.

She glared pure fire in his direction.

"Where's his body?" she demanded.

Seddon above. Salwark moaned to himself. *This was* not *going to end well in the least.*

"We . . . we gave him to the fire pit," he mumbled, wondering if the Balgothan woman had a knife on her person. He'd scream if she did. He'd scream like a ten-year-old boy hammering his finger with a maul.

"You what?"

"We gave him to the fire pit."

Zelia leaned back. "You burned him."

Salwark nodded, waiting, the rain falling on the roof every bit as furious as the woman in his study chamber. "We don't have burial lots here, good Zelia," he explained. "The fire was the way he would've—"

"He would *not* have wanted to be burned," she shot back, hating him with her eyes. "He wouldn't have. He would have . . . would have . . ."

But she couldn't finish the sentence. Her mouth clamped shut, and she stood that way, staring at Salwark with a mixture of undiluted hatred and disbelief, at a loss at how to proceed. In that space of time, the rain intensified.

"I'm sorry," he eventually said, watching her carefully. "Truly."

Her eyes moistened and sparkled in the torchlight, but then her face hardened, hardened with such effort that Salwark was struck speechless. Her emotions seemed on the very cusp of overwhelming her, but the Balgothan woman would not permit it, especially not in front of him. She inhaled sharply and rattled her head as if awakening from a healer's unfit medication that had done nothing for her condition.

When she spoke, her voice was a raspy, ugly thing. "What do you plan . . . on doing?"

"What?" Salwark asked uncertainly.

"What do you plan on doing?"

Salwark couldn't answer right away.

"You seem at a loss," Zelia said, face contorted from the effort of quashing her emotions. "I'll tell you what you're going to do, Salwark. You're going to select your best man this very night and tell him that he's going to kill Goll of Kree. Then you make arrangements for the blood match."

"The arena—" *is closed right now*, he was going to say.

Zelia cut him off with that murderous glare. "Tomorrow," she said. "That is what you're going to do. Tomorrow."

Salwark didn't know what to say, his mind fluttering. Thunder rattled the skies, flustering him even more.

"I'll be in attendance," she continued. "To see the execution of the man who killed my husband."

"There might be a problem," Salwark said, fearful of the Balgothan woman.

Zelia's face screwed up into an exasperated question.

"These things . . . take time," Salwark explained. "There is a process to a blood match. I have to speak with the Madea and inform him—"

"Tomorrow," Zelia said, cutting him off. "Do whatever you must, but do it tomorrow. Before the games."

Salwark shriveled under her gaze. "I'll . . . try."

That was the wrong thing to say, and the woman's face became a dark and evil thing.

"You did not come to me after my husband perished upon those sands," she said. "You burned his body without consent, and now you are hesitating regarding my wish for vengeance. Salwark. Son of whoever owns this place. Have you no idea how you've insulted me and my husband's memory? In Balgotha, this is no small thing. I do not ask you to do these things. I tell you. Carry out my wishes, or risk my wrath."

Salwark gawked at the woman before him. "You dare threaten me? In my own home? In what was my mother's *study*?" he said, his own anger rising.

"I do not dare," the Balgothan woman snapped back. "I *promise*."

With that, she slapped the nearly empty wine bottle to the floor, shattering it. Salwark flinched at the impact, and all fight left him.

"Do as I say," Zelia charged him. "*Tomorrow*."

She scalded him with one last withering glare and left the room. The manservant behind her promptly placed his back against the wall, allowing her passage.

Salwark watched her go.

Rain fell in a warm deluge as Zelia emerged from Salwark's residence. The doors closed behind her, the servants glad to be rid of the infuriated woman. Zelia walked into the storm, skirting a pathway's edge and marching toward the closed gates of the Slavol compound. Sorrow over her husband's death powered her. Outrage over his subsequent cremation threatened to drive her mad, and anger—at herself, for failing to convince Sorban to leave these games of blood and return to Balgotha with her—ate at her heart.

The rain soaked her robes to the skin not halfway to the gates. Her hair flattened against her skull, and water blurred her eyes. Great colorless beads dripped from her nose and chin, but the summer storm meant very little to the grieving Balgothan, who was dealing with a much more powerful, more crippling tempest within herself.

A pair of guards emerged from a nearby shack, their faces concealed by cowls and reduced to shadows. They lumbered into sight, their hands at their sides. They remembered her, and she them. They didn't stop her or ask any questions. One went to a smaller door set into the gate and opened it before stepping aside.

At least someone in this unfit hole showed her some measure of respect.

Zelia walked out into the deserted street. The gate door closed behind her, barring her from entering again. She didn't care. If she willed it, she would gain entry again, and nothing would prevent it.

Vengeance.

She was a woman without her husband, and all the dreams they'd had were lost forever. How she wished she'd persuaded him harder to leave rather than indulging him and his sport. All gone now. Her man was gone. Her dreams were gone. And she was alone.

She set her jaw and walked, barely conscious of the storm. Sheets of rain pummeled the city, the crashing loud in her ears. Most of the nearby buildings and houses had their shutters closed, but a scattered few had their shutters open, allowing a subdued light onto the roads. Water pooled in the shallows of the road. The yellow flowers and other greenery decorating the sides trembled and buckled under the stinging downpour. Forms lurked in alleyways, but they didn't venture out into the open. If they marked her as easy prey and sought to rob her, they'd get more than bargained for.

As if daring them, Zelia stopped and glared at the shadows, her little hands becoming fists.

The forms retreated, sensing the fight in her.

So she walked on.

By the time her house came into view, she'd reached new depths of misery. She stopped and beheld her and Sorban's little home—a hovel, really, with a tall roof to shrug off the winter snow. The storm had transformed the narrow strip of grass surrounding the property into a soggy, tangled morass. Other houses lined the street, the light from lamps or torches outlining their closed shutters, but no one ventured outside to meet or comfort her.

That was best.

Zelia studied her little home, her shoulders and frame trembling, her throat constricted and aching. The shutters remained open, but no light came from inside. The door was ajar as she'd failed to close it in her rush to leave. *Home.* It was no longer a home to her, not without Sorban. Now it was a reminder of wonderful memories, now barbed and painful, and lost opportunities.

Thunder rumbled, followed by white crackles that flayed the skies. Light flashed and heated the heavens.

Zelia heard a soft, grief-stricken note and realized she was moaning.

Sniffling, she went inside and closed the door behind herself, muting the sound of the rain. She grabbed one of two timbers lodged against the wall and fitted one then the other into place, preventing anyone else from entering. Then she closed the shutters and barred them as well. The house no longer smelled of honeywood but rather a dull ash, perhaps emanating from the fireplace. Standing in darkness, in the center of the main room, with the rain crashing down outside, Zelia croaked another sad note of suffering. She ripped her wet robes from herself and threw them into a corner. She listened, trembled, rubbing at her face and arms, and for a few heartbeats, let her pain swallow her as she sunk to the floor.

She cried for her dead husband and the children she would never have. No one should have to live through what she'd experienced. No one. Her bawling became monstrous wails of sadness. At some point in the long, wet night, she finished, believing she'd spent every tear in her person. She lay on her side, listening to the rain and those mighty barrels rolling across the sky. She wiped the water from her face and felt her soaked hair. Knowing the location of every possession, she found a thick towel in the darkness and rubbed herself down. When the towel became damp, she dropped it. A candle set rested on a shelf, and she struggled with the flint until finally she had light. She looked to a bedroom, hoping beyond hope that her man would emerge, but the candles revealed a dismal emptiness.

Zelia located another towel and surprised herself by crying into that.

She sobbed for what seemed like a very long time while the storm raged against the thin shell of the house.

Then, much later in the night, she ceased crying for good. Her chest stopped hitching. Her hands steadied and trembled no more.

Zelia looked up, wearing a tunic that Sorban had worn when alive and home and close enough to smell. She pinched the material away from her chest, not remembering when she'd pulled the garment over her head. His scent haunted the material, and she breathed deeply of it. The tunic armored her, so she continued wearing it, savoring every breath, left to her thoughts.

A blast of thunder got her moving.

Vengeance.

She realized why that miserable ass-licking punce of an owner hadn't visited her. He had dismissed her as unimportant. He saw her as only Sorban's wife, a figure in the prized gladiator's shadow, and of no consequence. After all, he'd visited her only at his chosen times, despite a few kind gestures of appeasement, which she realized were nothing more than shrewd efforts to keep Sorban close to the games.

We've coin enough. We could leave tomorrow.

Her own voice cut through her mind.

We've coin enough.

Oh, if only she'd been more forceful, more convincing. Zelia wiped at her cheeks. She looked around her empty home. The time for crying was over, and she was done with it. Sorban would not approve in the least. Nor would he approve of her next course of action, probably dismissing her as Salwark had, leaving the notion of revenge to his fellow gladiators and believing his wife incapable of such.

They were wrong. All wrong.

Especially the one called Goll.

4

"Damnation," Muluk grumbled, peeking out at the rain. He held the wooden shutter open only a crack, yet droplets speckled the sill and his face. He flinched at the contact.

"What?" Goll asked from inside Shan's healing house. After the Ten's victories upon the sands, where Junger had defeated one of Grisholt's gladiators and Goll had killed one from the Stable of Salwark, the once Free Trained house sought lodgings for the night within the city. They would travel home in the morning if the schedule allowed it.

"It's a right and proper downpour out there," Muluk said.

"Well then, close the shutters."

"Won't be able to see it then."

"Master Muluk . . ." Goll said with a sigh.

"Oh stop it with that 'master' gurry. Lords above, I'm tired of it already. I'm Muluk. Of Kree. Nothing more or otherwise. Call me Muluk or call me nothing. If I hear 'Master Muluk' once more, I'll stop and squat right there on the spot. And that's a promise."

Goll frowned. He sat alone at a table on the main floor, relaxing and basking in the afterglow of his return to the arena.

"Doesn't want to be called Master," Clavellus said, sitting one table over, along with a perpetually dour Machlann and a stern-looking Koba.

"It's his title," Goll said. "And it serves a purpose."

"He clearly doesn't feel that way."

"I clearly don't," Muluk said, still peering at the storm and the dark streets.

Goll gave up, not interested in arguing the matter. Rain hammered the roof and the walls in a constant hiss. The air had cooled considerably, and sleep would be a comfortable thing this night if the thunder would settle down. The booming was well and truly deafening—relentless. It was one of those summer storms Sunja was long overdue for, one that threatened to split the sky and drench the lands.

The other house members lounged or stood about the room where Shan would meet and examine people with various ailments. Junger sat in a corner, his head down on a table as though asleep. He'd gone back to wearing his shirt even though the spectators screaming his name had sought to rip the garment from his back. The man had said little after his performance on the sands that day, but one thing was certain: his reputation was growing.

The guards Valka and Pratos stood near the entrance. Shan himself puttered through the main chamber every now and again before disappearing through a back door to his living quarters and his waiting wife. His missus had been happy to see her husband, which was good. Goll didn't like seeing his healer under undue stress. More and more, he saw the good in convincing Shan and his wife to move out to Clavellus's villa.

Muluk turned away from the window. "I'll say this: we were wise to stay here for the night. If we chanced heading home, we would've been caught on open ground, trying to roll over bad roads and all that mud."

Clavellus shared a look with Machlann. A bottle stood on the table before them, but not much else. The taskmaster was in the mood for some drinking but lacked the alcohol and didn't want to brave the weather. They'd managed to purchase the wine from a merchant closing for the day but had no time for anything else. People had pursued the Ten from the Domis into the maze of backstreets, seeking a glimpse of the one called the Perician Wonder.

"Just think if we had gone," Muluk continued, "and, Lords forbid, become bogged down along the way? Miserable, miserable. Glad that we stayed."

Clavellus sighed, checked his cup, and frowned at what remained. "No letting up, is there?" he asked.

As an answer, Muluk swung the shutters open wide and stepped aside.

Rain. A black sheet of it.

The taskmaster looked away after he'd seen enough. Goll smirked inwardly. He knew the one bottle of wine would not last much longer. He recalled the earlier conversation then, centering on Junger's amazing victory in the Pit. The man had defeated a known killer without swinging his sword even once. Goll didn't mind the attention the Perician was receiving—not much, anyway. He had his own personal victory to celebrate, of returning to competition and once again participating in these grand games. Not only was he victorious, but having put down the one called Sorban sent a clear message to the enemies of the House of Ten.

Though only two fighters remained, the Ten were not finished.

Their victories had also brought fresh coin to the house's treasury. Not so much Junger, as the odds were greatly in his favor, but not many had believed Goll would vanquish the Balgothan, it seemed.

That brought a ghost of a smile to the Kree's face.

"You must be thinking about the coin," Clavellus put to him, still playing with his cup.

"Truth be known, I'm not."

"I'd be thinking about the coin."

"Maybe you would."

"There's a lot of it."

Goll knew there was, just above their heads on the second floor, in small sacks that made Clades and the other once Sujins visibly nervous while transporting it all from the Domis to the waiting wagons. They brought their riches to Shan's house and left it under the watchful eye of Clades, who would guard the money for half the night until someone relieved him.

"There's going to be little sleep for some of us," Clavellus said. "Have we decided who'll keep watch after the lads?"

Koba raised his hand.

"Thank you, good man," the taskmaster replied.

Junger lifted a hand as well though his head remained on the table.

"The Perician Wonder," Clavellus said. "Excellent. Is there nothing you cannot do?"

"I'll take a watch," Muluk said from the window.

"You're watching now," Goll pointed out.

"I'll do it anyway."

"At least go and sleep for a bit, then. Your head will only touch the pillow before you'll be rising again. Or so it'll seem."

Muluk agreed with his fellow Kree. He pulled the shutter closed and rolled his shoulders. Water had wet his beard and flattened parts of his hair, actually revealing the ghastly hole where his left ear had been. The brutish Kree was still an unsightly wreck from having battled a handful of killers weeks earlier, and he limped toward the staircase. He slapped his good hand upon Goll's shoulder and shook it fondly as he passed.

Something tapped Goll on his other shoulder. It was a hand, one missing three of its fingers, lopped off at an angle just above the knuckles. Muluk managed a fist with his mutilated paw and offered it to his companion.

Goll frowned and was about to press his own fist into Muluk's when the man drew back.

"Hold on," the hairy Kree grumbled. "Best not to. Here." He offered his other fist, fully fingered.

"You're certain?" Goll asked wearily.

"Go on, don't be a punce."

Goll pressed his fist to his friend's and held it until Muluk pulled away and retired for the evening.

"We should have at least one of them for the second watch," Clavellus said, indicating Valka and Pratos.

The once Sujins, both armored in leather and carrying sheathed blades, resembled a set of stern executioners who'd long since tossed off their black masks, revealing the graying hair and beards underneath.

"I'll take watch for one," Goll said. "I'm not ready for sleep."

"I'm ready," Machlann grumbled and rose. He went for the stairs.

"I believe that's it, then," Clavellus said and smiled. "We're ready for the night, such as it is. Good of you to take watch, Master Goll."

"Best for me to watch the door. Anyone else, and you might convince them to let you outside, and damned if I want to go hunting for your hide in that 'Row' place."

"Arbin's Row," Clavellus said fondly before his expression darkened with disappointment. "Not that I would. Not this night. The weather's unfit."

The taskmaster hobbled to his feet and stretched. He eyed the sitting Kree. "You did well this day, Goll. Very well. Your victory might've been eclipsed by that one over there . . ." He indicated Junger. "But you did well all the same."

"Thank you," Goll said quietly.

Clavellus nodded, drained his cup, and set it gently upon the table. He moved to the stairs. "Lords above. The heavens are pissing on us tonight. It'll be right and proper treacherous traveling back to the villa tomorrow. The roads will be thick with sludge."

"Worried, are you?"

"About this?" Clavellus pointed outside. "Not at all. We're comfortable here. If we don't return home tomorrow, it's no great matter. Nala understands the season and the nature of the games. Pratos. Valka. Who wants to get an early sleep and take watch some time after midnight?"

The soldiers regarded each other. Valka, being the older, shrugged and moved away. Pratos, younger only by a pair of years, smirked good-naturedly behind his companion's back. When Valka moved upstairs, the main chamber of the healer's house became a lot less cluttered.

Goll glanced at Junger's unmoving heap. The man sat at the table with his head buried in his folded arms—a poor way to sleep, but Goll left him alone. He stood and wandered over to the front door, where he nodded at Pratos. Muluk had closed the shutters, so Goll cracked one open just a finger's width and grimaced at the sight.

"The land needs the rain," Pratos said, his weathered face barely moving.

"There was rain a few days ago."

"Needs more."

"Why don't you sit for a while," Goll said, changing the subject. "No need for two of us here."

Pratos thought about it and did just that.

Goll was glad he did—no chance then of having a conversation. Goll was content to stand guard until midnight or so and listen to the rain. Water fell off the roof in a dark curtain, the likes of which he had trouble remembering. A few drops hit his face, but he kept the shutter open, watching the narrow street beyond. Anyone lurking outside would be in poor spirits indeed. His thoughts switched to Borchus and where the agent might be.

Junger appeared on the other side of the door, distracting the Kree.

"I thought you were asleep," Goll said with a frown.

"I was, Master Goll. For a short time. Man can't sleep while sitting up like that, however."

A soft snore interrupted the Perician then, and both men turned to see Pratos, sitting at a table, right and proper unconscious, his chin lowered to his chest.

"Well, most men that is, especially those who haven't done any soldiering in their life," Junger said. He unlatched the shutter on his side and threw it open. Fresh air flowed, and he filled his lungs.

Goll studied the empty streets.

"You did well this day," Junger said.

The Kree didn't really want to talk, but he dipped his head, appreciating the gesture.

"But . . . truly, Master Goll. These games don't have to be filled with blood or death. You don't need to kill every gladiator you face. It's better for the house if you don't."

"You ever pull that sword of yours?" Goll asked.

Junger stared out at the storm. "Do you plan on killing every one of your opponents?"

"I asked you first."

Thunder overhead, a long crackling that diminished into nothing.

"So you did," Junger said. "Yes, I do pull steel. When it's needed."

"It's not needed in the Pit?"

"No. Not really."

Irritated, Goll looked to the night. "Try to sleep, Perician Wonder. It's a long road back to the villa. Chances are we'll be pulling our wagons through the mud at least once."

Junger studied Goll's profile for a moment then turned his attention to the weather. "I'll wager we're not going anywhere tomorrow. This storm is far from spent."

Goll squinted. "We'll see tomorrow, then."

"We will," Junger said and, with an affable nod to his house master, wandered back to his table.

Goll was glad of it. Junger had left the shutter on his side open, so Goll closed it, annoyed about having to do so. He returned to his window and caught a trace whiff of wood smoke, mild and pleasant.

We're not going anywhere tomorrow, Junger had said.

Perician Wonders, ferocious rainstorms, missing agents, and a city filled with gladiator houses plotting revenge against the Ten.

Goll wondered what else might be happening this night.

5

The air was fiercely humid and thickened with the scent of exotic wood or perfumed water of a name beyond Torello. The woman with him called herself Shonni, which didn't rightly mean anything to him, but he didn't care as long as she was willing to hold his topper for a bit. They squirmed about on a grand bed, the edges hidden by a flimsy curtain the color of moonlight. Shonni was married to some merchant of some gurry or other—Torello really didn't need to know that either. All he needed was her to be supple and pliant and willing to do all those things underneath the blankets.

And she was.

He ran a hand over her chest and received a pleasurable sigh for his efforts. Her mouth clamped down on his with growing urgency while her hand fell from his chest, to his waist, to his—

Lords above.

She gripped him fiercely, and pressed him onto his back, back into the bed's softness. The blankets fell away, and Torello lay there as Shonni, in all her naked glory, rose above him, running her hands over her breasts and head.

She moaned again.

"I'll have you screaming soon enough," he whispered.

Shonni smiled with lewd intent and ran her hands over snowy hair, her dark-tipped breasts rising with the effort. She arched her back, glanced behind herself, and reached down. Another moan, louder than before.

Torello grimaced. "Seddon above, *easy* there," he cautioned her. "You'll bring the servants."

She looked away, past the curtains surrounding the bed. "What is it?"

She met his eyes. "You don't hear that?"

"Hear what?"

Shonni ignored him. "I said wake up!" she said in a suddenly very manly voice.

Torello's eyes narrowed. *That was disturbing.*

"Wake up, you insufferable bastard!" she yelled in that same misplaced, masculine tone.

The roof came off the bedchamber in a soundless explosion, and the walls dissipated into gray. Shonni's eyes widened, the surprise brightening her lovely face, just before Torello felt the frustrating pull of reality. He opened his eyes and fumed in annoyance.

He was back in his alcove, in his miserable straw bed. A few stalks stabbed him in the crack of his ass. Rain crashed against the roof overhead, and a discordant *plunk* of water striking wood came from deeper within the gladiators' barracks. Torello shifted, easing off those pointy shafts, and cringed at the warning flare of pain in his wrapped ankle.

A man's groaning stopped him on the mattress.

"You hear that?" a voice asked from the darkness, sounding a few alcoves down the way. Torello recognized it, even though he hadn't heard it much. It belonged to that one-legged fright with the haunting gray eyes.

"I heard," he answered.

"You're awake?"

Torello didn't bother replying.

"I said are you—"

"I'm *awake*, you unfit slab of gurry. I'm awake."

"Something's wrong with your friend," the voice said.

Garl. Torello remembered the name—a Sunjan from the city, once a gladiator until the arena took his right leg.

"He's not my friend," Torello said, wanting to clarify that right away.

The last friend he'd had died not too long before, and he wasn't even able to avenge Kolo's death. That bothered him to no end, despite Junger having righted the killing in a blood match.

"Well," Garl said, "you share this place with him."

"I don't share anything with that—"

An unfit squawking of released gas interrupted them, followed by a deathbed moan. The noise stopped Torello from continuing.

"Saimon's black hanging fruit," he finally muttered in disgusted wonder. "What was that?"

"That's what I said," Garl said anxiously. "He woke me up, and he's only getting worse. You best check on that lad."

Check on that lad? Torello thought, the notion alien to him. *Check on the Sarlander?* "I'm not checking on him, my ankle's unfit."

"Well, I'm missing a leg."

"I've seen you hop about on crutches."

"I'm *missing* a leg, man. Besides, he knows you. I'm new here."

"No better time to introduce yourself, then."

That silenced Garl, and in that beat of time, Brozz croaked—an organic clicking noise, sounding as though he was parched something fierce. Then the man stopped breathing entirely, as if a person had jammed a fist right down his gullet. Torello waited for him to breathe, waited, and waited a bit longer, knowing it was well past the normal tempo. *Snoring, that's all it is.* The Sarlander's tongue had slipped down his own pipe. He'd spit it out eventually and resume breathing. Guaranteed.

In that space of heartbeats, Torello's brow scrunched, and his concern grew.

And the silence stretched on.

"Breathe," he urged softly, "*breathe.*"

But Brozz did not breathe. In fact, the lack of breathing became even more alarming.

"Seddon above, he's passed on," Garl blurted.

"He hasn't passed on."

"Check on him!"

Torello thought it might be a good idea after all.

And right then, there was a click and a massive intake of air from Brozz's sleeping area, as if he'd just surfaced from an exceptionally deep pool. Then, having reached capacity, the sleeping man let it all go in a lengthy sigh. The breathing evened out, and the Sarlander shifted in the darkness.

"He's sick," Garl announced.

"He's wounded," Torello countered.

"He's *sick*."

"What do you know of it? You a healer?"

"I know sick when I hear it. And that man's unfit."

"He's resting."

"He's *dying*," Garl insisted. "And the longer you wait, the deader he's getting."

That worried Torello even though he didn't want to admit it. Brozz wasn't his friend, but Kolo didn't mind the Sarlander, not like that brute called Sapo. That one was a twice-dipped punce.

"All right." Torello relented and sat up, gritting his teeth at the unkind way his ankle disagreed with him. He lowered his legs to the floor and groped for his own crutches. "Brozz, wake up."

No response.

"Brozz. Wake up, you unfit pisser."

A wheezy snore came then, followed by another disturbing bout of silence, during which only the rain rattled the roof.

"Brozz?" Torello asked.

"Get over there and *shake* the topper," Garl pressed from the darkness.

"Why don't you shaddup?"

"That man's dying, Seddon above, and all because you're wasting time!"

Getting his crutches underneath him, Torello stood, wavered for a bit, and pulled back the curtain covering his little sleeping area. He scratched at his head and peered into the darkness just as another frightening gasp came from Brozz. The Sarlander sounded like a person being allowed to breathe upon another's whim.

"Brozz!" Torello barked unkindly, forcing a false tone of impatience into his voice. "Wake up! *Now!*"

No answer.

"The man certainly sleeps like a corpse," Torello muttered and shuffled along the hall, his night vision discerning the unlit corridor.

The air was warm and moist and carried a scent that was growing stronger. Then he realized what it was, having frequented enough alehouse latrines in his time. The sour stink of a released bladder.

"Anything?" Garl asked from farther back.

"Hold on, will you? Not there yet. Here we are. *Brozz!*"

Torello stopped and yanked a curtain across the opening.

And stared.

The alcove wasn't any different from his own, but the state of it was deplorable. Brozz's unmoving form lay upon his straw cot, his bare skin glowing in the dark with sickly perspiration. Not even the night could soften the wrecked appearance of the Sarlander. His broken nose remained in bandages, no doubt contributing to his breathing problems, while the rest of his features were an uneven surface of bruises and stitches. He lay coiled up on one side, facing away from the wall, his hands clutching at his bandaged gut. Piss had soaked through the bed's straw and dripped to the floor, but another smell lurked within the tiny chamber, one that Torello didn't like at all.

"Dying Seddon," he swore, taking in the grim sight. Brozz wheezed through his moustached mouth, which was enough for the crippled man.

"*You!*" Torello flicked a crutch across Brozz's bare legs.

The sleeping gladiator didn't move.

"*Wake up!*" Torello demanded and snapped wood across flesh and bone again.

Nothing. Not even a grimace.

"Brozz," Torello said and moved to the man's side. His feet touched wetness, and he scowled, knowing damn well he'd just shuffled through the Sarlander's piss puddle.

"Seddon above, *Brozz!*"

The unresponsive man didn't wake. Torello sized him up one last time, taking in the numerous stitches keeping the gladiator together.

"He awake yet?" Garl called out.

"No," *but he will be*, Torello vowed. He placed a crutch against a wall. Then, balanced on his one good leg, he leaned over and shook the Sarlander's large frame. One of Brozz's hands fell away, and in the low light available, Torello thought he saw an ugly blossom seeping through the cloth bandage covering the man's belly.

A chill enveloped the Sunjan. "Oh, you knobby bastard," he whispered.

He shook Brozz again, with both hands, letting his other crutch fall atop the unconscious man. The Sarlander rolled over onto his back, exposing the stained bandages for what they were.

Torello frowned and lowered himself, catching a whiff of wet, rancid meat. He recoiled from the stink.

"Well?" Garl asked impatiently.

Torello gingerly prodded at the bandages, and at the firmest pressure, Brozz released a groan of discomfort.

"Seddon above," Torello swore, rubbing his fingertips together and spreading the wetness there.

"*Well?*" Garl yelled.

"It's . . ." Torello drew back and took greater stock of the situation. "It's his gut. I think . . . it's infected."

"*What?*"

"Infected, you one-legged prick! Infected!"

"How's it infected?"

"*I don't know!*"

"Well, go fetch the healer, then."

Angry, Torello rolled his head. "Oh, aye *that*! I'll just start walking right this instant. Maybe I'll reach Sunja next year this time. You remember the healer's *away* in the city? With the others? He's gone!"

That silenced Garl.

And that uneased Torello just a little bit more.

Brozz covered his stomach once again.

Thunder crashed, reminding Torello a storm was on, and a right nasty one at that.

"You'll have to fetch someone," Garl told him.

"I know I'll have to fetch someone," Torello retorted, which was a ripe lie if he'd ever told one. "But who?"

"Let the lady of the house know."

As good as anyone, he supposed. "And you'll leave that up to me."

"*I've got one leg, you unfit bastard!*" Garl shrieked.

Torello ignored that. He grumped and replaced his crutches. "Stay there," he ordered Brozz. "And stop pissing yourself."

With that, he shuffled back into the corridor at best speed—which wasn't very good at all—cutting through the foul puddle covering the floor. He got to the corridor, turned left, and swung toward the common-room entrance.

"Tell her the lad's unwell!" Garl shouted after him.

"Yes, yes," Torello muttered, passing an assortment of tables and benches. Light flashed beyond the shutters, followed by a slow rattling not unlike boulders tumbling down the side of a very deep chasm. The door ahead was shut. He heard no wind, but the crashing hiss of rain didn't impress him in the least. Torello threw back a latch and kicked the door open before launching himself forward into the stormy night. Water pelted his face and head, staggering him, soaking him in an instant. No one was patrolling the walls, but then again, he could barely see the battlements through the pouring rain. Grimacing, he plodded forward, splashing through puddles growing amongst the sand. He didn't mind the water so much, knowing it would wash away the Sarlander's piss.

"Hey!" Torello shouted, looking toward the villa's ramparts. "Where are you?"

No one answered.

Dying Seddon. He spun around as best he could, splashing as he went, and peered into the night. The wooden outlines of the practice men stood upon the training grounds, as well as a few other implements of physical torture, but no sentries. Usually at night, two were posted upon the walls and one inside the courtyard. Now, however . . .

"I need a healer!" he shouted. "Anyone there? The one called Brozz *needs a healer!*"

No answer. He waited a few heartbeats more, scanning the darkness.

"*Wake up, you maggots!*" he finally roared, the last words almost lost in a frightening boom of thunder.

Torello waited, panting, his throat stinging from the outburst.

Lightning flashed again, and in that fleeting illumination, a guard appeared.

Nala lay in her bed and listened to the storm. A loud crash had pulled her free of her dreams not moments earlier. She blinked heavily as sleep sought to reclaim her. She resisted for a moment, content to listen. The weather didn't bother her. The villa was well-built and dry, and though a good many menfolk had gone off to participate in their violent sport, more than enough guards were about to protect the property.

So she shifted underneath a cover of old silk and slid a hand across her bed, just to make certain that her husband hadn't returned in secrecy. She found him still gone—for the best, really. She had watched those great bloated clouds come in from the east earlier in the afternoon. By evening, all windows were shuttered, and the rain soaked the property. Clavellus would stay in Sunja this night, knowing full well the roads would be treacherous for traveling. If the storm remained until tomorrow, she supposed he wouldn't be returning then either, for boats would be needed instead of wagons and horses.

He was safe from the weather, however. That was the main thing. She was safe as well, so she had nothing more to do than sleep and hope that the ceilings wouldn't surprise her with a leak.

Games, she thought, relaxing more while the night rumbled outside.

Her consciousness drifted.

A hand pounded on her bedchamber door, yanking her back with a fright.

"Lady Nala," a woman called. "Lady Nala, it's Ananda."

Upon hearing her young servant, Nala wiped the sleep from her eyes. "Yes, what is it?"

"It's one of the gladiators, Lady Nala. He's not well."

Not well?

"Just a moment," Nala said and slipped from her bed. The thought of one of their boys, as she'd grown to secretly call them, being unwell troubled her.

She quickly pulled on a few robes and tied them off at her waist with a belt. The rainstorm reminded her to grab a thick blanket, which she draped over her shoulders. Ananda waited at the door, worry clouding her pretty face.

"Take me there," Nala said, tying back her shoulder-length hair.

A single guard waited outside Nala's residential entrance and escorted her and Ananda along the training grounds. Ananda carried a lamp, and the flame wavered under the storm's power. Water and sand splashed over Nala's sandals, but she didn't allow that to slow her.

The barracks could barely be seen, and the rain had drenched them by the time they reached the entrance. When she entered the low building, she heard them before she saw them.

Another guard stood at the inner door leading to the sleeping area, a place Nala hadn't been since its actual construction. Shaking off the wet blanket, she tossed it onto a nearby table and allowed Ananda to take the lead into a narrow corridor.

The lamplight merged with that given by a pair of lit torches. Faces rose at the ladies' appearance, all of which she knew indirectly though they'd never been formally introduced.

"What is it, then?" she asked the gladiator with the injured ankle. The rain had flattened the man's black hair and stubble into a wet smear of pitch. A collection of scars covered his dripping features.

"Lady," Torello said with forced respect. "He's in there."

"He's suffering," said the one-legged man behind Torello.

Garl, she remembered.

Another villa guard backed out of the alcove and nodded pensively at her before getting entirely out of the way. He fixed a torch on a wall bracket. She moved past him cautiously and peered inside the sleeping quarters. Her breath froze in her chest.

Brozz. The tall, brooding Sarlander with the thick drooping moustache that made him both dashing and ominous, lay coiled up on his bunk as if he'd been stabbed through the middle. The torchlight transformed his flesh and the perspiration covering him into a sparking orange hue. Sweat coated his forehead and soaked his hair, but the thing that stole Nala's attention was the bandages covering his midsection . . . and the dreadful stain seeping through.

"What's that?" she asked with a calmness she didn't think possible.

No one answered.

She looked directly at the pair of crippled men.

"We don't know," Garl blurted. "He was making noise when I woke up, and it took me a few moments to wake up this one here."

Torello frowned at the somewhat implied blame. "It's probably his gut wound," he said. "He got himself pricked there in his last fight."

"Didn't the healer leave ointments for the lad?" Nala asked.

"Your guard picked this off the floor," he said and presented a small jar missing its cover. A glistening salve the color of smoke half filled the container. Deep grooves marred what remained, made by fingers scooping out a dose.

"So he put that on himself?" Nala asked.

"I didn't do it," Torello said sourly.

The nearby guard scowled at the injured gladiator, a warning to address the lady of the house properly.

"Well, I didn't," a heedless Torello repeated.

"Neither did I," Garl admitted in a small voice.

"He wouldn't have let us anyway," Torello gestured. "Not him."

Nala studied them before directing her attention to the sick man. She stepped inside the sleeping area with Ananda at her back. The Sarlander didn't look well at all. In fact, she feared for his life. She touched his cheek, considering that soaked bandage around his waist. "There's no healer about."

"That's what I said," Torello remarked.

"We'll have to take that off him," she continued, "see what's causing this."

That was greeted with silence.

"You, ah, something of a healer?" Torello asked. "My Lady?"

"Not at all."

"Well . . . might there be a healer around these parts?"

"The nearest healer would be in Pynn's Brook, and that's a very long way to travel at night. Especially in a rainstorm. And looking at dear Brozz here, I doubt he'd be alive by the time a healer returned."

Nala studied the two men. Neither Torello or Garl was capable of helping in their condition. The guard didn't look to be the healer type. She glanced at an uneasy Ananda and wasn't about to ask her to do what needed to be done.

Thus, the lady of the house stooped and began picking at bandages. She stopped a short time later and shook her head.

"You," Nala said to the young guard. "You have a knife?"

He nodded.

"Give it to me," she commanded.

He extracted a blade and offered it handle first. Holding the sizeable weapon, Nala stooped and studied the bandages again. On impulse, she leaned over the barely alive Brozz and thumbed back an eyelid. Fire glimmered across the eye's surface. She released the lid and returned to the bandages.

She pinched and cut away at the material, unleashing a stink that reminded her of bad meat and juices best kept inside a body. Blood beaded and dribbled to the cot's straw, but it wasn't a result of her cutting with the dagger. She peeled away long strands of cloth, the smell strengthening with each layer, the blood flowing a little thicker.

"Oh, that's right unfit, that is," Torello said, his lips becoming an unpleasant button.

Struggling with the smell, Nala cut away the last few strips of cloth and let them fall. She gazed upon Brozz's wound. The flesh had risen in a burial mound hard to the touch. The puncture hole drooled blood and pus. Brozz lay unconscious to the world while that foul, seeping bubble wrought the blackest magic upon him.

Nala wished Shan hadn't gone to the city with the others.

"Maybe," she started, "maybe this might help."

She looked at the container of ointment, the smell of onions nowhere near as offensive as the putrid aroma coming from Brozz's midsection.

"Begging your pardon, Lady," Garl said. "But if my memory's right, what you have in your hand is for cuts. Deep or shallow. That—" The once beggar nodded at the stricken Brozz. "That's infected. With a foulness I've seen before, in other people."

"What should I do?" she asked.

Garl half shrugged. "Clean the wound. At the very least. Don't suppose you have any healer medicines about this place?"

"Other than this?" she asked, indicating the container of ointment. "No."

"Oh. Well. That's unfortunate."

"What about cleaning it?" Torello asked, mulling the suggestion. "You said cleaning. What about that?"

Garl's expression lit up with uncertainty. "I don't know. I mean, I'm not sure. Perhaps some hot water. But that boil shouldn't be there. I mean, look at it. That's a leech if I ever saw one. It's what's going to happen that worries me."

"What's that?" Nala asked.

"The infection's already got a hold of him. Maybe too much of a hold. Look at him. He won't have any water left inside him by morning. And that's just one worry. I don't think that boil's going to get any smaller."

Dread fell over Nala then, and she heard her throat click when she swallowed. She could do nothing, letting Brozz fight his own battle, but that wouldn't sit right on her mind or heart.

"Clean it, you say?" she asked.

"Aye that," Garl said. "At the very least. Might . . . might give him a chance."

Nala looked to Ananda. "Bring me hot water and fresh bandages. From the kitchen. As fast as you can. And twine for stitching."

Her servant hurried off. The night rumbled while the rain intensified overhead.

"You're going to clean that yourself?" Torello asked.

"Neither of you look able," Nala said. "Nor does my guard."

The young man frowned at the assessment, but he didn't say otherwise.

"I'll do it," Torello said, casting an unimpressed look at the guard. "You're bound to slice off his topper. Or worse."

Nala didn't give up the blade. "You think I don't know my way around toppers?"

Torello glowered at the rebuke. "Truth be known," he said, "I don't think your husband would be too pleased you're doing this."

"You don't know my husband."

Torello's expression said, *true enough.*

"No, I'll take care of..." She couldn't finish the thought, so she nodded at Brozz's festering wound.

They lapsed into silence then, waiting for Ananda to return.

Nala hoped the woman didn't take too long.

What seemed like an uncomfortably long time later, Ananda returned with a covered pot and a satchel. The pot she placed on the floor next to Brozz. She then unloaded the satchel's contents: cloth bandages, towels, and a small cushion with a ready needle, as well as a spool of stitching twine. Nala dropped to her knees and organized the items, taking grim stock of everything.

Torello gazed on with ripe aversion. Garl appeared the stronger, watching with fierce concentration.

"You're going to have to cut through that infected skin," the once beggar advised. "Maybe even... peel it back. Then perhaps clean away anything that comes out. Anything rancid looking. There'll be blood, plenty of it, so I hope my Lady doesn't favor her clothing there."

Nala answered that with a frown. She might be many things, but she didn't place clothing above a life.

"Just saying is all," Garl muttered.

She studied the infection site. "How do I clean the infection, exactly?"

"That's the unfit part. I'd scald it with that hot water. That might help."

"Might?"

Garl's eyes flared with doubt. "I don't know for certain."

"You seem to know a bit."

"I was a gladiator once," he answered simply. "You spend some time in an infirmary, you remember things."

Nala supposed that would be true enough. She looked at Ananda. "Will you help me?"

The servant nodded, a touch fearfully, dreading what she was about to see.

"You there," Nala said to the guard. "Pirrus. Get the other one out in the common room. Both of you hold him down by the shoulders and the legs, just in case he wakes up."

The young Pirrus left and returned in short time, bringing a second guard. They moved into position, further crowding the narrow space.

"All right then," Nala said, once everyone was ready. She took up the knife.

"Drop that into the hot water," Garl said. "Cleans it, you see."

Nala did just that. She pulled it clear a few beats later and placed the edge to Brozz's bare skin. Firelight flashed along the metal, replaced by shadows. The stitches along his chest captured her attention.

Seddon above, Nala thought and wondered if she was still sleeping in her bed. There was one way to find out, she supposed with uncertainty. A nervous dread crept into her old hands, but she gripped the knife more tightly, choking it.

"All right," she repeated, looking upon Brozz's unconscious face. Nala dearly hoped he wouldn't wake up. Though she was displaying remarkable resolve, truth be known, she trembled dearly inside.

Taking one final calming breath, she started cutting.

6

In the city of Sunja, rain bounced off empty streets and flowed into sewers. Puddles formed and widened. Open barrels of garbage filled, floated, and spilled. The lamps and torches remained unlit, so the night became a black and fearful thing. Nights such as these, people deemed it best to simply sit and wait out the storm. And most did just that. However, a few determined souls with pressing matters could not wait for dawn. They wandered the streets, enduring the rains with canvas coverings and high boots. The odd drunkard also staggered about, searching for the next alehouse.

Other ones clung to the deeper darkness formed in alleyways or other such recesses, hoping to be mistaken for shadows.

The killer called Sunjack strode through the rain, his cloak and garments drenched and clinging to his person. He was a tall man, burly, and one of the more valued cutthroats belonging to the Sons of Cholla. He frequently butchered people on their behalf and rather enjoyed his work. Perhaps a week before, Sunjack and his partner, Bardal, had visited this part of the city and spoken with a long-bearded healer called Ivalo. They spoke to him about a man called Borchus. Word was that a gladiatorial house wanted Borchus dead. It appeared the man was an agent of the games, and it was common knowledge in Sunjack's profession that it was only a matter of time before an agent, *any* agent of the games, was targeted by a rival house. The Sons of Cholla had been tasked with this particular killing, which was passed on to Sunjack and Bardal by Jaro himself.

Busy times, Sunjack mused blackly, for one of the Sons—a right and proper hellion called Strach—had been discovered dead himself. The Sons very much wanted Strach's killer to be found. Thus, Sunjack, Bardal, and every dog and snake within their sizeable organization were charged with searching for that very man in addition to Borchus.

Thus far, not a hair nor a whisper had been detected of Strach's killer. No further attacks upon the Sons had been made. That suggested, at least to Sunjack, that Strach might very well have crossed the wrong person with that brazen tongue of his. A smart person who, upon cutting Strach's tongue out, had decided it wise to leave the city.

Or so Sunjack supposed.

Bardal agreed with him, so there was that.

So the hunt leaned toward locating Borchus. They found Ivalo, who might have treated a nameless man for a knife wound, a man matching the agent's description. Nothing more, however.

Still, it was a sniff. A good sniff, in fact. One to act upon.

And since no one had discovered anything in the search for Strach's killer, it was wise to show the Sons that at least *some* progress was being made. And who knew? Every snake and killer with working eyes and ears was watching the streets these days, listening in on conversations and twisting bells when needed. If Strach's killer remained in the city, they would find him, perhaps even while closing in on Borchus.

At least, Sunjack hoped they would before Jaro, the Sons' head enforcer, began crushing throats to motivate those scouring the streets.

All they needed was Borchus showing himself, but the agent was careful. Sly. Stealthy. Since taking up the hunt, no one in the Sons' considerable web had even seen the man.

Truth be known, Sunjack was impressed.

Borchus knew how to hide himself, knew how to move undetected about the city. There was a chance the agent had fled Sunja. Both Sunjack and Bardal agreed that was the smart thing to do. Sunjack, however, had a feeling that wasn't the case.

He suspected the agent remained in the city.

And truth be known, after a week of hiding, a rainstorm, the particularly *nasty* rainstorm currently drowning the city, would be a very good time for a man—a *hiding* man—to emerge and go about his business, whatever that might be.

Sunjack took shelter underneath a closed shop front with broad eaves, escaping some of the rain lashing the stone tiles in a furious applause. He adjusted a belt of daggers both long and short. The long ones he used like regular short swords. The smaller blades could be flung a considerable distance. The tall killer opened his mouth and caught enough water to swish around. He gargled and spat, narrowed his eyes, and took stock of the area before him.

Across the way, a figure emerged from an alley. Sunjack wouldn't have seen the man unless he moved.

Anything? Sunjack inquired with a hand signal.

Nothing, the man signaled back.

Disappointed, Sunjack wandered along, the rain bouncing off his head and shoulders.

Another figure, as still as stone, waited in a closed doorway. Sunjack asked the same question with a quick flick of the hand and received a similar answer. He sighed, frowned, and meandered on, traveling an open maze he'd routinely patrolled for nearly half a week. Shadows emerged from hiding places, but they never stepped into full view. They all reported the same.

Nothing.

No one had seen a thing.

Sunjack sighed again, a touch more impatiently. It was all damn disappointing. He'd been certain Borchus would appear this night—so much so that he'd charged everyone under his and Bardal's command to be vigilant. The Sons had deployed a sizeable pack to kill the elusive agent, a human net consisting of the most underhanded and vicious cutthroats ever assembled. Sunjack had even directed a few lads to keep watch at the arena, in case Borchus appeared there.

He continued walking and eventually stopped in an alleyway, placing his back to a door. A collection of balconies loomed overhead, providing some relief from the storm. He leaned against a wall, peered around a corner, and eyed a familiar door in the middle of a narrow lane, where white stone walls were marked with irregularly spaced doors.

The one Sunjack watched, however, belonged to one long-bearded healer.

"Anything?" a voice asked behind him.

He shook his head.

Bardal took up position against the opposite wall and cricked his neck. The shorter, blockier man was constantly cricking his neck, and it was beginning to get on Sunjack's nerves.

"He's gone," Bardal said in a low voice. "Probably halfway across Vathia by now. If not Kree."

"Why do you think he went south?" Sunjack quietly asked.

"No other way to go," his nefarious companion explained. "Anywhere northwest is the front. East is the marsh plains. No man would willingly walk across that miserable stretch of slop. Not after one night of this piss. North is Marrn, and who wants to deal with those bastards? Sooner or later, you're going to kill one."

Sunjack grunted agreement.

"So south it is," Bardal went on, adjusting his back. The short blades he adorned his thumbs with glinted in the gloom. He stuck his head outside and sighted the healer's door.

Sunjack frowned at the brazen lack of subtlety. "Why don't you just go on up there and knock?"

"Bit too obvious."

"What you're doing now isn't?"

Bardal fixed him with those deep-set, dangerous eyes, in which the light resembled fire-red needle points. Sunjack stared back and didn't break away, not with Bardal. To do so would invite disaster.

Eventually, the shorter man sneered, looked at his own boots, and shuffled back into the darkness.

Sunjack returned to watching the door, satisfied that he'd won that round.

"He's not coming back," Bardal muttered.

"So you think we should be doing something else?"

"Aye that."

"Like what?"

Bardal didn't reply.

"Maybe you should tell Jaro your thoughts?" Sunjack pressed. "If you're so convinced."

Bardal scoffed and cricked his neck as an answer.

"Why do you keep doing that?" Sunjack asked.

"Like the sound."

"It's annoying."

"Is it?" Bardal asked and popped his neck the other way. "That bother you?"

"Punce."

Bardal rolled his powerful shoulders, cracking those as well.

"You're thinking about the tar again, aren't you?" Sunjack asked.

Bardal said nothing, but the guilty silence said it all.

"I should throttle Paze," Sunjack whispered. "For slipping you that unfit shite."

"Not unfit," Bardal said. "You . . . go places."

"Imagine you do. Your coin goes places, too, I wager. But not in the same direction."

"Nothing else to spend it on."

"Plenty to spend it on," Sunjack countered. "You just don't want to spend it on anything else."

"It's my coin."

"Are you hearing yourself?"

The shorter man waved a hand, dismissing the conversation. The two of them returned to watching the door.

"I could throttle the man," Bardal suggested softly. "Root out an eye?"

"Root out an eye?" Sunjack repeated in distaste. "Who?"

"Him."

"The healer?"

"Mm."

"What's that going to do?"

Bardal didn't answer.

"That's going to do nothing," Sunjack answered his own question, annoyed. "Except get the entire street talking about how some brute fishhooked the eyes out of a healer's head. You think that'll bring the punce out into the open?"

"Maybe."

"If I thought that might work, I would've cut that that asslicker long ago."

Bardal had nothing to say to that.

The conversation reached a lull.

"He's gone," Sunjack said, echoing his companion's sentiments, and looked at his own boots.

"I'm not staying out in this all night," Bardal grumped. "Not right."

"No, it's not."

"I could piss myself and not feel a thing."

Sunjack didn't comment.

"The others can keep watch."

That notion tempted Sunjack, truth be known.

"What do you think?" Bardal asked.

"It's not yet midnight."

"How can you tell? It's blacker than King Juhn's blossom out here."

Sunjack didn't need to think about the ruler's blossom. "I feel it. I get weary around midnight. I'm not weary yet."

"Tell me when you're weary, then," Bardal said. "And let's get out of this shite."

"Not until midnight," Sunjack said, stealing another peek at the healer's door.

"Can you really tell when it's midnight?"

"Course I can."

"Then we go."

As much as he didn't like the idea of Borchus having escaped them, doubt was seeping into Sunjack's mind.

"Then we go," he agreed with a sigh.

7

The cellar door opened a crack, allowing water to flow down the steps. A few fingers appeared, struggling for a better grip. Borchus peeked out and gauged the storm, squinting at the rain and mindful of the stream flowing past his boots.

Unfit, he thought, and meant it.

He knew he should stay below ground and sleep, waiting the storm out, and hope for better weather the next day.

A couple of thoughts, however, prevented him from doing that.

A few days earlier, after speaking with his newest spy, Naulis, Borchus had taken the long way back to his old lodgings underneath the cobbler's home. That very day, he located a new hole to inhabit, just south of the arena. Deciding that staying hidden for a while would be wise, Borchus had a talk with the owner of the newest cellar. The man was a bowyer, and his shop contained an impressive assortment of hunting and war bows. An agreement was reached, and Borchus paid the man two weeks' lodgings in advance. The agent later informed the cobbler's wife that he would be leaving their cellar. They were sad to see him go but wished him well.

Sometime after sunset, Borchus finally settled into his new abode. There, stooping underneath the floorboards of the bowyer's home, the agent told himself he would stay for only a short time. No bed was there, except a blanket he'd brought with him. That went onto a dirt floor, along with a handful of candles, a change of clothing, and the old short sword he carried. He buried a small sack of coins in the center of the cellar and charged himself to remember his funds' location. The place had no latrine but did have a pisspot. When Borchus asked about this, the bowyer, a middle-aged soul with one squinty eye and a thick rash extending from his jawline to his scalp, handed him a hand shovel and gave permission to dig.

"But when you do, dig deep," the bowyer advised with a meaningful nod.

Borchus did as told—when he had to. It was either that or chance a public latrine, and with the way his luck was playing out, he didn't like the idea of being stabbed while reaching for a scrub brush.

At night, he lay back in the cool darkness smelling of dusty earth while voices rumbled above, and he attempted to figure things through. He wondered about Garl and if he was doing well with the Ten. He wondered about who had attempted to steal the Ten's coin weeks earlier, only to have Muluk thwart their efforts. He eventually wondered about who was trying to kill him and if the reason was revenge for his killing of Strach, to satisfy Garl's own need for retribution.

Mostly, however, he thought about Sindra . . . and what he might be able to do or say to convince her to spy for him.

No chance of that happening, for she'd made her thoughts on the matter—and him—quite clear the last time they'd talked.

Sometime during the very next day of his self-imposed seclusion, he admitted to himself he no longer cared about Sindra being a spy. Truth be known, that was only a convenient lie, a means of inserting himself back into her life, a reason for speaking to her, if he needed a reason.

Any reason.

Since then, Borchus had ventured forth into the city, always at the height and power of the afternoon sun, when the day's heat would dull a person's thinking and he could move about with a cowl over his head. His size and build was a problem since a person could recognize him, but he chanced it. He was careful, never buying food or drink from the same place in a day and constantly keeping at the center of flowing crowds.

Most of his travels seemed to circle closer and closer to Hadree's—now Sindra's—alehouse, which he would watch from a distance, usually from the shade of an alley.

Borchus intended to go there this wet and stormy night.

His hand drifted to his stab wound. It bothered him constantly, especially when he walked. His side ached just under the left side of his ribs, where the knife had opened him. The stitches tightened and pulled whenever he moved too quickly. He regularly applied ointment to it, purchased from another healer and generously applied, hoping the fragrant shite would work its properties quickly, as well as moisten the flesh, making it a little more pliable.

A vibe of trepidation coursed through him, poisoning his core, as he watched and breathed in the freshness of the storm. He knew the root of the problem, knew he had to address it, else it would plague him until the end of his days—just like before, when he'd left Sunja for fourteen years.

Sindra.

But unlike before, he was no longer wondering what she was doing. He was wondering who the man in her life was, and what he meant to her.

He'd left her alone since their last meeting, hoping his absence might douse the dislike she'd cast his way, but if he didn't talk with her soon, he believed he was going to burst.

He needed to know.

Once he *did* know, he believed he could move on—one way or another.

So he had smelled his clothing and deemed them clean enough, inserted his belt-buckle knife and readied it. His boot dagger was already in place, and the short sword hanging off his waist, in a scabbard, was concealed by a cloak and cowl he wore.

Peering out at the rain, however, Borchus didn't think the cloak would keep him dry for long. And he didn't relish the very real struggle of removing his boots upon returning.

He was about to leave then, but a chill overcame him, and the haunting voice of Hadree spoke, unexpectedly, at the back of his mind.

Stay in tonight, lad, said the alehouse owner, the man whom Borchus had thought of as a father at one point—a father he usually ignored, he supposed with a touch of regret.

"It'll be all right," Borchus whispered, which silenced the ghost in his head.

That was Hadree's way. If one warning wasn't enough, he'd keep his mouth shut thereafter.

Borchus rose from the cellar into the fierce weather. He closed the door and followed the alley to the main street. There, he paused at the corner, his eyes already used to the darkness, and scanned the way before him.

Not a soul was in sight.

Borchus waited as long as he cared to, then he clenched his cloak around his front and left the alley, keeping to the wedges, outcrops, and crevices offered by the street. The storm hurried him along, covering his passage. He moved like a wet rat, hugging the walls and scurrying for fear of being discovered.

Later, well before midnight, he stood between two buildings and viewed the lit and glowing windows of Sindra's alehouse ... and the man-mountain called Gurga guarding the entrance.

Seddon above, Borchus fumed, unimpressed with the sight, suspecting the enforcer would gleefully toss him into the street if he revealed himself.

After a right and proper thrashing.

The huge guardian stood beneath immense eaves, scowling a face that might've been raked by blunt nails. He wore breeches as black as night and a white shirt opened wide at the neck, with sleeves rolled up to midforearm. Hair flourished with oily vigor in those places, especially around the neck. As far as Borchus could deduce, one of the man's parents had to have been violated by a bear . . . or worse.

Gurga stood with his back to the doorway, hunched over with his skull barely clearing the beams overhead, appearing quite dry. A huge belt hung about his waist, and a frightening spiked club drooped from its length, as threatening as a battle-axe.

Borchus rubbed his face at the sight, knowing full well the challenge ahead of him.

Wait the bastard out, he decided and stayed back, watching the formidable enforcer from the depths of the alley.

The rain continued, penetrating Borchus's cloak, soaking it, and eventually reaching his skin. The agent did not move. Water seeped into his boots, toes and heels.

Borchus continued to watch Gurga.

The big man looked left every now and again, and occasionally right. Sometimes, he scratched his nose or chin. Once, he plucked at his neck. He was a massive guard dog of unknown hellion origin, glaring at both ends of the street and deeming it his. When he did turn his head, it was with ominous grace, a result of unseen counterweights and ancient cogs, casting his fearsome attention over every fitted stone of the street.

Borchus didn't believe anyone was in the alehouse, truth be known, and it didn't have anything to do with the weather. Gurga's presence alone would freeze the piss in damn near any decent soul.

He supposed he could try the back door, but he remembered it being barred from the inside, with two stout planks. Perhaps he could—

Sindra appeared in the doorway.

Borchus stopped thinking.

As lovely as ever, she stood in a flattering dress of red, both shoulders bare and glowing in the backlight from the alehouse's inner fires. Her hair was loose and flowing, and she reached around and gathered it all in a hand, as if considering tying it. She talked to Gurga, who listened like the obedient ogre that he was. Her other hand hitched upon her hip in a question then latched onto Gurga's hairy forearm. She smiled and broke away with a fond pat, leaving the big man on the alehouse deck, and that flash of happiness made Borchus's heart ache.

Lords above, he grumbled. For all his intelligence, for all his stealth and good intentions, though questionable at times, he watched Sindra disappear inside the alehouse and hated himself.

Fourteen years he'd been gone.

And she still filled his thoughts, stronger than ever.

Borchus shook himself, remembering the cold soak of water in his boots and clothing.

"Sweet Seddon," he muttered, glancing in Gurga's direction with an air of defeated reproach. *Undone by a towering temple slave.* "You . . . big . . . *bastard.*"

Miserable and knowing it was a long walk back to his hole in the ground, Borchus retreated into the shadows as if he'd been kicked right and proper in the plums.

When he was far enough away, he turned and disappeared into the night.

8

Boredom got him out of his hole.

The morning was dismal, the sun blocked by storm clouds not quite finished with the city. A fine drizzle enveloped Borchus as he climbed out of the cellar. He located a small stone, tucked it just so underneath one corner of the cellar's door, and opened it once again.

The hard nub of rock fell to the ground.

Satisfied, Borchus replaced the rock. If anyone attempted to enter his cellar, perhaps with the intention of stabbing him in the darkness, he'd know with a quick check.

No games would take place this day with the weather so unfit, but the gears turning behind the bloody spectacle wouldn't stop. And after having slept in the damp darkness, stripped down to nothing, Borchus *needed* to get out and walk around. His clothing and boots were far from dry even though he'd wrung most of the water from them. The stink, however, could not be warded off by hand alone. Perhaps he'd buy fresh clothes later in the day. That was an idea.

After he visited the Pit.

Though he'd charged Naulis with keeping an eye on the arena and the cesspool known as general quarters, he felt the need to check on matters himself, to find out who the Ten would be fighting later in the week and deliver some semblance of information to Goll. That was risky, even stupid, but Borchus didn't care. He needed the distraction. He always had the chance to reconnect with Naulis, to see if he'd heard anything new. Borchus could go to the man's house, but now that the lad with practically no chin was in his employment, he didn't want to risk the chance of revealing Naulis's home to any unseen spies.

So he marched along, keeping his head down and hood up, not appreciating the damp weight upon his shoulders. The cloak had been drenched, and the resulting smell was nose wrinkling, despite being in the open air. He stopped at a food stall and purchased breakfast, a quick handful of hard-boiled eggs that he munched as he walked. The potential for more stormy weather had thinned out the crowds, but losing oneself in the ebb and flow of people, carts, and livestock was still easy. At one point, Borchus kept pace alongside a covered wagon of caged chickens, patting down the rear as if familiar with the animals, mindful of the driver and anyone who came too close. He avoided the alleyways with beggars, knowing full well they could be plied for information if needed, and took the long way around to the arena.

By midmorning, the Gate of the Sea loomed ahead, a huge gaping maw set between a pair of black Vathian marble columns, at the base of a four-story shell of red brick and oak timbers. Fitted stone tiles remained wet looking from the night before, and rainwater had collected in some shallow depressions. The arena cast a gloomy shade over the fairway, further darkening the ground. Any other time, the majestic construction would generate a twinge of excitement, but not today. Borchus hung back from the arena and critically eyed the thin crowds before the structure. Places to hide were scant between there and the Gate of the Sea. He doubted the other side of the Pit was much better.

Casually, he glanced back at the way traveled and failed to see anyone following.

The way ahead beckoned.

Saimon's black hanging fruit, he thought and ambled into the open space. That very act alone felt similar to jumping off a cliff. Though his outer demeanor seemed carefree, he was scanning everything within his field of vision. A pair of Skarrs stood and watched him until he went by. A small group of men gathered to one side talked about the last night's weather. Borchus calmly moved past them. People going about their business drifted across his chosen path, but by all outward appearances, he paid them no heed. In reality, he was studying every one.

The welcoming darkness of the Gate of the Sea grew larger.

Someone laughed a little too loudly, distracting Borchus, but he kept his pace steady, not betraying the rising unease of being so exposed.

Footsteps rushed him from the right.

Borchus halted when a pair of children—a girl chasing a boy—bolted past. Smiling thinly and far from relaxed, he started walking again. He made a point of looking around for other children.

"Where're you going?" a man called out, sending a bolt of nervousness through Borchus.

"Getting breakfast," a different person replied. "Have you eaten?"

The warm laughter that followed failed to calm the agent's nerves.

Food stalls lay just ahead, on either side of the gate. People stood and grazed, jowls flexing, nodding at sleepy conversations. The smell of warm bread, sweet jams, butters, and salted meats attracted Borchus's attention. He even slowed, making a scene of deciding whether or not to stop before continuing on.

Natural. Have to look natural. No quick moves else any wolves about would pick up his scent.

The arena's shadow fell over him, and he proceeded inside the murky tunnel that was the Gate of the Sea. Another passage appeared on the right, and he entered it, embracing the rising stink that wafted past him.

General quarters. He secretly loathed the underground barracks as much as Naulis.

Torches lit the way as he followed the brick corridor.

Peeking up from a small meal of honey buttered bread, an unshaven stick of an individual chewed noisily and watched the drowned topper in a cloak pass by the food stall. Gray eyes followed the little traveler's every movement as he entered the Gate of the Sea, right up until the wet-looking knob tickler disappeared into a side tunnel. Once the punce was gone, the watcher stuffed the remainder of his food into his mouth, gave his face a quick wipe-down with a hand, and glanced around before taking up a brisk pursuit.

Before he vanished inside the tunnel, he coughed into his palm.

Alerting two other watchers nearby.

Borchus took a longer route, traversing the bowels of the Pit and bypassing the cramped morass that was general quarters. Torches set into iron sconces revealed bubbles of orange-hued brick interspersed with long shadows. He passed by the infirmary and glimpsed an individual standing amongst a row of empty cots. Borchus didn't dally, hearing the man's soft boots scuff along the floor. It had been a while since he'd taken a more indirect path to the owners' chambers, so he stopped once between two pockets of torchlight and reflected on the direction, studying the way ahead and behind him.

When he did, he heard the distinct halt of footfalls.

Borchus frowned. He hooked his cowl back from an ear and waited.

Nothing.

He started walking again, no faster than before. He felt no need to be alarmed just yet. The tunnels could be a hive of human activity at any time.

Borchus increased his stride, and that ghostly echo trailed him.

In short time, he linked up with the white tunnel and sought the Ten's private chamber. The door was closed, so he knocked and waited before trying the latch. It opened. Borchus peered back the way he'd come, checking on his pursuer.

The way lay empty.

A pair of Skarrs approached, patrolling the level, and Borchus paid them no mind. He slipped inside the room and immediately spied a scroll tossed onto the floor. That summoned a wry smile. The Madea didn't seem to favor the Ten in the least.

Freeing up his sword arm, just in case, Borchus picked up the scroll while placing his back against the wall. He scanned the contents, frowning at the message.

Blood match.
Stable of Salwark.
Demanding revenge for the death of one of their own.
Goll of Kree.
The next suitable day of the games.

Borchus sighed. He'd heard Goll butchered a Balgothan gladiator. The Kree was going to get himself killed, and probably by another Balgothan. The storms had doubtless stopped the Ten from leaving the city, so Borchus guessed they were holed up at Shan's house. He thought about visiting but disliked the thought of Goll's inevitable questions on his recent whereabouts.

Borchus placed the scroll on a nearby bench, where it should've been in the first place. Someone would find it, perhaps Naulis.

Footsteps in the corridor distracted him.

The agent returned to the door and listened. The footsteps grew louder as two robed arena attendants passed the entrance. One of them eyed Borchus curiously but continued with his companion. That was good.

Borchus stepped into the corridor, watching their backs.

Then he looked the other way.

A shadow grew along the tunnel wall, becoming a commonly dressed man, a man who kept his hands at his sides, his face drawn and stoic. Hollow cheeks and stubble darkened his features, and the eyes fixed upon Borchus.

The figure stopped in his tracks, studying him.

Borchus stared. He knew that look.

The two men watched each other then, waiting, undecided as to what to do next. Borchus recognized the taller hunter for who he was, all the while cursing his own brashness for coming to the arena.

Then he recognized an even greater opportunity.

Laughter drifted from the other end of the tunnel, from the direction of general quarters. Borchus considered returning to the Ten's chamber, but Goll probably would not appreciate that. So he decided upon another place.

He followed the pair of arena attendants.

And the shadow tailed him.

The attendants were unaware of the two individuals following them. Four Skarrs with their backs to the wall came into view. Borchus followed the attendants past the guards and glanced over his shoulder, to ensure his admirer was still there.

He was, watching his quarry and appearing even more determined. Or disgusted. They were headed toward the general quarters and the hundreds of Free Trained that resided there. The smell grew increasingly unfit with every step.

The attendants disappeared amongst the first ranks of swaggering gladiators. Borchus didn't follow them, nor did he seek to lose his hunter amid the hundreds of lounging pit fighters. He avoided the Madea's high desk and the half dozen Skarrs guarding him. Instead, Borchus passed by and continued to another tunnel. He walked along a series of shorter passages, much wider than the ones before. No gladiator was to be seen in this part of the Pit, and rightfully so.

Borchus again checked on his hunter.

He was still back there, still following, and walking faster.

The temperature increased, becoming uncomfortably warm. Borchus heaved off his cloak, dropping it upon the floor. Up ahead, the corridor opened into a broad chamber, and the crackling of a fire could be heard. He entered the chamber and grimaced at the spike in heat. Torches burned around the upper edges of the room. Red brick surrounded a broad landing, and two men had tilted a large cart off its wheels, while a third was about to drop to his knees. That one held a drooping brush and a small bucket of grease. A wall of chopped firewood, cords deep, lined the walls, while a chopping block with a heavy axe set into its splintered girth stood just to the left. A few barrels and crates lay scattered around the place, and straight ahead, the floor extended perhaps a dozen more feet before ending at an unfenced drop.

There, the arena fire pit waited, already burning and puffing smoke through the dark slots of an unknown ventilation system.

Borchus didn't know exactly why they were firing up the pit on such a damp day, but he didn't rightly care, either. Perspiring, he walked across the sizeable chamber. His shadow fell across the wall and the wood stored there. He stopped at the pit's edge and peered into its smoky red depths. Nothing about the fire pit was sacred—no podiums for sermons. The disposal area for dead gladiators was scalding hot and practical.

The hunter appeared in the entrance, eyes glinting in the firelight.

The three attendants stopped working and regarded the two new arrivals with genuine looks of puzzlement. The one with the brush appeared the most distressed, nervous enough to let slip a cow kiss.

Keeping an eye on his stalker, Borchus reached into a pocket and produced a few gold coins. These he held out to the attendants.

"Leave us for a while, would you?" he asked.

The three men traded looks. The one holding the brush and bucket plunked the items into the cart while the others lowered it.

They collected the coin with averted eyes and hurried out of the room.

The hunter paid them no mind, focused on Borchus. Neither man moved, studying each other for a time.

"My thanks," the hunter said quietly. "I wouldn't have paid them a thing."

The fire pit crackled. Air currents lifted glowing embers to the ceiling.

"Don't worry," Borchus replied. "I'll get my coin back. After I'm finished with you."

The hunter didn't smile at that. He walked across the room, taking his time, eyeing Borchus for any sudden moves. The agent backed away, giving the hunter space but staying close to the pit's edge. A dozen or so strides separated the two men. The hunter stepped to the fire pit's edge as well and, guardedly, peered below. What he saw summoned a scowl to his face, and he shied away. He reached behind his back and brought forth a pair of exotic, well-used knives, their lengths curved and wicked. The hunter lowered the blades to his sides. Firelight rippled along their edges.

Borchus pulled his short sword. "Who are you?" he asked calmly.

The hunter ignored the question and stepped forward.

"Who sent you?" Borchus asked.

Another step, the hunter's face becoming a stern and set thing.

"Why am I to die?"

Again no answer. The hunter flexed his arms and assumed a far more formal stance.

Borchus frowned. "All right then . . . Do you know who I am?"

The fire pit rumbled below, filling the silence left by the question. A bright ember floated past.

"You're Borchus," the hunter said, unblinking.

The agent smiled faintly. At least he'd gotten one answer out of the unfit he-bitch.

He fully intended to get more.

The three attendants stood further down the corridor. A yelp of pain caught their attention, followed by a guttural hissing.

TO THUNDEROUS APPLAUSE

There was a short burst of profanity, a barely heard scuffling, then nothing.

A short time later, Borchus strode by and eyed them darkly, warning them not to speak of their meeting or anything they might have seen. He left the three alone then, his thoughts occupied with other matters. His would-be slayer belonged to the Sons of Cholla. The pisser hadn't said as much—he didn't say much of anything, really, being annoyingly defiant to the end—but before Borchus dropped the man's bleeding carcass into the fire pit, he spotted the ink upon the hunter's forearms. Upon a further search, he discovered that the twisting chains and smiling dragons went up the man's biceps and extended to his chest.

That colorful ink had also decorated Strach's person.

Somehow, the Sons knew Borchus was responsible for Strach's death. He sighed wearily. At least Garl was free of the city. That was one worry off his mind though now he admittedly had much bigger concerns, dealing with and surviving the largest, most ruthless street clan in Sunja.

With a little more urgency to his stride, Borchus retraced his steps to general quarters, wanting to be clear of the Pit and somewhere safe. Free Trained gladiators, the lowest of the low, sauntered about, conversing or getting in each other's way. Borchus didn't pay too much attention to them until—

"I wager you'll do fine. Just fine. Good fortune to you."

Those few spoken words slowed Borchus down as if a poison had just reached his heart. He stopped mere strides away from the white tunnel and, with all the practiced calm he could muster, looked toward the twisting, churning maggot cluster of bodies.

There, removing his hand from a gladiator's shoulder, was a tall, well-groomed man, handsome even, in a cruel sort of way. He wore dark clothes including a vest of fashionable leather that shone in the torchlight. He was smiling, yet not, at a blocky Free Trained brute—no doubt some foreigner come to try his hand at the games. Borchus saw how the man's not-quite-a-smile dimmed and frosted over the instant he turned away from

81

the pit fighter. The face wasn't familiar, as it had been dark in the alley that night when Borchus first laid eyes upon Sindra's visitor.

But he remembered the well-oiled voice.

And the words.

I'll remember our time together and look forward to the next meeting.

Same voice. Same tone. Borchus pretended to study his fingers, rubbing them together while secretly watching the finely dressed individual. The roguish bastard greeted the Madea next, spoke to him, and received a scroll from the arena official. He flashed another unpleasant smile as if the punce didn't realize how unfriendly that display of teeth actually was.

"Until next time, good Madea," he announced and turned away, walking in that same lofty stroll that suggested a very high opinion of himself.

A good evening to you, sweet Sindra.

It was him.

The cold realization seized Borchus by the guts.

Forgetting about the Sons of Cholla, he pursued Sindra's man.

They exited through the westerly Gate of the Moon.

Sindra's man—a term that annoyed Borchus—was a fast walker, so fast, in fact, that he almost lost him on the fairway's open expanse. People were milling about the arena, so hurrying across that empty space would attract attention. Borchus forced himself to wait until Sindra's man was nearly across before he followed. The agent restrained himself from hurrying over the fairway. When he crossed over into the streets, he made two wrong turns before reacquiring the scent and continuing after his quarry.

Up ahead, Sindra's man emerged from a smaller lane and walked through the people moving about, cutting off more than a few.

Backtracking—perhaps to see if he'd been followed.

A skill usually practiced by a spy or agent.

Borchus's suspicions grew, and he became much more careful, well aware he'd only just disposed of one street snake. He checked his own tail to ensure he wasn't being followed, remembering a previous attempt on his life involving two killers.

Up ahead, Sindra's man walked close to the street's edge, along a section of wooden posts, parked wagons, closed doors, and merchant shops. He abruptly disappeared down an alley, and Borchus slowed to give him some distance. After a few heartbeats, he peeked around the corner.

Sindra's man, halfway through the alley, had pinned an old wretch against the wall and was hissing into the unfortunate bastard's face.

Borchus withdrew and pressed his shoulder to the corner, straining to hear.

". . . ask me for coin again, and I'll—"

A farmer shouted at a string of cows to move faster, blocking out the rest. One beast cried out and dropped a considerable kiss onto a stone tile. Borchus frowned at the interruption and peeked into the alley.

The old beggar was still there, but Sindra's man had gone.

Right, Borchus thought and entered. He approached the old man, whose wrinkled face had paled to wormish white, brought on by a rattling of nerves. When he noticed Borchus approaching, the old man pressed himself against the wall and moaned.

Borchus pitied the frightened topper, so he stopped, signaled for a moment, and rooted around a pocket. All while the beggar squeezed his eyes shut and squirmed as if much too close to an open fire.

"Here," the agent finally said and held out a fist.

The beggar moaned again.

"*Here*," Borchus repeated and forced a handful of silver and gold into the beggar's bony palm. "Take this—"

And he left the fellow staring at coin spilling through his fingers.

It hadn't belonged to Borchus. The dead man cooking in Sunja's fire pit had owned a bigger purse than expected.

Hurrying along while trying to appear unconcerned with the time, Borchus lost sight of Sindra's man at a small intersection. A nearby cook tried to sell him the previous day's odd-smelling strips of beef. Ignoring him, Borchus spied a puddle halfway up a lane between two whitewashed walls.

The puddle's water trembled as though having been recently disturbed.

Borchus cautiously proceeded. He stayed back at a comfortable distance, sometimes guessing wrongly but mostly reading the signs and following the trail.

And sometime just after noon, Sindra's man halted before a high wall of mottled stone. He rapped upon a closed gate set into the wall. An inset door opened, and the roguish punce bared those predatory teeth before entering. The door closed, and that was that. Borchus had located the private abode of Sindra's man.

Or at least his employer.

Either way, the agent's stomach twisted into fearful knots, the likes of which he'd not experienced for a very long time.

Even though fourteen years had passed since he'd last seen the place, the inner streets of Sunja's city remained the same, and though his memory had clouded, fragments became clearer with every alley he passed, every public well, fountain, and gathering square. If he'd had time to stop and properly size up his surroundings, he would've known immediately where he stood, but he couldn't spare a moment. And with each awakening memory, the sense of familiarity swelled, as did his trepidation.

For Sindra's man had gone from the arena to none other than the walled training grounds belonging to the House of Tilo. The former employer of Borchus himself, back in a time when Hadree was still alive and interactions with Sindra were far more pleasant to remember.

The compound's looming walls sent a jolt of fear through Borchus. At least three sentries would be posted behind the closed gate, where a slot could be used to peer out at visitors or passersby. Borchus had no intention of going any closer to the property. He eyed the walls' formidable heights, aware of the fortress-like walkway behind them and their patrolling sentries.

Knowing full well he'd stumbled into an exceptionally dangerous place, Borchus withdrew as calmly as possible while his heart screamed at him to run.

He slunk back into the nearby city maze, with every intention of returning to his hole under the bowyer's house.

9

Later that same afternoon, Naulis sucked in as much fresh air as he could into his unimpressive chest. He held that breath, savored it, and released it. He then ventured beneath the Pit, tasting the foulness pervading the stone passages and knowing it would make him sick. Moving as quickly as he could, he arrived at the Ten's private chamber, picked up the scroll within, and though perplexed to see it opened, promptly delivered the message to the healing house of Shan.

There, Goll waited just inside the main door.

"What's this?" the Kree asked, mouth slightly screwed up, irritated at the oppressive humidity and the weather's indecision to clear or rain.

Naulis shrugged.

"You didn't read it?" Goll asked, taking the document.

"I did not."

Goll unrolled the scroll. He read the contents and smirked. Clavellus appeared, so he handed the parchment to the taskmaster's shaking hand.

"Any sign of Borchus?" the Kree asked.

"None," Naulis said, scratching at his oily scalp.

Clavellus finished reading the message and tapped the scroll off a shoulder. "Blood match. The next day of competition."

"Aye that." Goll then looked at Naulis. "You have any idea where he might be?"

"No," the spy replied.

"No indication of who the gladiator might be," Clavellus noted.

"Won't matter," Goll said.

That piqued the taskmaster. "Why won't it matter?"

"I'll kill them anyway. Whoever they send."

That put a smile on Clavellus's bearded face.

Goll realized Naulis was still there. "Yes?"

"Anything for me to . . . ?" He trailed off.

"No."

Naulis nodded and remained where he was.

"We won't be traveling home, then," Clavellus said. "Not until this challenge sorts itself out. Just as well. Where's Shan?"

"Out back," Goll said. "In his residence."

"We'll have to stay here . . . with his wife's permission."

"Suppose so. Are you waiting for something?" Goll pointedly asked Naulis.

"Well, Master Goll," the man explained with embarrassment that seemed a touch forced. "Borchus and I—we had an understanding regarding payment. Particularly when I had to go down into general quarters. Or even go *near* general quarters. You see, I hate general quarters."

"We all hate general quarters," Goll interrupted and dug out a few coins from a pocket. "This enough?"

Naulis brightened.

"Off you go, then," Goll told him. "But report back if you learn anything, especially if you hear from Borchus."

Naulis left the house, and Goll faced the taskmaster. "Best you speak with Shan about staying here another day. I don't have the tongue for it right now."

"What about Borchus?"

"Your agent isn't doing his job."

Clavellus thought about that. "Then he's either dead or he's very busy. Either way, we'll be here for another night at least."

"You don't have to stay. If allowed, I'll stay here alone. Or somewhere else in the city."

"Wouldn't be right to leave you alone," the older man said. "Daresay the fight will be tomorrow, once this damned weather clears. The sun will dry out the roads quickly. Make it somewhat passable. Nothing really pressing at the villa. They'll be fine for another day."

"How is he?" Nala asked, returning after having reclaimed some of the sleep lost to her the night before.

Sitting on a stool, Torello looked up, straightening from where he'd leaned against the wall. He glanced at the unconscious Brozz, laid out on his cot. Sweat covered the Sarlander, and the pungent smell of onions ruined the air despite the shutters being open—a grim reminder of the gruesome bit of surgery Nala had performed upon the man, when she opened him up and attempted to clean the infection with hot water. Stitches closed the large cut afterward, but it wasn't an easy thing. Three times, the twine had broken, each sinewy little *pop* unnerving and frustrating her just a little more than before, until she heaped a gob of saywort into the raw fissure, hoping it would at least soften the flesh and make it somewhat more pliable. That had worked to a point, but getting a grip on the skin thereafter had been almost impossible. Her hands eventually cramped, and she could do no more, whereupon Ananda switched off and completed the task. In the end, the cut resembled a mouth sewn together much too tightly.

They'd smeared more ointment across the sealed wound and covered it with a thick wad of cloth.

"Half dead," Torello answered the lady's question and sighed wearily. "The other half like this. With the odd twitch now and then. Still alive, so there's that."

In the alcove across from Brozz's, Garl struggled to sit up from the cot upon which he'd been resting.

"Hasn't awakened at all?" Nala asked.

Torello shook his head. "Best that he doesn't, I think. I mean, look at that. You sliced him like a pissed-drunk butcher. Put him back together like . . . well, I don't know what. And that ointment? My eyes have been stinging the whole time I've been here."

"It's truly ripe," Garl agreed. "But the lad's still alive, like he said."

That will have to do, Nala supposed, gazing upon the still-sleeping Sarlander. Her eyes came to a rest upon that dreadful gash she'd inflicted upon the man. And Torello was right. The saywort stank. Her own eyes were on the verge of watering.

"Watch him," she said. "I'll send someone to relieve you both."

"He's not going to wake up screaming," Torello pointed out. "And if he does, we'll hear him."

"He needs a healer," she stated again. "I couldn't do enough."

"He's not dead yet," Garl reminded her.

"Mind you," Torello said. "There's a war going on inside him right now. I wipe down his face, but a short time later? He's all sweat again."

"Is that a good sign?" Nala asked. "I don't think it is."

Neither man said anything.

"I don't think Clavellus will return this day," she said. "I'm thinking about sending someone to Pynn's Brook. A rider could be there by nightfall. Perhaps in the morning, they could return."

"How far away is it?" Garl asked.

"Half a day."

Nala saw how the older man's face sank with doubt and decided to say something. "Thank you. Both of you. For watching him."

With that, she left them and walked into the deserted common room beyond. She stopped just inside the main entrance and studied the clouds overhead, clouds that rolled and became blacker as the day wore on. It had rained all night and morning, tapering off to an annoying drizzle, but by afternoon, the drops fell again. Puddles filled every rut in the training grounds' sand and the land beyond the villa's gates. The roads in particular were unfit for traveling.

It was a right and proper summer storm.

They'd been fortunate so far this season, but now a monster had found them and showed no signs of moving off.

Pynn's Brook was a half day away under the best conditions. A rider could get there, but neither he nor a healer would return this night.

Nala looked at the ground, uncertain of what to do. Brozz needed a healer. His life could very well be balanced on a very sharp knife, which was a thought the lady of the house didn't want to think about. Despite initially disliking the gladiators' presence at the villa, she'd grown accustomed to them. And the one called Brozz struck her as a man with a sad history attempting to somehow clean it.

The rain reached her standing just inside the doorway, wetting her robes.

Clavellus would return tomorrow. Shan would be with him.

It was only a question of Brozz surviving until then.

10

When the household guards opened the double doors to the meeting chamber, all conversation stopped among the owners gathered within. One or two voices sputtered with throaty rattles, while one actually groaned upon seeing the unexpected arrival.

The weather was unfit for fighting, so Curge had decided to call for a meeting among the owners. As Grisholt received very little notice about the gathering, he didn't feel bad in the least for arriving much later than expected, as indicated by the simmering glares of the assembled men. In fact, he was beginning to enjoy the effect his presence had on others. They thought they projected anger, but Grisholt sensed they were uneasy behind their masks. And so they should be. It was due. His name was no longer associated with weakness. So he ignored them all except Dark Curge, for they occupied his meeting room—but even that bald-headed topper didn't look particularly pleased to see him. Not that Grisholt cared.

"Good Curge," he said with newfound aloofness.

Curge's eyes narrowed with dislike, and he didn't return the greetings. Dressed in a white shirt and black trousers, he was the only one standing at a huge rustic table. Six other men, none of them happy to see Grisholt's arrival, sat around that round slab of wood that might've once served as a fortress door. An empty chair sat there, the very last one in fact, spaced well apart between Burco Ustda and the young kog representing the Stable of Slavol. Salwark was his name, and the lad appeared to be sitting on two ass cheeks full of shite.

Grisholt moved to sit between the two owners. He noted that his rivals were all well spaced around the table. The death of Gastillo had helped with that, as well as the noticeable absence of Nexus and the upstart House of Ten. Grisholt checked the faces a second time, and sure enough, no one new was in attendance.

He pulled out the chair between Burco and Salwark, meeting the poisoned looks from Vandu, of the House of Vandu, and Razi, of the House of Razi. Grisholt ignored them, knowing full well they'd be right and proper unfit and seeking revenge for the deaths of their pit fighters.

"May I?" Grisholt said, indicating the chair. Burco paid him no heed, and Salwark went right on fidgeting.

"Sit where you like," Curge said.

"Perhaps he can sit where I like," a graying Razi said hotly, wasting no time. "Which is right outside that unfit door."

The outburst brought a smile to Grisholt's face, which really wouldn't help matters.

A red-faced Razi became even more angered. "You're smiling *now*, you ass-packing punce, but I guarantee you—"

"Razi," Curge warned, turning his attention upon the fat owner. "Control yourself."

The man's lips twisted. "He's a shiteberry of—"

"*Razi.*"

The elder manger quieted but, with looks alone, wished death upon Grisholt.

Curge watched the white-robed manager as though his stare alone would instill better self-control in the man. To his credit, Razi kept his mouth shut though he squirmed, fumed, and flashed raw hatred in Grisholt's direction.

Grisholt wisely kept quiet.

Curge eventually regarded him with simmering annoyance.

"I would have been here earlier if I'd gotten word earlier," Grisholt explained, smoothing his pointed beard. "As it was, it breaks up the day. Weather's too foul to return to the villa. The wagon wheels would sink in the road."

Dark Curge showed no indication he'd heard. Then he sniffed mightily, clearing his senses, and got down to business. "I called this meeting to address a matter concerning us all, which you're aware of. Prajus, a gladiator of some skill, belonging to the House of Gastillo, was challenged by Gastillo himself. In the fight that followed, Prajus killed his owner."

"In front of witnesses," Vorish said, earning a glare from Curge.

"Witnesses or not," Burco Ustda said, "I've heard this Prajus is a right and proper nuisance and that he goaded Gastillo at every opportunity."

"Witnesses or not," Curge repeated. "Public challenge or not. That dog *willingly* killed an owner. That will not do. You'll notice that Nexus does not attend this meeting. He was not invited. That bloodsucking leech has revealed his true face in this matter by taking Prajus in and allowing him to fight on his behalf. This displeases me greatly. It should displease *you* greatly. By sheltering Prajus, Nexus—a merchant, no less, who's been *dabbling* in our business for his own personal amusement—has pissed on not only us but the history of the games because he believes Prajus capable enough to become champion."

"He is capable enough," Razi grumped, "truth be known."

"I believe so," agreed Vorish.

Old Tilo's chin bobbed on his sunken chest as if lost in sleep, his great beard serving as an unfit pillow. Upon hearing the owners' voices, however, he lifted his head and paid attention to the discussion.

"He will not become champion," Curge ruled with grim authority. "Because he killed Gastillo. And because Nexus took him in. Those are inexcusable crimes. And as a group, we must agree on the punishment. For Prajus. And Nexus. Prajus requires no thought. He'll die in the arena. He's dead. If it's your hellpup facing that unfortunate bastard, then order him to kill the brazen maggot. Are we agreed?"

Hands rose around the table, accompanied by murmurs of agreement. Even Grisholt approved.

"Good," Curge said, pleased with the owners.

"That's to be done inside the arena?" Plump Vorish asked, squinting, mouth opened enough to show his tongue. The overweight bastard breathed like a punctured bellows, and the very sound turned Grisholt's guts.

"What kind of question is that?" Curge demanded.

"Well . . . I mean . . ."

"Of course it's to be done inside the arena, you unsightly tit." Curge then glowered with some poisonous afterthought, as if killing Prajus outside of the arena wouldn't be frowned upon.

"Will the Chamber support this decision, Curge?" Burco asked innocently enough. He was the second youngest, while his family was unquestionably one of the wealthiest, making their coin first on cloth before, as an afterthought, financing a house of gladiators. Burco had never fought in the Pit, despite having kept himself in some degree of fitness. Nor had his father, Unglo, before him. Neither man had ever managed to field a potential champion for the games.

Most of the owners, including Grisholt, smiled cynically at the question.

Curge did not, however. "Who do you think makes up the Chamber, young Burco?"

Burco's posture stiffened, and he realized he'd spoken without thinking. His face became red as his usually twinkling eyes dimmed just a little. He knew who the members were or once were. One only had to notice the scars and missing body parts amongst the order. They were primarily old gladiators, some once champions and those who had nearly seized the title. Then there were the few who were inducted simply from bloody experience in some form or other.

"Gladiators past," Burco answered quietly, clearing his throat. "Mostly."

Curge grunted, not seeing the need to further embarrass the lad. "And it's because of the Chamber that I summoned you all here today. If I had not done anything, they'd be wondering why we haven't acted. They're expecting us to punish Prajus. Although, truth be known, if we fail, they'll probably take matters into their own hands. Your thoughts, good Tilo?"

Frowning, Tilo chewed, or at least his jaw rolled over as if grinding away upon gristle, making his wild nest of a beard shake with infernal life. Despite some eighty-seven years or more pressed into his shrinking frame, Tilo appeared nowhere close to dying. He nodded, perhaps pleased to be asked for his opinion, and when he spoke, Grisholt noted how Vandu, sitting closest to the old owner, pulled his head back.

Tilo's breath was as foul and fragrant as a morning shite trough.

"Aye that," the old topper practically gargled, his throat sounding as if it were filled with sloppy butter. "They'll do something." His voice smoothed. "Without question. They're just as poisoned about Gastillo's death as the rest of us. There's little they can openly do against Nexus. He's paid his fees, like the rest of us, and the Chamber loves their coin. Mostly, though, they'll leave the cleaning of this pisspot to us and watch us use our tongues. If Vavar Slavol were here, he'd agree."

At the mention of his ailing father's name, Salwark nodded in understanding though Grisholt wasn't exactly sure what Vavar Slavol's son *thought* he was agreeing with—or whom he was fooling. Salwark was the youngest of them all and widely considered to be woefully inexperienced.

And like Tilo, Salwark's breath reeked. The unscrubbed crack of a dead man's ass smelled better.

"If we can't kill Prajus in the Pit, then they'll act." Tilo's little black eyes brightened like coals catching a breeze. "They'll kill the dog. Or maim him. Secretly, of course. Perhaps an accident of some sort. A fall from a great height. Maybe... choking on a piece of fruit. Some gurry like that. They'd prefer something much more... public, however. So they'll let us go first. See how we manage. Nexus and his school, however, will be handled differently. They'll leave that to us as well, with an eye on forcing him out of the games."

"To that end," Curge said, "I'll have my gladiators punish anyone belonging to Nexus."

"Punish?" Salwark asked, looking uneasy.

"Maim," Curge clarified. "Ruin his pit dogs. For competing. For even staying with him."

Salwark blinked in dread.

"Maiming is always a danger in the Pit," Old Tilo explained. "It comes with the profession, but intentionally maiming is a cruel act. One that's frowned upon but allowed, as you've no doubt seen in Sunja's fair streets. It's just as good as death and perhaps even worse to a gladiator, without the concern of a blood match. The Madea doesn't consider hacking off a limb reason enough to offer official retribution, so that bit of revenge is usually, ah, denied."

Tilo let that last word sink into the younger man's thoughts.

"If you dislike maiming then just kill his fighters," Curge said. "Either way will serve our purpose."

"Nexus's gladiators will dread entering the arena," Vorish added eagerly. "Morale will crumble. And as word spreads, the merchant won't be able to attract new blood to his school. No one wants a mark upon their heads for a deed they didn't do. Choking off the flow of new blood into his school will end him."

Silence fell then as the idea sank into their heads.

"I'm for it," Vandu said with a shrug.

"As am I," said Vorish.

Tilo raised his hand in agreement, and the others joined in, even a reluctant Salwark.

It pleased Curge to see such participation. "I'm taking extra measures," he said. "I'll not tolerate Nexus's presence in the viewing box from this day forth."

That surprised them. The upper viewing box was a coveted privilege, a trophy seat, and reserved only for the houses with the best overall showing from the previous year.

"How do you intend on doing that?" asked Vandu. The man was short, shaped like a boulder, and possessed a thick gray beard. Three scars of a questionable nature decorated his right cheek. Vandu's hooded gaze met Curge's head-on as neither man liked the other.

"I'll make it so," Curge answered, finally breaking the stare.

"How?" Vandu pressed with bored impatience. "Harsh looks? Extra sword arms? Then keep that splendid perch all to yourself, for the rest of the season?"

"Yes," the towering one-armed owner said.

"The Chamber won't care," Vorish added in that piggish squeal of his. That annoying knob of flesh sat next to Vandu.

Razi sat across from them both. Studying each man in turn, Grisholt wondered if the three pig bastards were dropped from the same mother.

"Not after what Nexus has done," Razi grumped in agreement. "That unfit—"

"Many thanks for telling us your intentions," Tilo said to Curge, cutting off the other owner. "Everyone at this table should follow your example. I'll further punish Nexus in my own way. In and out of the arena."

"As I will," echoed Razi, not appreciating being cut off by the eldest owner.

"Never liked the dog blossom," Vorish added. "Carries himself a little too high, for my taste."

Burco and Salwark grunted neutrally, but they'd follow the leads of the others. Grisholt also nodded, remembering his own dealing with the merchant: seven hundred gold pieces in exchange for his man, Barros, killing Junger and keeping the bargain a secret—all payable upon the Perician's death. However, Barros failed to kill Junger, and Nexus refused to pay. Grisholt had thought about going after the he-bitch for some of that coin by threatening to reveal the bargain to the

Chamber, but now, with the problem of Prajus and seeing the minds of the other owners, he decided it best to keep the matter to himself. Nexus had officially made himself an outcast, and any association or interaction with him would reflect badly on Grisholt. Though he possessed a newfound confidence and swagger because of his stable's recent successes, Grisholt was still somewhat rooted in the past. His own departed father had once warned him about how a determined and united group of owners could destroy an out-of-favor house.

And Nexus was clearly out of favor.

"The man doesn't associate with us, anyway," Vandu pointed out. "He's a merchant. The games are merely a diversion for him. Anything we might do won't truly hurt him. I don't believe there's much else we can do beyond butchering his lads."

"And that's a greater risk than keeping him from your precious viewing box," Razi grumbled.

"So we're agreed," Curge said, dismissing the last point and growing tired of the meeting. "Prajus is to be killed in the arena. Maim or kill any other gladiators fighting for the school of Nexus. And as for Nexus himself—"

"I'll decide how I deal with Nexus," Vandu said, steel in his voice. "Not you."

The two owners stared off again, clearly not pleased with each other.

"We've all decided," Tilo rumbled, breaking the tension. "Kill Prajus. Punish the other gladiators. But for any of you who might think otherwise, to do nothing informs Nexus you're fine with him taking in Prajus. The majority is not. If you choose to do nothing or very little, you risk facing the wrath of those around this table. Consider that. And if your lads fail in taking a few of his heads, then do a little more outside of the arena, to show your disapproval of what the merchant's done."

Curge waved his stump. "That chinless stain sees his dogs as investments. Maim or kill any of them off—*especially* Prajus—and you hurt him."

The weight of that charge quieted the owners.

"*If* we can kill off Prajus," Razi muttered. "The man's no slouch with a blade."

"Make no mistake," Tilo said. "That unfit drop of piss will perish."

"This might very well start a war between the houses," Salwark said.

"Then start a war," Curge countered, not bothered by the prospect. "Nexus doesn't care. Not yet, at least. He will, however. In fact, he's started one already."

"What of the Ten?" Burco asked, changing subjects.

"What of them?"

"Shouldn't they know of our plans?"

"No," Curge said flatly.

"The Free Trained shite isn't fit to grace this table," Tilo said with a grimace.

"A poor joke by the Chamber," Curge added, "recognizing them as a house."

That thought hung in the air.

"A joke?" Vandu said with a tired but sarcastic smile. "Really, Curge? Didn't that joke kill a pair of your pit fighters? Or have you forgotten?"

The temperature in the chamber rose as Curge straightened his broad back, eyeing an unflinching Vandu with dangerous intent.

"Good fortune," Tilo said, coming to Curge's defense and breaking the tension. "Nothing more."

Vandu's sleepy eyes narrowed into puzzled slits. He leaned toward the oldest owner. "Good fortune? Is that what you think? That's truly surprising coming from you, Tilo. I mean, if you believe it *was* good fortune, then I'll be smiling all the way back to my hole. But I've seen the Ten fight. I know what good fortune is. Dismiss them at your own peril."

"Dust specks clinging to each other are still dust specks," old Tilo said. "They're only larger. Easier to see. And to wipe away."

"Remember," Curge said before anyone else could speak. "In the beginning, there weren't even ten of them. They were Free Trained kogs stumbling from match to match. The scroff of the sands. Remember again, not two days after the Ten declared themselves a house that the Free Trained, the very gurry they separated themselves from, *decimated* them. Now, there are... what? Three gladiators remaining? My spies tell me that one of the three had to be helped from the arena and looked right unfit. He isn't expected to fight again. That leaves two."

A scowling Curge let that sink in.

"In the days to come, there'll be none," he finished.

"The season's longer now," Salwark pointed out.

Curge silenced him with a harsh look. "What does that have to do with the Ten? Nothing. These games, these glorious games, have *always* been a contest of endurance. And skill. And *will*. This year's no different. The weak will perish. The unprepared will drop into the dust. The strong will be right and proper tested, and only those truly worthy will advance to the final eight. A bloody journey that concludes with one gladiator surviving all, becoming victorious over all. So don't despair over the long days of the season. This year's games are the truest test yet."

Smirking, Vandu glanced from one owner to the other. "Say what you want. *Think* what you want. The Kree's returned from the grave. He's a threat. Their Perician's undefeated. He's an even *greater* threat. In fact, from what I've seen, the Perician's unstoppable."

"The Perician's a dead man," Curge rumbled, averting his gaze to the walls. "Just like the other one. By my hand or someone else's."

"You *hope* someone else's."

Another black look from Curge.

Vandu didn't flinch.

"Have you issued a blood challenge?" Burco asked Salwark across the table, defusing the standoff. "For the Kree?"

The son of Vavar Slavol frowned upon being asked of his plans, but he nodded.

"Well then," Curge announced, weary of the meeting. "Any further thoughts on the matter?"

In answer, Vandu gripped his chair's armrests, preparing to rise.

"Then . . ." Curge gestured at the chamber door, signaling their business concluded.

Chairs rattled and squealed as the owners rose. Vandu flatly made it a point to not look at Curge and strode briskly toward the exit. Guards opened the door in time for the man to march through.

Curge didn't move to leave, and old Tilo remained seated. Both studied Grisholt, to a degree that momentarily uneased him. He remembered who he was then and lifted his chin. The old Grisholt might've nodded at the two owners, showing some measure of respect. Things had changed, however, and he no longer saw either man as his peer . . . or his equal.

Straightening his clothing, Grisholt left the room.

When the owners were gone and Tilo was alone with Dark Curge, he looked at the one-armed ogre and smiled. "Vandu doesn't like you in the least."

Curge's scowl provided all the answer Tilo needed.

"We've already crossed blades this season," Curge said. "We'll cross blades again."

Tilo nodded, supposing that would be so.

"My thanks for your thoughts, good Tilo," said the menacing owner. "And support."

"No need," the older man said. "I agree with you. You're perhaps the only one in these games who I understand. I don't understand the others nearly as well. And I don't care to. The younger ones turn my guts rancid. Vavar's bastard there is a pretty worm. Burco is the same. Neither man should be gracing the Pit. Your father would've said so as well."

Old Curge no doubt would have. The son nodded, remembering his long-departed father.

"What you said is true," Tilo assured him. "About Nexus. About the Ten as well. There's only two or three of them remaining. With the seasons being stretched out, they'll soon begin to feel the weight of the arena. The ever-improving quality of the competition. No doubt they're questioning whether or not they have the strength, of body and of mind, to continue. Then, there's the knowledge that the entire arena is looking to take their heads because they dare compare themselves to us, to call themselves gladiators simply because they paid the Chamber's fee. What gurry is that?"

Tilo's features soured as if he'd gotten a whiff of his own mouth.

Curge again nodded.

"Did you see that lavender-dipped weasel at the end of the table?" the older man asked.

"Grisholt?"

"Aye, Grisholt. See his finery?"

"I don't really notice how another man dresses, good Tilo."

"Well, you should. Your father would. You can tell an animal by his fur, and that's one maggot who's enjoying life far too much. For a maggot."

Curge's features became pensive, and he looked toward the open door.

"If you need to talk," Tilo muttered, his rancid breath curling around Curge's nose. "You know . . . where I am." With a knowing dip of the head, the old man stood and exited the room.

Curge ran a hand over his face as if cleaning it, then took a purifying lungful of air. He thought of Grisholt then and decided Tilo was right. Old Curge would've made note of Grisholt's clothing and how he'd managed to pay for it all, when the punce had been all but done financially at the beginning of the season. The games could change one's fortunes, and Grisholt's fortunes had certainly changed. So had his gladiators'—all for the better, and in a very short time.

That thought remained with Curge as he strode out the door. He had other business to attend to.

The weather wavered between drizzling and pissing down upon Curge's bald head. He wandered outside and stopped just beyond the protective cover of eaves. Rows of gladiators practiced upon the wet sands, splashing through puddles, lifting heavy timbers, and hacking out punishing routines upon wooden skeletons. Squat and thick-necked Baris nodded in his direction, and Curge returned the gesture. The taskmaster's face looked oddly flat, as if he'd been bashed with a plank upon being birthed. Baris squinted in the rain and watched a great beast of a man struggling upon the training grounds, chopping away at a practice target. The brute was using a wooden axe upon his stationary foe and clearly wasn't having a productive session.

Sapo.

Despite his face resembling an overripe plum, courtesy of a pounding bestowed by the Ten's Sarlander, Baris had deemed the huge gladiator fit for training on this wet day, much to Sapo's ire. Yet because of his facial wounds and bruises, Sapo believed himself unfit to train.

Curge watched him from the edge of the sand. Sapo chopped without heart, paused with ill-concealed loathing for the task, and reset with a dramatic groan as if speared through the guts. After another poor swing, Sapo shook his head and looked at the dismal rainclouds, clearly annoyed with the weather, as if that had some bearing upon his performance.

Dark Curge wasn't impressed.

"Sapo," he called out, and the man turned in his direction.

Curge waved him over, and like a great hairless dog, Sapo obeyed, his battered face scrunched into a question. Swollen lips, broken teeth, stitched cuts, and purple welts covered his features. The man was a mess, but his eyes were clear, his nose well enough to breathe through, and his frame practically untouched.

The big man stopped before Curge, looking him in the eye without fear. Just a finger or two in height differentiated the men, but Sapo made it a point to be taller, to straighten his back before the owner, as if suggesting anyone in his presence should be impressed.

"Master Curge," he said with a quick, almost affable dip of the chin. His inflated lips warped his words just a touch.

Curge forced himself to be pleasant. "How goes the training?"

"The training?"

"Yes, the training."

Sapo frowned. He then attempted a smile. It didn't work. He looked at the heavens. "Terrible day to be training, truth be known. And I'm not in the best condition." He indicated his face. "I'm not making my cuts like I think I should be."

Curge didn't immediately respond, and the sound of gladiators training in the background replaced the lack of conversation.

"You're not making your cuts," Curge quietly repeated.

"Aye that," Sapo said and made a show of thinking hard. "Perhaps in a day or two. After some rest. Let my face heal a bit. Remember, I only just fought."

Curge nodded. "So you did. Only just."

Sapo quieted then, appearing pleased, then the silence stretched on, puzzling him.

"So I'm free to retire for the day?" he asked, not bothering to hide his hope.

"Retire for the day?"

"Yes."

"You think that might help?"

Sapo actually shrugged. "I do. Just getting out from this weather will help."

Curge stopped himself from repeating that thought. He made a point of inspecting the gladiator then the man's bare torso.

"The Sarlander," the owner began, "he punched you. In the face. You landed on your back."

"Aye that."

"Any trouble there?"

Sapo thought about it. "I don't think so."

"Any bruising?"

The big man shook his head.

"Turn around."

Shrugging, Sapo complied, showing off a heavily muscled torso. Cords of flesh flexed for good measure.

Curge wrapped his arms around the big man's neck, enveloping it with unexpected speed and expertly locking it in a choke hold. At the same time, he drove his hip into Sapo's lower back, placing him off-balance and partially lifting him off the sand. Though Curge's left arm was missing midway, it was his right that served as a throat-crunching vise.

That, he squeezed with killing force.

Sapo released a short, pipe note of surprise. His eyes bulged, and his face swelled. He gripped Curge's arm with one hand while the other shot up as if waving at a person far away. He kicked as if realizing he needed both feet on the ground to escape, then he stomped—before his struggling weakened under that terrible pressure.

Curge bore down on his right arm with the remainder of his left. The cords of his neck stood out, and his face became a hellion shade of red. He grimaced, teeth bared, but did not relent.

In fact, he squeezed harder.

Sapo slumped, becoming nothing more than massive slab of meat.

Red-faced and scowling, Curge didn't let go, didn't let him drop.

Instead, he lugged the man back, well away from the training grounds. The unfit blossom was a dead weight in his clutches, and Curge didn't want to kill him anywhere near the sands, for fear it might summon all sorts of superstitious gurry amongst his true gladiators, of which Sapo never had been. He briefly wondered if Sapo's leaving the House of Ten and crossing the sands wasn't in fact an elaborate ruse planned by Clavellus.

That made Curge squeeze Sapo's corded neck all the more.

The other gladiators had stopped what they were doing. In twos and threes, they turned their attention upon Dark Curge and the man he was killing.

Hissing with exertion, Curge tightened his hold even further. No neck could tolerate that crushing pressure. He held it, took a breath, and applied even more strength, arms and shoulders flexing. Blood thumped ominously in his ears and temples. Flesh creaked.

A satisfying pop of bone reached his ear.

Curge released the dead man.

The corpse flopped onto its back a dozen strides away from the training grounds. Sapo's eyes were bloodshot and staring, his face the color of an overripe plum about to burst.

Breathing hard and feeling an ache in his shoulders, Curge flashed a look at his remaining gladiators.

Who promptly returned to their afternoon drills.

Curge returned to his front door. He continued breathing hard and resisted the urge to nurse his aching shoulder. Such a thing would not do, not before an audience. Sapo had been removed from the roster, however, and the satisfaction of doing the deed himself eased his hurts just a little.

In his wake, Taskmaster Baris walked over to the dead heap crumpled in the grass. He stood over the man, sizing him up from one end to the other. He finally motioned to a few gladiators, indicating that they dispose of the carcass fouling the property.

And do it quick.

11

The cellar door creaked open just a crack.

Nightfall had come, and rain continued to lash the city. That cellar door remained opened, the exposed darkness studying the alleyway for potential threats. Sensing all was well, fingers wormed around the edges, gripped, and pushed. Borchus rose, cringing when the cellar door's hinges groaned. He quickly got clear and lowered the lid, glancing this way and that, scanning the shadows for danger.

Nothing charged him. No one tried to kill him.

His clothing only marginally drier than before, Borchus had dressed himself, slid his weapons into place, and covered himself in a cloak that smelled faintly of cellar dirt. Not feeling particularly clean or well-fed, he picked up his little rock, fitted it into place along the lid's underside, and slunk to deeper shadows.

It was late, well after supper, and the gloomy weather was once again keeping most people off the streets. Water streamed over stone tiles in fat rivulets. Wooden walls glistened underneath shuttered light. A few figures walked about, but Borchus avoided them when he could, watching them for signs of changing course and following him. Thoughts of the one he called Sindra's man had troubled him during the day, urging him to travel to the alehouse and question her. After feeding a gang member to the arena's fire pit, however, Borchus had decided to remain belowground until night.

Miserable yet anxious to see her, he forced himself to take the long way to Sindra's alehouse—deciding the business name sounded just as pleasant as Hadree's.

Later that night, he stood between two buildings and once again spied the alehouse's lit windows. As before, the enforcer called Gurga guarded the entrance. His mighty arms were folded, his expression unhappy. The same spiked club hung from his belt, and Borchus wondered if the man went to bed wearing it.

Figures moved inside the alehouse, glimpsed through the open door, but Borchus couldn't identify who. He decided to wait, so he retreated a step and leaned against a wall. Water dripped and hissed around him. It seeped into his boots and touched his feet. He sighed and looked at Gurga's unflinching form. The brute had outwaited him the previous night as well.

The enforcer didn't move. He stood there as if carved from a slab of unpolished Vathian marble. Voices traveled to Borchus's ear, coming from the alehouse, but Gurga didn't seem to mind them. A pair of customers soon left the alehouse on swaying ankles. Gurga watched them, turning his head ever so slightly, but that was the only thing he'd done since Borchus had arrived.

Stone. The enforcer was stone.

The night stretched on, and Borchus became ever more impressed with Gurga's vigilance. Once, the enforcer stuck a finger in his ear, rooted it around, and sniffed at the findings. Seeing nothing amiss, he wiped his hand on his trousers and resumed his watch.

Another pair of customers left the building, a man and a woman. The lady clasped a cloak about her shoulders while her companion kept a hold of her waist. She giggled, a pleasant sound, and almost tumbled away from her escort, who caught her at the last possible moment. Laughter from both of them lightened the rain.

But then the woman lurched with an audible *yuh*, bent over, and violently emptied her stomach.

Gurga frowned at the display. Right in the street, too.

"Oh, I'm sorry," she said weakly, almost spinning from the force.

The man supported her again and asked if she was all right, or so Borchus thought. Her companion mumbled.

"Quite all—" she heaved again, without warning, releasing another foul gout onto the ground.

Borchus looked away, paused, and leaned out to better watch the pair.

The woman bent over what appeared to be a flower bed, disgorging another blast of drink and wasted coin, while her helpful companion held up her long hair, ensuring that it stayed clean. Gurga eyed them as well, his face contorted into fascinated disgust. She continued heaving into the flower bed, her back relaxing before tensing up with each soupy yawn.

Dying Seddon, Borchus swore in wonder at the lengthy episode.

The spasms and voiding lessened, becoming an occasional, quite noticeable *yuh*, in which nothing was produced. She straightened, a little wobbly, but felt well enough to continue. She wiped her mouth with her bare hands, and cleaned those on her dress. The pair went on their way. A stoic Gurga watched them, and Borchus watched Gurga.

Who went right back to cleaning his ear.

"Seddon above," Borchus said under his breath and thought again of the alehouse's back door, the barred one leading to the kitchen.

No way was he going to get past Gurga, and he suspected the man slept in one of the alehouse's upper rooms. To make matters worse, the rain had increased, furthering dampening his resolve to speak with Sindra.

His feet soaking, Borchus looked at the entrance guardian once more, then the ground, then the enforcer one last time.

Sighing, he rolled his shoulders and grimaced at his cloak's weight.

Outdone by a temple slave yet again, Borchus thought. *Unfit.* He blamed his growing lack of patience upon getting older.

Not quite believing he was again abandoning the night, he turned, and in that lack of attention, his right boot hooked what might've been a few discarded shards of wood, perhaps tossed into the alley by a passerby.

The clatter froze him.

He glanced over his shoulder and saw Gurga was staring right back at him.

But he was not moving.

Borchus froze, waiting for the enforcer to look away . . . or to charge.

Gurga did neither, however.

Fighting down his impulse to flee, Borchus slowly receded into the alley, sliding his feet along the ground and placing them only when he was sure of his footing. He kept his eyes on the enforcer, quite ready to bolt like a discovered thief if need be.

In the end, he didn't, however. A few heartbeats later, Gurga's unmoving frame slid out of sight, hidden by a corner.

Angry at himself for such a lapse of concentration, Borchus slunk deeper into the dark, moving away from Sindra's alehouse.

"What are you looking at?" Sindra asked as she wiped down a table just inside the entrance. She studied Gurga's stern profile and realized he hadn't heard her. "Gurga?"

The enforcer heard that time. He met her gaze with a questioning frown.

"Did you hear me?" she asked.

"No."

"What are you looking at?"

Gurga's frown deepened as he stared across the street. "Something."

"Something."

"Hm."

"Well, no doubt you've scared it off."

He didn't comment and kept looking off into the night.

Telda came out of the kitchen, wearing a cloak and carrying a basket. Her round eyes narrowed as she stopped beside Sindra, studying the big man just outside the door.

"What's he looking at?" she asked.

"Something," Sindra replied.

"Something? He didn't see what it was? Doubtful he'd miss much of anything, as tall as he is."

"Well, he missed whatever it was out there."

"Well," Telda said in mild disbelief and fixed a cloth over the basket's contents. "Still raining out there."

Sindra stepped before her friend and pulled the cloak tight about her shoulders. Telda grimaced at the stormy night.

"You take the last of those buns?" Sindra asked.

"I did."

"Tell Novus about the roof."

Telda rolled her eyes. "Don't worry. He'll do it."

"Thank you."

"Can't have the roof leaking. Bad for everyone. Leaves the beds smelling."

"And makes more work for us."

"For me, especially."

Sindra smiled agreement.

"You think he'd be able to fix a roof," Telda said pointedly, indicating Gurga.

"He's certainly able to reach a roof," Sindra said. "Gurga?"

The enforcer turned, saw Telda, and nodded. He ceased guarding, stooped to clear the doorframe, and entered the alehouse.

"What did you see out there?" Telda asked. "Someone lurking? About in the shadows?"

Gurga shrugged massive shoulders concealed under a loose-fitting white shirt.

"You wear that cloak there," Sindra told him, pointing at one hanging on a wall peg. "I put it there for you."

He did so without fuss and pulled up the hood, flattening his gray hair. His beard, equally gray, puffed out the front.

"Man looks like a hairy rock," Telda said. "Well then, let's go. Before this roast gets any colder."

"You took all of it?" Gurga asked with alarm.

Sindra sighed. "There's a chicken back there waiting for you. And whatever fresh bread Telda left."

That calmed the big man. "Thank you," he said. He unhooked his spiked club from his belt and hefted the thing.

"Right, we're off," Telda said and winked at Sindra. "Kitchen's all cleaned."

"Have a good night, then," Sindra said, moving to the door.

"Sleep well. Until tomorrow, then."

Gurga stepped outside, and Telda followed. Sindra closed the door halfway before looking at her enforcer. "Stay under the eaves as much as possible. And mind your feet. If you drip over this floor, you'll be cleaning it up, understand?"

The enforcer nodded.

Sindra closed the door. She struggled just a little in placing one timber across its width, barring it from the inside. Once finished, she went to the nearest window and closed the shutters, hooking those on the inside as well. She repeated the process for the other windows. Gurga would return after escorting Telda back to her husband and two children. Rainy weather didn't do much for business, but they still prepared for it. And when it didn't happen, they still cleaned, though not as much as if they'd had customers.

Sindra pushed a few chairs against their tables. She double-checked the door and windows then inspected the burning lamps, soon to go dry. Those she would replenish in the morning. Walking through pockets of warm light, she made her way back to the kitchen.

Resting on a table and covered by a white cloth was the chicken waiting for Gurga. A small basket of leftover buns lay nearby. Sindra checked on the bread then peeked at the chicken. She pinched a strip of meat from the bird and ate it, looking over things and seeing if anything more needed to be done. The back door had already been barred, and two solid planks lay across its width.

She stopped, noticing that Telda had forgotten to take out the garbage—a large uncovered basket.

"Telda," she said, cleaning her fingers. She peered inside the container, made a face, and hesitated. The basket was only a quarter full, but discarded vegetables filled the bottom, crowned by the flowering smell of raw guts.

Raw chicken *guts*, she knew. And by the morning, the whole of the kitchen would stink. Sindra scowled. If she placed the container outside this night, the street cleaners would carry it away at dawn. She could wait until Gurga returned and let him do the deed, but he would be soaking wet and would drip across her floor, and she didn't like the idea of having the enforcer plodding about her cooking area with a mop.

And, Seddon above, that stink was getting stronger with every passing moment.

She considered the back door. It wouldn't take long, not long at all. In and out, and done.

The awful smell of decaying chicken guts wrinkled her nose.

Sindra sighed. She went to a counter where an assortment of knives, ladles, and other kitchen utensils hung on a board. She selected the biggest knife, a worn butcher's blade from Hadree's day, which she and Telda frequently used to slice up fresh meats. Sindra hefted the knife, approved, and went to the garbage. The basket wasn't heavy, just unfit, so she carried it to the door. There she hesitated, thought again, and went to a barred window. She placed the blade upon a nearby counter and unhooked the shutter. She opened it a crack, straining to see. Rain crashed down, becoming even heavier since Gurga and Telda had left. The alley was a black, wretched place filled with water, and again she considered just leaving the garbage for her enforcer.

Sindra listened, scanned the space around the door, and saw no one lurking in the alley.

Lurking, Telda whispered in her mind.

It was too damn wet out there anyway, Sindra thought and closed the window. She returned to the door.

The two planks came away easily as she just lifted then placed them to the side. The weight wasn't bad, but once again she reminded herself to get a sliding bolt—perhaps five of the things—just so none of them would have to keep hefting these damn planks. Thinking on who she could get to do such a service, she gathered everything up again. With the knife in one hand and the basket balanced on her hip, she reached for the door's handle.

The door exploded inward with a burst of wind and rain, and a figure sprang into the kitchen, driving Sindra back.

She didn't scream.

Didn't panic.

Having experienced and evaded countless groping attempts, she reacted instead. She dropped the basket and jabbed the butcher's knife.

The intruder slapped the blade away, rattling it onto the floor. The figure grabbed her about the throat and shoved her. Sindra bounced off the counter and landed hard on her back, banging her head. Squinting through the pain and anger, she glimpsed her attacker's face and felt her stomach twist into frigid knots.

Senturo.

With his usual not-quite-a-smile best suited for a corpse, Senturo stood above her, sizing her up with approval while throwing back a very wet cloak.

"Dear Sindra," he said in a whispery huff. "Lovely to see you again. I've been counting the days."

Sindra crawled while on her back, working her elbows and feet until her head clacked into a counter post. She barely felt the connection.

Dripping as though he'd just stepped through a waterfall, Senturo's smile remained in place as he inspected her legs.

To her chagrin, she realized the hem of her dress had risen, exposing a leg to her knee. She quickly covered up and glared.

Then she screamed.

The sudden blast stunned the agent, but not long enough. Nor did it dissuade Senturo from his intentions. He rushed her. Avoiding her kicks, he dropped a knee into her midsection. She swung at him, which he batted aside before grabbing her throat again.

Much harder this time.

Sindra couldn't breathe. The pressure behind her eyes swelled, on the verge of exploding. She clawed at his chest, but he pressed her down, wedging her between his knee and the counter. She pounded his knee, dug in her fingers, and attempted to pull his leg one way and then the other. He absorbed it all with that same maddening grin, even swatting away her hand shooting for his crotch. She gasped, burning through her air, and realized she couldn't get any more. That sent her into a thrashing panic. He held on, strangling her, and pressed his knee into her stomach even more. The sounds of her struggling receded into a white waterfall of noise as Senturo's face loomed above her. His face shimmered then wavered. Bright suns exploded before her eyes, and her strength, once furious, ebbed away.

"There we are," he whispered, staring into her face. "There we are. Just a little more. Don't worry, good Sindra, I'm not going to kill you. No, no, no. Just taking the fight out of you, is all. Make you a little more—"

The door creaked on its hinges.

Senturo abruptly jumped off her, spinning as he went.

And there, standing inside the kitchen, was the wet and very dangerous-looking Borchus. Short sword pulled and gleaming in the lamplight.

Borchus lunged, slashing for Senturo's head.

Senturo ducked behind a counter, evading that killing blow, and scrambled along the floor. He flipped a table as he went. Bowls and utensils flew. Borchus went after him, his wet cloak flapping. He stabbed repeatedly, but Senturo was quicker, evading everything until he bolted for the opposite side of the room.

There, he spun about and pulled his own short sword, stopping Borchus in his tracks.

For a shivering instant, the two agents studied each other while the rain fell outside.

Sindra gasped for air, watching them while massaging her throat.

Poised behind his weapon, Senturo showed teeth in that unsmile of his, and his eyes narrowed with recognition. "The cattle man. From Plagur's Reach."

Borchus didn't comment. Behind him, Sindra held her neck while barking a series of coughs.

"You're not a cattle man, are you?" Senturo asked slyly.

"Not really."

Borchus attacked.

For moments, the two agents traded blows in the lamplight, steel crinkling at each thrust, slash, and parry. The pace of the exchange increased, becoming as impressive as it was lethal. Borchus sought to get in close, to better use his smaller but heavier frame, but Senturo circled for the door, jabbing and keeping his foe at bay.

"You're not leaving," Borchus said with a scowl.

"No?" the taller agent asked.

Senturo charged.

Borchus parried a straight-armed stab, lifting his adversary's sword up and away. He ducked under the arm and barreled into the Senturo's chest. Both men crashed into a counter, twisted, and staggered back into the kitchen. They landed on the floor, with Borchus on top. Senturo lost his sword. Still holding his blade, Borchus hammered the wrought-iron pommel twice into his adversary's face—hard punishing blows that burst apart a cheek and grazed an eye.

The blow to the eye did more damage.

Senturo shrieked, bucked, and threw up an arm, effectively locking up Borchus's sword arm at the elbow. Senturo twisted, heaving the smaller agent into the closed door that led to Sindra's private room. The hard grain of worn planks sanded Borchus's face.

Senturo released him and grabbed for his dropped weapon.

Borchus backhanded, whipping a fist at what he thought was Senturo's head.

The taller agent ducked and stabbed. Two feet of steel sank through the private room's door, close enough to Borchus's ear that he felt the barest lick of the blade.

Senturo quickly released the weapon. He punched the shorter man's face, splitting open a cheek. Then a dagger was in Senturo's hand, having magically appeared.

Borchus kicked out one of the knees of the bigger man, who collapsed upon him. There was a frantic sprawl then, a wild shivering tangle of limbs. Borchus released his own blade and tried to catch Senturo's weapon arm. They wrestled, rolling over the other, grunting and groaning all the while. Senturo stabbed too quickly for Borchus to avoid. He jerked his left forearm up in time to deflect the knife, the blade slicing him to his elbow, until Borchus caught and seized the other man's bicep.

They lay on their sides, half locked in an embrace.

Senturo rammed his forehead into the smaller man's brow.

"Cattle man," the smiling agent said. "I'm going to—"

Nowhere near as stunned as the Senturo believed, Borchus smashed his bleeding forehead into his opponent's face, returning the gesture. The blow took all the fight from Senturo. He grunted as his eyes squeezed shut. Torrents of blackness shot forth from his nose like water spilling from a cooking pan.

Borchus scuttled atop the man, pinning his knife arm under a boot. From high above, the blocky agent proceeded to pound Sindra's attacker, smashing a series of hard fists into his stunned face.

Senturo's nose squished to one side.

Teeth rattled onto the floor.

The flesh and bone around an eye purpled, blackened, and burst in a spurt of unpleasant jam. Blood spattered the floor in perfect blots. Borchus didn't relent. So great was his fury that when Senturo's head lolled, on the very precipice of unconsciousness, he grabbed the man's destroyed nose and twisted. Senturo released a nasal, practically piggish squeal of agony . . . until Borchus finally stopped punching.

Delirious, Senturo gasped and panted, his head rolling as his cries tapered off into a maddening giggle.

Borchus drew back, the fury of the combat dissipating, and studied the mauled features of the man trapped beneath him.

"Cat . . . cattle muh . . . man." Senturo grimaced, revealing the red remains of his ruined teeth. He spat and chuckled with insane mirth, the sight horrifying. Blood dappled his neck and chest. A tooth slunk along the curve of his chin before dribbling to his throat. The flesh surrounding his one eye inflated to the size of an egg, squeezing it closed. "Yuh . . . you're no . . . no cattle man."

Borchus's bleeding features squinted in puzzlement.

Then a shadow fell over both men.

Senturo looked up into Sindra's disheveled but hard face. She avoided him, stepping in close to where Borchus had pinned the agent's torso to the floor.

Senturo's one good eye focused on her. "Good . . . Sindra," he croaked, his face in full red bloom.

Sindra beheld the wrecked features of the agent. Her hands became fists . . . just before she stomped on the man's throat.

12

Borchus flinched at the unexpected strike and rolled off the dying agent. He stood, cautiously eyeing Sindra, while Senturo clutched and clawed at a crushed windpipe.

Sindra watched the weakening death throes of the man she'd just killed.

Senturo was no longer smiling, and in time, his struggles became twitches . . . until he ceased moving entirely.

Outside, the rain intensified.

"Well," Borchus said wearily, uncertain as to what to say.

"Is he dead?" Sindra asked.

"Oh, I'd say so."

"Can you check him? Please?"

Borchus supposed he could although he'd seen enough corpses in his day to know Senturo was now one of them. So he moved around her and dropped to a knee, feeling things pull and stretch when he did so. At some point during the fight, the stitches beneath his ribs on the left had burst apart. A fine sparkle of pain flared into existence, complemented by a disturbing wetness spreading to his waist. Knowing he'd have to get that looked at, he paused, tired from the brief but extreme battle, and gripped the dead man's chin. He moved it left to right, then back again, discovering that unsettling rattle of flesh and bone.

"Dead," he reported.

"You're sure?"

Borchus chided her with a scathing look.

She didn't say anything, didn't acknowledge the agent, and went on staring at the corpse. "He was called Senturo."

"Hm."

"He worked for old Tilo. The one who owns the gladiator house."

"I know who Tilo is."

"Oh," she whispered, distracted by something. She nodded at the dead man.

Borchus followed her gaze. *Well.* The carcass with the broken neck was in the process of pissing itself.

"Does that happen?" she asked.

"Sometimes."

Her hand rose to her throat.

"Are you all right?" Borchus asked, wincing as he stood.

"Just a little off is all," she said. "He was a pig."

"He was that."

"He was waiting for me . . . for me . . . to unlock the door. I checked outside before I opened it, but I didn't see him. He was hiding out there. Maybe even more than just tonight, to know when I was going to toss out the garbage, so he could . . ." Her face turned red and pensive. She pursed her lips and nodded her final thoughts.

"No doubt he was," Borchus said.

Sindra turned her shaken attention upon him. "You saved me."

"I'd say . . . distracted him. You would've fought him off. One way or the other."

Sindra studied his face, hers containing emotions Borchus thought might've been shock. She looked at the floor, and her features scrunched into a question.

Borchus looked as well.

Blood dappled the floor beneath his left arm.

The agent frowned, feeling the sting along the length of his limb to the elbow. For a brief moment, he thought he was going to empty his stomach, but that passed. Then a chill enveloped his legs and stayed there. He lifted the arm as Sindra took a step toward him.

"Seddon above," he swore.

He prodded the wound, realizing it had happened during the fight when Senturo tried to stab him. Blood soaked the green sleeve of his shirt, turning it black. He peeled back the cloth, not surprised to see the material split right up the middle.

"Oh my," Sindra whispered and yanked a cloth off a small hill of baked buns.

Borchus continued to unwrap his arm, revealing a drooling cut that started halfway up the outside of his forearm and continued to his elbow, where he didn't really want to look. But he did, glimpsing that dull whitish pink of bone, bone that worked visibly when he flexed the limb.

Sindra covered everything up with a kitchen cloth. Borchus hissed at the contact.

"That hurt?" she asked.

"A little."

"What about this, then?"

She pulled the cloth tight, and Borchus straightened his spine.

"Thought so," she said, tying off a knot. "That'll hold you for a while, but you're going to have to get it taken care of. It's beyond me."

"I'll do it later," Borchus said, looking at her face.

"You'll do it now," she warned and hesitated, gathering her thoughts. "Thank you for this, Borchus. Don't think I'll forget what you did here tonight, but there's history between us. Wounds that stitches won't ever close. I'll need a night to think on things. Until then, you'd best leave else I remember the bad and forget the good. Understand?"

"I suppose," he muttered. "What about him?"

"Senturo?" Sindra shook her head as if discovering a dead rat. "I'll take care of it. Or rather, I'll have Gurga take care of it. You best go now."

"I'll return."

"Borchus," Sindra said. "Don't say you'll return. In case you haven't noticed, you never return when you say you will. So just shut up and leave. Do that small favor for me, will you?"

She knew him well.

Borchus gripped his bleeding arm and moved to go.

"And if you find a healer this late at night," Sindra said, "have him look at your cheek too. It looks like that dead bastard scrubbed your face with a rock."

Borchus was about to touch that very spot but realized his fingers were wet with blood.

"I'll . . ." Then he remembered what she'd told him, so he shut his mouth, nodded, and left the alehouse through the kitchen's back door.

The fight had exhausted him, and the rain reminded him of that. He breathed deeply, drawing some measure of strength from the night air. On impulse, he glanced back at the open doorway and saw Sindra moving about Senturo's corpse. She felt his eyes upon her and looked up, as still as a framed painting.

His arm aching, his clothing soaked with blood, Borchus slipped away, leaving her to her task. He had to get to a healer, and this time, he imagined he'd be walking home without any clothing. He would certainly be needing new ones in the morning—another task but not the most pressing one.

Healer, he thought. He needed a healer. There was Shan, but the Ten were there, and he wasn't so keen on meeting up with Goll this night, not cut up as he was. There was the other one, the long-bearded one who had helped him before. The old man was a walk away from Sindra's alehouse, but Borchus didn't have a choice.

Holding his arm and hoping he wouldn't bleed to death before getting there, he walked off into the night.

At times he stopped, dizzy from the effort, and leaned against the nearest wall for support. When he regained his senses and the streets stopped rolling, he continued on. The downpour strengthened, heavy sheets dropping from the night sky, ridding the streets of life. Water bounced off the stone, the crashing hiss loud his ears. At one point, he stopped underneath a narrow eave and leaned gratefully against a wall. He inspected his arm, pinching away the covering cloth, and uncovered a grim sleeve of meat for his bones. The parted flesh stung even more when exposed, and gazing upon that lengthy slit made his stomach flutter.

Borchus covered up, composed himself, and marched on, forcing himself to stay deep in those watery shadows and not to hurry through the city.

Just before midnight, Sunjack was practically falling asleep on his feet. The Lords above were once again pissing upon the city, making the night a miserable one. Worse still, it was *boring*. Twice, he'd caught himself drifting and lifted his head only to see Bardal watching him, and that was a disturbing thing to notice even during the day. Great beads of water cascaded before Sunjack's eyes, so he leaned out from underneath the eaves and doused his face. Shaking off the rain, he withdrew into the alley shadows.

"Better?" Bardal asked.

"Not really."

"Another night of this, and I'll be ready for the coast."

Sunjack peered in the direction of the healer's door, set in the middle of a narrow lane. "You think he's any good?"

"Who?" Bardal asked back.

"The healer."

"Suppose he's good."

"Not many people visiting him."

"The weather's unfit."

"Suppose. Perhaps people have spotted us lingering about."

Bardal shrugged. "So what if they did?"

Suppose. Sunjack eased back, placing his back against the wall's damp stone. He stared off into the night and sighed.

"Tired?" Bardal inquired, sounding weary himself.

Sunjack grunted he was indeed.

"Nearing midnight," the other murderer pointed out, with the slightest note of hope that their shift might be nearly finished.

"Suppose it is," Sunjack agreed. "I like the way you think, at times."

No sooner had the last word left his mouth than Bardal held up a hand, calling for silence. Sunjack became quiet and, like a pair of drenched hounds catching a scent, they watched the open lane.

They waited.

A midnight darkness was settling over the city, and the heavy shower poured down relentlessly, but they were still able to discern a hunched figure halting at the healer's door.

Drenched to the bone, Borchus rapped on the healer's door and waited, not daring to knock any harder. The weather prevented him from hearing anything inside the house. He glanced left and right, spying two nearby alley mouths choked with darkness. He studied one then the other, squinting, rain dripping from his brow.

His arm buzzed as if having been stroked with a hand saw, the sensation dulling his senses, but still . . . he sensed movement in the nearest alley.

A scrabbling of chains from inside the house distracted him.

The door opened a crack, and the long-bearded healer appeared there.

"I need help," Borchus informed him.

The healer frowned, his face shadowed, before drawing back in alarm, shattering his usual stoicism. "Get on!" he whispered harshly, looking past the agent. "They're looking for you!"

And if the wreck of his arm had dulled his danger sense, those few words reignited a powerful warning within Borchus. "What?"

TO THUNDEROUS APPLAUSE

The healer made to close the door.

Borchus slammed a palm against it, stopping it. The healer peeked out in horror, looking past the agent. Borchus glanced over his shoulder, toward the street.

A short barrel of a man slammed into him.

The two men exploded through the healer's door. The slab of wood snapped back with the force of a bow, knocking the healer away. Borchus and his attacker rolled inside the house in a harsh rattling of furniture and breath. A table got smashed aside. Two chairs clattered to the floor. Lamplight flashed. Borchus landed hard on his back just before two hands clamped down on his head. Thick fingers dug into Borchus's cheeks. Silver glinted an instant before pain lanced his face and metal gouged bone.

Borchus grabbed a set of wrists. A face appeared above him, the features dark and determined to plunge a pair of weaponized thumbs into his eyes.

"*Lords above, Lords above!*" someone was shouting.

Drawing on reserves of strength he didn't think he had, Borchus pulled those wrists to the right while twisting underneath his attacker's legs. The man with the bladed thumbs fell to the side, mashing his face into the floorboards in a jarring clap of wood.

Borchus untangled himself and regained his feet.

His attacker did the same. The man shook off his daze and regarded the agent. Deep-set eyes glared in undisguised fury.

The healer backed himself into a corner, wanting nothing to do with the fight.

Borchus pulled his short sword, the steel backing up his adversary, but not far enough to send him running into the night. Incredibly, the short man—whose stocky build mirrored his own—crouched and looked ready to charge.

"Do that, and I'll cut you deep," Borchus warned.

And right then, the doorway to the healer's house filled with a much taller individual, his drenched clothes sticking to his skin.

"Haven't killed him yet, Bardal?" the tall man asked with genuine curiosity.

Bardal didn't answer.

"Nimble little punce, aren't you," the tall man said and rolled up the wet sleeve of his right arm, exposing a length of inked dragons and snakes coloring his forearm.

The Sons, Borchus realized, knowing he'd been sloppy.

The tall man pulled forth a short sword, the steel rippling in the lamplight. He widened his stance, effectively blocking the door. He studied Borchus for a moment, his eyes latching onto the agent's battered features, before his cruel face lit up with knowing. "Ahhh," he said, "you're bleeding."

A chill ripped through Borchus's spine.

"Kill him," the tall man said.

Bardal snatched up a nearby chair, and charged.

Borchus retreated, unwilling to exchange blows, and whipped a table into Bardal's path. The obstacle slowed the man long enough for Borchus to run. He shot past the terrified healer and crashed through a doorway and into a short hall. Sounds of pursuit behind him, Borchus plunged into a pantry of sorts, the walls divided into two tiers of worn cupboards. He spotted a shuttered window.

No time, his mind said.

Bardal rushed into the room.

Borchus turned as those bladed thumbs pawed at his right shoulder. He spun and lashed out with his sword, but Bardal blocked the cut with a raised chair. Bardal lunged then, tackling the agent, driving him back into the cupboards. Wood crackled. Borchus dropped his short sword. Spools of bandages, slivers of metal, and containers filled with liquid spilled forth, tumbling over the two combatants. Flasks bounced off the floor as the men wrestled without grace. Bardal sought Borchus's face again, and the agent fended off those deadly hands. One of Bardal's thumbs whisked across Borchus's temple, creating a black field of stars where the killer's face filled the center.

On reflex alone, Borchus punched, a straight-armed thrust, which crunched into the other man's throat.

The effect was immediate. Those soulless eyes cringed, and Bardal staggered back with a pained gargle, holding his neck. A wall stopped him. He gasped and wheezed, attempting to draw breath.

He looked up just as Borchus stabbed with his recovered short sword . . . straight through the man's eye.

A raspy intake of breath was abruptly cut short, and a mighty reflexive twist nearly disarmed Borchus, but then all life fled Bardal's stocky frame. He crumpled into a boneless heap, his chin bounding off the floorboards. Borchus put a boot to the dead man's ribs, gripped the blade, and pulled the weapon free.

Just then, the tall man stuck his head into the healer's supply room.

"Bardal?" he asked, his mouth dropping in shock.

Borchus retreated, scrambling amongst the medicinal debris littering the floor, until his back clipped the corner of a set of cupboards.

The tall man eased himself inside that wooden box and regarded Borchus in disbelief. "You killed Bardal?"

With nowhere to go, Borchus charged, stabbing for a face.

The tall man jerked himself out of range, only to counter-thrust, his short sword seeking to spread Borchus's guts across the floor.

Borchus parried the cut to the outside, closed the distance, and punched—a curving left-handed blow, not nearly as sure as his right, but powerful enough to snap his attacker's head back.

The tall man collapsed with an expression of complete bafflement.

Drawing in deep, pained breaths, Borchus straightened and took a moment to study the half-unconscious man at his feet.

"Aye that," he got out. "I killed Bardal."

He put his sword to the man's throat. "And it was damn easy."

With a dismissive thrust, Borchus stabbed the tall man through the gullet. He worked the blade so there would be no mistake then yanked it free. A mess sprouted from the corpse, forcing the agent to withdraw a safe distance. He looked toward the shuttered window and felt the weight of his wounds. No way was he was crawling through that. Not now.

With two quick wipes, he cleaned his sword on the tall man's shoulder. Borchus then peeked into the hall—no one. He sheathed the blade and went to the main room, where the healer immediately backed himself into a corner again. The old man appeared relieved at first, but then fear took him again.

"I had nothing to do with it," he blurted. "I didn't know you'd be back. I don't even *know* you. They've been here over a week now, waiting."

Borchus didn't respond. He hurried—*lumbered*—at best speed through the room, crashing against and overturning a table and chairs. He reached the main entrance, the door open. The rain hadn't stopped but only fell harder. It didn't surprise him.

"Anyone else?" Borchus asked the healer.

"What?"

"Is there anyone else?"

The healer faltered. "I . . . I don't know."

"I'll return," Borchus told him, but not unkindly. "I don't hold you responsible, healer, so rest easy on that."

The man didn't appear to believe him.

Borchus let him be. The agent had other worries. *A week*, the healer had said. Those two killers had been waiting about for a week. More might very well have been out there in the dark, and he suddenly felt unsafe lingering about the healer's residence. He tasted blood and dabbed fingers across a cut along his upper lip—a hurt he couldn't remember receiving.

"You have sewing string?" Borchus asked.

Eyes blinking, the old man nodded.

"Get it for me. Now. And some of that sour-smelling shite that speeds the healing of cuts."

The healer went to a cabinet, moving more quickly than Borchus had ever seen him move. Items tumbled off shelves as the old man pawed through his supplies. Once he had the materials, he joined Borchus at the door. The agent took a small container and a spool with a pair of needles sticking out from the top.

Borchus stored everything away in a cloak pocket.

"My thanks," the agent said. "I'll pay you for this later."

"There's no need," the healer said, backing away.

Borchus didn't agree but didn't argue. With the mood the old man was in, he could drop dead from fright alone. It was time to leave.

I'll return, he was about to repeat, but then he heard Sindra's voice.

You never return when you say you will. So just shut up and leave.

So he left.

The healer's house wasn't safe, or so he suspected, so finding another practitioner of the arts would be best. Borchus cursed himself, knowing full well he'd made a mistake coming back to this place. It had almost cost him his life. The streets appeared empty, so he eyed the deep, welcoming portals of the nearby alleys. Bracing himself for the journey ahead yet not sure where he was going, Borchus stalled just outside the door.

A chill overcame him, one that had nothing to do with the furious downpour hammering at his person.

The streets.

The dark and menacing streets.

Like specters emerging from the cracked entrances of tombs, figures materialized, detaching themselves from the surrounding gloom. Traveling cloaks hid their features. The crashing rain concealed their footsteps as more of them drifted into existence, converging upon the healer's house. Borchus counted four, then eight, and those were the closest ones. They didn't hurry, and he realized it was because of his size. In that wretched wet darkness, they probably believed he was dead Bardal with the thumb knives.

He glanced at a nearby alley, a nearly black corridor.

Forcing himself to not yield to the panic bubbling in his guts and chest, Borchus took a deep calming breath and walked toward the alley, trying very hard to look unconcerned.

He would not have much time.

13

"Bardal," someone hailed, a whisper barely heard above the thrashing rain.

Borchus ignored it and entered the black pitch of the alley.

And collided with a man.

The pair disengaged, swatting at each other to create space.

"Bardal?" the dark figure whispered once the surprise ebbed away.

"Aye that," Borchus muttered back and punched, connecting with the gang member's gut. The cutthroat doubled over with a pained wheeze. Borchus pushed him back into the darkness. The Sons' killer stumbled and fell amongst unseen debris.

The agent hurried past, following the otherworldly lane, knowing that his ruse was effectively over. He brandished his sword and held it at the ready.

Dark, so damn dark. Borchus nearly squashed his nose into a wall after missing a turn. He blinked away water as he tumbled along, hearing men kicking wood behind him. The alley continued straight, but a second route materialized, looking like a black rectangle cut into a wall. Borchus stuck out his bandaged arm, feeling his way along, the very movement causing him discomfort. He spat blood and pressed forward, disappearing into an even narrower passage. The rain lessened in places, blocked by overhead balconies.

Not too far behind him, someone stumbled and released an angry stream of curses.

Borchus increased his speed. He turned a corner and raced along an alley that had him angle his shoulders straight on to better fit. Ahead, the darkness appeared lighter, and water cascaded in a gloomy sheet. He slunk through a narrow aperture into a dim street.

Whereupon he ducked.

A blade sliced through the air where his head had once been. Borchus sprang from his crouch and sank half an arm's length of steel through the waiting killer. That soft yet stubborn resistance yielded a startled intake of breath from the man just before he fell back. Metal tinkled on stone. Borchus stumbled along, freeing his sword as he went.

Frustrated, he swore at the corpse as he hurried away, chancing a quick look back. *Another one.* How many snakes did the Sons have hunting him? He wasn't going to escape by leaving a trail of bodies in his wake.

But damnation if he wasn't getting tired of the Sons of Cholla.

And damn Garl for using him to kill Strach in the first place.

His sword gleaming dully, Borchus drifted toward the middle of the deserted street, where no one would be waiting for him behind corners. He stopped, stooped, and pulled the dagger from his boot, and that movement alone caused him considerable pain. Everything seemed to be bleeding. His cloak and clothes had taken on far too much water weight. He gripped the spare weapon tightly and marched ahead.

A shadow detached itself from a closed shop front, a wide, hunched-over cone of a man. The figure took two steps, watching Borchus hesitantly, as if confused. The figure's hand appeared, ghostly in the lack of light, and the fingers went through a series of signs.

Borchus scowled and walked forward.

The figure stopped signaling, sensing wrongness, and reached for a blade.

Borchus lunged, stabbing the man through the guts. The figure hissed sharply and buckled, and Borchus hammered his dagger into the offered neck. Fluid burst onto the stone tiles as the street snake dropped to his knees. Borchus twisted the blade free and strode away, leaving the dying man, who toppled with a wet thump some three strides later.

Borchus marched on.

But a rush of footsteps reached his ears. He glanced back, and his heart, already pounding, fluttered violently.

The street.

About half a dozen shadows were racing after him, heedless of the rain.

That was half a dozen bastards too many to deal with.

Borchus spied another alley and disappeared into its depths. The walls narrowed the farther along he got, and he knew the Sons' minions were closing in behind him. He turned twice when he could, sputtering all the while. He hurried along a short corridor, knowing he was passing doors despite being unable to see any, and too much in a rush to search for latches. Someone said a few words behind, speeding Borchus along even more quickly. The fear of being caught by those shadows lent him a renewed, though desperate, reserve of energy, one that was fading fast.

The night became a maze of alleys and narrow spaces barely the breadth of a man's shoulders. Borchus twisted and turned, moving quickly enough that he believed he'd lost the killers trailing him, but in his efforts, the tall, dreary, brick-and-timber confines of the city's guts confused him.

He wasn't sure where he was.

Reaching another street, Borchus rushed across it, his footfalls splashing. Out of the corner of his eye, a pair of figures launched toward him, their movements as silent as floating ghosts.

He saw their knives a heartbeat before he dove into a twisting, angular alleyway with several unexpected turns. Twice, he stopped because he ended up in a dead end. The second time, he clearly saw his pursuers filling the corridor before they spotted him. He backtracked, fear giving him yet another boost of strength. He stumbled through a short passage and emerged into a deserted lane, perhaps even a main road. Voices approached, but the weather hid what they said. Borchus quickly stepped to the corner and placed his back to a wall. He readied himself, knowing he had to deal with his hunters.

One figure burst into view, followed closely by the other.

Borchus slashed for a head and missed. A shadow stabbed for his gut, which he twisted to avoid. He pushed a face away, hacked at a leg, and connected. One shadow let loose a shrill wheeze and dropped to the ground with a splash.

The other chopped at Borchus's head then his arm.

He parried both blows, spun to get in close, and buried a foot of steel up under his hunter's chin. With a warbled croak, the man shivered and fell as if he possessed no legs.

A heartbeat later, Borchus stabbed the other, still-living squealer though the middle and left him writhing in the puddles. Noise from the alley urged Borchus to hurry. He ran, not caring who heard or what came of it. Every footfall splashed. The city streaked by as he looked for a hiding place. The road ended up ahead, in a small square of sorts, where the city edges seemed to drop off into blackness. A shape came into view, and it took him a moment to realize it was a statue of a gladiator poised for battle. Heavy rain bounced off the figure, which stood upon a stone dais in the center of a public pool. A low wall rose to waist level, where water overflowed into the street. Borchus stopped there, bending over and placing an elbow on the stone wall, gathering what little strength he had remaining. Thunder rumbled overhead. He glanced around, his weapons drooping, but couldn't see anything a few strides beyond the pool—only the gladiator at his right and the fitted stones beneath him, which stretched off and disappeared into the ever-strengthening downpour.

Unfit, he thought, *and frightening*. The entire city had seemingly vanished within the storm, leaving only a stone island in a wet squall of madness.

Movement hooked his attention.

Just ahead, walking out of the gloom, was a man carrying a short sword. To the right of the swordsman appeared another gang member, wielding a pair of curved knives. The steel gleamed unnaturally bright.

"Damnation," Borchus whispered, wondering how the pair had gotten ahead of him. He raked a hand across his forehead. He retreated a step, turned, and stopped as if slamming into a wall. At the absolute edge of his vision, three more figures materialized, sauntering forward with all the wary solemnness of hunters having trapped their prey.

Five total—five against one, who was already damn near death.

But then, better death than capture. That much was clear. Borchus had no intention of being caught.

"Bit wet out tonight," the agent muttered and swung a leg over the pool's wall, entering it. More water spilled. He waded toward the gladiator, an imposing figure with sword and shield raised, as if ready to lop the head off a foe. For the life of him, Borchus couldn't remember such a statue ever existing in this part of the city. Water sloshed at his waist as he crossed, taking six or seven steps to reach the statue. A wide circular platform supported the figure, and the agent clambered onto it with audible gasps. His cloak weighed him down, so he let it drop from his shoulders, where it landed with a splash in the pool. Once freed, Borchus staggered and almost fell, but the statue stopped him.

Panting, he looked up at that dark, indifferent face and smiled.

"My thanks, friend," he rasped. "Stay there now. Watch my back."

The statue didn't reply, and Borchus supposed that was a good thing.

"Did I . . . ever mention . . . I once wanted . . . to be a gladiator?"

Rain rippled and flowed down the stone features.

Borchus looked to the pool's edge, and for an instant, he didn't hear the storm or feel the hammering in his head and chest.

The hunters had caught up to him. Five shadowy killers gathered at the pool's wall, their features hidden. Rain rippled along their unsheathed swords and daggers.

Borchus smirked. "So close," he said, his voice carrying with bedrock strength. "What's a few more steps? Come on and finish this, before I fall asleep."

He brandished his weapons, wanting to be done with it all.

The five killers glanced at each another, hesitating.

Then a series of legs rose as they entered the pool.

"Keep watching my back," Borchus whispered to the gladiator and tightened his grip upon his short sword and dagger. The next few moments would be very brief and very, very bloody. *Sindra,* he thought, feeling an instant's remorse.

Then he readied himself. "Come on, then," he muttered.

The five slogged across the pool. They spread out, seeking to engulf him like a closing hand.

Borchus noticed they hadn't discarded their cloaks.

That realization summoned a spike of energy he hadn't thought he possessed. Borchus jumped into the water, on the far left, and attacked the nearest figure. He parried an overhand chop before leaving his dagger in his attacker's guts. The first man toppled like a falling tree, the water frothing around his torso. The other men splashed toward Borchus, but the floating body hampered them. They also realized how they'd lost their advantage. Instead of swarming their quarry, they'd allowed him to flank them in an arena of his choosing, where he could face them one after the other.

In that gloomy, disorienting downpour, Borchus attacked.

A gang member gagged, wheezed, and clutched at his throat, his lifeblood suddenly spurting through clutching fingers.

The killer behind him pushed his dying companion out of the way. He lunged, underestimating how the water would impede his charge. He stumbled to his chest, his sword flailing and missing his target completely.

Borchus cleaved his skull in two.

The two remaining killers hesitated and looked at each other. The one farther away splashed around the statue, intent on attacking Borchus from other side. Borchus withdrew, watching the closer one wait for his companion to circle the statue's stone base. Borchus couldn't rightly see the man's expression, but he imagined it was very angry. Soaking, Borchus backed away from them both, into the wall, and weakly scissored his legs out of the pool.

The effort exhausted and pained him.

"You can't let me go," he informed the two gang members still in the water. "And you can't go back to the Sons without my head."

That got the pair moving.

One of them, a lout with two daggers, stayed in the pool but just beyond the agent's reach. The other one climbed out on the far side.

"Not so stupid after all," Borchus muttered, eyeing the knifeman while distracted with the approaching killer wielding a short sword.

The swordsman rushed Borchus, driving him back in a hurried retreat. Borchus parried a slice for his head, a stab for his chest, and a low sweeping slash seeking his legs. Borchus knew full well that, although he might've *wanted* to be a gladiator at one point, he did not possess their hard-drilled abilities with a sword.

And the swordsman swinging for his head was genuinely worrying him.

After two more narrowly avoided cuts, Borchus's arms became lead. The swordsman sensed him slowing and doubled his efforts. Borchus blocked a series of thrusts, each connection sending a painful shiver up his weakening hands. The swordsman slashed for his head, and Borchus ducked, swinging at a knee. Steel licked bone in a gush of blood, and the swordsman collapsed.

The knifeman appeared, then, long free of the pool. Borchus stood and shook out his arms. He lashed out, and the knifeman actually jumped over the sweeping blade. The agent scrambled back, sword pointed at his remaining adversary. The knifeman harried him with feints and thrusts, his twin daggers flashing.

Then the worse thing possible happened.

All life left Borchus's fingers, he dropped his weapon.

The knifeman charged. Borchus grabbed the man's wrists as his foe crashed into him. They landed hard on the stone tiles, with the knifeman on top of Borchus's upraised legs. Borchus tried to kick out, to push his adversary away, but the knifeman bore down, pressing the agent's knees into his chest. Joints popped and screamed. Borchus groaned and pulled the knifeman off-balance, and the men rolled across the street, struggling for an advantage. The agent landed on top of the killer, who immediately bit at his face. Strong teeth sank deep into the agent's cheek. Borchus squealed and pulled back, drawing that hateful face up with him.

The knifeman struggled for balance with one hand, but the other still held a blade.

Feeling his face ripping, Borchus grunted, groaned, and drove his head forward, smashing the knifeman's skull off the stone tiles.

The knifeman released the cheek.

Borchus hammered his forehead into the man's face twice more. He reared back, inspecting the bloody mask beneath him, when he heard the wet slap of boot soles upon the street.

The swordsman.

Borchus threw himself off his dazed foe as a sword sliced him, cutting through drenched cloth and parting the skin and muscle covering his ribs. Borchus spun on his back and kicked—kicked *hard*—and drove a heel into the swordsman's leg. The swordsman dropped. Borchus scuttled over him, reaching the man's face. The agent punched him twice, hard strikes that rocked the killer. Then, gripping that dazed face, Brochus sank his thumbs deep into the swordsman's eyes. The swordsman screamed, but only as long as it took for the agent to free one hand and slam an elbow into a throat.

A different sound erupted from the swordsman, but one that quickly died away.

On the absolute edge of exhaustion, Borchus slid off the body. He saw the sword, grasped it, and held on. That last effort had drained him, so he waited a moment, refilled his burning lungs, and released the blade in an exhausted huff.

Movement attracted his eye.

An unsteady knifeman was rising to his hands and knees.

With an exasperated moan, Borchus snatched up the sword again. He half lunged, half fell at the rising knifeman, and stabbed the street snake through the guts. The knifeman seized up with a whimper, clutched at the killing blade, and rolled over onto his side. Borchus held onto the weapon and worked it deeper, past what might've been a spine.

The knifeman stopped moved.

Borchus left the blade in the man, just to be sure.

Wheezing, his heart hammering, and his face seemingly on fire, Borchus crawled away from the dead men, pausing only to scan the night for more attackers.

None were there.

Grimacing, bleeding, and stricken by hot, piercing needles of pain, Borchus clawed his way forward. Water beaded off his gray hands while thick rivulets flowed through his fingers. His temples throbbed, and a vast sense of unwellness overtook him. He felt sick, felt like emptying his stomach in the street. He stopped for a moment, puzzled at the growing sensation, and patted himself down.

His hand stopped on the last place he'd been stabbed. The blade had split him open right between the ribs.

He should be dead.

Chuckling darkly until he coughed, he resumed crawling until his forehead softly tapped a wall.

The pool with its gladiator statue.

Borchus placed his cheek against wet brick, then his back. He eventually righted himself. His sparkling collection of wounds screamed for attention. Before him, rainwater thrashed and flowed around the two corpses in the street. Oddly enough, the streams shone as if touched by moonlight.

"Not good, Zhiberian," Borchus croaked and blinked as if very, very tired. He wondered why he'd said that. Then he remembered and, against better judgment, struggled to sit up a little further so that he could lay eyes upon the statue at his back.

The stone figure held its pose, but it appeared much more obese, as the Zhiberian had been.

"Not . . . good," the agent whispered as he rested his chin atop the wall. An evil chill enveloped his frame. "But . . . not bad, eh? For a . . . nuh—novice."

The statue didn't move, but Borchus thought he heard a haunting *yes* somewhere in the stormy night.

Then he wondered why it was so dark.

His cheek slid down the pool's wall. Coarse brick clawed at his face. Skin parted and snapped back into place. The heavens continued to piss down in hateful, crashing sheets, prickling his face and scalp. Thunder crackled, leaving the scene and sounding frustrated with how events had played out. The storm's grumbling burrowed deep within his skull, while the thumping of his overtaxed heart slowed to a very ominous beat.

The world tilted . . . and crashed.

14

A fist banged upon the door three times, paused, and banged again.

Sindra stopped what she was doing, cleaned her hands in a cloth, and hurried to the entrance.

"Gurga?" she asked, dreading that it might be anyone else.

"Aye that," he answered in that cave-bear growl of his.

Relieved, she removed the timbers securing the door and stacked them nearby. She pulled the door open, and there stood her main—her only—enforcer. The rain had doused him well, rendering his usual greasy appearance even slicker.

The brutish face looked upon her with unchecked horror.

"It's not mine," she told him.

He frowned as if he'd just downed a mug of very unpleasant medicine, and he entered the alehouse. Sindra got out of the way, checking her appearance yet again, as she'd done several times since having killed Senturo.

Blood stained her clothes. A lot of it.

"What happened?" Gurga asked, leaning his spiked club against the door frame.

"There was trouble," she informed him. "Senturo. He was waiting in the back alley. Knew I was alone. Probably saw you leave with Telda and decided to attack me."

She turned and pointed. There, on the floor where she'd dragged him, was the man wrapped up in a dark blanket.

Gurga huffed, becoming angrier with each passing heartbeat.

"Calm yourself," she said. "He's dead. I killed him."

"Killed him?" he asked, taken aback and perhaps a little disappointed that his employer had done his job.

The reaction annoyed her. "Yes, I killed him. What's wrong with that? You don't think I could put a man into the ground?"

Gurga's frown returned as he showed rare wisdom in declining to answer. He went to the wrapped-up corpse, dripping rainwater with every step. The enforcer inspected the body and nudged it with a boot.

"Oh, he's dead," Sindra assured him. "Guaranteed. I need you to take him away. Put him somewhere where the Street Watch will find him."

"Street Watch?" The very words summoned a look of distrust to his face.

"Yes, Street Watch. And then you forget about ever doing such a thing."

After a while, Gurga eventually nodded.

"And if Tilo asks, you don't know what happened to Senturo. Understand?"

Gurga nodded again, not that he would ever report such a thing to the gladiator house owner. She didn't question Gurga's loyalty. Over the years, the big enforcer had become her right-hand man and one of only a select few Sindra completely trusted.

"Go on then," she said, "and hurry back."

His task given, Gurga gripped the ends of the rolled-up corpse and easily hefted the package off the floor. Sindra paid scant attention to the effortless display of strength. She'd seen him do far more in the past. She remembered one instance with a customer who'd thought himself quite powerful. The man actually grabbed and attempted to wrestle Gurga to the floor. The brazen kog would've had more success attempting to uproot a tree. Sindra remembered the scene, the laughter from the onlookers, and Gurga throwing his attacker through the front door.

She watched the enforcer tuck Senturo's drooping length under one arm and check on the ends.

"There's no blood," she told him. "Or very little. I cleaned up what I could. Get going. And return quickly."

His orders understood, Gurga carried the body to the door as if it were no more than an unwieldy length of wood. He reached for his spiked club.

"You truly think you need that tonight?" Sindra asked.

"Might."

"No one's going to bother you. Not with him."

Gurga didn't appear so certain of that. He wasn't one for overconfidence. Hefting Senturo's corpse, he took the club with his other hand. He stepped back out into the weather, where the rain immediately pelted him.

"Hurry now," she said and watched him wander off into the night.

She closed and barred the door and returned to the kitchen. Blood still coated the floor as she'd been more occupied with finding a blanket. Inspecting the gruesome mess before her, she grabbed a cleaning cloth, filled a bucket of water, and dropped to her hands and knees.

While she scrubbed, she replayed the night's events, right up to the unexpected arrival of Borchus. She shook her head at the memory. Leave it to that one to show up at the worst of times—except, she easily admitted, the agent had saved her. She sighed and scrubbed harder.

Blood. So much blood. It didn't surprise her anymore, having cleaned up her share of it back in the early days, but the sight appalled her and left her cold.

A knocking upon the door caught her attention, just as she finished her cleaning. Wiping her hands, she hurried to the main entrance.

"Gurga?" she asked.

"Aye that."

She quickly let him in, noting that he carried only his club. Water dripped from his huge frame. "Where did you put Senturo?"

"Near the Street Watch post. They'll find him."

Sindra sighed. "Did anyone see you?"

"No."

"Did anyone follow you?"

Gurga shook his head.

Relief surged throughout her person. "Oh Lords above. Excellent. Thank you for that. It's been a busy night, and not in a good way."

The enforcer watched her, waiting for further instructions.

"That's all I need of you," she said. "I'll bar the door. You go on. And thank you again. Make sure you give me those wet clothes tomorrow, and I'll see that they're washed. Can't have you stinking around here."

Washing his own clothing wasn't one of Gurga's skills, and if she didn't remind him to hand his garments over for a weekly scrub and soak, she believed he would just continue wearing them until they rotted away. Or at least that's what she and Telda suspected would happen.

Gurga turned toward the stairs while Sindra looked to the open doorway.

She gasped.

The sound stopped the enforcer in his tracks. He whirled about, following her gaze.

Standing there, with one hand braced against the door frame, was the wretched form of Borchus. The rain had flattened his hair to his skull, and his clothing clung wetly to his body. His other hand pressed his side, as if keeping himself together. In the diminished light of the alehouse, Borchus's hard features looked ravaged. All color had deserted his face, leaving it ghoulish. Sindra wasn't completely certain he was even alive.

But then he staggered inside, nearly falling over as he crossed the threshold. Sindra rushed over and caught him, soaking herself from the contact. She faltered, unable to support his weight alone. Borchus dropped to a knee, his arms falling to his sides.

"Gurga," she called out.

The enforcer stomped across the floor. He grabbed the smaller man underneath the armpits and raised him up as if inspecting a grain sack. Borchus's head rolled, but he lifted his face just enough to see Sindra before him.

"What happened?" she demanded. "Who did this to you?"

"Sons."

Sindra scowled. "Who?"

"Cholla."

A spike of fear lanced her then, and her voice failed her.

The Sons of Cholla. She knew full well who they were. She'd even encountered an unfit bastard belonging to that hateful clan years before, having discovered him in her alehouse like unwanted vermin scurrying about the floorboards. She made it clear to Gurga to watch for the Sons' inked flesh and turn anyone wearing such patterns away at the door. Over the years, the Sons had left her alone because of her ties to Tilo, or so she suspected. Whatever the reason, she was grateful. She'd heard plenty of worrying stories about the gang and their nefarious activities, especially with business owners.

"The Sons did this to you?" she asked.

Borchus's chin dropped. Sindra grasped his head and shook it, trying to wake the unconscious man.

"Dying Seddon," she swore and looked at Gurga. "Take him upstairs. Put him in one of the rooms."

"On a bed?" Gurga asked, his mouth twisting in dislike.

"Aye that, on a . . ." Sindra reconsidered—the agent was a bloody mess. "Put him in a chair and keep him there. I'll be up after I bar the door."

Gurga nodded and adjusted his grip on the man.

"And don't hurt him," Sindra warned. "He's close to death already."

His orders received but clearly not liking them, Gurga hoisted the unconscious man into his arms. The floorboards creaked as he took the stairs.

Sindra barred the door and the shutters and doused all torches and lamps except two. One lamp she left burning low on the main floor, while she took the other upstairs. She found both men in the first room on the right. Gurga had placed Borchus in a chair and was holding him there with a hand.

"All right," Sindra said. "Keep him in place while I get his clothes off."

Gurga scowled in distaste.

"What are you making that face for?" she asked. "I'm the one doing the work."

The enforcer didn't answer, so Sindra let him be. She focused on Borchus, studying his face and the punishment inflicted there: cuts, bruises, and what appeared to be a bite, as if someone had thought his cheek was an apple. The purple around the bite wounds worried her. Then there was his arm, which was a mess. She peeled away a cut sleeve, hissed at the damage there, and went to work unbuttoning his ruined shirt. The material came off and landed on the floorboards in wet clumps.

When his shirt came off, Sindra drew back in horror. Borchus had been stabbed at some point earlier, and the stitched wound had broken apart, becoming a dismal mouth that dribbled blood. A new gash—bright and disturbingly red—had been inflicted on his right side.

"Keep him there," she ordered Gurga.

"Is he dead?"

"No, he's not dead," she said and went for the door. "But he will be soon. We won't be able to just put him to bed and be done with him. Not this night."

She rushed down the hall to a closet stuffed full of spare blankets, the same place she'd taken one to wrap up Senturo.

She grabbed a fresh one, hesitated, and took three more. Once loaded, she hurried back to the room.

"He's bleeding," Gurga informed her when she entered.

"I know. I have these."

She dumped the blankets on the bed and spun toward her enforcer. Her hand shot out. "Knife."

Gurga immediately reached down and pulled a blade from his right boot. Sindra took the weapon and instantly regretted it. The knife wasn't quite the size of a short sword, but it was close . . . and heavy. She started cutting up a blanket. Once she had enough bandages, she got to work binding Borchus's wounds.

Gurga kept him in place.

Sometime deep into the night, when everything that bled had been bound and tightened, they put the agent to bed. Thick bandages covered him, and a cloth strip kept a wad over his ugly bite wound.

No sooner had the agent's head hit the pillow than his eyes opened, wide and black and not healthy in the least.

"Buh," Borchus said weakly and attempted to rise.

Gurga stopped him with a hand. Sindra leaned in and touched Borchus's forehead. "Lie down," she whispered. "Lie down. You're safe now."

The agent looked at her in confusion. Sindra pushed him back until he hit the pillow.

"You're safe," she repeated.

"Sindra?"

"Aye that."

"You're . . . not angry."

"Oh, I'm angry," she said. "But we'll talk when you're able to. I owe you that at least."

Borchus's deep-set eyes drooped, but he stayed awake. "Sons . . ."

"Of Cholla. You said so. Don't worry. They won't find you here. Did they cut you up like this?"

The agent blinked, and that very effort alone seemed to drain him. He swallowed thickly, his eyes never leaving Sindra's face. "Yes . . ." he managed in the end.

"We'll take care of you," she said. "I'll take care of you."

That brought a moment's puzzlement to the agent's face, but he didn't have the strength to do any more. His eyes closed. Sindra kept a hand on his forehead, studying him, until she saw his chest rise on its own power.

"He's damned near dead," she whispered.

"Damn near," Gurga agreed.

Sindra shot him a stern look, shaming the man into silence.

She checked on the bandages then the unused blankets at the foot of the bed. "Cut those up. No, wait. I'll cut those up. You go on and get some rest. It'll be morning shortly."

Gurga looked toward the ceiling, as if catching a whiff of something unpleasant.

"I'll keep watch over him," she said.

"Sons of Cholla," Gurga said. "The little man has big enemies."

"The biggest."

"They might come here."

"Then we'll turn them away."

"They might come back."

"Then we'll turn them away *again*," Sindra informed him sharply. "As often as needed. Do you understand, Gurga? This one saved me tonight. That means something. I'll save him in return or at least protect him until he can leave here on his own power. And I don't care who the Sons of Cholla are, what their reputations might be. I don't like owing debts to anyone, and certainly not this one." She indicated Borchus.

Gurga nodded pensively.

"I mean it," Sindra continued. "There's only one staircase here. Watch it. And keep watch over everyone who comes inside the alehouse. Look for the ink. On the arms and around the neck. You know the Sons' mark. If you see any of them, you have my permission to throw them into the street. I'll trust your judgement."

Gurga's expression lightened at that.

"I go," he rumbled and went to the door.

"Good night," Sindra said. "And thank you, Gurga. For everything here."

The enforcer nodded again and left her.

After he'd gone, she looked back at the unconscious Borchus. The air was warm and humid, but she pulled up the bed's blanket and tucked the ends around the agent's chin.

Borchus, she thought, studying his face and sighing at the predicament of it all.

"Seddon above," she muttered and turned her attention to a spare blanket.

He would need fresh bandages in the morning.

15

The rain still fell though it had lessened when dawn's light peeked around the window's closed shutters. Garl woke, sighed, and sleepily scratched at his nose. He studied the ceiling, taking in the dark planks without a thought. A wind rose and fell, rattling the shutters. That sound alone sank the man's spirits. He drew another deep breath, listened to the storm beyond the walls, then rolled onto his side.

He looked at his legs.

The right one was still gone, tapered below the knee like a pointed beach rock. He flexed the nub that remained and felt straw stab skin. The one blanket he was lying upon and the coarse fabric of his pants failed to protect him. Garl reached down and felt the knob of skin there. *Still gone*, he thought. His secret wish was that one day, he'd wake up and see the right leg beside the left, fully restored, just waiting to be used. He'd lost the damn thing years before, but his head refused to accept that it was gone and kept telling him the limb was still there, despite the reality.

Every unfit morning. Garl thought it cruel to be tortured by his own mind. He tried to make do and got around as best as he could, but a deep misery had taken root within him, permanently dousing whatever spirit he had. In a world where a person was only as good and useful as his trade, Garl was nothing.

He was a sack of skin and bone waiting to perish. On mornings such as these, when the sun refused to shine, the hateful part of his mind reminded him of exactly that and dumped him into a hot stew of wretchedness.

He flexed the nub again and adjusted the pants Borchus had bought for him.

Then he remembered why he was sleeping just across from the Sarlander. He listened and heard breathing, but from the wrong direction. Garl struggled to sit up, and when he did, he looked over into Brozz's alcove. A dark, unmoving shape lay splayed out on a cot. No one was beside him.

"Torello?" Garl asked, looking around. "Torello?"

The breathing continued, and he realized it was from Torello's own quarters.

That poisoned him.

"Torello!" he shouted, his voice crashing the morning stillness.

"Uh?" came from deeper in the barracks.

"Wake up!"

Nothing then, but Garl sensed a groggy movement just beyond his walls.

He heard a thump, a rustling . . . then silence.

Garl waited, waited, and realized the unfit bastard had returned to sleep. "Torello!"

"Yes?" came the immediate though bewildered reply.

"Get up!"

After a pause the unseen man asked, "Is it morning?"

"Yes, you punce, it's morning. Get up and get over to Brozz. See if he's still breathing."

"Right, right," the other man mumbled and inhaled sharply in an effort to clear his mind.

Garl knew the routine well enough. They'd shared those duties all through the previous day. *Watch him,* the lady of the house had charged them. Garl didn't know about Torello, but for him, it was the first bit of honest responsibility anyone had given him in a long time.

He heard a clatter, then a muttered curse. Another racket was followed by an even more energetic *"Damnation."*

"What are you doing?" Garl demanded.

"I'm getting up."

"I told you to get up, not move the unfit furniture about."

"Watch your tongue, old man."

"Maybe I'd rather just tell the Lady of the house how you decided to leave Brozz's side and return to your bed for the remainder of the night. You were supposed to be right *there*, you brazen he-bitch."

"Hard to tell anyone anything if I yank your tongue from your head."

The threat opened Garl's eyes in offended disbelief.

Torello appeared in the corridor directly between the sleeping quarters. The injured gladiator scowled at the older man. He then checked on Brozz before finally settling on Garl.

"He's sleeping," Torello reported. "All right?"

"You haven't checked him."

"I checked."

"You didn't. I saw."

"I just looked."

"And I just looked," an angry Garl informed him, locking gazes. "From *here*. And from here, he looks *dead*. Get in there and hold your hand over his mouth. Check his breathing. His bandages."

Glaring hard enough to ignite the straw of Garl's bed, Torello grudgingly did as told. He stopped at the Sarlander's side and inspected him from head to toe but made no further movement.

"What are you waiting for?" Garl asked.

"Just wondering . . . is it catching?"

"What?"

"The infection."

"You can't catch an infection caused by a weapon," Garl sputtered in annoyance.

"How do you know?"

"I know! I said before you learn a few things while you're in an infirmary. And I've seen and smelled enough infected wounds to know. Then there's seeing the healers tend to those same wounds."

Torello's brow knotted in curiosity. "How often were you in the infirmary?"

"I said I was a gladiator in a past life."

"You obviously weren't a very good one," Torello remarked and placed the back of his hand to Brozz's mouth.

"No, I suppose I wasn't," Garl admitted. He settled down, however, upon seeing the other man checking Brozz. "Well?"

Torello's harsh glare returned. "Quiet."

"Quiet? Why? You aren't listening to—"

Torello sat on the edge of Brozz's cot and lowered his face to the man's mouth. He listened, turning his head, and stayed that way for a few moments.

"He's breathing," he finally reported. "Barely."

"Is he sweating?"

"No."

"Check the bandages."

"I don't want to check the bandages."

"Check them."

"You're brave for an old man just a few strides away."

"You should hear me at the far end of a field," Garl said. "I'm damn near fearless, then."

Torello stared, and the one-legged man stared back. They stayed that way for a very long time. Garl didn't know what was going through the young punce's head, but he wasn't going to relax and do nothing while a fellow pit fighter lay suffering and dying a few steps away.

As if sensing that iron resolve, Torello wavered and reluctantly focused on Brozz. He exhaled wearily and pinched one of the Sarlander's cloth bandages, giving a quick peek at what lay beneath.

His lips curled back in distaste. "Dying Seddon."

"What?" Garl asked.

"She cut him something fierce."

"Is it bleeding?"

Torello squinted. "Hard to say. No. It's all crusty and such. Wait." He leaned in closer and studied the underside. "Perhaps a little."

"Does it smell?"

Clearly not pleased about having to do such a thing, Torello lowered himself and sniffed. His face turned sour.

"Is it bad?" Garl asked.

"I mostly smell that shite the healers use. It reeks."

"Saywort."

"My eyes are already watering."

"At least it woke you up. Can you smell anything else?"

Torello grimaced as he took another whiff, then another. "Not much. There's a little smell of something there. Faint, but not good either."

"It could be healing," Garl said.

"And it could be just gathering its strength again."

That set both men to thinking.

"Suppose you want me to tell the Lady about this," Torello said.

"That would be wise, I think."

"I've seen you move about on those crutches," Torello said. "You get along better than I do."

"Spend a few years with them, and perhaps you'll manage just as well."

"I don't think so."

"Then get going," the one-legged man said. "I'll stay here."

"Scream if you need anything."

"You'll hear me scream if you don't get going this instant."

Looking annoyed, Torello stood, retrieved his crutches, and swung himself out of the alcove. He stopped just inside the hall and regarded the older man.

"Just to be clear," Torello said. "Don't make me angry. I won't care if you have only one leg or two or none. You scream at me like you did this morning, and I'll hurt you. I'll hurt you bad enough that you won't want to see me ever again."

Garl was hit in the wrong place by the brazen words. "Truth be known, I don't want to see you ever again *now*. I don't know what manner of pit fighter *you* are, but that's a sword brother over there, one belonging to this house. In my day, we took care of our brothers."

The man's back straightened, and Garl knew he'd said something that struck him and struck him hard, perhaps harder than intended.

"I take care of my brothers," Torello stated quietly. "Don't you worry."

"Well, I worry, so keep your saucy threats to yourself, you knobby bastard. I'm not afraid of you. I survived the Pit and much, much worse. At the hands of some truly frightening cutthroats. There's nothing you can say to me that hasn't already been said. Nothing you can possibly do that hasn't been done. You remember that, youngster."

Torello's hard eyes softened just a little around the edges. He kept his thoughts to himself, however, and just when Garl thought the young man was going to say something cutting, he straightened, bent over his crutches, and swung himself out of sight. The slide and thud of the crutches receded in the distance, and when Torello was far enough away, Garl slowly released his breath in relief.

Lords above, he thought, aware of how his hands were shaking and his heart hammering.

He couldn't remember when he'd last showed anyone that amount of iron, but it felt good. It felt very good. Truth be known, he didn't think Torello would do anything to him. He knew the type: loud and brazen but not truly evil. And if Garl was wrong, well, he'd scream. Long and loud. The people around the villa would come to his aid, not like those in the city, who would only walk faster to distance themselves away from his screams—and whoever was smashing his face at the time.

Around here, they actually cared for him. To a point. But any point was good in his mind.

Garl's thoughts drifted then. He watched the unmoving Sarlander, but his mind remained on the villa and the sense of safety he was becoming accustomed to. A pleasant sense of wellness settled in then, one he hadn't felt in a very long time.

After so many years of absolute misery, fear, and pain . . . life had mysteriously improved.

Over the villa walls, storm clouds filled the sky and hid the world. Gray sheets poured onto the land, soaking it, even flooding it in places. The weather didn't seem to wish to move along just yet, and Nala found that disturbing. She stood inside the doorway leading to her balcony, where her husband usually roosted. Movement below attracted her eye, and she spied Torello limping along the edge of the training grounds. She drew back, smoothed out her robes, and organized her thoughts. The rains fell all of yesterday, which she believed had prevented her husband from returning, not that she worried about him. Her man could certainly take care of himself, especially with the number of trained swordsmen he traveled with.

She did worry about Brozz, however.

She hadn't sent anyone to Pynn's Brook for the healer there, for Brozz's condition had seemed to improve just enough to hint at a recovery. So she charged the two men—Garl and Torello—to watch the unconscious man and left them with an abundance of bandages and the remaining saywort.

"Lady of the House," Torello bawled from directly below her balcony.

She placed her fingers to her temples and went outside. "Yes?"

"The lad's the same, my Lady."

"You've checked the wound?"

"I did," he reported, squinting in the rain. "It's not pretty in the least, but it's no worse."

"That's not quite good enough," she said more to herself than the man below. "I'll be down shortly."

And she was. She gathered Ananda as well as the young guard Pirrus, who fell into step behind her as soon as the two ladies left the residence. Ananda covered them both with a traveling cloak, held above their heads, to ward off the weakening rain.

In short time, they arrived at Brozz's alcove.

"Lady," Garl greeted formally.

"He's still asleep?" Nala asked.

"Ah yes. He is. But he doesn't look so bad this morning. I mean, not any worse."

Nala studied the unmoving form. "How long has he been like this?"

"A day and a bit now," Garl answered.

"Doesn't he have to eat?" Ananda asked. "Or drink?"

"He does," Nala said. "But he hasn't."

"When the need becomes strong enough, he'll awake," Garl said.

Nala thought about that as well. She then reached out and plucked the container of saywort from the window sill. She opened it and examined the remainder with a frown. "How often have you been using this?"

Garl and Torello exchanged looks.

"Sparingly," the old man said. "We dabbed some on in the afternoon and a dab more last night."

"There's not much left," Torello added.

"No," Nala agreed and covered the jar. She examined Brozz with a concerned gaze. "Unless the weather improves, I don't expect my husband to return this day. We don't have much saywort left. Keep watch over him. If this rain stops, perhaps my husband will return with the healer. If he doesn't, I'll have to send someone to Pynn's Brook."

Garl cleared his throat.

"You don't agree?" Nala asked.

"No, no, Lady," he blurted. "I was thinking the very same, but perhaps you should send someone today. Just as a precaution. While it's light outside."

Sound advice, she thought, and scolded herself for thinking otherwise.

"All right," she said. "I'll have someone travel to Pynn's Brook and bring back the healer there."

She took a hand cloth from near Brozz's head and wiped his face clean. His sweating had ceased since she cleaned the cut. A good sign, she believed.

"Until then," she said and handed the cloth to Torello as she left.

A light breeze blew rain into the faces of the women, despite Ananda attempting to shield them both. They skirted the edge of the training grounds, avoiding puddles that had grown in size. Brozz's suffering troubled Nala, and she decided Garl was right, sending someone to Pynn's Brook right away was best, while the days were long. Every wasted moment might prove costly for Brozz's recovery, and she realized she was taking a gamble waiting for Shan's return.

Nala stopped at her front door.

"Pirrus," she said, addressing the guard just behind her. "You know the way to Pynn's Brook?"

"I do, my Lady," the young man answered.

"It's terrible weather, but that man's life is at risk. I want you to go to Pynn's Brook and get the healer. Bring him here. Tell him we'll pay whatever he wants."

Pirrus nodded. "And if he refuses?"

Nala didn't like thinking about that. "If he refuses, then tell him about Brozz's wounds and what we've done thus far. Get instructions on how to take treat him as well as whatever medicine he might recommend. Then, return here as quickly as possible. And by that I mean no later than tomorrow afternoon. Understood?"

"Clearly, my Lady."

"Then gather your things. Outfit yourself for travel. I'll have Ananda pass along some coin for you."

Pirrus turned to leave.

"And Pirrus?"

"Yes, my Lady?"

"Be quick . . . but careful."

"I will." With that, Pirrus hurried for the stables.

Feeling somewhat better now that she'd put a plan into motion, Nala opened her front door and disappeared inside the main residence.

All the while, the man called Ajik watched them from underneath the relative dryness of his forge, where he slept. When Nala and Ananda entered the house and were out of the weather, Ajik's dark eyes lingered on the door then the guard heading to the stables.

A short time later, he turned his attention to the barracks.

16

Arrus retired for the night and spread out the blanket covering the creaky framework of his cot. The straw underneath stabbed at his skin in places, for the blanket provided limited protection. He lay down and stared at the stone ceiling. The air was warm, but not uncomfortably so. A soft orange glow from the burning brazier outside his cell pushed back the darkness, and the dungeon sounds became distant as sleep overtook him.

He dreamed of his parents and his brother Kra. They sat down for a meal, around a fine table his father had built from the nearby forests bordering Nordun and Norjos. The room was redolent with the smell of cooking rabbit. His mother was talking, and she looked quite young. Arrus discovered he was a boy again, and that alone made his heart soar. His father told him to settle down, to settle down *now*, while his mother served them supper. Kra was all smiles before kicking Arrus under the table. The scuffle didn't go unnoticed, and their mother swatted both boys across the heads before placing a warm hand upon Arrus's shoulder. He looked up into her face, and she smiled.

That alone was worth closing one's eyes.

His throat tightened. His sinuses filled. Arrus woke to the sound of someone kicking his water bucket. He tensed in the darkness, lifting his head and focusing on the iron bars of his cell door.

It remained closed.

The brazier light flickered, and something scraped against the nearby wall *inside* the cell. Puzzled, and just a little on guard, Arrus searched for the source and jerked his face back as his water bucket floated by his nose.

Ivus's Grace, he thought.

Voices cried out, belonging to the other prisoners. Some were frantic, some were angry, and all were loud. A foulness polluted the air, one of raw sewage. Arrus winced at the stink. He watched the bucket bob and drift past his cot. The same bucket had been just inside his cell door when he went to sleep. On the floor.

Curlord, he thought and sat up, swinging his legs over the cot's edge. His feet splashed into water, just two fingers away from the lower frame. The Nordish man stood and found himself knee deep. Fire shimmered across the oily surface, revealing lost strands of straw and clumps of excrement. Arrus grimaced and flinched as one of those bobbing nuggets brushed against his inner leg. He backed himself against a wall and looked toward the corridor. Water invaded the passageway beyond, slapping against the brazier's metal hull. The prisoners cried out, trying to alert the jailors to their predicament. Arrus looked toward the back of his cell, distracted by a gurgling of bubbles emerging from the corner where he squatted to relieve himself.

The dungeons are flooding.

"Arrus?" Heelslik called from across the way. "Are you seeing this?"

"Seeing it? I'm tasting it! With every breath."

"The water's still coming in," the Norseman called Rullik shouted over the wailing Sunjans. "They're calling for the jailors."

"What's happening?" Arrus yelled.

"Heavy rains," Rullik answered and paused. "Draining from the city above. That's what I'm hearing. Someone heard the jailors talking of a bad storm overhead. The sewers . . . are filled. First time in memory the rains are so bad. Can't take any more. The water has to go somewhere."

"So it comes here," Heelslik said and laughed. "If it wasn't bad enough."

"We've had it good," Rullik said. "Wait."

The sound of a hand slapping water caught Arrus's attention. A stream of Norjos swearing stemmed from the next cell over.

"Curlord above," Rullik cursed in wonder. "There's rats in the water."

Arrus's eyes went wide. No sooner did he hear the words when several of the vermin paddled by his cell, their wet faces gleaming in the firelight, their tails creating little wakes. One latched onto the bars of his cell. Arrus sent a wave into the little creature, dislodging it entirely. Other rats tried the same thing, their claws scrabbling on metal, the sound chilling the Nordish man's guts. He washed them away as well.

"Damnation," he whispered, searching the waters for more. Plenty were visible though none invaded his cell.

"Jailors!" Heelslik shouted. "We're drowning down here!"

"Hush," Rullik warned. "Let the Sunjans call them. They'll move faster. They'll certainly understand them."

"They'll understand my tone."

"And ignore you," Rullik reminded him. "You're just a Nordish dog blossom, remember?"

That dampened the other man's urgency. "This is unfit," Heelslik said and splashed at the water. "Oh, this is unfit."

"What?" Arrus asked.

"I just slapped away a knob of shite. Thought it was a rat but there was a rat just behind it."

"It's getting hard to see." Rullik said.

Arrus didn't think it would ever get that hard to see, at least not for him.

"Watch what you're swinging at," Rullik warned. "And keep your cell clear of the little bastards."

A wedge of rats swam for the closest brazier, cutting across the shimmering blackness of the water. The foremost vermin hooked their claws over the container's hot metal lip, squealed, and fell back. Those behind didn't have the sense to understand what was happening, so the scene repeated itself for several heartbeats. The little screams frayed Arrus's nerves just a little more. Then he wondered how high the water would rise.

The Sunjans shouted as if they were dying in their cells, perhaps encountering the rats. The fellow prisoners' distress needed no translating. The water rose to just over Arrus's knees, and he cringed at the growing smell.

"It's lifting my cot," Rullik reported.

"And mine," said Heelslik.

Arrus looked at his own bed and saw the water seeping through both straw and blanket. Straw floated while the blanket became a wet curl of sludge. The wooden frame didn't rise, however, which left him wondering why.

"Perhaps they don't want us fighting in their games anymore," Heelslik said. "And they're content to let us drown. A shame."

"They knew you were enjoying yourself too much," Rullik said.

"No doubt."

Arrus didn't laugh, enduring the water's touch and other foul delights. It continued to rise. Twice, he pushed away the muddy chunks surrounding him. Every breath was a mouthful of filth, the smell thick and tongue curling.

"*Skolla*," Arrus whispered, wincing. "I'm breathing in shite. I'm *tasting* shite. Are the jailors coming?"

"What makes you think they'd come at all?" Rullik asked. "I've got shite nuggets bobbing all around me."

"Be almost bearable if it was mine," Heelslik said. "But it's not. I haven't been that well-fed."

"It's not these floating cow kisses that bother me. It's the filth already dissolved into a *slop*."

"Oh," Arrus gasped with unchecked disgust and studied the depths. "Oh... that's..."

On cue, the Sunjans' screaming increased.

"Curlord," Heelslik swore. "They sound like children."

"They have something to scream about," said Rullik.

The memory of sitting with his family around the supper table was long gone, and Arrus wanted nothing more than to be gone with them. The water crept up to his midthigh, showing no sign of retreat.

"How high could it go?" he asked.

"The water?" Rullik asked.

"Aye that, the water."

"Good question. How far are we below the surface? Three, four levels?"

"At least four," Heelslik figured.

"Say four, then," Rullik said. "I've no idea how deep the sewers go, but I believe we're deep enough."

"To drown?" Arrus asked in undisguised horror.

"In rats and shite?" Heelslik added.

"Aye that," Rullik answered. "High enough to drown in rats and shite."

"You don't sound worried," Arrus said.

"Of what? Drowning? Only means I'll be free of this place."

Arrus didn't comment, knowing the Norseman had been inside a Sunjan dungeon for a long time. He suspected the man was more than just a little unfit in the head.

The water rose to the braziers' lips, producing steam. The Sunjans continued screaming until a clang of iron erupted from farther back in the dungeon.

"What was that?" Heelslik said.

"Wait," Rullik replied from beyond.

Arrus cringed and waded to the other side of his cell door. He pushed away all manner of floating debris and attempted to see up the corridor.

"The jailors are here," Rullik said. "They're talking."

"What are they saying?" Arrus asked, recognizing the voices.

"Wait..."

"Seddon's unfit *crack*," Runson whispered in horrified awe and pushed against the dungeon's iron door, forcing it open. Water rushed through and quickly wet his feet and sandals. He jerked away, bumping into a jailor called Gulsha—a round-faced individual who was relatively inexperienced with the finer points of jailing.

"Back up," Runson scolded the man.

"What?"

"Back *up*, I said."

He was too late, however. The water had already soaked his feet. Gulsha hurried to the stairs not a dozen strides away and climbed the first few, escaping the flow. Runson didn't bother. He stood in the rising water, ankle deep, and glared at his fellow jailor.

"This is your fault," he said.

"What was my fault?" Gulsha asked, the space between his eyes knotting up in puzzlement.

"This. My feet are wet."

Gulsha studied the man's ankles then the stairs. "Oh."

Not impressed, Runson sloshed to the door. He peered inside the dungeon, noting how the steps and floor were already submerged. Water flooded the entire chamber, at least to midthigh. Runson grimaced at the sight, baring that upper half rack of teeth.

"Seddon above," he groaned.

"How bad is it?"

"It's bad," Runson reported and moved so that the other man could see.

Gulsha saw. "Well, they were screaming."

"They're still screaming." Runson looked around. "The storms. Happens every year. Some years worse than others."

"How bad?" Gulsha asked as he'd become a jailor only weeks earlier.

"Bad. Quite bad, in fact. Or so I understand. Every year the area floods, though not like *this*. Not that it matters much, considering who's down here. With the rains overhead, it was only a matter of time. Now, however, I can see for myself . . ." He shook his head again. "Best get Balazz."

"Should I get him?"

Runson frowned at the man. "Yes, you should."

Gulsha hurried up the stairs. Runson grimaced at the sight and wondered how the idiot had ever gotten his position over in the king's dungeons—probably had relatives who put in a good word for him. Runson scratched his nose and then his substantial gut hanging over his belt. He inspected the rising waters, thinking of his own extended family and knowing no one would help him find another profession. He was stuck with what he had, not that he would change if he had the opportunity. He loved his work.

"Saimon's black hanging fruit," he muttered, spying rats through the growing clouds of steam.

"What are you waiting for?" someone shouted from within the dungeon. Frantic faces pressed between the cell door bars.

"Get us out of here!" another shouted.

"Get us *out*!" yelled yet another.

Their demands amused Runson, who knew nothing of the sort was going to happen.

"We're drowning here!" one shrieked with all the terrified anger of a child being abandoned by his parents.

That got on the jailor's nerves. "Shaddup, you unfit *tit*! You're nowhere near drowning in there! Be sensible!"

Instead of getting silence, the noise only intensified. Runson sighed as he realized his mistake. Now the whole dungeon block knew a jailor was present and listening.

"What's going on?" Balazz asked as he lumbered down the stairs, blotting out the torchlight from above.

TO THUNDEROUS APPLAUSE

The head jailor's fleshy bulk grazed a wall. A thick layer of fat covered the man, but Balazz was in no way weakened because of it. Muscle lurked underneath that coat of hairy lard, and the man would use it to punish anyone stupid enough to upset him. Balazz approached, appearing vaguely curious as to what all the yelling was about. Gulsha followed the jailor a stride behind.

"Dungeon's flooding," Runson reported.

"What?"

Runson stepped aside and gestured at the rising water.

"Saimon's swinging fruit." Balazz groaned softly and exchanged looks with Runson. "How long's that been going on?"

"Long enough, I suppose."

"Summer weather," the head jailor fumed, clearly annoyed. "Let me see."

He shambled toward the door, a roll of that bear fat brushing Runson's own considerable gut as he passed. Runson didn't enjoy the belly-to-belly contact.

"Dying Seddon," Balazz swore as he peered one way and then the other. A chunk of shite floated toward him, and he kicked it away with a splash. "She's right and proper gone."

"She's gone," Runson agreed.

"This never happened in the king's dungeons."

"Well, those were the king's dungeons, weren't they?"

Balazz scowled at the man, sending a message to not get overly saucy. The prisoners shouted and pleaded, but Balazz appeared not to hear. His expression softened into tired resignation. "Well, that's it, then."

"That's it?"

"Hm," Balazz grunted in the affirmative. "Nothing I can do. Nothing you can do."

"So . . . we do nothing?"

"Nothing at all."

"Well . . . all right," Runson said.

Balazz shut the door and began securing the assortment of sliding bolts.

"Might they drown?" Gulsha asked from behind.

"The short ones might," Balazz replied easily enough, as if discussing the weather. "The taller ass packers don't have anything to worry about, I suppose. But, yes, if the water goes any higher, the short bastards will probably perish."

"Short ones always go first," Runson explained. "In any flooding. Like piss drops in a river."

"And we're going to leave them?" Gulsha asked.

Runson and Balazz exchanged puzzled looks.

"You trying to start something?" Balazz asked him pointedly.

"No, not at all," Gulsha said. "But . . . think . . . didn't Master Soranthus—"

"One of the lads called him 'Sore Ass,'" Runson interrupted, and both senior jailors shared a smile at the memory.

Gulsha didn't take to the name. "Didn't he mention something about the prisoners? And I mean *all* the prisoners in *all* the blocks."

"This block is divided into smaller ones," Runson reminded him. "All behind that door." He indicated the one currently shut.

"And I'm not going in there," Balazz announced. "Are you going in there?"

"I'm not going in there," Runson answered.

Then the two old jailors stopped smiling. They both remembered at the same time.

"Saimon's dew-slicked topper," Runson swore in annoyance.

"Unfit bastards," Balazz growled with equal ire, looking toward the secured dungeon. "We're supposed to keep them *alive*."

"He said, 'Try not to maim or kill them,'" Runson clarified, recalling the conversation. "*Try*, that's what he said. And he didn't say anything about drowning. Especially like this. It's purely accidental. And completely natural."

"Completely natural," Balazz scolded. "Do you hear yourself? Try explaining that to him once he learns the whole nest perished in the summer storms. Just try."

"We can't let them perish," Gulsha said.

Runson looked at the younger man. "I don't remember you being there, Gulsha, or talking to the man."

"I wasn't talking to the man, but you told us later. You said to keep them asslickers alive so they could put on a show in the Pit. That's what you said."

Balazz and Runson exchanged suspicious looks.

"That was for the Jackals," Runson explained as though searching for an excuse to leave the lot to the rising waters.

"No, that was for all of them," Balazz grumbled, remembering and none too happy about it. "I remember. Damn my ears, but I remember. We can't let them drown."

"Wait." Runson held up a finger. "He said we could *kill* one or two just as an example. To bring the rest in line. If needed."

"Now you're being unfit," Balazz scolded. "You're better than that."

"I just don't want to go in there."

"You think I do?"

"Of course not."

"We can send him," Balazz said, nodding at the new man.

"Me?" Gulsha exclaimed. "What did I do?"

"You . . ." Runson stopped and looked at Balazz. "What's the word?"

"Clarified."

"Aye that. *You* clarified the situation. That's what you did. And reminded us of the unfit particulars."

"And I'm head jailor," Balazz said. "And what I say happens."

Runson nodded in agreement.

"So go clarify the rest of the prisoners," Balazz charged the younger man. "Pick your jailors or your Skarrs—"

Runson shook his head. "Unfit to send Skarrs in there. Not with all that gurry floating about. You know they'll be unhappy about it . . ."

"Jailors, then," Balazz corrected himself. "You pick your jailors and ensure none of them hellion-born he-bitches are drowned in their cages. If there are, you get the perished ones out. Just be mindful. Whoever you pick to go in there with you . . . will be right and proper angry for doing so."

Gulsha clearly didn't look forward to the duty, and the head jailor picked up on it.

"Or . . ." Balazz drew out. "You could stand here and simply look in every now and then. Unless the water rises so high you can't open the door."

"And if any of them perish," Runson continued, "we'll simply say they were being unruly."

"No one needs to know," Balazz added.

"Certainly not Sore Ass."

"Certainly not him."

"He'll probably never come down here to investigate, anyway."

Gulsha wilted before the combined might and reasoning of the two jailors. He reluctantly nodded.

"Good," Balazz said. "You're one of us, after all."

"Truly one of us," Runson added.

"Don't concern yourself with them," Balazz said, indicating the dungeon door. "Truly don't. They're scroff. The unfit scutters of decent people. The very gurry that deserves to float along with the shite bobbing in that water. So don't concern yourself with those maggots because if they're in there, they're maggots. And maggots deserve everything they get and worse."

The water was lapping at Arrus's crotch when he heard the clatter of a door being locked. Some talking had reached his ears before that, what he could hear over the Sunjans' damned screaming, but even that died away when the door closed.

After only a moment, however, the screaming resumed, more frantic than ever.

"Well," Rullik said over the racket. "That's it."

"What did they say?" Heelslik asked.

"I couldn't hear much. Not over the yelling of these kogs."

"Did you hear anything at all?" Arrus asked.

"No, nothing," Rullik admitted. "The jailor told them all to shut up. That was it. They closed the door. That says everything we need to know."

"They're just leaving us to die?" Heelslik asked.

"I'd say they're leaving us to suffer."

That quieted the Nordish men.

Arrus looked at the rising water levels, and hot anger surged through him. *Leaving us to suffer*, Rullik said.

Their Sunjan jailors were certainly doing that.

17

Dense clouds as grim and dark as thunderheads hung and coiled in the sky as if nailed there. Rain continued to fall, though not a downpour as before, but as a steady, dampening shower that soured the spirit. At times, the clouds lightened and the rain slacked off, becoming nothing more than a hopeful drizzle, but then the sky darkened with renewed vigor and purpose, and the mist transformed into droplets again. Gray sheets dripped from eaves. Walkways and streets filled with water, unable to drain quickly enough. Streams formed between puddles. Stones were washed and left gleaming. That slick, shiny look didn't reach the foundations and wooden bones of buildings, however. Foul shadows fell across those, creating a wretched twilight.

Clavellus stared out at the narrow backstreet, inspecting the miserable weather.

Rain. It simply didn't want to stop. That pulled a sigh from the old taskmaster, one much longer and louder than intended. No doubt the men behind him had heard. He didn't care, having already passed that mark long before. He stood at a window while his left hand shook relentlessly. His hand continued to do so even when he clenched a fist, trying to control the trembling. He couldn't maintain the fist for long, however, as an annoying cramp overtook his hand, always starting in the joints then seeping into the muscle. Worse still was the *craving* settling into his chest and the back of his throat, a despicable ache that grew with every passing moment, drying out his gullet.

Soon, Clavellus knew, it would demand action, and he'd be powerless to resist.

The thirst.

He knew it well enough but was able to keep it away most times. Truth be known, he was able to *drown* it most times.

This was not one of those times.

Water dripped before the open window. Clavellus watched it but did not see it. The growing buzz within his right ear, one that seemed curiously linked to his parched throat, had fish-hooked his attention. He licked his lips. He wiped his mouth. He wanted to glance over his shoulder at the ones behind him, only he knew he'd done so only a few heartbeats of time earlier. To do so again would only draw unwanted attention to his agitation.

So dry, he thought, and cleared his pipes. The sound rivaled thunder in his ears. Clavellus sighed, huffed really, and reached out for the window's shutter. He pulled it close, hesitated, and opened it again just a few fingers. A shimmering curtain fell off the eaves, splashing into puddles. Clavellus shifted from one foot to the other and shook out his fist, only to clench it again. *Water.* There was so much of it, truly a storm of the season. He raked his beard and smoothed it out, gripped the whole thing and gave it a tug. *Nala.* He wondered how his wife was doing back at their home, envisioning her in all her glory, but *the thirst* interrupted him, dispelling the thought and seizing his attention. The rain outside didn't seem so bad anymore, certainly not as heavy as before. He could steal away to the nearest alehouse. Perhaps even find a merchant selling Sunjan firewater. That was the stuff, the real drink, with enough bite to snap a man's spine. Even a few mugs of the black would satisfy him. Even wine appealed to him—his least favorite drink.

Firewater, however. That sounded right and proper to him. Clavellus scratched at his throat. His eyes shifted side to side before inspecting the dark sky. He could do it. Just head on out and find what he wanted, what he needed, and truth be known, what he deserved. Just a little gift for a job well done.

Clavellus straightened his back, hearing a *crick*. Shan would have a traveling cloak. Koba could go with him for protection. He could even take along one of the once Sujins for extra protection though not many would bother him with the fearsome trainer at his side.

Clavellus turned and jumped at the sight of Goll right before him.

"Saimon's red crack, I didn't hear you," Clavellus blurted, his shaking hand going to his chest.

The Kree's eyes narrowed. "Are you all right?"

The question took Clavellus off guard, and he was well aware of the other men lounging about the lower level. Machlann and Junger in particular looked in his direction.

"Of course I'm all right. Why wouldn't I be?"

Goll didn't stop staring.

"I'm not ready to perish here, I'll tell you that. Not during a summer storm. Just bored is all. Bored. Need something to do. To . . . to occupy my mind."

Goll's stare was unwavering.

"Have no concern about me," Clavellus said and did a double take of the Kree. "Seddon above, Goll. Look someplace else, will you? You're starting to bother me."

"I can see that."

"Oh you can, so then you continue staring just to annoy me?"

"No need to raise your voice."

"I'm not raising my voice."

"I can hear you well enough."

"I'm *not* raising my voice," Clavellus insisted and noticed the stern but curious gaze of Machlann. Not that he cared. He'd cracked heads with his trainer often enough in the past to have lost all fear of him. "I'm simply telling you to *stop* looking at me like that."

In the stillness that followed, someone's chair creaked. A man coughed upstairs, and Goll eventually looked past the taskmaster toward the streets outside the window.

"Unfit weather," the Kree said.

Clavellus nodded that it was and backed up a step, finding the man much too close. Goll glanced at him again, just a glance, but Clavellus didn't like it, didn't appreciate it. In fact, if the damn foreign he-bitch looked his way once more...

"I was thinking," the Kree began, scrutinizing the weather, "about heading out there and looking for a merchant. Perhaps pick up a few bottles for the lads."

Those words straightened Clavellus's spine, and suddenly, he was listening very, very closely.

"Just a few bottles, to get us through the day." Goll continued, unaware of the attentive expression on the older man's face. "I doubt Shan's wife would want this place to become an alehouse. We're fraying her nerves as it is, staying here."

Clavellus nodded.

"What do you think, then?" Goll asked. "A few bottles? Beer? Mead? Just to take away the boredom? Something to sip on with a meal."

"I think," Clavellus cleared his throat. "I think... that's a fine idea."

"Someone will have opened their doors this day. People still need to earn a living."

"Most certainly. Just a matter of going out there and finding them."

"So you don't object?"

"No, no, not at all. A fine idea, I said. Very fine. I'm a little surprised at you for even suggesting it. Must be because of your victory on the sands."

"Must be. Might as well enjoy them while we can."

"May you win more often." Clavellus chuckled softly. "Maybe I'll toss in a few coins for the drink as well."

"Not necessary." Goll smirked. "The house's finances will take care of it."

"Well, that's very kind of you, Goll. Very kind. It'll be good for spirit. The lads will appreciate the gesture. Ah, might I request a single bottle of firewater?"

"I think I can manage that."

The words were sweet to the taskmaster's ears. "Thank you."

"You're welcome."

"Who do you think that is?" Goll asked abruptly.

Clavellus frowned and glanced out the window.

There, standing in the middle of the street, were two very wet-looking travelers, their faces shaded by a rain cloak held up by the taller of the two.

"No idea."

"They're looking this way."

Clavellus studied them. "Perhaps they're looking for Shan. The man's a healer, after all."

"I'll see to it," Goll said and stepped outside. He approached the pair huddled under their cloak. Clavellus watched them talk for a moment, but Sunjan firewater filled his mind—a storm to combat a storm.

Goll returned shortly, his clothes soaked. He pulled the door closed and looked at the taskmaster. "They don't want Shan."

"No? Who then?"

"They want him." Goll nodded at Junger, who straightened in his chair.

"What's that?" the Perician asked, awakening from a bout of boredom.

"You have a pair of admirers outside," the house master informed him.

"I do?"

"They're waiting for you."

That dampened Junger's curiosity. "In that? The weather's unfit."

"I know it's unfit. And so do they. They said so themselves, but they still wish to speak with you."

The Perician frowned. "What about?"

"They wouldn't say."

"Go on out," Clavellus told him. "At least say hello. Only proper you speak with them. Just a few words."

Goll fixed the taskmaster with a sarcastic eye. "Like the way you first talked to us?"

"That was different. You were Free Trained shite then. Now you're a house."

Goll's reply was interrupted by Junger getting to his feet. The Perician went to the door, opened it, and grimaced, clearly not excited about heading outside.

"Go on, then," Clavellus said.

Not happy in the least, the Perician did as told. Goll closed the door and joined Clavellus at the window to observe.

Junger braved the storm and greeted the two men. One was clearly old, perhaps well into his years, while the other was probably his son, who appeared to be in his thirties.

Goll and Clavellus became quiet, straining to hear the exchange but got only whispers.

The old man clutched at the Perician's arm and smiled, shaking his head as if greeting a long-lost friend. Junger gripped the old man's hand in return and nodded, but the words were too faint to hear.

"Can you hear anything?" Clavellus asked.

"Nothing."

Junger shook his head then, and the old man's smile dimmed. More words were spoken, and the son looked from his father's face to the Perician's.

The old man slowly shook his head, clearly disappointed. He released the gladiator's arm and patted it fondly. After more words, the pair departed, quickly disappearing up the lane.

Junger returned, closed the door, and shook himself. Water flew from his person. His shirt was soaked and clinging.

"What did they want?" Goll asked.

"They thought they knew me."

"Did they?"

"No. Not at all. I looked like someone the older man once knew. When he was younger."

With that, he walked back to his seat, pinching his shirt away from his chest.

"About that drink, then?" Clavellus said.

Goll looked from the Perician to the departing strangers to the taskmaster. "Yes. Right away . . ."

Not much later, Goll returned with a small keg of beer, some bottles of Sunjan wine, and one bottle of firewater, accompanied by Pratos. Clavellus relieved Goll of the firewater when he entered. The rest were placed in the middle of a table, and the men gathered around for an afternoon libation. Mugs were brought in by the pensive Shan. Muluk snatched one from the healer's hands, drawing a look from the man.

"This is for your missus," Goll said, distracting Shan, and handed over a bottle of wine.

The healer took it without thanks and leaned in close. "Don't make too much noise. This isn't an alehouse."

"I didn't bring enough for that."

"Suppose not." Shan observed and headed for his inner home. Goll considered the various drinks on the table. He'd spoken the truth. He didn't want anyone to overindulge, with Clavellus being the exception. The taskmaster had been growing increasingly twitchy without his daily drops. Anyone with eyes could see that, and Goll still remembered the verbal scalding the taskmaster had delivered a handful of weary gladiators weeks before.

He didn't need a repeat of that, not here.

Muluk cracked open the keg and was already filling his mug.

"Take that slow," Goll warned. "There'll be no more."

"You should've gotten more," Muluk replied.

Goll ignored that and watched the House of Ten settle down to enjoy their drinks. His attention stopped on one man, so he walked over to where Junger was sitting and joined him.

"Question on your mind?" the Perician asked.

"Just about those two men."

"Strange business, that."

"Who were they?"

"A father and his son."

"The old man thought he knew you?"

Junger shrugged. "I have that kind of face, I suppose."

"Suppose you do. Who was the person you reminded him of?"

The Perician smiled in sympathetic disbelief. "A warrior from long ago. Helped saved his village once, apparently. Then disappeared."

Goll watched him.

Junger detected the scrutiny. "That was all, I swear."

"Nothing else?"

"What else is there? The old man is an old man. Eighty at least. The mind can fade in that time. I met him because it made him happy, and it was interesting to hear what he had to say, but truth be known, that rain's wet. I would have talked longer if it had been a young woman, but he wasn't."

Goll checked on the others. He turned back to Junger. "What do you think of it all?" he leaned in and asked. "The season, I mean."

Thoughtful, Junger drank some of his beer. "It's longer."

"So it is."

"I don't know how much longer."

"Nor I," Goll said and studied the man. "You seem distraught by that."

"I do?" Junger said in surprise. "Well, truth be known, a longer season means more fights. More fights means more chances to be cut into pieces. Or outright mauled. I was hoping to get through these games without either one happening to me."

"Seems the king has other plans."

Junger paused, thinking, and his expression took on a decidedly darker, more contemplative nature, as if he'd just been informed he had only days to live. The transition was so obvious that it caught Goll off guard. Junger's eyes flittered about the room, checking on the whereabouts of the others.

He motioned Goll closer while keeping an eye on Clavellus. "I know what you did for the taskmaster."

That surprised Goll. "What do you mean?" he asked in a low voice.

"The firewater. That was kind of you."

"I didn't do anything except hand over a bottle."

"You did more than that. Clavellus looked like a man in desperate need of a pisspot over there, standing at the window. Anyone could see that. That hand of his . . . ?"

"I did nothing."

"You helped him. That's all I'm saying."

Goll straightened with a scowl. "Good. Then I'll stop listening." He stood. "A warrior from long ago? Is that what he said?"

"He did."

Seddon above. Tired of the conversation, the house master shook his head in distaste. That was all he needed, an old man spreading such sorcerous nonsense amongst the masses. The whole notion stank of bad Perician theater, yet the people would lap it up like parched dogs. They'd seek Junger in even greater numbers.

An unpleasant burning sensation, one of poisonous jealousy, bled to life in the depths of Goll's guts.

He left the Perician to his beer.

18

"You sleep here."

The trainer called Rezzo pulled back a curtain and revealed some uninspiring quarters. The area was sparse, as befitting a gladiator's cave, but clean. A single blanket covered a straw bed, complete with a lumpy pillow. At the foot of the bed stood a short table with a few shelves built into it for personal belongings, not that Prajus had any. A familiar, underlying taint of sweat lurked about the entire gladiatorial barracks, the sour kind that seeps into the wood and clings to it.

That didn't bother Prajus.

"Magnificent," he said with a cold smile. "Truly."

Rezzo studied the newest—and exceptionally controversial—addition to the School of Nexus with undisguised dislike.

"You don't like me much, do you?" Prajus asked.

Rezzo's eyes narrowed in distaste, as if he'd caught an unfit child picking up shite and flinging it at people. In answer, the short trainer smacked his lips and sighed. "Breakfast is in the morning."

"When it usually is," Prajus added, maintaining his smile.

Rezzo's expression remained as unmoving as stone. "Be there with the others. Or get fed nothing. Rain or sun, you'll be working."

"Rain or sun," Prajus repeated seriously, tucking his amusement away for a moment. "Aye that. Good . . . What was your name, again?"

Rezzo didn't answer. Instead, the trainer looked around the corridor, meeting the gazes of the curious few who watched and listened to their conversation. As in any other gladiatorial barracks, very little privacy existed.

Then the trainer spoke, his voice clear and crisp and laced with just a twinge of resentment. "Now, listen. Master Nexus has deemed that no harm is to come to this one. Not one. Not one bruise. If there is, you'll be punished for it."

The words cut through the building's quiet interior. More men slowly filled the corridor, emerging from the nearby alcoves, drawn to the trainer's voice and the new arrival. The gladiators of Nexus were huge brutes, tall and brooding and bare chested, their eyes resembling black rocks that twinkled in the torchlight. They gathered like a pack of trained ogres, waiting for the command to feed. More than one lowered brow was aimed at Prajus, more than one murderous stare.

He didn't blame them at all for the cold reception.

After all, he'd butchered two of their sword brothers during the games.

"They'll listen to you, won't they?" Prajus asked with a feigned note of nervousness that sounded perfectly natural to his ear. In truth, he didn't fear any of these hellpups, though he thought it wise to at least put on a show.

"You best pray they do," Rezzo answered.

"Oh, I'll pray, all right," Prajus said in a distracted tone. "My thanks, good Rezzo. For your time."

If the trainer was about to leave, that one string of words stopped him in his tracks. "That's *Master* Rezzo."

"What's that?"

"You heard me," Rezzo warned with a lingering eye, "you pale slip of maggot shite. I'll not warn you again."

Fine, Prajus's expression said, glad the discussion was over. He studied his quarters behind the curtain.

Rezzo seemed about to speak but decided against it. He walked by the pit fighter, ramming his shoulder into Prajus's arm as he went. The hard blow wobbled the gladiator, but not much else. Rezzo was shorter and smaller, but he was solid around the chest and middle. And as Prajus discovered with that little nudge, the trainer was still able to use his weight when he wanted . . . the sour-assed blossom that he was.

Prajus stepped inside his new quarters and drew the curtain closed behind him. He had nothing to drop onto the floor, not having had any time in fleeing Gastillo's training grounds less than a day before. Leaving his few remaining possessions bothered him more than Gastillo's death. His armor, in particular, had been fashioned for his form alone, as had his helmet. The sword was merely another sword, but the piece he missed the most was the shield. That had the black iron head of a dragon upon its surface, a particularly striking piece of art. Perhaps he could get another in its likeness.

Or perhaps he'd get the original.

He stood over the cot. He lifted it easily enough, sighed, and let it drop to the floor. It was no better than his last one, so he sat down upon it, put his elbows to his knees, and held his head. He thought of Tulka, Savul, and Kall, the three companions Nexus had refused to take. The house master's decision didn't surprise Prajus, really. Tulka wasn't one for the games, Savul's lust for coin was greater than his actual skill, and while Kall showed promise, he lacked desire. All three were louts and lacked sense, thinking themselves much better than the rest of Gastillo's roster, with the exception of Prajus. They did have their good points, being that they followed Prajus without question. He didn't know what he'd done to deserve such loyalty, but he supposed they were drawn to his skill, style, and confidence.

They would survive the city, not that he cared about their wellbeing. They weren't his friends, not in the least. Once or twice, Prajus had given thought about just what those three asslickers were to him, and he'd decided they were shields of meat.

He could get others, even in this place.

He studied the wall. *The School of Nexus.* The merchant knew greatness when he saw it and was far more intelligent than Prajus had given him credit for. He wondered just how intelligent the old bastard might be. Prajus had to admit the man wasn't Gastillo. Nexus had a familiar look about him, one Prajus had encountered often in the arena and even a few times in the open streets. The merchant possessed the aura of one not to be challenged, who believed all others were nothing more than meat, waiting to be used and slaughtered. If Prajus didn't bring him what he wanted, he had no doubt the merchant would cast his carcass aside without a second thought.

Prajus didn't worry about being cast aside. He'd meant what he said back in that fancy chamber. Even now, he considered this change of stables nothing more than a slight skip upon the path to becoming champion, and a new territory to impose his will. Throughout his entire existence, since he could remember, he'd been yanked from one road to another, only to right himself and continue moving forward, toward competing in the grandest of games.

His parents had been slaughtered by bandits, leaving him an orphan at five, and while an ordinary person might unconsciously suppress those painful memories, Prajus's mind did no such thing. He remembered everything, from helplessly watching his parents die by chopping swords, to screaming at their killers. That pain motivated him, sharpened him, as Prajus made his way from village to village.

A Lancer called Vellic found him begging in the countryside and took pity upon him. Vellic raised him as if he were the son of a neighbor who had gone missing. He was Prajus's first taskmaster, educating him in the ways of the sword. Sadly, Vellic disappeared when Prajus turned thirteen. The Lancer went out into the westerly plains of Sunja's realm and never returned. People talked of the Dezer ambushing and killing Vellic's patrol, but Prajus never learned what exactly had happened to his missing guardian.

Seeking out Vellic's killers—a notion that amused him later in life—Prajus traveled to Vathia and was discovered by a disgraced trainer by the name of Shoor. Shoor enjoyed the drink far too much, craved the bite of firewater, and regularly guzzled thick warm beer. Prajus remembered a number of women as well, but none of them ever stayed with the man. That love of carousing had cost the taskmaster his position with a local gladiatorial house. The knowledge and skill remained with Shoor, however, even though no one ever offered him work ever again. Prajus was never sure if the drunken trainer recognized his natural ability and potential or simply wanted to fashion a gladiator one final time.

And create a gladiator Shoor did, one of the finest in Vathia, despite his age of only sixteen. Prajus killed his first opponent in a much smaller, more personal pit fight organized by Shoor and a few others. He was a Vathian called Serbone, three years older and utterly shocked when Prajus plunged half an arm's length of steel through his gullet.

The memories flowed, bringing a terse smile to Prajus's face.

The curtain to his alcove slid open, and a man—a big man—peered in, distracting Prajus from his thoughts. The brute had taken something of a beating about the face, so his nose had swollen into a truly eye-catching feature, and several other cuts had been stitched closed. A furry chest had a patch shaved away, where a line of stitches ran just above a nipple. Mildly surprised, Prajus waited for the gladiator to speak, for he was clearly annoyed about something. More men gathered in the corridor beyond, their shadowed faces just as stern, their shapes blocking the sparse light.

Not that Prajus cared. "Yes?"

The big man stared at him. "You killed Malo."

Prajus's eyes narrowed in thought. "Who?"

"Malo, you bastard, Malo. And you killed Parek."

More silence. Prajus drummed his fingers off his chin. He really didn't have patience for such gurry. "I see. And?"

"You're not welcome here."

"Really?" He considered the words. "That's surprising. Well, your house master—or is it schoolmaster since this is a . . . ? No matter. Nexus—you remember him? Well, he has a different opinion about me being here. Ask him if you like."

That didn't budge any of them. The hard looks remained. In fact, the hard looks intensified.

"I wanted to butcher you myself," the big man said with a slow shake of his battered head.

Prajus absorbed that thought, thinking it best to get this expected unpleasantness out of the way. "Right. Well. You certainly can't do it now. My apologies."

"Who says I can't?"

Prajus didn't think mentioning Nexus again would help. Not since the school owner had already made his thoughts clear on the matter.

"He's a right and proper asslicker," someone seethed over the big man's shoulder.

"Why not just smash his head, Colcus?"

"Do it, Colcus."

"Aye that, do it."

The big man seemed to consider it.

"Colcus, is it?" Prajus asked, untroubled and deciding to take the initiative. "Yes, why not just smash my head? Just smash it. You look capable enough. And willing. You've probably smashed plenty of heads. And here I am. Defenseless. Without a weapon. Armor. Nowhere to go except through that."

He jabbed a thumb at a shuttered window.

"And I'm not about to go through that. Not with you right here. So why not smash my skull? Smash it right in. Lords above, I certainly could use a good smashing, with all the things I've done. The lives I've taken. The people I've angered and tormented. The animals I've kicked or outright killed. Just out of pure . . . delight. And I do remember those two lads, by the way. Somewhat."

All the while as he spoke, Colcus's expression went from grim to frightening. The man's breathing increased, causing his mighty chest to rise and fall. He was considering some smashing, a right and proper pummeling about the head and shoulders, that much was clear.

Prajus stood and studied every unfriendly face glaring at him in the flickering lamplight. Quite a few were jammed in there, all looking to snatch a peek at the new arrival, even to help with the smashing if necessary. Prajus could appreciate that.

"He's a brazen one," someone muttered.

"Too brazen," said another.

"A long-tongued pig bastard."

"Pull that tongue out from his head."

"Stretch him out and put the boots to him."

Prajus frowned, having enough of such gurry. "All right," he said, a hard edge creeping into his voice. "So I killed a pair of lads from this school. One I even remember taking the head off with one cut. But that's the Pit for you. Seddon knows they would've chopped me down if they had the chance, and then it would've been *my* sword brothers going after you. But I killed them first. Without hesitation. Am I guilty? No. These are the *games*. We all know what can happen during the games. Men perish. All the time. Some more brutally than others. I killed them, yes, but can any of you say it wasn't a quick and clean death in both cases? And I didn't cripple them, so think on that. But . . . you're entitled to your revenge, so if you want it, here I am."

Colcus glared but, surprisingly, didn't move. Nor did anyone else. An unmentionable force kept them at bay.

"He put down his house master." One of the men behind Colcus sneered, an ugly he-bitch with an unsightly array of scratches and stitches covering his face, as though he'd crawled free of a barbed honeypot. "That's the word on the streets," he informed his companions.

"Aye that," said two others.

"So I did," Prajus admitted. "I did kill my house master. But he challenged *me* first and made it clear he intended to kill me. Instead, I killed him, so I'm not guilty of murder. Your schoolmaster knows this. He knows. I would not be here otherwise."

"I think . . ."—Colcus eyed him dangerously—"that you'll say just about anything to save your unfit hole."

Not so stupid after all, Prajus thought, but what he said was, "That's to be seen, isn't it? There's just the one of me. There's at least two dozen of you. I'm trapped, obviously, but I'm not about to turn my back. So I'll make it clear, like that idiot Gastillo made it clear to me. If it's just you, good Colcus, we'll fight. You. And me. Right here. To the death or otherwise. I don't care. There's very little I care about. We'll fight, and I'll use only these."

Prajus lifted both fists with solemn intent, the knuckles whitened from tension.

"But know this," he quietly continued. "If any of those savages behind you tries to help you, or if you all charge me at once, that's a different matter entirely. It's about survival then. I'll forget about being honorable. I'll forget about avenging a dead sword brother. I'll hurt you. I'll hurt as many of you as I can. Oh, I'll be either crippled or murdered or unfit in the head at the end of it all, guaranteed. But I'll leave my mark on a few of you unfit bastards calling yourselves gladiators. You hear that? I'll leave my mark."

His threat given, Prajus adjusted his stance, tucked in his chin, and watched them all from under a lowered brow. He waited for the rush from behind his fists.

In the ensuing silence, no one spoke.

Then Colcus blinked. He straightened his neck, thinking deep thoughts. He appeared torn between a gladiator's vengeance, personal honor, and outright slaughter, which was Prajus's very intent. Behind Colcus, the ugly blossom with his face stitched together looked as if he'd swallowed something barbed and unfit.

Uncertainty hung in the air. Prajus could sense it, and damned if he didn't enjoy it.

"He still killed Malo and Parek," the ugly one reminded his sword brothers. Grunts and nods of assent followed.

"I did," Prajus agreed. "And I understand you want blood. What about this? On my honor, if I'm not struck down during the remainder of the games, I'll offer you the chance to avenge those two lads. Out there, on the open sands. One last fight. To ease your minds. I'll take on all challengers then. One at a time. Or all at once. Your choice."

Indecision seeped into the harsh faces before him, but the one called Colcus wasn't convinced, and neither was the asslicker with the stitched face. They gave him more looks, but not as hard as before.

Showing no fear, Prajus squared his stance and cracked his shoulders. "What will it be, then?"

The pack wavered, then wavered again, glancing at one another. They weighed their desire to hurt Prajus and avenge their dead companions against their own honor. A challenge to a blood match would have made things much easier.

"I'm for the end of the season," someone muttered.

"You gutless bastard," said another.

"I say we paddle him right now."

"He can't fight all of us."

Prajus scowled behind raised fists, ready to crack whoever decided to take a swing at him. He hadn't lied. The first unfit kog to charge in would forever regret it.

"Well then . . . go on, Colcus," one gladiator said.

But the big man didn't. Colcus frowned. "You go on if you're so damned eager."

"You're right there."

"I can fix that easily enough."

The pack shuffled and fidgeted.

"The punce is right," a tall pit fighter rumbled in the back, turning heads. "These are the games. Malo and Parek knew that as well as anyone."

"He *killed* them," the scratched-face asslicker blurted. "And his house master."

"He killed them in the Pit. Not in some back alley. As for his house master, I've heard the same. That the gold-faced topper challenged him."

"He was taunting the man."

"Aye that, but what house master would fight one of his own hellpups? In the middle of the season? Nexus would've put his house guards on us and been done with it."

The pack took that thought and chewed upon it. The stitched-face man sensed the mood shifting and appeared ready to burst.

"You seem to want his blood the most, Rigger," the tall one said directly to the stitched-face man. "Kill him if you're able, but I'd just as soon scrub old Nexus's ass crack with my bare hands than foul them this way. The season won't last forever. I'll fight him out there on our training grounds at the end. If I'm able. And if he's still alive. Not until then. And not like this."

With that, the tall one left the pack. Two others muttered agreement and went away as well. Then the entire group fragmented and drifted apart, with glares and looks of loathing in Prajus's direction.

"He killed Malo and Parek." Rigger threw the words at the disintegrating group. "He killed them *both*."

"Wait till season's end, Rigger."

"Leave it alone, man."

"Blood matches are for out there, not while the punce is sleeping."

"He's right *there*," Rigger said but failed to convince his sword brothers to remain.

Prajus could barely hide the delight in his twisted heart. To do so would lose this gamble and bring the entire barracks down upon his skull, so he kept on with his defiant face, making it clear he was ready to perish.

Colcus remained, not completely decided, along with two other formidable pit fighters and the one called Rigger. All four wore only leggings or loincloths, displaying an assortment of cuts and bruises upon the imposing physiques of men in their prime.

"We'll do it, then," Rigger said to the other three before regarding Prajus with undiluted contempt. "There's enough of us."

Prajus was beginning to dislike him.

"You don't speak for me, Rigger," Colcus rumbled, not taking his eyes off Prajus. "And I can see this was a mistake. The man speaks truth, and I'll not partake in a senseless beating. Not for nothing."

That mortified Rigger. "It's *not* for nothing! We're avenging Parek and Malo!"

"When the games are done," Colcus said. "And perhaps not even then."

"Those two were your friends."

Not caring for the reminder in the least, Colcus fixed Rigger with a dangerous look. "I know who they were, you long-tongued punce. I don't need you to tell me who they were."

That silenced Rigger into submission.

"You're wiser that you look," Prajus said.

Colcus swung his attention back to him. "Make no mistake, maggot. I think Nexus is wrong in bringing you here. I sense you're as poisonous and treacherous as a slanted ass crack, and it's better to cut one's own throat than trust the likes of you."

"I'll do my best to convince you otherwise," Prajus said, lowering his fists just a little.

"Stay away from me," Colcus warned. "Else I forget myself and put you facedown into the dirt."

The gladiator left then with parting glares at both Prajus and Rigger.

The three remaining pit fighters stared after the departing Colcus. Rigger recovered first and confronted Prajus. He took greater stock of the newest addition to the school. "You're a sly one," he said, "I can see that now. Very sly. You might've convinced the pack to leave you alone this day, but I'll be watching. I'll be watching."

Prajus lowered his hands completely and shrugged. "Watch all you like. Watch me squat over a shite trough, for that matter. Just let me know when you want to pull steel on me. And remember: I might've killed those two, but I didn't do it while they were sleeping."

"We'll talk again," Rigger said, pointing at the floor.

In answer, Prajus took two steps toward the three, who braced themselves for a fight. Prajus stopped, frowned at the men, and pulled the curtain across, hiding them from sight.

"We'll talk again," Rigger said from beyond and punched the fabric.

Prajus went into a ready stance, expecting all three to rush him. Nothing more happened, however, and he sensed them moving away. A hand slapped a wooden post outside, perhaps out of frustration.

Prajus relaxed.

A short time later, he smiled.

19

When Borchus opened his eyes, he saw two things. One was Gurga, standing over him like the grim-faced bastard he was. The other was a halo outlining the enforcer's mighty frame. That disturbed the agent. He didn't want to think that Gurga was all that waited for him in whatever life lay beyond death.

Gurga unfolded his arms and leaned over the unmoving agent. "You alive?" he asked, his breath hot on Borchus's face.

The agent screwed up his nose. "Aye that."

"Not dead yet?"

"No."

Gurga grunted in disapproval and straightened. He backed away, his heavy footfalls crashing in the agent's ears. Borchus was glad the enforcer was out of his face, not wanting to be that close to the brute ever again. He frowned and felt his skin tighten around his cheeks and forehead in unpleasant ways.

Stitches, he realized, just before his strength ebbed away, taking his consciousness with him.

Moments later, he didn't know how long, someone, or some *thing* was breathing on his face: Gurga, standing right over him.

"Dead, now?" the enforcer asked with genuine curiosity.

Borchus sighed and managed a frown. "No, you punce. No. I'm not dead."

Gurga scowled back, not appreciating being called a punce. "You looked dead," the man said after a short time.

"Well . . . I'm not."

"Feel a little dead?"

Borchus squinted in weak annoyance and saw that the enforcer very much expected an answer. "I do not. I *should*. But I don't."

"You don't look so alive."

Borchus sighed and closed his eyes. No, he probably didn't look so alive.

"You rest," Gurga said. "Check on you again. Later. See if you're dead."

"I won't be dead."

"You could be."

"I will not."

"You might."

Borchus didn't have the strength to argue.

"I'll come back," Gurga said.

"You do that."

And that little exchange sapped what energy Borchus had remaining. Sleep took him under, and in those floating depths, he heard voices and detected a presence. He didn't dream, nor could he understand what the voices were saying.

When he opened his eyes again, Gurga wasn't standing over him. He looked left and right and saw that he was in a bed, in a room—an alehouse room, if his memory still functioned properly. He remembered slogging his way through the backstreets toward Sindra's alehouse and crashing on her floor.

Then he was here.

Sons of Cholla, he thought, and a buzz of alarm sounded in his head. They would be searching for him. At least, he had to assume they would be searching for him. That meant Sindra would be in danger. He had to get away, to get out of what used to be Hadree's alehouse, before the Sons arrived. With a groan, he reached up and grabbed a blanket's edge where it was tucked under his chin. That discovery drew a frown from Borchus, as he didn't think Gurga capable of being so motherly. Pushing that thought aside, he pulled the blanket down, stopping twice, before unsheathing his legs. He struggled to sit up, did so, and felt a chill.

His clothes were missing.

Borchus inspected himself and couldn't, for the life of him, understand what he was looking at. He was naked, freely dangling, with his upper body trussed in bandages. That discovery caused him to feel the bandages over his face and head, as well as dressings covering his arms, especially the left one. A memory flared across his mind's eye then, of a fight in the falling rain, and him parrying a knife or a sword with his forearm.

Youuu punce, Borchus scolded himself. Sitting on the bed's edge, he fumed and gripped the frame. That took a considerable amount of strength, and he weakened quickly, much to his dismay. Then he remembered the Sons of Cholla, which prompted him to rise.

The room tipped and twirled in a dizzying rush. He thumped back down upon that straw mattress, and when his senses returned, he wondered how he'd gotten there. Then he filled his lungs and called upon his legs to get him out of bed. His arms gave out almost immediately, and his legs became boneless an instant after that. He thumped back on the bed again, took stock of the situation, and became aware of his racing heart. His vision narrowed, and he focused on the bedroom's only door. A deep and disconcerting sound came from beyond, a constant, whispery chewing, like that of worms feasting upon the edges of a scroll. Borchus listened, skin shivering while his innards flared with heat. Sweat beaded upon his face, and a feeling of unwellness rushed in and overcame him.

His eyes closed, and he sensed himself falling, just dropping, even though he was certain of not moving from the bed. The fall took a very long time, and the final impact didn't bother him in the least. A voice righted his senses, but that didn't last long. At some point, Gurga returned, breathing into his face.

Borchus opened his eyes and saw it wasn't Gurga after all. It was Sindra.

And the concern in her face was balanced with clinical curiosity.

"He dead now?" Gurga asked from behind her.

"He's not dead," Sindra said derisively. "But he's far from taking a walk in the garden. Are you able to speak? Can you hear me?"

"Aye that," Borchus finally croaked.

"You sound thirsty," she observed. "Can you drink some water?"

Water. His throat practically seized up at the word, and a deep, desperate need overtook the agent. "Yes."

"Gurga, pass me that pitcher, would you? And a mug." Sindra looked back at Borchus. "How do you feel?"

He shook his head, which almost sent him under once again.

"You should be dead," she told him.

Before Borchus could comment on that, Sindra was tipping a mug into his face. He didn't see Gurga passing her a pitcher or even pouring water into the mug, but there it was. She held his head in place and angled the mug until, finally, water went down his dusty gullet.

Sindra pulled the mug back, and his eyes narrowed in an unspoken question.

"Slowly," she advised. "See how that stays with you first. You've been sleeping for a while now."

Borchus's eyes narrowed even more, tightening his stitches.

"A day and a bit," she told him and gave him another, much longer drink. "I'll tell you one thing, I don't know how much blood is in a person's body, but I was damn certain all of yours had seeped out onto my floor."

That softened his expression. "I'm sorry."

"For what?" Sindra asked. "You didn't stab yourself, did you?"

"For everything. Especially for coming here. For troubling you. With this."

For several heartbeats, Sindra did nothing. Then she tipped the mug into his face again. He drank until the water was gone.

"I should go," Borchus said.

"You're not going anywhere."

"You can't stop me."

That comment creased the space between Sindra's eyes. "I can't stop you? I don't *need* to stop you, you idiot. Don't believe me? Try standing again. Go on. I could do with a smile. I came up here to see if you'd finally died and found you uncovered, your blanket cast aside, bare ass down on the bed and looking dead to the world. Barely felt a breath coming from you. I thought you were a corpse, which was a shame, I'll admit, since I'd done a lovely job piecing you back together. I don't think I've ever done so much sewing my entire life. Then there were the bandages, and that reminds me: you owe me a new pair of blankets. And then, just as I was thinking how to get rid of your carcass, your eyes started to move behind their lids. But that's all beside the point. When I say you can't go, I mean you're *unable* to go. Anywhere."

Borchus stared at her before speaking. "Suppose you're right."

"Oh, I'm right. Am I right, Gurga?"

"Very right," the enforcer said.

"Head on downstairs, to the door, will you?"

Gurga left.

"I'll go as soon as I get my legs back." Borchus said.

"You're as white as a tablecloth." Sindra studied him. "Why the hurry to leave?"

"The Sons. They'll be searching for me."

"Why did they do this?"

Borchus winced, unwilling to speak.

"I think I deserve an answer," Sindra pointed out.

"It's best you not know."

She pursed her lips, shrugged, and appeared uninterested. "While I don't doubt those maggots are searching the streets for you, I do know that you've been here for two nights now, since you saved me from Senturo and then bled all over my floor. If the Sons were going to find you—or take you—I think they would have done so by now."

Borchus considered that and decided she was right. He relaxed.

"That's better," Sindra said. "Keep doing that. Can you eat?"

"Yes."

"Telda has some soup down below. I'll send her up with some. If you can eat it."

"I can."

"Good. Maybe get some color back into your face. Some real color. You lost a lot of blood, Borchus. And you look like one of Telda's roasts carved up by a set of very sharp knives. Rest a bit. Get your strength back. And once you're able, you can leave."

Borchus didn't say anything to that.

Sindra placed the mug on a nearby bed table and stood. She smoothed out her dress, a green one with a high neck, and studied him. "Thank you again for stopping by when you did. When Senturo was here."

"You're welcome. Thank you . . . for keeping me here."

That quieted her. She seemed about to say more but changed her mind and turned away in the end. Sindra stopped at the bedroom door and looked back at the recovering agent. "Gurga's on guard down below. This door is locked, and I have the only key. No one will bother you. If someone does, I think it's best you leave if you can."

Borchus frowned in puzzlement.

"Because," Sindra continued, "it probably means I'm dead. That Gurga is dead. Chances are, if that happens, you'll soon be killed." Realizing what she'd said, Sindra nodded once and left.

The door locked, the sound very loud in his ears.

A short time later, a knock came at the door. Metal scraped metal until a key finally fit the lock and the tumblers gave away. A woman entered, carefully carrying a large bowl trailing steam.

"You awake?" she asked.

Borchus grunted that he was. He tried sitting up, but his collection of wounds stopped him.

"Don't get up," the woman said and walked over to his bedside. She stopped, placed the bowl on the nearby table, and pulled up a chair. She swiped a few strands of brown hair from her face, smiled a yellow smile, and planted herself next to him.

"Now, then," she said and retrieved the bowl. "Supper time."

"Supper?"

"Aye that, supper." A spoon appeared in her hand, and she stirred the soup.

"I only just closed my eyes," Borchus said.

"And a day went by, is it? Happens to me all the time. Especially since I got married. Don't ever get married. Unless your husband's a soldier that plans on being away for days. You won't be tempted to kill the bastard in his sleep. Or when he's awake. Lords forbid you have to do it then. A true mess. Anyway. You think you can eat some of this?"

Borchus stared at the woman, blinked, and slowly, cautiously, nodded, keeping her in sight all the while. "You're Telda?"

"I am."

She leaned over, a smell of pleasant herbs surrounding her, and positioned the spoon in front of his mouth. "Open."

Borchus did so, and Telda did the rest, unloading spoonfuls into him. The soup was a broth of beef and vegetables and very good. Much like the water, the food hitting his tongue made Borchus realize how he badly needed it.

"That's what I like to see," Telda said, smiling that ferociously yellow smile. "A willingness to eat. A sure sign you're getting stronger. There you are. Eat that, and we'll get more into you."

"It's good."

Telda chuckled. "You must be hungry to say that."

"It's very good."

"Oh, lovely," the woman said, feeding him. "I can listen to compliments all day if I have to. Perhaps even longer."

"Where's Sindra?" Borchus asked.

That halted the feeding. "Ohhh, interested in where the missus is, are you? Care for some bread?"

That wasn't a bad idea at all. Borchus nodded.

"I'll get you some bread," Telda said and set the bowl down. She stood, smiled fondly at him, and left, locking the door behind her.

Borchus watched her go, his stomach wanting more of the soup. He stayed there, unmoving, and stared at the bare timbers of the ceiling. The door opened a little later, and Telda reappeared.

"Here we are," she said and began shredding the one piece of bread she'd brought with her. "Not so busy out there, this day. Still somewhat overcast, but the rain's stopped, at least. Water everywhere, you know. Some parts of the city's flooded. Terrible. Terrible, terrible. Turn one's stomach, seeing what's floating up from the sewers. Worse still watching the youngsters splash through it all." She shivered for dramatic effect, stuck her tongue out in disgust, and deposited the pieces of bread into the soup. Once she was done, she gave it all a quick mix and loaded up the spoon once again.

"Here we are," she said and leaned over him.

Wary, Borchus opened his mouth.

As he ate, Telda's demeanor went from jolly revulsion to morbid curiosity. "Lords above. You truly are a mess, and I've seen a few right nasty fights in my time. Not while working here, mind you. Not with the likes of Gurga minding the place. One look at that beast would take the will out of a bloody army, let alone a few brazen pissers. You, now... you've had boot heels put to you."

It didn't take a sharp eye to deduce that. Borchus was fairly certain the stitches and bandages were the only things keeping him in one piece.

"Imagine the other fellow looks worse," Telda said.

"Has Sindra spoken . . . about me?"

That question drew the woman back. "You're very interested in the missus, aren't you?"

The silence was all the answer she needed.

"I don't blame you. She's quite the piece of fruit. Some ladies don't like that kind of talk. Quite the berry, quite the flower, quite the drink of wine. I do. I speak that way all the time. And she is. Never married. Oh, she's had her suitors, have no doubt, but she never showed any interest in them. I imagine you're not entirely unfit to look upon, before someone tried to bite your face off, that is. Mind you, she's particular, our Sindra. Very particular."

Borchus knew.

The soup disappeared, and Telda dabbed at his mouth with a hand cloth. Once done, she gathered up the bowl and inspected him from head to toe.

"Sweet Seddon above and all the Lords combined," she marveled. "You're fortunate to be alive, you know that?"

"Yes," he said, already growing weary.

"You just lie there. Get better. Once Sindra takes care of someone, she won't let them go until they're right."

Borchus wondered about that.

"Sleep, now," Telda said, going to the door. "Not much else to do. There's a pisspot underneath the bed. If you need help, just shout. I'll hold it for you."

His eyes narrowed.

"The pisspot." Telda chuckled, enjoying the flirtation. "But if you do need help with anything else . . ." she drew the thought out, "I'm happy to help. Don't hope for Sindra. It's either me or Gurga, and you don't want Gurga. I've seen him eat whole chickens. Cooked, of course, but one look at the man would make you think otherwise."

She laughed softly, the sound rasping but not unpleasant. The door closed. Footsteps receded. Borchus exhaled and stared at the ceiling again. *It's either me or Gurga.* That thought was enough to tie his pisser into a knot. Telda had only been giving him a jab, one that summoned a fearful smile to his face, and smiling hurt. Part of him, however, feared she was serious.

Gurga. He frowned, his eyelids growing heavy.

The battered agent fell asleep.

Sindra heard Telda's shoes clapping the worn boards as if a drunken bull were descending from the second floor. She reached the bottom and rounded the counter, paying no mind to the regular evening patrons filling the alehouse. The lamps were lit, and bands of pipe smoke hung between tables. Telda parted some of those dreamy ribbons as she walked behind Sindra.

"How does he look?" Sindra asked in a low voice.

"Dead. Or just about dead."

That stark assessment tightened Sindra's face. Count on Telda to tell the truth.

"But . . ." her friend said, stopping and checking on the nearby wall of kegs and bottles. "He's awake. And he seems right enough in the head."

"He does, does he?"

"Oh yes. Gave him a few jabs. Purely fun. His eyes were like this." She opened her own to their maximum potential. "Such fun."

A little smirk spread across Sindra's face. "Yes, I'm sure he enjoyed that."

"It's my way of seeing if he's well or not," Telda explained. "See if he's still in this world. And he is. Just looks near death right now is all. He'll recover, I'm sure. He ate everything I fed him. That's a good sign."

A good sign, Sindra thought.

"He was asking about you." Telda smiled.

That brought her to attention. "What?"

"Oh, he's taken with you. Easy to see. Just in his manner. He tries to hide it, but he's smitten. I can tell."

"I don't think so."

Telda leaned in. "I know so. Perhaps better than you. Give this one a chance is all I'm saying."

"You do remember you were in favor of Senturo?"

"I only said he was a handsome fellow. Or something like that. This one isn't so handsome *now*, but there's a quality of iron about him. A very strong will. Spend some time with him. You can kick him out when he's able to walk. That's all I'm saying."

"When he's able to walk," Sindra said, peering straight ahead, "he goes out that door."

Across the dimly lit interior, Gurga stood guard at the main entrance like a sleepy but wary cat. His mighty arms folded, he studied the alehouse's small crowd before swinging his attention outside.

"If I didn't know better," Telda carried on, "I'd say he was a gladiator. He's not a gladiator, is he?"

"Borchus?"

"Yes."

"No, he's not."

"Oh," Telda said with disappointment. "That's unfortunate. He's probably too short for that, I suppose. Though I've seen short gladiators before. All those cuts and bruises and bites. Someone was desperate indeed, to try and bite his face off like that."

Sindra agreed. "Desperate. It'll take a while to heal."

"A long while. But . . . if you like, there are ways of speeding up the healing. People who make it their trade."

"Healers?" Sindra asked. "You mean the saywort?"

"I could get some for you if you like. Just a small jar."

Sindra thought about it. "That ointment smells. And it's costly."

"But if you want him to leave sooner," Telda said, "or seal up the important parts. It might be wise not to rely on stitches alone."

Sindra's silence suggested agreement.

"And it will get Borchus on his way faster. If you want him gone, that is. Since you don't like him."

"I don't."

"Of course."

Sindra folded her arms, leaned back against the counter, and studied Telda. Then, having reached a decision, the alehouse owner went to one section of the bar and reached underneath the countertop. She pulled out a small leather purse and stuck her fingers into the top, widening its opening.

"Not quite sure what you're playing at," she said, "but I know you're playing."

Telda blinked innocently.

Sindra reached underneath the counter again and dipped her hand into an open coin box. "Here," she said, bringing up a fistful and counting the coins off as she stuck them into the purse. "Thirty gold. Go on and find a healer. Get whatever saywort you can and bring it back. Might as well slap it on him while he sleeps. At least I won't have to speak to him then."

Telda took the small bag of coins and hefted it. "You're certain you don't like him?"

"I don't. The sooner he's gone, the better."

"I see. Which is why he's sleeping upstairs this very moment and you're paying for his healing."

An old patron with graying whiskers walked up to the bar. The two women quieted when he stopped and inspected the kegs. On cue, Barrud, the regular barkeep, emerged from the kitchen and immediately addressed the customer.

Sindra leaned into her friend. "That's payment for helping me when he did that one time," she whispered.

"Well," Telda whispered back. "You know what you're doing."

"I do."

Telda looked toward the alehouse's entrance. "The clouds are breaking. Daresay there'll be games tomorrow."

Sindra didn't comment.

Telda tucked the coin away in her dress pocket. "It's not too busy. I can get to a healer and be back again before too long."

"Go on, then."

"If I get this, you'll have to put it on him."

"What do you mean?"

"I mean you'll have to put it on him. Some will say that ointment smells like onions, but I think it's much more like cat's piss. And I'll be cooking this night. I can't be cooking with that on my hands."

"Then wash them."

"The smell *clings*. You know what it's like."

Sindra shook her head. "Go on. Get back here quickly. I can't spare Gurga."

"I'll stick to the main streets," Telda said. "And scream if I need to." She walked out from the bar then, not bothering with a rain cloak. The weather was improving, the storm clouds breaking up and moving off. After a few nights of hardly any customers, Sindra suspected tonight would be quite busy. She'd welcome the diversion.

It would take her mind off the man upstairs.

The rain ceased, the storm clouds began a sullen retreat, and people returned to the streets, grateful to escape their houses and eager to be rid of rain cloaks. They always felt that way after a right and proper dousing of the city. Those last few days had been much more powerful than any in recent memory, but it was summer. Gladiatorial sport and storms were to be expected.

Tall and skinny, like a malnourished dog on the verge of losing its fur, Paze leaned against the corner of an alehouse at the head of a junction and inspected his fingernails. He was a gnawer, a biter, and he nibbled at his nails constantly, his fine teeth flashing, trimming the troublesome bits. Paze took care of his teeth. He constantly cleaned and protected them. As a result, he retained a full set at the prime age of thirty, when most people had already suffered at least one loss, if not several, especially in his business. Not many dogs ran in the Sons' pack with the teeth he possessed. Most of them didn't care about their teeth, but not Paze. His best features lay in his mouth, and he knew it, even as he snipped and spat the pieces of skin into the street.

A pair of ladies walked by, well-dressed and carrying folded rain cloaks just in case. They glanced at Paze as they strolled past, horrified by his energetic nibbling. Paze caught their stares while still pruning at some more stubborn pieces. He spat the clippings to one side and then unleashed his most charming smile upon the women.

They quickly hurried away.

Paze's smile disappeared just as quickly, and he returned to snacking, snipping at the corners and sampling the skin there. He did that when there was nothing left to his nails. As an afterthought, he swung himself around and glanced down the street behind him, just past the substantial girth of the alehouse. Several high walls were down there, some adorned by metal barbs to dissuade thieves. Doors were set into those walls, and Paze watched one in particular.

Behind that entrance was a healer's street-side house.

Not many people had visited the place during the day, making Paze's task of watching and remembering an easy one. A mother had pulled a young boy inside the house around midmorning. An old man and his nearly crippled wife went in early in the afternoon. A young man had gone in at the midafternoon mark and left some time later, but Paze didn't think anything suspicious of him either. The fellow had walked past Paze with barely a bruise or cut on him.

That's what Paze was looking for: cuts and bruises.

Jaro, the Sons' head enforcer, had tasked the gang members with finding a man—or men—who had been in a fight. A *real* fight, where eyes were clawed out, bones broken, or throats partially crushed. Two nights before, Sunjack and Bardal and a pack of street snakes had surrounded a healer's house, suspecting that the man called Borchus, an agent marked for death, would return there. Borchus *had* returned and proven he was no easy mark for anyone, killing not only Sunjack and Bardal but also several other gang members. The death toll had been so significant, so disturbing, that Jaro was even grimmer than usual. Paze had been present when the enforcer visited the long-bearded healer and grabbed him by his neck—a flash of movement even more shocking since Jaro rarely exerted physical force, relying on sheer intimidation in most cases. Paze *had* been intimidated, as the biggest and most dangerous of Cholla's sons had damned near strangled the healer even after obtaining the details of Sunjack's and Bardal's deaths.

Paze suspected the demise of Jaro's most reliable killers had brought out the worst in him.

Cuts and bruises.

Two nights before, amidst the pouring rain, the surviving Sons had removed their dead from the streets. The downpour concealed their efforts, and when morning arrived, every corpse had been removed.

The search for Borchus began in earnest.

Jaro had deployed all hands to the streets. Not a healer in the city went unwatched. Sunjack and Bardal had set their trap around a healer's house, and Jaro believed their thinking had been sound.

Paze shifted from one foot to the other, teeth whittling at a thumbnail already reduced to a jagged quick. Borchus had killed eleven of their number—*eleven*—in one rabid night of butchery. The man might've killed even more if the Sons' snakes hadn't been so spread out while searching for him. All those deaths would have been considered an act of war by another street clan. One had survived, a lad who'd been gut-punched and left gasping in the storm. The bastard was fortunate. Paze suspected he'd lived only because Borchus had very little time to kill him.

Eleven dead.

It was no longer just a simple killing of one man. It had gone beyond that.

Now, it was a point of pride.

Jaro couldn't believe Borchus had escaped without taking at least one cut, perhaps even more than just cuts. And if the agent had been wounded, he would need healing soon enough.

Paze had lurked around the corner of the alehouse for two days since, long enough to feel a little uncomfortable about his watch. He strolled around the structure when he could, only to hurry back. The post was an awkward one, very much in the open, only to become busier with the clearing of the weather.

Fear of Jaro kept Paze in place, however.

So when a plain-looking missus walked up the street and stopped at the healer's door, Paze was there to take notice. She wasn't eye-catching, not at all, and her grayish dress very effectively concealed her figure. She stood there, waiting, looking up and down at the door, until it finally opened. She smiled a greeting—displaying teeth that looked unhealthy, to say the least—and disappeared inside.

Right, Paze thought, and spat dead skin. He shifted from one foot to the other and sighed. He wasn't looking for a woman shaped like a small beer barrel. He was looking for a battered and bleeding agent.

Eleven dead, he thought again, marveling at the number. One of those unfit punces *had* to have stuck a blade into the bastard. One of them must've inflicted *some* measure of damage to Borchus. If they hadn't, the entire incident would greatly tarnish—if not outright ruin—the Sons' reputation as ruthless and effective killers.

Borchus had to be bleeding somewhere.

That idea lingered in Paze's head, refusing to be dismissed. If Borchus *was* bleeding, he mused, then how could he seek out a healer's services? Wouldn't he leave a trail? Perhaps the man was unable to walk. Paze then wondered if the agent would even risk visiting a healer after escaping the first attempt on his life. If the agent was indeed badly hurt, he might decide it wise to send someone for a healer, or maybe *bring* a healer to his place of hiding.

That bit of reasoning made sense to Paze. He had to admit he'd done some damn fine thinking there.

So when the woman emerged from the healer's place of work and closed the door, disappointment seized his foul heart.

She clutched a small cloth bag to her waist and walked toward him. Paze didn't panic, having practiced the game enough to assume a look and posture of indifference. She noticed him soon enough, her face crunching with bemused curiosity.

"Enjoying supper?" she asked as she walked by.

"Aye that, and thinking about dessert," Paze replied without pause, flashing a brazen smile.

The woman didn't care for the remark. She increased her stride and quickly walked away. Paze chuckled to himself. He spat a few lingering shreds of skin to the ground and waited, keeping her in sight all the while.

When she'd gone far enough ahead, he followed.

20

Nordish Front

Thunderheads crept across the fiery evening sky, smothering the heavens as the Second Klaw's forward elements reached the waiting Third—or rather, the entrenched Third.

On the southeast side of a small valley, the army group rested, completely obscuring what might've been a green slope. Far below the incline, over pitched tents, weapon racks, and hastily constructed walls of pointed logs, flowed a black river that traversed the entire valley floor. The Sunjan forces stopped on the shores of that wide and forbidding rush of water. Grassland rose on the other side, freckled sparingly with rocks. Imposing timberland ringed the opposing incline's heights, creating a wall made all the more impressive under the last few rays of sunlight.

The head of the Second Klaw halted just below the ridgeline, while farther back in the column, Tubrius and his Koors stopped upon the crest and gazed out over the darkening slope. Firebugs with glowing bellies drifted across their field of vision.

Seddon above, Tubrius thought blackly as he assessed the setting. The place was an arena. The Second had marched along beaten pathways left by the Third, slowly turning north, where the forest leaned over and threatened to crash upon their heads. *Three days*, Jusek had vowed. That's how long the two army groups would take to join, and even though the slog through the humid wilderness had punished both man and beast, the Second had done just that, arriving just ahead of a beast of a summer storm.

"Lords above," someone muttered behind the Right Koor.

"It's a great big bowl waiting for a war," said another.

"Our archers could douse that treeline," a voice commented, indicating the forest upon the opposite rim of the valley.

Tubrius frowned at the assessment. "Not from here, they couldn't."

"Where's Paw Savage territory?" another man asked.

"Look around you," someone answered.

Look around you, indeed, Tubrius thought pensively and lifted his rump from the saddle, making the leather creak. If they weren't in Paw Savage land, or what had once been their territory, the two Klaws weren't far from the borders. The armies were close enough to be uncomfortable, despite the size of the encampment, the rough-hewn palisades, and the vigilant patrols. One never truly relaxed when near Paw Savages.

And that was just the Paws. The Nordish Ikull was out there as well, a great thrashing machine of an army, devouring all that opposed it, responsible for the demise of the First and Fourth Klaws.

Campfires were few, Tubrius saw, which meant the Third expected trouble. Infantry and supporting staff of the army stopped eating or marching and looked upon the arriving Second. Faces broke into smiles. A few hands lifted in greetings, but voices were kept in check.

"Welcome to the war," Tubrius said to himself, sensing truth in the words. The valley felt destined for some serious bloodletting.

"What's that, sar?" asked a nearby Lancer Koor called Malos.

"Nothing. Talking to myself. Pretty, isn't it?"

"Right now it is. We'll churn it all into a bloody gurry before we're done here."

"Aye that," Tubrius supposed. "Maybe in a day or two if we're fortunate."

"A day or two would be nice. If we're fortunate."

"What's that noise?" someone asked.

Malos turned in his saddle. "Shaddup back there."

Tubrius heard it as well, however, and held up a hand for silence. The Lancers quieted, and over the din of the encamped Third, the Right Koor strained to hear, to pick through the sounds.

Then everyone heard it—the great single blaring from a deep horn that rose above the subdued bustle of the encampment. Tubrius had never heard the likes of the horn before, perhaps stolen from Seddon's own temple, producing a note powerful enough to make one's skull ache. It was a dire instrument of the Lords, of Seddon above, and perhaps even Saimon below. That teeth-aching sound drifted over the valley as if heralding the arrival of the Second. Helmets turned to the north, distracted, and peered across the valley. Patrols slowed to a stop, and men ceased whatever they were doing. That single ominous note hung on the air for an impossibly long time, well past the capacity of any mortal player. Sunjans traded disbelieving looks as that melancholy call stretched on and on. Tension thickened. Lancers shifted in their saddles. Some muttered oaths while others swore in growing trepidation, and still the deep horn sang, as if a great, solitary hinge of a malefic hell gate was slowly being pried open. The sound reached out and squeezed hearts and rib cages. It crushed conversations and left the Sunjan armies mystified and haunted. Tubrius waited for that flat metallic dirge to end, and when it did not, his apprehension grew. His superstitious side took hold, and he scanned the forest walls on the valley's far side.

The deep horn blew on, rumbling down the slopes like an unbroken death knell fit for a mountain.

A voice shouted, from deep within the valley and on the Sunjan side, breaking the spell of that evil instrument. More voices rose, and the men of the Third sprang into action. A wave of activity sped across the expanse as whole lines of soldiers bolted for palisades or hefted shields. A shimmer of chain-mail vests adorned with breast- and backplates clambered toward the river's edge while a clattering of weapons rose in answer to that dreadful horn. Spears were hiked and rammed into the earth. Rows of archers readied bows while campfires were stoked to greater strength.

That eruption of activity reached the Second. Flags rose into the air and whipped about, delivering orders.

"Stand fast," Tubrius said upon spotting the colors. Malos relayed the command, bellowing the words hard enough to break the sorcerous hold of the deep horn. The Second flowed into a state of battle readiness and waited for further orders despite having just finished a punishing march. Tubrius gripped his horse's reins and placed a hand to its neck, calming the animal. The activity continued all around, but all that became secondary to the Right Koor. He waited for that ungodly wailing to end as he scanned the distant hillsides. Not a single bird broke from those dense dark swells. Not a single set of wings graced the skyline.

And still the deep horn sounded, carrying through the valley, impossibly loud.

"Stand fast," Tubrius repeated, and Malos again relayed the order.

Others took up the command, and the two armies braced for whatever was about to venture forth from the other side. They waited long moments, and Tubrius caught a different sound, of one breath coming to the aid of the first, just as the note began to falter. The second horn swallowed up the dying breath of the first and rose in strength.

"Hear that?" Tubrius asked his second.

"Heard that," Malos reported.

"And where there's one, there's thousands more, I wager. Just out of sight."

At the front of the column, a flag rose and waved, calling forth the entirety of the Second's commanding officers.

"I'm to the front," Tubrius told Malos. "Keep the lads ready."

"Keeping the lads ready, sar."

Tubrius urged his horse forward, past the Lancer lines of the Second, until he arrived at the column's head, where a handful of officers surrounded Jusek.

"Right," Jusek addressed his Right Koors. "No time to waste. We'll find Ronus directly and see what's afoot."

"What's the meaning of that deep horn, sar?" a Koor asked.

"No idea. But I'll wager it's nothing good. This way."

The commander led them deeper down the valley slope, past rows of ready archers. Next came a wide formation of spearmen, who paid little attention to the knot of officers riding toward the Third Klaw's center. Tubrius thought he detected movement atop the forested valley's ridge in the distance, but he was unable to determine exactly what he was looking at.

Jusek reined in his horse, stopping his officers before a group of Lancers. There were no formal greetings, but one of the riders, a gray-bearded hound of an individual, wearing the stained and battle-scratched armor of a commander, faced the new arrivals.

"Good timing, Lord Jusek," Ronus said with a sly smile. "This pot looks about ready to boil over."

"Good timing indeed. Where do you want us?"

The Third Klaw's commander indicated the Sunjan-held side of the valley. "Keep your Lancers and regular horse at the back. The ground's unfit, and that river below is treacherous. This fight's going to be decided by foot and not in the saddle. Split your spearmen to either side, to cover our flanks, and send your Sujin to the front to join up with mine."

"Archers?" Jusek asked.

But just then, a shout distracted the gathered officers. Fingers pointed toward the high treeline on the opposite side of the valley. There, armored shapes emerged and fell into formation all along the valley ridge. One line of soldiers materialized, then a second, followed by a third, while the deep horn played on. The Nordish ranks steadily deepened, while those in the front began a slow march downward.

"Seddon above," someone muttered.

"That's the Nordish Ikull," Ronus announced with a nod. "My Cavaliers and scouts ring this great bowl, keeping me informed about the Ikull's whereabouts. The Nords have been forming up just over that ridge. Streams of them coming from all directions, all coming here. To this." The Third Klaw commander studied Jusek's face. "This is where the war ends. Right here."

"Tonight," Jusek said, distracted by the ever-growing masses upon the valley slope. "Damned nuisance. Daylight's confusing enough."

"There's light enough," Ronus said. "Just enough for them to assemble on the field."

"And descend."

"And descend," Ronus agreed. "But I don't mean to engage them at night. When they're in range, we'll douse the lot with arrows. Drive them back. Keep them in place until the morning, and that's when we'll end this."

"Damnation, that horn's unfit."

"The Jackals like their music, don't they? We use flags. They blow on horns. Makes one wonder how we're losing this war. You had no trouble finding us?"

"None at all. Only one of your messengers reached us. We found the others along the way. Killed."

The two commanders resumed watching the Ikull as it seeped through the upper valley woodland, growing larger with each passing moment. The emerging mass had no shape, just a solid tide of armored men stretching from one end of the valley to the other.

Tubrius shifted uneasily in his saddle.

The Ikull was no military force broken up into segments like Sunja's army. The Ikull was a thickening metal carpet that slunk forward with all the ominous, sluggish grace of burning pitch. Nords blackened that broad expanse, and the sight made Tubrius more than just a little nervous. He'd been in a few skirmishes with Jackals, marauding Dezer, and even bandits, but this day would be his first major encounter with a sizeable enemy invader, a concentrated enemy force. He glanced around, checking upon the Sunjan forces surrounding him.

Grim spearmen were braced and waiting.

Archers were poised with readied bows.

Stoic Sujin had lowered visors and raised shields.

All stood steady, all unwavering and set. The sight of the combined army groups ready to crack skulls quickened the heart. The Sunjans resembled an immense field of meat and steel waiting to be unleashed. They appeared every bit as formidable as their northern adversaries.

Tubrius hoped the advancing Nords got a good eyeful of the Sunjan Klaws.

"Ronus," Jusek suddenly said.

"I see it."

As did everyone else. Upon some unheard command, a ripple of steely quills appeared along the Nordish Ikull's foremost ranks, from one end to the other.

"Spears," Jusek said.

"Three lines deep," added Ronus with a detached professionalism. "No more."

"Their heavy foot will be behind that."

"And their archers behind that."

"Best to return to the lads," Jusek said and turned to his fellow commanding officer. "Watch yourself, Ronus."

That summoned a wry smile. "And you, young Jusek."

"Have a drink after all this this is done?"

"At least a keg."

"Call on us when you need us."

"I will. Send along your spear and Sujin. And remember, watch the flanks. Have your horses in the rear and ready, just in case the Nords do decide to press the issue. If they do, I imagine we'll have need of that river in the morning."

The sound of a second deep horn carried over the valley, followed by a thunderous third. The combined horns imparted an even greater sense of doom upon Tubrius. Jusek and Ronus exchanged well-wishes, and the Second Klaw's officers were then moving back to their own ranks at a brisk trot.

"Tubrius," Jusek said, "Make way for Bovello and his boys. We'll get them down here prompty. Tubrius?"

The Right Koor heard. "Sar?"

"The horns bothering you?"

"They are, sar."

"Well, don't let them."

"I'll do that, sar."

"The horns are just a means of relaying orders."

"But what orders, sar?" Tubrius asked. "The Jackals do nothing without purpose. I suspect that's how the First and the Fourth got the chop. Something was missed."

"If you can decipher their meaning, then tell me straight away. Until then, let's just hope that they don't play that gurry all through the night."

They parted ways then as Jusek halted his horse at the Second's head, while Tubrius rode on, quickly spotting the advancing form of Bovello. The Lancer passed his lancers and eventually stopped alongside the Sujin officer.

"Bovello," Tubrius said. "You have your orders."

"Oh, I have them," Bovello's spotty smile widened in disdain. "Straight to the front while you're heading in the other direction. Seddon's crack, if I get out of this alive, I'm buying a horse and strapping a few plates of iron to its blossom."

"Where are your runners?" Tubrius asked, referring to the groups of light-armored Sujins assigned to locate and kill any Jackal scouts.

"Still out there. I intend to keep them out there until I hear otherwise."

Jusek didn't mention anything about the runners, so Tubrius didn't press the matter. He left the Sujin Right Koor, not having the time or patience to listen to the man's complaining. The three horns continued to play throughout the valley, becoming an odd melody that filled and warped the air. The Ikull's menacing numbers blotted out everything as they descended farther down the slope. Their prickly battle line advanced slowly, as if very much aware of the Third's archers.

"Orders, sar?" Malos asked when Tubrius reached him.

"We're pulling back."

"Aye that. How far, sar?"

"Behind them all. The spearmen will guard the flanks. We watch the rear and stay there until needed."

Malos's gaze flickered to the approaching Ikull and kept his thoughts private. Tubrius appreciated that.

A short time later, Bovello and his company reached the Third's waiting Sujins. The Second's archers moved into position just above the Third's. Tubrius grimly watched the maneuverings as the deep horns caused his head to ache. Malos sat in his saddle beside him, taking the discordant music much better.

"Why are they doing that?" Malos asked.

Tubrius thought about it. "It's unsettling, for one. Maybe the Nords used it to effect in other battles. Maybe they think it'll drown us out. If we're attacked on our flanks."

"Seems a wasted effort."

But it wasn't, at least not on Tubrius, and he kept that to himself. That jaw-grinding song rubbed at his nerves, so he tried concentrating on other matters and focused on the positioning of the army groups below. Rows of helmets stopped behind the Sunjan lines, reinforcing the companies of spearmen and Sujin positioned upon the riverbanks. The vast array of mail shirts and armor plating seemed all the more intimidating in the fading light. Their defenses looked well entrenched and nearly ran the length of the valley floor but were noticeably thinner, compared to the advancing enemy. The Ikull had descended a little farther, their numbers still oozing from the distant forest heights. Their front lines marched over white rocks, immediately hiding them from view. As the ground dipped in places, the Nordish army sank and rose, creating massive ripples in their ranks. Though nowhere close enough to discern details, Tubrius could see the bristling spears as well as broad shields meant to provide protection from arrows. Heavy infantry marched on the spearmen's heels, glimpsed every now and again as sections of the Ikull climbed and fell with the land.

The Nordish army was immense and nowhere near as thinned out as believed.

Tubrius looked over the two Klaws numbering nearly ten thousand men and saw how they didn't flinch in the face of the approaching enemy. He had confidence in his homeland's forces, but the approaching battle would be a very near thing.

All the while, the horns wailed.

"Lords above," Tubrius muttered as the Ikull's massive bulk crept closer.

"I don't see any horses," Malos commented.

Tubrius squinted. "Nor I."

"No Lancers?"

"Doesn't appear to be. Not yet. Perhaps they're somewhere in the back, as we are."

Malos peered ahead, scouring the valley heights for any sign of warhorses. "They couldn't be thinking of flanking us. Not here. The spears would gut them."

Tubrius checked the sky. Violent, black thunderheads rolled over the valley, darkening the evening and promising a wet night. Those clouds soured the officer's mood all the more. He could smell the moisture on the air. Koors shouted on the Sunjan side, ordering their men to stand firm. Another roared encouragement in the face of the approaching Ikull. Shadows deepened across the land until it was difficult to discern the enemy upon the far slope.

The tension thickened even further as the armies drew closer. The archers kept their bows pointed down and at the ready, waiting for orders. Any moment, the first exchange in the coming battle would be the winded sizzle of fire arrows slicing through the air.

Tubrius glanced to his right, checking on the Second's spearmen posted there.

Movement caught his eye.

A single man bolted from the surrounding forest and immediately fell. He did not rise again. Concerned, Tubrius twisted in his saddle, attempting to make sense of what he'd just glimpsed. A Koor from that quarter shouted, and the spearmen under his command tensed. Tubrius heard the order to stand fast an instant before the deep horns ceased playing. The sudden absence of that dreary melody caught him by surprise, and he exchanged looks with Malos.

Then the arrows started falling.

Hard sheets of iron hissed and zinged from the forest depths, twanging off Sunjan armor or sinking into flesh. A dozen spearmen crumpled in the otherwise solid front. Others quickly followed. Cries of pain went up from that quarter as more arrows fell with deadly accuracy. A Lancer's horse reared up and broke into a crippling gallop, the rider clutching its reins. Another rider fell from the saddle entirely. A Lancer clutched at his shoulder where a red-tipped arrow had pierced his back and exploded out the front, bypassing an armor-bearing leather strap. Yet another rider had his head snapped back when an arrow took him through the eye.

"Watch yourselves!" Tubrius shouted, gripping his horse's reins and steadying the animal. "They're in the trees!"

The Lancers and regular horsemen weren't the only victims. Having no infantry to support and protect them, half the Sunjan spearmen hoisted shields over their own heads and that of their nearest companion, hunkering down underneath that punishing squall of arrows. As a few scrabbled to lift their metal barriers above themselves, falling arrows sank into shoulders and necks. Bodies collapsed, sometimes falling into a man standing nearby. The forceful patter of arrowheads smacking upraised shields replaced the deep horns. Wails of pain became the new noise.

Tubrius and his Lancers attempted to move their horses, but arrows continued to flay their ranks. Riders fell from the saddle with startled grunts. Horses bolted, slamming into other animals and causing havoc. A few Lancers rode into the middle of the wagons belonging to the numerous traveling tradespeople that supported a five-thousand-strong army. A man and woman, perhaps cooks or some other needed profession, stood in their wagon seats before arrows struck both of them down. A bare-chested man wearing a leather apron and sitting on a box rose only to have an arrow slam into his face. He fell over into a campfire, which burst into a cloud of embers. Livestock wasn't spared as cows and horses were hit and either collapsed or ran screaming through the encampment.

An enormous pig with three shafts sticking out from its considerable hide streaked across the path of Tubrius's own horse. The warhorse reared up, and the Right Koor fought to avoid being dumped. When he regained control, Tubrius became aware of the screaming, not of fear, but of rage. He turned in his saddle as did nearby Malos—still managing to stay by his officer's side—and gawked at what rushed the company of spearmen on the right flank.

Men.

A mob of bare-chested, white-painted men charged the Sunjan lines with furious intent. Sinewy arms brandished clubs and flung spears into the still-firm Sunjan ranks. Where the spears hit, the savages followed, grappling and striking the Sunjans.

Savages.

Tubrius's heart nearly stopped in shock, glimpsing a wave of attackers bursting from the treeline not only on the right, but also on the left.

Paw Savages.

Fighting with *the Nords.*

The realization struck him as the primitive tribesmen, long considered a poisoned thorn in Sunja's side, ripped into the spearmen lines. All the while, hidden bowmen released sheet after devastating sheet of arrows into their disciplined numbers.

"Sound the horns!" Tubrius yelled, flinching as an arrow flashed by his cheek, close enough for him to smell the feathers. Hunched over, he glanced around and saw several Lancers forming up around him.

"Sound the horns!" he shouted and pulled his sword free from a scabbard, the curved steel flashing in the fading light. "After me!"

He kicked his horse's flanks, urging the animal toward the Paw Savage offensive. A horn bellowed behind him before squawking into silence. An arrow bounced off his shoulder plate, the impact powerful enough to straighten him in the saddle. Two more arrows struck his breastplate, keeping him upright for a jarring instant before he pulled himself down over his horse's neck. Determined Lancers appeared on either side of him, creating a broad wedge, and they raced toward the spearmen struggling with white-painted Paw Savages, their frightful war colors blazing against the forest background.

A break appeared in the line, and Tubrius led his Lancers toward it. Waves of Paw Savages wielding spears, short swords, and crude war clubs poured across the open space between the forest and embattled spearmen lines. A clatter of weapons rushed over the field as the two forces grappled.

"After me!" Tubrius yelled again, cutting through the breach. Two Paw Savages, their eyes blackened and their mouths twisted by hate, screeched as they charged the Right Koor Lancer. Tubrius's horse ran down one while he personally split open the head of the second from jawline to forehead. The blow snapped the primitive's skull back in a spray of gore.

Then he was among the attackers, but not alone.

Lancers and savages slashed and stabbed at each other. The Paws had no fear of the horses, and they clubbed or slashed at the animals' legs. Riders and mounts crashed to the ground in plumes of dirt or gouts of white flesh. Some horses reared up, kicking out iron-shod hooves with grisly results. One savage was lifted into the air with his chin cleaved, landing several strides away. A warhorse trampled through a thick knot of savages, driving them into the ground. Tubrius rose in the saddle and stabbed a charging Paw through the mouth before ripping the blade free in a flash of blood and teeth. He righted himself and hacked at a head on his left. Lancers supported him on either side, thundering over the ground, raking it, and killing several of the war-painted hellions.

But these were Paw Savages.

And in battle, Paws were fearless. Relentless. And fought with a fury bordering on suicidal. Their reckless, truly terrifying ferocity rendered them the monsters in many children's tales of the Sunjan wild.

The sheer masses of the tribesmen stalled the Lancer line, and the Sunjans struggled to cut through the waves. Paw Savages swarmed riders and spearmen alike, becoming a deadly wave of clutching hands and stabbing or smashing weapons. One war-painted screamer plunged a spear into the haunch of a Lancer's horse. The animal crashed to the ground, taking its rider down as well. Tubrius tried to bring his line around, to save the fallen Lancer, but he'd only half turned when a half dozen Paws enveloped the fallen Sunjan and his horse and began stabbing and clubbing. More horns called for aid. Tubrius battled his way toward the group of savages and reared up his warhorse. Hooves cracked one skull and hammered another Paw to the ground. Tubrius chopped at one savage, removing an arm at the shoulder in a burst of black matter. Another white-faced Paw stabbed a spear toward the officer's midsection, where the weapon bounced and slid off his armor plate. Malos appeared then, maneuvering his mount to the broad side before splitting the Paw's head down the middle with one chop. The dead man fell, twisting the sword free of Malos's hand. The Lancer pulled a second blade from a saddle scabbard and sought a new target.

Plenty were there.

Hundreds of Paw Savages engaged the Sunjan spearmen and Lancers—perhaps thousands, even. The sheer number and scope of the attack mesmerized Tubrius as bloody swaths of destruction were cut on both sides of him. Men screamed, and horns blared, rising above the frenzied clatter of iron upon iron. Arrows split the air, ricocheting off armor or sinking deep into their targets. One Lancer toppled from his saddle with an arrow dead center in his face. Another was pulled down into the rabid embrace of the Paw Savages and quickly chopped to pieces.

Tubrius hacked at leering, white-painted features. His sword rose and fell as his horse plunged forward and turned, churning through a tide of naked flesh. A red mist exploded with every strike, and the Right Koor fought on, driving for the heart of the Paw onslaught with Lancers on either side of him. They eventually cleared a small area, whereupon Tubrius reared back and chanced a look across the way.

He balked at the sight.

Paw Savages were ruling the day, and a veritable horde had crushed the company of spearmen there. Tribesmen leaped at the horsemen and Lancers galloping about attempting to aid their fellow countrymen. All cohesion had broken down among the Sunjan forces as primitives attacked the legs of horses, bringing the riders down with the animals. As Tubrius watched, one Lancer fell over sideways when a pair of savages leaped from the ground and tackled him.

But that wasn't the worst, for his attention was grabbed by events transpiring farther down the valley.

Waves of arrows speckled the evening sky as the Nordish Ikull and Sunjan Klaws exchanged pointed pleasantries. The sheer spectacle of that deathly downpour froze the Right Koor's mind as he sought to discern if any of the arrows were about to fall upon him or his Lancers. They were not, he realized, as the Ikull was too far away to inflict any damage upon them.

The front lines massed about the river, however, were a different matter.

TO THUNDEROUS APPLAUSE

Arms hefted shields to the sky, taking the brunt of those lethal flurries, as men died on both sides of the valley. Archers unleashed continuous volleys, strafing enemy bowmen and soldiers alike. As the two armies drew closer to each other, the shield-bearing soldiers huddled under their shields, waiting for their chance to get within arm's reach of their foe and do some meaningful cutting.

Tubrius realized he could no longer see the river.

Worst, he glimpsed the vast reserves of the Nordish Ikull, still emerging from the forest along the valley ridge. Infantry and horsemen covered the slope in nightmarish numbers, and no end was visible. The Ikull was *huge*, and Tubrius blinked at the size and scope of it.

Malos was on his left, swinging his blade at the Paw Savages crowding him. The action brought Tubrius back to the present. White faces reached and clawed for his legs. He killed one man with a single slash across the eyes, stabbed another through the face, and plunged half his sword into a chest. He left the weapon and pulled his second blade.

A Lancer on his right tumbled to the earth, his horse's throat erupting in a gush of black. The pair were swarmed by angry tribesmen. One savage bounded onto the horse and sprang off its quivering rump. He crashed into Tubrius, knocking him from the saddle. The two men toppled over, slamming down upon on painted bodies. They rolled, and Tubrius landed on his back, pushing a hateful black-eyed face back while clutching at poised hand axe. The Paw Savage leaned in, forcing his weight downward as horse hooves danced upon the earth near Tubrius's head, the impacts causing him to flinch.

The Paw Savage above him angled the axe toward Tubrius's face. The officer noted the weapon was an old Sunjan-style axe, the steel colored by rust and blood. The Paw Savage leered and forced the weapon closer. Horse hooves exploded into the ground closer to the Right Koor's head.

Tubrius felt a scream coming on, perhaps the last sound he'd ever make, just as a sword sank halfway through the Paw

Savage's neck. Blood splashed onto Tubrius's face. He pushed the body off and scrambled to his knees, facing the broadside of a warhorse. The Lancer who had helped him flailed at savages. His mount turned, kicked, and moved, revealing the filthy, quivering, white-painted ass of a Paw Savage backing up toward Tubrius's face, the crack barely covered by an even filthier skrag of animal skin. Thick naked legs pumped and flexed as that loathsome section of primitive anatomy rushed the rising Right Koor.

Then a metallic *gong* damn near deafened Tubrius as much as it surprised him, and all strength left his person. He fell over, driving his fingers deep into mud and blood. A heavy weight crashed over him, but he didn't know what. He rolled onto his back, blinked as if he had all the time in the world, and held up his hands as if surrendering. The urge to help Malos filled him then, though he had no idea of the man's whereabouts. Then he wanted to ride deeper into the valley but didn't understand why that was important. All fight deserted him, so there he stayed, dazed and gasping for breath, while brutal ghosts fought over him in the flashing heavens.

His mother and aunt filled his thoughts, accompanied by the smell of baking bread and a yearning to be with them.

And somewhere in that odd-sounding space of memories, sparkling lights, and underwater screams that lasted forever, Tubrius sank into blackness and knew no more.

21

"So, then, it's not all bad," Halm said as if assuring himself. "I do a little bit of cleaning about the alehouse. She tells me what to do, and truth be known, she knows what I can do more than I do right now. I clean off the tables and chairs. Wipe down the counter and the mugs. Dust off the kegs. Simple things. Every day. If there were two people in the alehouse or twenty, everything still gets cleaned down. All looks very clean to me. Spotless. But perhaps my eyes are getting old. Well, anyway, I clean. And I read. Oh yes, I'm learning how to read. And write the characters."

Halm stopped and quietly marveled at that. "Quite the step for me. Never could read or write at all. Daresay she'll have me sketching characters into whole words before too long. Oh—she wants to put clothes on me. Me! Clothes! Ha! Well, a shirt at least. Might be a bit warm at first, but I think I'll get used to it. I'll need one for the winter, so it's a good thing. And that's it. Might sound a bit dull, I suppose, but I'm content. And now that the rain's finally ended, I'm able to get out around for a walk. Not that being inside with Miji for a few days is a bad thing. Quite cozy, in fact. She's charmed me, that one. Charmed me utterly. So. What about you, then?"

Lish—the Dish—didn't seem to hear. Or was bored. The old gelding that had carried Halm from Clavellus's villa to

Karashipa—or at least carried him half that distance—stood in his open stable pen and stared with brown-eyed weariness. Lish blinked then snorted. An ear twitched.

Bored, Halm realized and sighed. The horse looked plainly uninterested in the news, and the Zhiberian supposed he would be to, truth be known. It wasn't very exciting—not the cleaning bits, anyway, and certainly not the reading bits though he was pleased with actually sitting down and attempting to learn how to read and write. It wasn't learning combinations of strikes or actually facing a brute trying to take your head off, but it was important, essential even, and a lot less dangerous.

Halm studied Lish's uninterested expression.

"You look well, at least," he said and glanced over at the animals sharing the stable. "The others are treating you well?"

Lish looked away, toward the stable's open door.

Halm frowned. He suspected this might happen and had prepared accordingly. He opened the small sack he carried and peered inside.

Lish turned his head.

"What's this?" Halm asked in a surprised voice. "What is *this*? How did this get in there?"

As if knowing exactly what the man had, Lish took a step closer, nostrils flaring, pressing his nose up against the bag.

"What? I'm suddenly interesting, now? All because of a bit of fruit?"

Lish prodded with more force, and despite his years, the large gelding could push when he wanted to.

"All right, here." Halm pulled out a large apple.

Lish made half the fruit disappear in one bite without nipping any fingers.

"You haven't changed," the Zhiberian accused softly. "You unfit animal. Understand this . . . I've been busy. That's why I haven't been about. Not that I've forgotten about you. I mean, I'm here. Now. Aren't I?"

Lish ate the rest of the apple. As soon as the fruit was gone, Lish chewed and slobbered just a bit and nudged the bag again.

"Not so cheap, are you? Here then."

Another apple went into the animal's mouth. Halm had one left, which he readied—no sense in teasing the bony-backed creature. He sensed Lish would know, anyway. It was a small price to pay to gain the horse's friendship. For some reason, that seemed important to the Zhiberian.

"See," he said, holding out the last one when Lish was ready for it. "Who else brings you that? Hm? And all I ask is for you to listen for a bit. Just a bit. Not like you're busy out here."

The horse took the final apple and got to chewing.

"You think that's good?" Halm asked, watching the animal eat.

He was going to continue that thought by explaining what Miji had been feeding him, but the sight and sound of the horse eating silenced him. Feeding the beast felt good. It felt even better that he still had his fingers. Lish took his time, staring off at nothing while he chewed. At one point, he turned his huge head toward the sun shining in through the stable doors, but then he looked away.

Once the food was gone, he looked at the Zhiberian.

"Gone," Halm informed him and held up the sack.

Lish inspected both, wet nostrils flaring, not quite believing him. Satisfied that the fruit was indeed gone, the horse looked toward the open stall and sauntered past the Zhiberian, letting the man know that the horse was done with him.

"Yes, get out of there and walk yourself," Halm said, watching the animal go. He reached out and lightly patted Lish's side. "No cow kisses, now. Listen, I'm glad you're well. Thank you for listening."

Lish walked off, so Halm shut up. He saw the stable hand looking in his direction. Lish continued outside and turned right, wandering into a small area nearby that had been fenced off. Three other horses strolled about, one seemingly leading the other two, but Lish stayed away from them.

Halm looked at the stable hand. His name was Calvo, a man perhaps in his late forties, with a head of gray hair. He wore a green bandana over a long scar that spelled out *punce*, cut into his head by the long-dead Tarcul. Halm remembered the stable hand, remembered how he'd told him how Tarcul and four others carved that insult into the width of his forehead. Tarcul must've had some very sharp knives indeed. Or perhaps he'd had some very blunt knives. That would be even worse. Or nails—nails would also do the deed and no doubt be exceptionally painful. Even then, it would have taken a handful of men to hold Calvo down as they etched the word across his forehead—an unpleasant time, to say the least, Halm figured. He then wondered how long Calvo had taken to recover from such a scarring, if he ever had. The thought of asking occurred to Halm then, but he barely knew the man and so thought it impolite.

But, Seddon above, such a mark had to sting.

"Ho, good Calvo, how does the day treat you?" Halm asked.

"Good morning to you, Halm of Zhiberia. The day's a fine one thus far. Be better once the land drinks down the recent rain."

"The ground's feeling soft, isn't it?"

"It is." Calvo stopped and looked at the animals. "Your horse is doing well?"

Halm joined the man just outside the stable doors. "As well as can be expected, I suppose."

"How old is he?"

"Twenty-three, twenty-four perhaps."

Calvo nodded. "My guess was twenty-four."

"My thanks again for taking care of the beast."

"For you? No thanks is needed. You did a great thing for us here."

Killing Thaimondus and his brood, Halm knew.

"How are you taking to the village life?" Calvo asked, scratching at his temple with a thumb.

"Here? Ah, it's not Sunja—"

Calvo smiled and shook his head.

"But I like it," Halm finished. "It's quiet. There's something to be said for that."

"Plenty of quiet around here."

"You lads drink much?" Halm asked.

"No, not really. The alehouse was the one place where Thaimondus and his sons frequently visited and, as such, most others avoided the place. Oh, some might have wandered over there, but only after that sour pisser had gone. Or any of those unfit dewdrops grown to manhood. Now that he's dead, no one really has the taste . . ."

"Oh . . . unfortunate."

"Not that they don't enjoy a drink now and then," Calvo added. "It's just that most people here have simply gotten away from it. And having stayed away from it for so long, not many truly think of it. Or miss it. That will change in time, I'm sure."

"No doubt," Halm said, understanding why the alehouse business was so dismal.

"Well, must be off. Life would be easier if the animals cleaned up their own shite."

Halm released a little chuckle for the sake of politeness and left the stable hand to his work. He looked at Lish, who stood studying the nearby forest, chewing on something or other. The animal did not glance in the Zhiberian's direction.

He hadn't expected the horse to do so, but he was a touch disappointed all the same.

The narrow road to Miji's alehouse wasn't very busy, but the houses built farther back bustled with activity. A few village women cleaned clothes in wooden washtubs, while others sat on chairs outside their doors, stitching shirts or cleaning rabbits. Children played, running circles around the property. The menfolk hammered or chopped or measured wood. Four of the villagers, all men, walked around a house corner and marched toward Halm. They carried axes and wore rough work clothes, with thick bandannas wrapped about their heads.

"Halm," said one of the men and lifted a hand. The fellow wore a pair of thin-looking pants, but everything else he might've worn was concealed by a truly monstrous black beard. Two dark eyes crinkled around the corners, revealing the upper part of a face lurking underneath that dense chin rug of curls.

"Damnation, lad," Halm muttered. "You're one right hairy bastard."

The other smiled. "I've been told. Why don't you come along with us this morning?" he said and gestured with his axe.

"Where are you going, good . . . ?" He paused, realizing he couldn't remember the man's name despite that memorable bear fur that stopped at his waistline.

"Bromull," the man supplied through a mouth visible only when he smiled. "Out back of the village. There's a cutting ground. Winter's not that far away, and we'll certainly need the firewood."

"You're cutting wood in this heat?"

"Certainly. You're welcome to come along. You look like you could swing an axe."

That reminded the Zhiberian of a fight he'd been in, in this year's games, when he faced the ogre-spawned beast called Samarhead, who wielded a double-bladed battle-axe in one hand, where any other man would use two.

Halm smirked at the memory. "Daresay I'd burst at the seams if I did."

"There's no need to take down a tree in one cut," Bromull explained. "You could work at your own pace. Do away with your boredom."

"Not bored in the least . . . but perhaps another day, Bromull." But then he reconsidered. "I suppose I could manage it. If the axe is sharp enough."

Bromull smiled again without insult. "As sharp as any of your gladiatorial blades."

Halm thought about it. "Ah . . . no. I've changed my mind. Best not."

"Another day, then." With a flex of his brow, the woodsman and his companions walked on, heading for the woods.

Halm watched them go, intrigued by the thought of chopping wood. A squeal distracted him, and he turned to see a group of children becoming tangled into a knot. A young boy of no more than eight or nine stood at the center, roaring like a newborn hellion and pushing his three smaller companions to the grass. The youngster set his legs and whipped his playmates around by the arms or pushed them flat on their bums, whereupon they bounced back into the fray. One little dark-haired girl, however, rebounded much faster than the others. Where the boys attempted to wrestle, she punched, throwing straight-armed shots from the shoulder in what Halm thought of as a little-girl way.

Her punches landed around the older boy's shoulders, eliciting a peal of pain. He grabbed her in a hug, lifted her off her feet, and threw her down.

The other boys stayed out of the match, sensing the escalation.

The girl screamed, all sense of fun gone, and jumped to her feet. She grappled with the older boy, and they pushed back and forth, letting off grunts, teeth bared in snarls. The boy forced her back until he set his feet and tossed her to the ground. The little girl landed on her chest, released a scream of pain and rage, and scrambled to her feet.

The mother emerged from the house nearby, drawn by the scuffle, and yelled for all to stop. The older boy ceased immediately, but the girl did not, and she staggered him with an unexpected two handed shove straight to the belly. They readied themselves for another clash when the mother stepped in and grabbed her little arms.

Halm resumed walking, the hint of a smile on his face.

The alehouse door was open and draped in the fine mesh keeping the bugs outside. Boots clomping on the walkway, Halm made his way inside and appreciated the slightly cooler temperature. Miji appeared in the kitchen archway, wearing a white apron over a green dress faded by much washing.

"You're back," she said with a smile. "Did your horse like the apples?"

"He did."

"All is well?"

"Aye that."

"Good," she said and pointed toward the counter. "If you're ready, you can start wiping everything down. The cloths are right there."

Halm saw that they were. He picked them up, separated them without protest, then looked for the small water bucket he used.

"Behind the counter," Miji informed him.

The Zhiberian lifted a finger as he remembered and went around the bar.

"Halm."

"Yes?"

"Do you miss it?"

"Miss what?"

"The games."

"No. Not at all." But he wondered if any fights would occur that day since the weather was fine.

"Truth be known?"

That stopped him. "Of course. This is all new and wonderful. I've become a creature of the cities, but I *was* one of the hills and forests a long time ago. I'll grow accustomed to this as well."

Miji stopped at the counter's edge. "But . . ."

He smiled, careful to tuck his teeth away. "Perhaps I'm a little impatient . . . to be done with all the bandages and ointments and such. I miss being able to move about. Being a little more, ah . . ."

Miji waited, her hands folded over the corner of the bar.

"Doing more," Halm finally said. "Not just sitting. Waiting to heal."

"That sounds like boredom to me."

"Perhaps a little."

"Did you talk with Calvo?"

"I did. He's a pleasant-enough sort."

"He is. A very nice person."

"He's busy, however."

"Very."

"I met a lad called Bromull."

"Slim lad, all beard?" Miji clarified.

"That's him."

"He's a good man as well."

"He was going to chop wood," Halm said, meeting her eyes. "Asked if I wanted to come along. Thought maybe I might next time."

"And swing an axe?"

"Possibly."

"You'll tear yourself apart."

Halm dipped his head in amused agreement.

"Just as long as you return to me," Miji said. "And not hurt yourself. I'd like you to help me manage this place, Halm of Zhiberia. If you're interested in that."

"Manage this place?"

"Aye that."

"What's to be done?"

"Just a little more than what you're doing. But not much."

He stepped toward her. "I'm interested."

"This place isn't the games," Miji went on. "And it certainly doesn't have the reputation of Sunja's city. But it's quiet. Even more so now that Thaimondus is gone. There are chores to be done every day, and some days will be busier than others, but I go home feeling content. As long as people come here, I'll stay at this."

Halm took her into his arms, and she slipped her hands around his considerable waist. For moments, they stood that way, studying each other with little smiles.

"Will you need an enforcer?" he asked.

"Perhaps," she allowed. "Best to have one than need one. You know of any?"

"I know one."

"Is he reliable?"

Halm grunted that he thought so.

"Dependable?"

He grunted again.

Her face loomed in front of his. "Is it you?"

He nodded.

"Are you any good?" she asked with a sly smile.

"Oh, I'm good."

"Being an enforcer?"

Halm carefully smiled back. "Fighting. Breaking bones. Heads."

That made her frown. "Why did you ever take up that life?"

"What life?"

"That life."

"Fighting?"

"Aye that."

He shrugged. "All I was ever good at."

Miji sighed. "Well. There are no games here. It's not the arena. With Thaimondus and his sons gone, I don't think you'll have many heads to break around here."

Halm agreed with her.

However, not so deep within him, one part hoped that wasn't so.

22

The skies had cleared, allowing the sun to dry out the land. Puddles spotted the streets, already withering under the growing heat of the morning. Jailor Balazz walked through the last clutter of buildings, through crowds grateful to wander outside without being drenched. He ignored them, walking toward the architectural splendor that was the Pit. He squinted at the cloudless blue overhead but avoided looking into the sun. Rivulets ran down the sides of his face, and he glowered because of it. Perspiration soaked the fresh stubble of his shaven head and the gray shirt and pants he wore. The storms had moved off, but summer had returned. He didn't like such scorching weather. The cooler temperatures of the past few days were much more to his liking. In fact, for his evening bath the night before—a solemn, personal ritual he always partook in when he returned home from his job—he actually took the time to boil the water going into his washtub, which was a rare pleasure indeed during the season. After dwelling and working in filth for two or three days at a time, scrubbing the dirt and lice away was imperative—especially the lice.

The returning heat, however, made him feel unclean, even more so considering what he did and where he worked. Lords above, he hated the summer. He was a creature of the cold. If he ever came into a large sum of coin, he thought he would move north, perhaps to the Ice Kingdoms, where the summers were short and the winters long.

That put a smile on his meaty face.

He walked toward the arena's bulk, seeing the Gate of the Sun and despising the way it glowed in the morning. The stone tiles were already hot enough to roast a slab of meat upon, and he was wearing sandals.

How he longed for the cold.

The low stone-and-timber booths comprising the Domis were to the right of the arena gate. Their shutters were closed, but that didn't prevent a handful of eager maggots from gathering about the premises. As he approached, Balazz's eyes narrowed in contempt. He enjoyed the games just as much as anyone else, but to gather in front of those coin grubbers early morning, just to be the first to place wagers, signaled a problem in his mind. About eight or nine men, their faces glistening, stood before a booth, chattering like hens.

They were all punces in the jailor's mind.

One of them sensed being watched and actually cocked his brow in the jailor's direction. The watcher was an old fat man with a fighter's face, and he eyed Balazz something fierce, just one shade away from sending a verbal jab toward him.

The jailor slowed and glared back, sending his own message.

Changing his mind, the fat man returned to the discussion occupying his companions.

A wise decision, Balazz knew, because with the rising heat and the sweat running down his crack, only a single unkind word would be enough to make him raise a fist. And Balazz was a large man, intimidating, and would clap the ears of any topper beneath his station if insulted—clap the ears and, if the pisser fell to the ground, perhaps stomp on something important. He didn't care. He was a jailor. The prisons held no fear over him.

Shade filled the gate's inner tunnel, and even though the temperature would be still warm, at least he wouldn't be cooking under the raw sun.

Balazz made for that shade.

He walked by the men standing around the Domis and caught some of the conversation.

"The Jackals will be fighting, guaranteed," one of the men said. "Though I wouldn't place coin on them maggots."

"Nor I," said another.

"Why's that?" asked someone.

"Principle of the matter," someone else answered. "We're fighting those crack lickers. Who's going to wager coin on the likes of them?"

The words hung in the air for Balazz, as if time slowed. He almost stopped, believing he'd just overheard something very important, a fat piece of information relating to the Jackals and their place in the games, but he didn't understand what it was or realize the significance.

The welcoming shade flowed over his sweaty hide. The air was still uncomfortably warm, but just being out of the sun was enough to make him forget about the conversation he'd overheard. He walked the stone passages, strolling through bubbles of flickering torchlight, navigating the maze to the lower levels and the jailors' common room. The large chamber was located one level above the dungeons. The common area wasn't much better than general quarters in terms of lighting and quality of air—not really, truth be known, but it smelled somewhat better, and the latrines were regularly cleaned . . . to a point.

"Sun's hot this day," Runson said in greeting when Balazz entered their dimly lit room. The lower jailor scratched at his oily scalp, where his black hair gleamed in the lamplight. They were the only two present at the moment although a hall adjoined near the back, where the on-duty jailors would sleep at night.

"Unfit hot," Balazz grumbled and wiped his face, flicking moisture to the floor.

"Another day in this wondrous temple."

"Shaddup." Balazz stopped at a bench and shelf, where his leather hung from wall pegs. He pulled his shirt off, cringing at the garment's sticky slide and one or two protesting seams.

Runson wandered over to where he undressed. "I decided to check on the flooded section yesterday."

Balazz regarded him as he was about to pull on his jailor garb. "What do you mean 'I'? Didn't I decide on Gulsha? That was me deciding that. Yesterday. Just before I left here."

"So you did. Anyway, I sent Gulsha down there."

Balazz smirked at that, only guessing at the unpleasantness waiting for the young jailor.

"Some unfortunate news," Runson continued. "A few prisoners drowned."

"Drowned?"

"Drowned."

"How did they drown? And don't be saucy and say something like by not being able to breathe water. I'll clap your ears if you do."

Not pleased at being so thwarted, Runson frowned and gathered his thoughts. "Seems the engineers didn't level the ground as well as they thought. There's a slant in the floor in the worst flooded block. Ever so slight, but it's there. I felt it. Anyway, the dungeon extends far back and then descends those steps, right?"

Balazz's shook his head in annoyance, knowing *exactly* where the story was leading.

"Well," Runson went on, throwing in a few well-timed gestures with his fingers. "The water ran down there, first submerging the lower cells. All that yelling we heard was from those at the other end, the one closer to us. Those other far-off ones were already long dead. They probably drank as much as they could before they went under, but they drowned in the end."

"Drowned," Balazz rumbled, clearly not liking the taste of the word.

"Drowned. Gulsha said their bodies were floating when he got down there—when the water receded enough so that he *could* get down there. Lots of bodies. As white as eels. Twenty-three dead, total, including a few of the Jackals. I mean, they would've died anyway, with the rising water—but with that incline, everything simply gathered on their end first."

"Does Soranthus know?"

"No." Runson scoffed at the mention of the Chamber member. "Course not. Not that I'm worried. He won't be back here. You remember how he was. Couldn't wait to be clear of the place. As long as we feed the Pit a few Jackals now and then, I daresay those dead bastards won't be missed. They're never missed. More food for the fire pit."

"You've burned the dead?"

"Aye that. Can't imagine the stink if we didn't. It's bad enough down there as it is. Worse than before."

The head jailor turned. "What do you mean?"

Runson sighed. "Well, it was never fit to breathe down there. I mean, it's not general quarters, but the potential's there. Now, after shite's been floating about, along with everything else choked out of the latrine, well . . . it's bad. Gulsha says that as the waters go down, it's leaving a skin over everything. A rancid skin. A right and proper grease slick unfit to smell and touch. The entire area's in need of a scrubbing."

Balazz chuckled. "Doesn't concern me. I say let them rot."

"Aye that, but . . . remember what I just said. Soranthus wants at least a few Jackals to fight in the arena. Simply for color. If the lot of them gets *sick* . . . and there's a chance they might, that'll draw him down on us."

That morsel of information made Balazz think. "What are the chances of that happening?"

"What happening?"

"Them getting sick, you idiot."

Runson thought about it. "Good, I'd say. The bastards always get sick if they're around their own filth long enough. I don't know rightly how, but it happens. They start coughing. Sweating. Then the color leaves them. The trembling. You know how it is."

Balazz did. "What're you suggesting?"

"We either clean those cells or not. If we don't clean them, there's a chance they'll get sickly and perish."

"That'll take some time."

"But we've never had a flooding as great as this," Runson pointed out.

Becoming impatient, Balazz waved a hand. "Are you going to clean those cells?"

"Lords above, no, not me. I was thinking Gulsha."

"All of them?"

"The worst ones."

"He'll hate you for it."

Runson shrugged, unconcerned.

"No," Balazz said, feeling better with his jailor garb on. "That's too much. He doesn't deserve it. He could manage those pissers as they clean their cells, but that's still a huge undertaking."

"The season's longer."

"He'll need extra men. Skarrs as well. Just in case."

"Aye that. All that."

"Look after it, then."

"Me?"

Balazz studied the other man. "Yes you, since you understand the situation so well. Do it. Get it done. And by that, I mean manage it. I'm not asking you to get in there and wipe down every damned stone by yourself. Offer the rags and water to the maggots. Let them choose if they want to scrub their holes. Give them something to do before they finally perish."

The jailor didn't like the idea, but he reluctantly nodded. "The smell might remain."

"Won't smell worse than general quarters."

Runson agreed. He didn't know who cleaned the latrines there—if they ever were cleaned.

"Get it done," Balazz repeated. "Any other news this morning?"

Runson shook his head and scratched at his bulbous gut, hanging over his belt.

TO THUNDEROUS APPLAUSE

"Good," the head jailor declared. "Then there's work to be done. There's games today."

The braziers had been snuffed out long before, leaving them all in perpetual night. During that period, the water level rose, creeping over his knees, cupping his man bits, and rising past his navel—eventually, above his waist. At its peak, the water touched Arrus's chest and stayed there for a good long time. He couldn't see the water, but he'd felt it, the cloying pressure nestling about his person as he stood, dreading its touch, wondering if it would rise any higher. Men had shouted, frantic in the beginning before becoming despondent, some reduced to tears as they well and truly thought they'd perish there, in the wet and rising depths of the darkness.

They didn't, however.

The water stopped rising, and though it didn't recede, Arrus had been grateful. Heelslik and the Norseman Rullik had been grateful as well, even the Sunjans calling out from the darkness. The relief in their voices was unmistakable and loud enough to draw a smile from the Nordish man, despite who they were or what they'd done. They might die in the arena, but at least they wouldn't perish by drowning in that impenetrable darkness.

That had been only the beginning, however.

The Sunjans called for the jailors, who did not appear, not even for feeding. The prisoners were left to those unpleasant waters, wondering when it would decide to rise or fall. Twice, Arrus relieved himself while he stood chest deep. The water was warm and not entirely unpleasant, as long as he didn't think too long upon what lurked below the surface. Every now and again, wet clumps of unseen matter had brushed against his naked skin, keeping him awake during the first night—or what he suspected was the first night.

No one had slept. No one *could* sleep, for as soon as they succumbed, their chin dipped or worse, and they woke up with a splash.

243

So they stood at attention the entire night—or what seemed like night. It was difficult to say.

Rats had perished in the flood, perhaps exhausted by swimming or slapped dead by prisoners. Their hairy little bodies floated in the darkness. Arrus had discovered three in his cell simply because their saturated corpses brushed up against him. When they did, he removed them and hoped the bars would prevent them from drifting back inside.

Men cried out during the night, angry at the situation, angry at their jailors. Voices cracked, some miserably so. Arrus didn't like listening to those pitiful sounds. Criminals they might be, but he still pitied them . . . pitied them all.

As time dragged on, the pressure on Arrus's chest affected his breathing, making it shallow. His limbs grew heavy, and he grew aware of the unpleasant sensation of being underwater for much too long. His senses drifted as he was too tired to truly function yet unable to rest.

A long time later, perhaps more than a day, the water level began to drop.

Arrus thought it was a dream.

The cot gradually sank, and when it was low enough, an exhausted Arrus returned his bed to its original place and sat down on a submerged blanket and straw. Just being off his feet was a relief. Arrus made himself as comfortable as he could with his lower bits still underwater, and he rested. The dungeon was silent during that time, drowned by exhausted sleep. No one talked or moved. At times, bubbles gurgled softly from his cell's latrine, but not often. His head drooped, and with a weary sigh, he closed his eyes.

An image of Kra flashed through his mind. They were in a forest and the air good to breathe. Rain fell in soft sheets though fragmented sunlight flashed between the trees. His brother was just ahead, running, bounding through green passages. Every footfall crunched through the underbrush. Arrus chased, laughing, having a grand time with the sport although his brother quickly outpaced him. He fell behind, losing sight of Kra entirely.

TO THUNDEROUS APPLAUSE

Kra noticed, however, and Arrus saw that he'd stopped. He waited between a pair of mighty oaks, head shaking and smiling, one hand reaching out with the sound of metal rattling . . .

Arrus cracked open an eye and looked toward his cell door. Voices filled the dungeon, and torchlight shoved back the darkness. Men stirred. Some of the angrier ones cursed, and Arrus recognized a few words from his limited lessons with Rullik.

Shadows swarmed the corridor. An uncomfortably bright torch came into view, followed by the jailor carrying it. The man swung the light over the doused iron carcass of the brazier. He grunted and swore softly as he inspected its metal depths, his hand straying to his huge belly for a scratch. Once finished, he looked into Heelslik's cell before turning and peering into Arrus's.

The jailor stepped up to the bars, the one called Runson. Arrus recognized the moustached face and missing teeth.

A number of Skarrs appeared behind him.

"This one," Runson said, pointing.

Arrus guessed his meaning.

A dozen men escorted the Nordish prisoner back to the world, where the temperature rose considerably the closer he got to the surface. When they arrived at the gatekeeper, one of the soldiers turned and offered him a short sword. Arrus frowned, not quite recovered from his watery ordeal, and didn't take the weapon straightaway.

The Skarr cracked a metal-skinned hand across his forehead, driving Arrus to his knees.

In that stinging, ringing afterglow, the Nordish man grimaced and dealt with the pain. The soldier had clipped him in a tender place, close to where the prisoner called Brill had tried to scalp him. Arrus prodded the gash with his fingertips and found the crusty scab still intact. That was good. The cut had taken a very long time to stop bleeding, so much so that Rullik and Heelslik had actually teased him.

The same Skarr who had struck him spoke. Arrus didn't respond right away, but he eventually stood. The soldier stepped directly before him, emotionless eyes studying the Nordish man, quietly warning him.

Arrus stared back.

Instead of striking him for insolence, which Arrus fully expected, the soldier surprised him. The Skarr took a short sword from another, turned the weapon around, and offered it hilt first.

Above, the crowds stirred, the sound of thousands excited to see the resumption of the games.

Arrus took the blade.

The Skarr stepped away from the stairs behind him, keeping his eyes on the Nordish man all the while.

"Go on," the gatekeeper urged from the side. "Go on . . ."

More words were said, but they were too fast, too warped for Arrus to understand. He thought about striking the Skarr, actually using that blunt length of metal and cracking it across the man's helmet, but he didn't. The barest breeze descended from the tunnels' steps and grazed Arrus's bearded features, distracting him, removing all thoughts of violence. The breeze passed although he lifted his face, hoping to catch another.

Air. Fresh air lured him forward, where the portcullis at the top of the stairs rose with a well-oiled clatter. Arrus climbed the stairs toward the great blue at the top. He took his time, feeling a soft wind, the currents cleansing him in ways he didn't rightly understand.

Daylight flittered across his face, warm and so good, and Arrus closed his eyes against the light. Heat flowed over him as he entered the arena. A blast of unkind sound blew past his ears as well—the crowds voicing their feelings. Arrus didn't care. He squinted uncomfortably, shying away from the brightness but grateful to stand in its brilliance once again. His hands surprised him, as they'd become a pasty white and shriveled, much like the rest of him. Dressed only in a loincloth and nothing else, anyone could easily see how the dungeon flooding had affected him.

He wandered a few steps away from the entrance, arms hanging at his sides, and absorbed as much of the light as he possibly could in the time given to him.

Which was not much.

To his left, a stick of a man ranted atop a podium. He was old and dressed in gray robes, with a shock of white hair that moved with every gesticulation. Behind him were the Sunjans themselves. Arrus slowly turned as an entire nation greeted him. The audience was a multitude of faceless heads and shoulders draped in faded colors, and every one of them seemed to curse his miserable existence. They spat and flounced their arms in his direction, venomous in their hatred. Arrus spared them a glance and nothing more. He walked along, taking his time, simply enjoying the open space. The arena was merely another cell, true enough, but it allowed him a freedom, limited though it was. A freedom he discovered he'd very much missed . . . and very much needed.

His opponent appeared on the far end of the Pit, a dark outline materializing beyond the heat shimmers while the portcullis lowered behind him.

He was damn near naked, like Arrus, and with a sword.

The Nordish man inspected his weapon: dull, without a proper edge, and flecked with rust—a blade that had become a club. That didn't matter, though.

Not to people such as these.

The shouting and screaming prickled the back of his neck—scalding hatred, vile and wicked and projected solely at him. Arrus couldn't make out all the faces of the crowds, but there was no mistaking their loathing, their need to see him die.

Feeling very tired, Arrus peered at the crowds, saw their livid faces, and took their heat.

Then he looked at his own bare feet, feeling the hot sand penetrating his soles, but not unpleasantly so. That soothing contact removed him from the present. The smell of his warming skin captured his attention, and he relaxed. He took a calming breath, flexed his limbs, and realized, with a fatigued gladness, that everything still worked, that he was still in one piece... and standing under the bright weather of a summer's day.

The old man had stopped talking.

Arrus looked across the sands and saw his opponent approaching, hurrying along as if in dire need of a squat. The Nordish man would've liked a few moments more to appreciate the sands, the sun, and even the sounds, oddly enough. But that was not to be. He hefted that sick length of old steel and tightened his grip upon the weapon.

Then he readied himself for what was coming.

Tasian was the other prisoner's name, or at least that's what Arrus thought he heard the old man shout. Tasian was tall, a few fingers more than Arrus but hunched about his narrow shoulders and apparently devoid of fat. His frame was bony, his belly concave and practically missing beneath his ribs. He looked sickly, as if he'd been pulled out of the ocean after floating there for days, but Arrus knew the real reason behind that, having lived it himself.

Tasian's face appeared hollowed out, his cheeks as nonexistent as his belly. His mouth was a snarl beneath a long, wet beard of grey, while his eyes were hard and black and gleaming.

Arrus could see that Tasian was every bit as angry as the people filling the arena, perhaps even more.

And with that visible, palpable anger, Tasian bared rotten teeth and increased his stride, charging forward as if believing Arrus was the source of all his misery to this point in time... and he very much intended to punish Arrus for it.

An overhand chop started the fight, followed by a sweeping, shrieking slash to the head, which led into a straight-arm punch that shot out from Tasian's shoulder.

Arrus sidestepped the chop, ducked the slash, and stumbled in getting out of the way of the surprising fist.

Tasian sprang forward, arms pumping, pressing his advantage. He slashed, and Arrus lunged, rolling into the sand as he went. The Jackal scrambled, kicking up clumps, sensing wild-eyed Tasian right behind him, and frantically leaped one way and then the other. Steel bit him across the back of a thigh, and that hot sting propelled the Nordish man forward. He stumbled to his feet, digging his knuckles into the sands for balance, and took off for the far wall.

The crowds exploded in shrieks of delight.

Arrus glanced over his shoulder.

Sacred Curlord.

Tasian was right behind him, mouth twisted and rotten teeth gleaming, chasing him as if the Sunjan were driving a naughty child from a kitchen.

Arrus couldn't turn to face him. If he did, that one fleeting instant would allow the Sunjan to close and take his head off at the shoulders.

So he ran.

In fact, he bent over and *sprinted*, burning whatever energy he possessed.

Tasian ran after him.

The crowds brayed and cackled, enjoying the spectacle. A Jackal chugged over the arena sands with a wide-eyed hellion right behind him. Both men breathed hard from the footrace, and sweat shimmered and fell from their frames.

The Pit's wall loomed before Arrus, so he shot to the left, planting a steadying palm against the stone to help complete the turn. He avoided crashing and pumped away, his own frantic breathing in his ears. He glanced back.

Tasian swiped at him, and the short sword lit up a line from Arrus's left shoulder blade all the way down to the upper cheek of his ass. That crackling whiplash of pain energized Arrus, who immediately lengthened his lead by about two or three paces.

Still not enough to turn and fight, not without getting cut again.

The audience howled and brayed laughter at points. Fingers stabbed in Arrus's direction. He forced himself to run harder, faster—hearing, sensing the hunched-over skeleton of a Sunjan closing on his heels. Arrus followed the curve of the arena wall and pounded feet toward the other end. Half-eaten apples and suckled peach pits rained down, pelting him. A wave of something warm drenched his head and shoulders and left him sputtering, but Arrus didn't stop or slow.

He blinked away whatever was in his eyes and worked harder.

He glanced back and was horrified to see that underfed hellion still on his heels, just fingers away from giving him a crippling chop. Tasian's face was contorted, red, and glistening. Black gums housed blacker teeth. Arrus tore his attention away to concentrate on maintaining that slimmest of margins between them.

One thing was certain: if he turned, he would be split down the middle or stabbed straight through the guts.

A stone wall became larger, and Arrus labored and squeezed out a few extra drops of power, to get just a little further ahead of Tasian before he ran out of arena. Arms swinging, he veered to the right, checking on his chaser and knowing it cost him some speed. Tasian pursued with the same feral intensity, too busy with maintaining the speed to swing at his opponent.

Arrus swung around, eating up the space needed to make the turn, and raced for the far wall yet again. He'd run the length of the Pit twice, and his strength was fading fast. One fleeting peek informed him that Tasian, powered by fury alone, was creeping closer.

Blessed Curlord, Arrus swore, straining, pushing his heart further, rattling his ribs.

He realized how this fight was going to end.

Tasian was going to continue chasing him until he got close enough to cut Arrus down or the Nordish man finally fell. There was another way, however, where Arrus would stop and spin—or simply spin while on the run—and lash out with his blade, hoping to connect.

And Tasian would strike with his own.

The faster man would live to fight another day.

TO THUNDEROUS APPLAUSE

The arena wall approached with a speed that made Arrus momentarily think the place was shrinking. His limbs burned, and his heart was close to bursting. The crowds' hateful energy filled his ears, and he knew, just knew, before he reached that wall, he would have to spin and whip his blade across Tasian's black teeth. No way was he going to run the arena floor a third time.

Arrus glanced back, checking on how close the Sunjan was, then he checked again, a flicker of the eyes, gauging the time and distance needed.

And in that instant—in that flashing prelude of time before Arrus could execute the life-saving spin and cut he intended to chance—Tasian lunged.

Perhaps the man was tiring himself. Perhaps he truly was sick, or perhaps he was becoming frustrated with all that damn running. Whatever the reason, Tasian apparently recognized that he was gaining on the Jackal, realized he was creeping forward just a little bit every time the Nordish man checked over his shoulder, and decided that the very next instant the Jackal glanced back, he would put his blade through the man.

The Sunjan lunged, stretching himself out as he dove forward, extending his arm in a ballista shot of power straight at the Jackal's spine.

And in a fearful burst of energy, that kind that explodes in one's limbs to save one's life, Arrus darted out of the Sunjan's way.

Tasian crashed into the sand, landing hard on his chest. His left hand twisted badly under his weight, while all the wind left him in a bark. Grit scrubbed his face. He gasped and groaned in a panic, visibly stricken as he attempted to draw breath. Tasian glanced over his shoulder just as Arrus fell on top of him, driving the point of his short sword down in a two-fisted stab through the meat of the Sunjan's back. That terrible thrust transfixed the man in place. His limbs shivered like a half-crushed spider. Tasian gasped a second time, spitting out whatever air he'd clawed into his chest before collapsing. One eye, flecked with grit, fixed upon Arrus's exhausted form. The eye twitched, even winked.

Then stopped.

The killing stunned the audience to a person, and a hushed silence fell over the arena.

On his hands and knees, Arrus pushed himself away from the dead man. He fell onto his back. He lay there panting but not receiving the air he needed... or so it seemed. Garbage struck him as the crowds slowly became animated, screaming displeasure at the fight's ending. Arrus rolled onto his belly, feeling the sun on his shoulders and the cuts sustained: one behind his leg, the other the length of his back. He winced, bone weary and aching. Both cuts would be a problem to tend to.

His portcullis opened a few moments later, and he slowly hauled himself to his feet. He dusted himself off, slap wiping his hands. Lumbering along at best speed, he reached up and wiped off his head, drawing away fragrant sweat.

Except it wasn't exactly sweat.

Arrus lifted his fingers to his nose.

Beer?

It wasn't Nordish beer, and perhaps half of the drink was in fact sweat, but it was beer all the same.

He stuck his fingers into his mouth and tasted the few drops of the finest beer he'd ever had the pleasure of drinking. When he was done, he squeezed his hair for more and only stopped when he started spitting sand.

The portcullis drew closer, and Arrus lingered at the opening, looking hopefully up into those furious, hate-spewing faces.

If he was fortunate, someone might toss more garbage at him, preferably one of those gnawed-down apples or bare peach pits to suckle. Arrus didn't care.

He wanted a bit to eat.

23

Gazing out at the arena, Salwark watched the last fight amongst the criminal element introduced to the games. He set his jaw and frowned, understanding full well why the people disliked the matches. They were shite. Complete and utter shite. He saw the mistakes the prisoners were making, the lack of style and thought, the art reduced to nothing more than sheer butchery. Bringing in Jackals was an interesting idea, but they were trained soldiers with experience, and the two pairings he'd witnessed that day had resulted in quick, disappointing deaths. And the one that had become a footrace up and down the Pit was laughable until the Jackal decided that enough was enough and nailed his opponent to the ground.

Salwark smoothed a hand over his hair then the window's stone sill, feeling the coarse grain of the brick. None of those fights had been a proper distraction from the real problem he faced, and that was the blood match his lad would fight later in the day.

Blood match. The very thought disturbed him. Zelia had demanded the fight, and truth be known, he was obligated to pursue one, out of respect for both Sorban and the stable's honor. And, yes, even the grieving wife.

But the opponent... the opponent was a fierce one. Defeating Sorban would have been no small thing at any time, but the fact that he'd been dispatched in such convincing fashion unnerved the acting stable owner. Salwark hadn't been in the games for long, but he suspected—no, he knew—no one in his current roster was better than Sorban. Not even Blacktooth, who'd had his ankle smashed by the man called Brontus and thus was no longer participating in the games.

Salwark continued to run his hand over the brickwork, seeing yet not seeing, lost in his thoughts. He finally glanced back at the man chosen to avenge Sorban. Zillari wasn't the best, but he was capable, or so the stable owner's son believed. The Marrnite was tall—with an impressive physique and dark, handsome features—and admittedly quick with the blade. Zillari was also a smiling kog, thinking himself unbeatable, despite having been put down twice already during the games. He exuded a stink of arrogance that most found offensive, including Salwark. Though adept with his sword and shield, with plenty of speed, he wasn't anywhere as good as he perceived himself. He made mistakes, placing flash and style over efficiency, and enjoyed the audience a little too much when he should be swinging.

Yet he was the only one eager enough to face the Kree called Goll. Salwark knew some would question his decision, even calling him stupid, but he believed enthusiasm was better than fear.

The man might even surprise them all at the end of the day.

If not, Salwark had other gladiators who were much more capable than the Marrnite, though not in the same class as Sorban.

Salwark wandered from the window and stopped before the taller man. Zillari wore a polished coat of ring mail, along with dented but still serviceable bracers and greaves. His helm—the upper portion fashioned into the likeness of a child while the iron jawline was that of a beast—had taken a few hard knocks that had been hammered out. His weapon was a heavy broad sword, thick and with a fine cutting edge, while his shield was a replacement. His previous one had been split down the middle.

"How do you feel?" the owner's son asked.

Zillari smiled like an unshaven bandit. "Good, Master Salwark. Very good."

"You're not nervous?"

"Not at all. Eager, if anything."

And he meant it, Salwark could tell. He nodded at the gladiator and considered the four others in the stable's private chamber. None of them would fight this day, but they'd come along in support of Zillari. Blacktooth was present as well, his two crutches placed against a wall while his smashed ankle healed.

"Eager," Salwark said. "Good. That's good. You've taken on a fine task this day, lad. A fine task."

"I welcome it."

"The lad's an animal," Salwark said. "A well-trained animal, but an animal. He's been feasting on Balgothans up to this point, but you'll change that. I mean that he won't feast upon you, is what I mean. Nothing else."

Salwark smiled feebly, reorganizing his thoughts.

"I'll put him into the dirt," Zillari promised. "He'll realize soon enough he should have never come back."

"Good," Salwark nodded. "Keep that mindset. This will be your—"

A knock at the door interrupted him, distracting everyone including Zillari, who glanced back with a question on his face. The other gladiators looked from the door to Salwark. For moments, the only things in motion were dust motes riding a sunbeam into the room.

"Open it," Salwark said.

A thickset unshaven brute walked to the entrance, boots clicking on the stones. He opened the door, peeked outside, and glanced back at Salwark with a concerned expression.

The owner's son motioned that he'd best open the door all the way.

The gladiator did that, though none too pleased about it, and a heartbeat later, Salwark understood why.

There, standing like an unhappy queen, was Zelia, Sorban's wife, dressed in a well-made dress of black and red, with a neckline that began and stopped at the throat.

Salwark's heart sank at the sight of the woman, and his voice croaked when he finally used it. "Lady Zelia, what are you doing here?"

She regarded him with controlled disdain, from which one slip would bring about a verbal lashing. "I'm here to watch your gladiator kill the man who killed my husband."

Salwark's mouth dropped open in surprise, exposing that fine set of teeth of his. "You can't watch it here."

"Why not?"

"Well, you—you didn't give me notice."

"I told you I'd be in attendance the last time we spoke," she said coldly, her eyes dry and staring.

The assembled gladiators waited for the owner's son to comment. Even Zillari gave him a puzzled, if not concerned, look.

"I thought you meant out *there*," he blurted, gesturing toward the window. "Among the crowds."

"No," she said. "Not for this."

"It's simply not done," Salwark countered, not knowing how to best explain the superstitious nature of the games.

"It's being done today."

With that, she glared a challenge at the thickset man holding the door. He retreated without question or even permission from the owner's son. That rankled Salwark to his bones.

Zelia entered. She immediately studied the gladiators present. "Which one is it?"

Silence answered her.

"Lady Zelia," Salwark said, "these games are an old—very old—tradition, and there are those who are very, ah, wary about . . . who is allowed within a house or stable's private chamber. The wrong individual could have a . . . unfavorable influence upon the match."

She studied him critically. "Are you saying my presence is making you uneasy?"

Another round of silence. The assembled gladiators didn't say a word. One man shifted his weight from one foot to the other, and his leather armor creaked.

"Well . . . yes," the owner's son said. "Truth be known."

"Salwark, I'm at the end of my patience with you and your unfit lack of conduct concerning my husband's death. Need I remind you I had to come to you to find out my husband had been killed? That you burned his body without my permission? And that, despite my informing you that I would be in attendance for the blood match, to personally see my husband's killer killed in turn, I still had to walk the streets of Sunja, alone and without an escort, to get here. I was expecting at least one of your brutes to arrive at my door and walk me to this unfit place, but in the end, I had to walk by myself. For fear of missing the event."

Salwark lowered his head and stuck a tongue to his lips, burning from the shame of that initial meeting and the latest breach of manners. "Apologies for that. You're right. I should have come straight to your door that very instant. And today."

Zelia's chin rose ever so slightly, acknowledging victory. "So where is he?"

He pointed at Zillari.

She inspected the gladiator from head to boot, scrutinizing his armored frame without comment.

"Is he any good?" she finally asked.

"Of course he's good."

"Because I expect your best."

"He's . . ." Salwark caught himself, very much aware of the lads present and listening. "Determined to avenge Sorban's death."

She stared coldly. "But is he your best man?"

Salwark couldn't rightly answer, which prompted Zillari to enter the conversation. "Don't you worry your pretty head," he said with that slick bandit smile. "I'll give that bastard the chop he deserves."

Silence then, and Salwark knew that all the latrines in Sunja would not be able to cope with the shite about to drop upon the brazen Marrnite's head.

The Balgothan woman unleashed a death stare upon the much larger gladiator, powerful enough to strike anyone else dead in their tracks. The temperature noticeably cooled within the room, but no one dared speak of it. Zillari's smile faltered just a bit, no doubt puzzled why his usual charm and handsome features weren't working upon the widow.

Salwark covered his eyes with a hand, fingertips rubbing at temples. "Zillari. Shut up. Lady Zelia—"

"Does this punce know he's fighting to avenge my husband?" she asked curtly.

Salwark sighed before answering. "He does."

"My *dead* husband?" she carried on in a haunted yet lethal tone of voice. "Yet he's brazen enough to try and flatter me, to assure me that all will be well, like some common honeypot he might meet in an alehouse."

Zillari's smile disappeared entirely, and he glanced ruefully at the owner's son.

"He's brazen enough," Salwark said, rubbing his head. "Truly brazen."

"I hope he can fight better than he talks."

The Marrnite's back straightened at that, but he had the sense enough to lower his gaze and keep quiet.

"He'll avenge your husband," Salwark said, forcing a shot of confidence into his voice and wishing he could do the same for his heart. "He will. You'll see. From right over there. Beside me. We'll watch it together."

Zelia left Zillari alone and looked toward the window. She walked to the sill, the men promptly getting out of her way. The arena held her attention, and she took her time studying the structure and the gathered people.

TO THUNDEROUS APPLAUSE

With a warning glare at Zillari, Salwark joined her. He studied the arena as well, nodding in assurance.

"This is . . . the Pit," he eventually said.

"Don't speak to me."

Salwark studied the woman's stony profile. In the end, he cleared his throat and settled down for the next match.

24

Fully armored, Goll was standing before Clavellus, who asked, "Ready for this?"

After the past few days of constant rain and sitting about a much-too-confined healer's house, Goll was more than ready to get back to competition. His face screwed up into a question.

Clavellus answered with a forget-I-asked frown. "Just keep in mind . . . if you kill him, they'll send another after you."

"And if I spare him, the house will still send another."

"They call themselves a stable, but aye that, there's a chance they'll send another."

"If I kill him," Goll said coldly, "they'll realize it's best to forget the matter."

"If you kill him, you'll anger the rest of their gladiators. They'll beg their owner for the chance to fight you. You'll truly be hunted, then."

Goll fixed the taskmaster with an impatient gaze. "Do you always do this?"

"Do what?"

"Put conflicting thoughts into your fighters' heads? Before their match?"

Clavellus sighed and looked toward the arched window.

TO THUNDEROUS APPLAUSE

"Have a pitcher of water waiting for me." Goll turned to meet a concerned Muluk.

"Watch yourself out there," his countryman said.

Goll went for the door, passing the rest of the gathered house members. Junger was the only one perhaps not looking worried. The Perician nodded, wishing him good fortune. Goll walked out. He didn't need the well-wishes. He certainly didn't need it from Junger. He needed very little, except to prove a bloody point.

These were the games, the great and legendary games of Sunja.

He'd trained all his adult life to compete in this competition of blood, in pursuit of becoming a legend himself, as had they all.

Outside the Ten's chamber, he met the arena attendant coming to fetch him. The gray-robed man pointed, indicating the direction the gladiator was to go.

Goll strode past without comment. *Lords above.* He was getting tired of people telling him what to do and where to go.

Sunlight struck his helmet, and the temperature soared. Goll lowered his head against the hot glare and waited for the Orator to finish introducing his opponent. The Slavol gladiator was present and waiting, standing at the other end. Blood spattered the sands between them. The man was a Marrnite called Zillari, and judging by the disturbing make of the gladiator's helm, he fancied himself a villainous character in some grand story.

Goll had neither time nor taste for such theatrics. His own armor was a basic vest of hardened leather, with a cloth padding underneath to absorb his sweat. Nothing was notable about the design, no guise of some woodland beast or underworld monster that he felt projected his inner self. Nor was there anything impressive about his sword and shield. They were well-kept tools that he trusted, but they weren't the most valued or important. Goll possessed far more important attributes—skill, speed, strength, endurance, and the willpower to lash it all together.

"Begin!" the Orator yelled, chopping a hand toward the arena.

The crowds erupted with cheers and applause, expecting blood. Thousands roosted above the arena's walls, and against that stone backdrop, Zillari strode forward with purpose, hefting a broad sword and shield. An unfit hellion face covered the man's helm. The piece's lower jaw was fashioned in a needle-toothed sneer, while the rest of the head resembled that of a child. The helm was striking, but in a disturbing way, and Goll wondered what manner of man would wear such a depiction of evil.

The Marrnite stopped some ten strides away, and that hellish helm yelled to be heard. "I've been sent to kill you, Kree."

Goll supposed he had and tightened his grip on his short sword.

"That's right, you Kree pisshead," Zillari said, assuming a battle stance. "Take a moment to smell the air. I'll give you that. Just that . . . and then I'll take your head."

Goll crouched, raising his shield, and crept forward.

"Yes," Zillari said. "You walk to me. Right over here. Come here."

The crowds lapped up the Marrnite's tormenting and added thoughts of their own. Goll ignored them all, focused only on his opponent, stopping within three paces of the man. Upon an unseen signal, the two gladiators circled each other.

Zillari pulled his shield in close, his dark eyes twinkling from within the abomination's face. "Swing that sword, Kree," he said, the mask lending a metallic timbre to his voice. "Let's see this unfit speed of yours. I mean, you must be fast. You killed the mighty Sorban of Balgotha. Not that I mind, you see. The man thought himself unbeatable. You could tell in his swagger. I'm glad you killed him, truth be known. Even happier after I take your head. They'll be speaking of me for years. I'll be known as the man who killed the kog who killed the mighty Sorban and Baylus the Butcher. Come on, *Goll*. Show me how fast you are."

TO THUNDEROUS APPLAUSE

Goll stepped closer.

Zillari feinted, but Goll didn't react, didn't even flinch, knowing the gladiator wasn't within striking distance. Zillari feinted again, stomping a foot forward to further sell the lie.

That time, Goll retreated a step.

"Touchy," the Marrnite noted with amusement, as if discovering a guarded secret. "Come on, Goll, you sweet, sweet honeypot, you. Swing at me. Take my head off. Or an arm or leg. My house master was well and truly uneased when I said I'd fight you. He thinks I can't kill you. Thinks I'm going to be killed. I'll prove him wrong. I'll prove them all wrong."

Goll studied the Marrnite over the border of his upraised shield.

"When I take your head," Zillari growled.

He attacked, breaking into a combination of cuts and chops, the broad sword flashing.

Goll avoided it all, twisting, parrying, and finally backing away when his foe spun and whipped the blade across his face in a flat plane.

Someone in the crowed screamed, then the whole crowd joined in, appreciating the action.

The hellion child nodded in appreciation. "Well done, Goll, well done. You're a nimble bastard, I'll give you that. Come on then. Give us a stab. Stab that blade into me. Show me the man who butchered the butcher, who butchered Sorban and left his wife a widow."

A widow? That was news to Goll.

Sensing a lull in his foe's movements, Zillari feinted and then lashed out, causing Goll to duck and jerk away. The Ten man kicked up sand as he dodged the broadsword whistling down in a blistering, over-the-shoulder chop. Goll retreated, forgoing any attempt to take the initiative.

Another round of cheering arose for the Marrnite, who sucked it all down and gestured for more.

The hellion child leered and pointed. "Oho, you were a touch slower that time, my Kree honeypot. Struck a nerve, did I? Didn't know that Sorban had a wife, did you? Well, he did. A little ripe peach of a missus, he had. She's watching right now, in fact. And daresay, if I make a right and proper meal of you, if I split you up through the middle and make you howl, I'll gain her favor and perhaps even a few bedside delights. She's right over there, if you wish to take a look."

Zillari pointed, but Goll kept his eyes on his opponent.

"So serious, Goll," the Marrnite taunted, enjoying himself. "Surprised Sorban had a wife, are you? Surprised that she wants you dead? Oho, she does. She *does*."

Zillari charged. He chopped for Goll's head and missed. He slashed for a leg and couldn't connect. Then he made a sweeping cut for the Kree's midsection and had his steel edge blunted on a shield. He rushed Goll, and their shields clapped together an instant before Zillari sliced for a sword arm . . .

Only to miss.

Goll backpedaled, shrugging, shaking out his limbs.

Zillari threw open his arms, as if to plead. "Where are you going, Goll? The arena's not that big. No doubt bigger than the pisspot in Vathia, I suppose. Come back, Kree. You're running about too damn much."

As if agreeing, Goll stopped retreating and waded forward, lowering his head in determination.

Zillari braced himself behind his shield. "Excellent, Goll, excellent. Come closer. Just a bit more—"

The Marrnite sprang forward, drawing his broadsword back while simultaneously snapping his shield out at his opponent's helm, punching the edge at Goll's eyes.

Goll ducked and stabbed, striking inside Zillari's guard, crowding him. They wrestled briefly. Zillari slammed his sword's pommel into Goll's twisting spine as if pounding a table in order to gain a barkeep's attention.

Then the Kree was disengaging, his sword trailing, dripping blackness.

He took several steps back from his staggering opponent.

TO THUNDEROUS APPLAUSE

Zillari was no longer talking. He dropped his sword and clamped a hand to his neck. A jet of black pumped through his fingers while a thicker soup spilled over his front and back in a glossy stain, reaching his legs. The crowds quieted as Zillari stumbled to a knee and fell over onto his hands. Fingers scrabbling at his chinstrap, he clawed at his helm and pulled it off as if in dire need to breathe. More blood spilled onto the arena floor. A spectator screamed as a surprising dollop of fluid splashed onto the sand.

Goll stood by, watching the doomed gladiator collapse onto his chest. Blood continued to pump from Zillari's neck in thinning spurts though the light in the man's eyes had already dimmed, his mouth caked with sand. A hand remained pressed against the inflicted wound, in a small area unprotected by Zillari's armor. Goll had noticed the gap after the Marrnite's first assault—a gap he'd just exploited. Just a parting of metal, revealing a strip of flesh no wider than a finger, opening and closing like a lipless mouth each time Zillari moved his head.

Goll waited, watching the gladiator pass on, and while he did, those in the crowd favoring him let their support be known. The rest quickly drowned them out with jeers and curses. The Marrnite seemed to have been popular though Goll didn't understand why.

He wasn't that good.

But he had supplied an interesting, though troubling, piece of information. The Balgothan had a wife, and she wanted him dead for the killing of her husband.

Unfortunate, Goll thought, hoping the man didn't have children as well. He scanned the open archways dotting the sand line of the arena, each one belonging to a house or stable. Some were empty, but some were filled with figures he didn't care to identify or remember. He located the window looking into the Ten's private chamber. The arched brickwork appeared clogged with a collection of approving faces, all of them watching, even Junger.

See that? Goll projected at the Perician. *I can dance as well, when needed.*

"Your *victor*!" the Orator declared with a grand flourish of hands.

With a parting look at the crowds, Goll gave his sword one last shake and left the arena.

25

Salwark fidgeted like a five-year-old boy in dire need of a piss at the first meaningful but bloodless exchange between the two gladiators. He shook his fist with every cut Zillari made. He covered his mouth when the two gladiators broke away and even glanced at Zelia's stern profile to see if she was watching. Sorban's wife wasn't moved in the least by the gladiator's efforts. Salwark was. Zillari was talking to his Kree opponent, but Salwark caught only pieces of that one-sided conversation. Zillari liked to taunt his adversaries, thinking it distracted them.

Perhaps it did. The tactic certainly appeared to be working upon Goll.

Right up until the Kree rushed in and grappled with the Marrnite.

Unholy Saimon himself piss-sprayed on everything after that.

"What's happened?" Salwark heard himself mutter as he stopped and stared. Out there, in the white glare of the sands, Zillari toppled, blood spewing. The flow became a shocking torrent when the Marrnite raked the helmet from his head.

"What's *happened*?' Salwark repeated. "Oh Lords above. Oh sweet Seddon."

Zillari lay unmoving upon the ground. His hand, the one held to his neck, fell away though the blood continued to stream with dying pressure.

Salwark clasped his hands before his nose as if in prayer, his attention divided between his dead gladiator and the departing Goll.

Then he remembered Zelia standing right beside him.

"Ah . . . my Lady," Salwark got out before his mind became a white rush of terror.

Zelia didn't look at him, her eyes firmly set on what had transpired within the Pit. Her face darkened into a thing of anger and terrible beauty.

"What was it you said to me?" she finally said. "About him being determined to avenge Sorban?"

"The Kree fighter is very good," Salwark blurted.

"Send another after him."

"What?"

Zelia turned, her anger gathering strength, and Salwark retreated from that terrible heat.

"Send *another*. The best you have. That one was not your best, and he rightfully perished. Now do what you should have done."

"It'll take—"

"*Do it!*" Zelia snapped, her lips twisting into a red button of rage. "Choose your best from any of them." She waved at the gathered gladiators, and they flinched as if doused with hot water. "And do *not* disappoint me this time, Salwark Slavol. Do not think you can pacify me by sending your gurry after the Kree. That Kree is a gladiator. It will take your best to kill him. Anyone less, and he'll perish, much like that piece of scroff bleeding out there upon the sands. Give him to the fire pit."

She turned to the gladiators behind her. "Who here is capable of avenging my husband's death. Who? Speak truthfully."

No one answered her.

"Not one of you?" she said in horrified surprise. "You call yourselves gladiators? You called Sorban one of your own? I know he's even *helped* some of you with your training. One of you must be skilled enough to kill the Kree."

None of the gathered men would meet her gaze.

"I'll talk to them," Salwark advised, coming to their rescue. He stretched out an arm, to guide her to the door without actually touching her. Salwark did not want to make contact, for fear of her ripping off his arm.

Zelia did not move, however. She glared away the arm, and Salwark clapped his hand to his robed belly.

"Do not *talk* to them," she said. "*Command* them. They live and fight under your house name, so choose. The best."

Salwark nodded.

"I'll return tomorrow," she told him. "To watch the next fight. Right here."

"We can't be sure that—"

"Make it so with whoever you have to. Arrange the next fight for tomorrow. It's a blood match. They'll arrange it if you demand it. And I demand it."

"There's no guarantee," Salwark persisted. "You must realize these matches are—"

"Make it so," Zelia snapped, her voice rising over the owner's son.

Salwark relented, nodded, and scratched at his head. "I'll do . . . what I can."

"And do it today. I'll wait here until you've done that very thing."

That mortified the man. "You can't wait here."

"Make the challenge right now, and I'll leave. I'm not returning home until I know there's another blood match tomorrow. Given your recent past, I prefer to stay until I hear word."

"I'll do it. I promise. Lady Zelia. Please. There's no need to wait here. Here, one of the lads will escort you—"

But she returned to the window and stared into the arena.

Salwark saw that she wasn't about to move, let alone leave. "All right. I'll do it now. Right this instant. Lads, stay here with her. I'll return. Aidas, come with me."

A well-built man with a light beard followed the owner's son out the door. Salwark entered the white tunnel and quickly strode away from the stable's private chamber. When he felt he had placed enough distance between Sorban's wife and himself, he glanced worriedly at his companion.

"You saw the fight?" Salwark asked.

"I did," Aidas replied neutrally.

"Can you defeat him?"

A slight pause. "I can."

"Can you kill him?"

"I can."

Salwark stopped and whirled upon the pit fighter, tapping the man's broad muscular chest with a finger. "Can you kill him? For certain? I need to know. *She* needs to know."

Aidas wasn't a huge gladiator in any means, but he was swift, strong, and gifted with considerable skills. His face was lean with few scars though his faded green eyes stared as if he'd seen far too much conflict in his short life. He met Salwark's imploring gaze and nodded.

"I can kill him, Master Salwark."

"You can? Good. Because if you don't, you'll probably be dead yourself. And I'll be left with *that*." Salwark gestured at the private chamber far behind. "And truth be known, I think I'd rather be dead."

Aidas didn't comment, and Salwark was grateful. After having endured Zelia's displeasure at the failed blood match, he needed a little more commitment from his lads.

"This way," he muttered and resumed marching toward general quarters. "Perhaps the Madea will be sympathetic . . ."

26

Dark Curge leaned back in his seat after the competition and contemplated the Ten man called Goll and his unflinching willingness to put down an adversary. A part of Curge grudgingly admitted he liked that. Houses needed pit fighters willing to lop the head off an opponent every now and again, without a care for consequences. It was good for the games. Kept the dogs on their guard. The Orator would call it good theater.

Curge drank from a silver goblet, sunlight twinkling off the metal. A bead of perspiration ran down his left profile despite the sun-blocking tarp stretched overhead. He expected some theater this very day, in fact—right there in the viewing box—a bit of drama he discovered he was very much looking forward to.

Nexus, however, the unfit kog that he was, had not yet appeared.

Even though the opening matches were no more than untrained gurry being slung about, Curge had been present to watch. He'd arrived early to watch, in fact. The fight with the Jackal had been the only one of interest, and in the worst possible way. Seddon above, displays like that in the arena no doubt had the Chamber members reaching for whatever firewater was nearby. Curge himself had to limit his drinking to only two goblets since he wanted his mind sharp for the approaching confrontation. But the true reason for his early arrival wasn't only to watch those opening acts of untrained butchery, where an ass crack's scrub brush had more purpose, but to settle into the viewing box well before Nexus so that he could properly greet the brazen he-bitch.

Along with the two dozen armed guards he'd brought along to the arena that day.

Six of those men stood at the rear, filling the area with their intimidating bulk and assortment of weapons. Black-bearded Demasta was back there as well, grim and glaring and fit to split skulls. Upon Curge's request, his household's head guard had gone out into the city and quietly recruited the small army, and what imposing butchers they were. Curge had inspected them not a day earlier and very much approved. They were frightening individuals, each one memorable in his own unique way. Some were scarred or missing teeth, fingers, or even ears. Some had haunted looks about them while some simply looked unfit in the head, but in a civilized way. All were well-built, muscular, and dangerous looking to begin with, and after being outfitted with the house's standard crossed leathers and a few garnishes of armor, they appeared even more unsettling.

Curge very much approved indeed.

Truth be known, he wanted to turn the entire pack loose on the first unfortunate topper that crossed him, but he refrained from such, knowing it wouldn't do.

The next pair of gladiators was introduced. Korzo, from the House of Razi, lumbered into the arena. The sight of the warrior interested Curge, for he remembered the fight between the lad and another called Ithas from the House of Tilo. Korzo was a tall, imposing bull of a man, and his helmet actually sported a pair of forward-pointing horns. A vest of hardened leather fitted his torso so snugly it seemed almost poured, while his meaty arms were bare to the forearms, where spiked greaves began. Spiked greaves covered his lower legs, and a crenellated skirt of leather protected tree-trunk-sized thighs. The truly disturbing thing about the man, however, wasn't his obvious physical attributes, but his chosen weapon. He carried a war hammer of considerable size in his right fist, long shafted for both hands if necessary, with an impressive brick of black iron the size of a horse's head. One look at that hunk of metal might leave a person doubting whether Korzo could effectively wield it in battle, despite his size.

He could, however. Curge remembered him doing so.

And this day, Korzo appeared ready to smash down walls.

His opponent was a noticeably smaller man called Trydas, from the House of Ustda. Trydas wandered into daylight to lukewarm applause. He wasn't broad in the shoulder, but the sun reflected off the bronze plates nailed to the leather strips adorning his frame. The choice of armor revealed a physique chiseled around the ribs and midsection. A pair of bronze wings stretched out from the sides of his helmet. The eye slots were rectangular, bestowing a decidedly noble, if a bit wizened, appearance to his visor—especially when compared to the monster waiting for him across the sands. Even his choice of weapons seemed pure of heart, with a curved sword and rounded shield. Curge thought Trydas looked damn near holy out there, with all that polished bronze twinkling under the sun. Perhaps the lad had joined the Salish after his last fight. Some had been known to do that.

Curge frowned. *The punces.*

If one looked closer, however, as Curge presently did, the edges of cloth bandages could be seen underneath both gladiators' armor. Their previous matches had cost them blood— the way of the games.

These glorious, glorious games.

The Orator yelled to begin, and both pit fighters went into their ready stances. Korzo marched toward the smaller Trydas while the cheering rose in a warning pitch. Trydas stood like a defiant weed facing down the wheel of an approaching wagon.

Korzo whipped that massive war hammer at his foe, and Trydas quickly got out of the way, much to the vocal disappointment of about half the arena. Korzo pressed forward, his horn helmet lowered in stoic determination. He swung that hammer as if it were an extension of his fist, a series of fast, looping arcs and darting jabs, forcing Trydas to the defensive, backing the man up.

A pounding came from the viewing box's door, distracting Curge. He frowned, watching the sand about Trydas's feet fly as the smaller man evaded Korzo's deadly affections. The Dark One fidgeted and hesitated before glancing over his shoulder. The manservant, holding an empty platter to his chest, backed himself out of the way. Demasta was already at the door.

A blast of approval went up from the crowds.

Curge looked back to the Pit. Trydas was no longer darting about. His sword had fallen to the ground, and the man shook his weapon arm as if attempting to awaken it. All the while, Korzo reset himself, the horned helmet tracking his foe.

"Master Curge," Demasta called.

Lips puckering up in annoyance, Curge stood and turned his back on the match. He hated doing so, but then he expected the next few moments to be even more interesting.

"He's here?" Curge asked.

"He's been spotted."

"Excellent."

Demasta and the other guards lined up on either side of the entrance while Curge filled the middle. He wanted to see Nexus's expression when he stopped him at the threshold, wanted to see the shock and then the rage on that chinless dog blossom's falling face.

Curge waited, focusing on the door's stout timbers.

He waited . . . and waited.

The shouting and cheering behind him rose and fell as if the crowd were witnessing something truly entertaining. A series of metallic *pings* and *claps* sprinkled the air, and Curge took a breath, wishing for the wine merchant to crack open the door.

Nexus did not, however.

TO THUNDEROUS APPLAUSE

Time dragged on, and Curge's bald brow crinkled in annoyance. He made to reach for the door, thought better of it, and resumed waiting. A startling cheer flew up from the audience, distracting him. He glanced over his shoulder but couldn't see what was happening within the Pit. That put his blood to boiling.

Curge regarded the door before yanking it open, surprising one of the guards posted outside, who was reaching for the latch at the same time. Dressed in plain clothing so as to not alert the wine merchant to their presence, the guard withdrew and shook his head.

"What?" Curge demanded.

"The wine merchant didn't come this way."

Curge scowled a question.

"He went for a side passage, leading a pack of guards away from us."

"How many men?"

"Perhaps a dozen."

Even though he trusted his man's word, Curge stuck his head outside and glanced one way up the brick corridor and then the other, where sunlight blazed through series of columns and stairwells leading to the arena's stands. Commoners strolled along, chatting, ignoring the tall owner as he scanned the area. His guards posted outside the door, however, suddenly straightened and looked all the more lively.

"Keep watch," Curge warned his lads and closed the door.

Nexus had to have known about his waiting reception. That told Curge that his men had been spotted. Spies—an agent even. *Seddon above*, he fumed. One couldn't do a damn thing anymore without being watched. Then again, Nexus wasn't stupid. Perhaps he'd anticipated Curge's move and decided to retreat to the private chamber below the arena, where the house gladiators waited for their time within the Pit.

Just like Nexus to disappoint him.

Curge shook his head. "That sly crust of maggot—"

Another mighty blast shot up from the thousands still watching the fight. Demasta and the other guards moved aside as Curge pushed through them, going for his chair. The two gladiators came into view, both men sprawled out atop the sands, the match all but finished.

Korzo lay on his back, arms spread wide, while Trydas lay on top of him with the edge of his shield poised upon the man's throat. Bits and pieces of armor lay around them, black and gleaming, like fragments cast off from a shocking collision.

The one called Korzo lifted his arms, palms up, in the traditional sign for *I yield*.

Curge turned away from the fight's conclusion, disappointed a second time.

But then anger bubbled up within him.

The guards posted outside Nexus's chamber visibly tensed as Curge approached with wide, purposeful strides. Eight of them were there, divided and standing against the walls. Skarrs stood nearby as well, ever present and watchful, and their visors followed the house owner's procession as they marched through the white tunnel.

Ever since his meeting with the other owners, Curge had looked forward to confronting Nexus, to yell in the man's sallow face. Curge didn't care if the merchant sought to avoid him, having somehow detected or anticipated his waiting armed force. That only emboldened Curge, stirring up an even greater desire to have a right and proper shouting match with the maggot.

The nearest guard rapped on the door as he eyed Curge and the approaching force. The man stuck his head inside, and a second guard appeared. Curge recognized the face, one of the pair he'd squared off against when the merchant had brought his armed dogs into the viewing box.

The familiar guard withdrew, leaving the eight outside.

Those eight quickly formed into a battle line that stretched across the corridor. Shields were turned out though swords were not yet pulled.

The Skarrs behind Nexus's men and farther up the hall became animated, their armor clinking as they moved away from the walls. More Skarrs appeared from behind the others, and the two groups merged and thickened.

Curge assumed the city guard behind him were doing the same.

He stopped not a stride away from the merchant's armed force. Demasta stood at his side, and two dozen sword arms were at his back. The area about the entrance was suddenly quite crowded.

"Nexus!" Curge shouted, ignoring the impassive faces before him. "Get out here now, or wade through the blood afterwards."

Silence answered him.

To their credit, the merchant's guards didn't flinch. They certainly didn't budge. Demasta was right there, black bearded and murderous looking, making his thoughts known and just waiting—*hoping*—for the word to start chopping. Curge very much appreciated that kind of loyalty.

Skarrs filled the space behind the opposing forces even though no one had pulled steel.

"Get out here, Nexus," Curge demanded, "or the only way you'll be going home is by crawling out onto—"

The door opened.

Scowling and red-faced, Nexus appeared. He glanced at Curge, the two forces squared off against each other, and then the surrounding Skarrs.

"What do you want, you hairless pisser?" the merchant fired back.

Curge pointed a knobby finger. "I want to talk to you, you rancid dewdrop of a pig bastard's topper."

"Talk? Why in Seddon's sweet ass crack would I talk with the likes of you?"

"Because I said so, you sick sleeve of shite."

"This is my chamber, Curge," Nexus yelled, gesturing with a hand. "Mine. Since you've decided you want the viewing box so much, I've decided to give it to you. This is much more to my liking anyway. The wine is superior, as is the company."

"You saw my lads waiting for you. That's the reason you slunk off here to mix with your gurry."

"Believe what you want, you unfit stream of pig piss."

"I'm giving you official word, merchant of shite," Curge blared. "You can stay down here with your maggot scroff. Don't return to the viewing box. If you do, you best bring along more of these pretty dog blossoms of yours. And plenty of rags to soak up their blood."

Nexus's face screwed up in disdain. "You don't make such decisions."

"I made that *very* decision, and with the support of the other owners. You're a tick, Nexus, suckling off a dead man's hole, and the gladiatorial houses know it. We all know it. Now, it's official. You've been judged and found lacking. You keep Prajus. Keep him. For as long as he still draws breath, that is."

"He'll live longer than any of the unfit scroff you'll send against him, in or out of the arena."

That rankled Curge. "What do you mean by that?"

"Pah!" Nexus spat and waved a dismissive hand. "Go back to your perch, you one-fisted ass packer."

"Don't come back to the viewing box," Curge warned. "There'll be blood if you do, and plenty of it."

"There'll be blood *here* soon enough," Nexus said, his old face scarlet and quivering as he stepped closer to the backs of his front line.

While they traded jabs, Curge was aware of more guards flowing out from Nexus's chamber—another dozen, at least, including a few hard-looking individuals he suspected were gladiators. They weren't dressed for combat, but they wore swords.

They didn't concern Curge.

The Skarrs, however, were much more numerous.

And closer.

Nexus glanced around as well, making his own conclusions.

"You wanted a war, Nexus," Curge said, his voice dropping in volume but his tone much more lethal. "You wanted a season of carnage. Isn't that what you said? What you failed to realize . . . these games sometimes go beyond the Pit. That's your mistake, maggot. That's your mistake."

Nexus scowled and batted at the air as if driving off a troublesome fly. He returned to his chamber and slammed the door behind him. His guards remained, however, including the pair who'd prevented him from leaving the viewing box not too long before.

Curge fixed them both with hard looks.

"You lads best get out while you can," he warned. "That one is walking an unfit road to ruin."

Another of Nexus's minions spoke then, to the lead guard.

Curge's brow tightened in puzzlement. The brazen he-bitch was speaking a different language. It took him a heartbeat to identify the words as Marrnite.

"You're not Sunjan," he muttered softly, studying the familiar guard.

The man didn't reply.

A light of understanding went off in Curge's head. These men weren't afraid of him because they didn't know his reputation. They were foreign bastards—foreign *mercenaries*—from Marrn.

The Skarrs were practically right behind Nexus's Marrnite guards, as well as Curge's group.

He looked at Demasta.

"I've said enough," Curge growled. "We go."

27

With the sun just past its zenith, a pair of men and a woman wandered up the steps to the alehouse. They were smiling, chatty, and joking, looking forward to a little midday drinking and eating.

Gurga stopped all that when he appeared, stooping to clear the entrance's upper frame and preventing the three people from entering.

"Let's see your wrists," he said, scowling underneath a sparkling sheen of perspiration.

The three visitors exchanged puzzled but worried looks. One of the men, the taller of the two, smiled and squinted in the afternoon light. He shrugged and held up his wrist.

"Bare it to the elbow," Gurga said.

Processing the odd request, the man good-naturedly did as told.

Gurga inspected the goods. "The other one."

The man showed that one as well.

"You're good," Gurga said. "In you go."

Pleased, the tall man stepped up and edged around the enforcer.

"You." The enforcer pointed with his chin. "Show me."

The second man held up his wrists. He smiled at the woman as he did so.

"All good. In you go." He waved the woman through. "You as well."

"Not going to check my wrists?" she asked.

Gurga shook his head. There was no need. She had her sleeves rolled up to her elbows, revealing skin drizzled with fine hair.

All three wandered inside, casting looks at the enforcer. The tall man stopped and returned. "Ah, I'm just wondering, good fellow," he said. "Why did we have to show you our wrists?"

"Looking for ink," Gurga replied as an afterthought, grimly studying people roaming the street.

"Ink?"

Gurga didn't bother saying anything more.

"What kind of ink?"

"The kind that marks you as street clan."

"Oh. They're not welcome here?"

Gurga shook his head.

An impish smile spread over the man's face. "What would you have done if I wore this ink?"

"Smash your face," Gurga replied while looking one way and then the other. "Toss you out."

That took all interest out of the tall man. The two waiting inside the alehouse cast fearful glances at the enforcer and urged their friend to leave the big man alone. So he did.

Gurga continued watching the streets.

Water beaded off Borchus's forehead and ran down his face, causing him to flutter his closed eyes.

"You're awake," Sindra stated without any feeling. "Good. Now I can get to work without worrying about waking you."

He scowled. A faint whiff of sewage and heat soiled the air, while his blanket clung to his skin. The room was unfit hot. He looked toward the window. The shutters had been thrown wide open, and daylight brightened the room.

"It's bright," he muttered.

"It's daylight. Supposed to be bright. Appreciate it for what it is. Unless you want the heavens to start pissing down on us again."

Borchus did not. "No. Had my fill of rain."

Sindra wiped his face and settled back. "We all have. Stay still now. It'll be easier to slap this slop on you."

"What slop?"

She held up a small container.

"Oh. That."

"Aye that. That. You sure your mind wasn't damaged somehow? No blows to the head? Besides the cuts, I mean."

"No."

She sat back and studied him. "No, you're not sure?"

Borchus squeezed his eyes shut. "No blows to the head."

"All right, then. Bring yourself forward," she instructed, which he did, with some effort. He was rewarded with the smell of clean skin. The barest hint of perfumed water—though pleasant—became secondary because she leaned forward and reached around to the back of his head. Her fingers fiddled with the knots of his bandages. That woke him up. She was very close, so he peeked and glimpsed her chin and frowning lips just above his forehead. The red dress she wore was done up to the neck, and a long tail of dark hair—colored with a few strands of grey—drooped over one shoulder.

"Enjoying yourself?" she asked as she continued working on the knots.

"Yes."

That deepened her frown. She drew back, but not far. And Borchus could see she wasn't entirely annoyed either.

"Don't get any ideas," she said and went back to work. "I'm just slapping on some of this and leaving, leaving you to stew in it."

"Thank you."

"You've said that before."

"Sorry."

"You've said that before as well. I must say, I like hearing those words, especially coming from you. A welcome change."

She unraveled a long strip of cloth and drew back. Borchus was disappointed for a bit until he realized she'd be wrapping him again.

"Maybe I was struck on the head," he said warily.

"Don't tell me that. I'll be tempted to bat you about. Just to see if it improves you any more. I've heard about people regaining their senses when they got a second clap across the skull. It's worth a try, don't you think?"

"Aye that."

Flashing him a scolding look that was more amused than harsh, Sindra opened the container and dabbed her fingers into the ointment. A moment later, she applied a portion to his forehead, his cheeks, and anywhere about his face in need of a fresh coat. Borchus closed his eyes, enjoying the moment.

"They look a little better," she reported. "How are you for walking?"

"I haven't tried since last time."

"Not even a step?"

Borchus opened his eyes. "I get dizzy when I sit up to eat. Not enough to fall over, mind you, but it's there."

Sindra studied his face, scrying for untruths.

"It's true."

She didn't answer.

"I swear," he said. "Once I'm healed, I'll be on my way. Have no fear of that. Best that I leave, anyway."

"Because of the Sons."

"Aye that."

She dipped her thumb into the ointment and tucked in her lips, indicating Borchus do the same. He did. She gently applied a layer over the stubbly cut across the two ridges beneath his nose. Her expression softened just a bit while her thumb slowed ever so slightly, almost stopping there.

Then her face became a stern thing.

"Probably best," she said and inspected her work.

"I don't want to leave, Sindra," Borchus told her. "But bad fortune follows me about, it seems. It's the business, and while I'm in it—"

"You're a smart man, Borchus," she said, cutting him off. "One of the smartest people I know. Or knew. It seems to me if the business, as you put it, was indeed so bad, wouldn't a smart person make strides to get free of it?"

"And do what?"

"Something safer? Anything that doesn't have inked killers trying to stab you in the dark?"

Borchus sighed. "You have a point."

"Of course I have a point, you idiot."

He didn't comment.

"I mean, are you getting rich doing this?"

He didn't answer.

"All right," she continued, "so you're not getting rich. So then, do you enjoy what you're doing?"

He sighed again, and with it came a rush of memories: creeping about the darkness, hiding in cellars, listening and wary of every creak and whine of floorboards; then the people upon the streets and glancing over his shoulder to see if he was being followed, taking the less-traveled roads in and around the city; placing people like Garl, who wasn't a bad sort in the least, in harm's way; leaving folks like Hadree and Sindra, especially Sindra, when it looked like his very presence might lead to one or both of them getting hurt or even killed.

"Well?" Sindra asked again, those huge brown eyes watching him.

"I don't know anymore."

"You don't know. Well, that's probably as much of an admission I'll get from you on the matter. How long before you think you'll be able to walk?"

The question confused him. "What?"

"You heard me."

"I don't know."

"Say a day or two? No more than three?"

"I suppose. At the latest. If all is well."

"You're eating well enough, and the cuts and bruises are healing." Sindra leaned forward, placing a hand on the other side of his covered thighs.

Her closeness quieted him.

"I think," she said, gazing into his face. "While you're here, resting, that you take that time and think about where you go from here. What you do. *Especially* what you do. You're no longer a young man."

She said that with a note of regret before looking at her drooping hair. Then she straightened and inspected his face once again. "I have clean bandages here, but I think I'll keep them off you for the rest of the day. Let the air get at those cuts. I'll cover them up later. Perhaps after supper."

She studied him.

Borchus knew her hand was right there, not a few fingers away from his own, and his entire arm buzzed with the urge to reach out and touch it. The buzz became a burn, an uncomfortable silence where only the sounds and chatter from the street below could be heard.

He refrained from doing anything, due to some unknown fear he wasn't sure of.

"You're enjoying the soup?" she asked.

"What?"

"The soup."

"Soup?"

Sindra frowned. "The *food*, Borchus."

"Oh. Ah, yes. Quite good. Thank you."

"Good. More soup for you."

"I . . . look forward to it."

She rose, her hands going to the small of her back, stretching it. "I'll return, then. Or Telda. One of us. If it's me, we'll talk again."

Borchus grunted.

She went to the door.

"Sindra."

She stopped and turned, a hand on the latch, a question on her face.

Borchus cleared his throat. "It might very well be wise . . . to leave the business. I can see the wisdom in doing so. But as you've said . . . I'm not a young man anymore. I'm not sure what else there is I can do."

She studied him again with those lovely brown eyes of hers. "Well," she said plainly, "you can learn, can't you?"

He thought about the question. "Suppose so."

Sindra gave him a well-then-there-you-have-it look.

And left him.

Sindra descended the stairs slowly, recognizing the little shift in her heart and loathing its brazen treachery. And her brain had played a part—all that talk about Borchus not being a young man. *Seddon above.* She shook her head and cursed herself. All those years she'd spent wondering where he'd gone, the hope for his return rotting into hatred, and the hatred ebbing away into nothing.

Then he finally did walk back into her life.

And here she was actually planting seeds in his mind, in hopes that . . . that he'd stay. That he'd *consider* staying.

She stopped halfway down the stairs, staring at a stout wall of timbers while people lounged and moved about the first floor of the alehouse, unaware of her patient lying in a bed above them. A bright shard of sunlight streaked in from the main entrance with nary a fleck of dust upon it. The truth hit her, then. Borchus would not stay in Sunja, not while the Sons of Cholla hunted him. He'd leave at first opportunity, guaranteed. So why was he looking at her so? She'd had enough suitors over the years to recognize the look when it was fixed upon her.

She stopped herself from thinking any more of the situation. She couldn't risk wondering about the future, about *her* future. Her hand gripped the wooden railing, old and polished and anchoring her, every bit as fine as her adopted father Hadree.

Borchus would leave, but would she follow?

You can learn, can't you?

The thought stabbed her, and she got moving just to avoid thinking more on it, for she would, and she didn't need to be tempted in such a way—not after all those years of being alone, of hoping and being disappointed. She hated herself for being so weak, remembering how she'd wished Borchus would return just so she could drive him off. He'd given her hundreds of reasons to hate him, to despise his very presence, and now that he was back, she knew that if he strung together the right words, with the right amount of emotion . . .

The broad back of Gurga came into view, standing just outside the open door. A good crowd was filling the alehouse, but he was enough to manage them. The thought of the Sons lurking about disturbed her, however, and even though Gurga was a match for anyone, he had to sleep eventually.

"Gurga," she said, joining him outside and squinting in the brightness.

The big enforcer swung his gaze upon her. Sweat dribbled down his face and soaked his hair and beard. His shirt was open, exposing that broad tangle of oily pitch covering his chest.

"It's hot," Sindra said, and meant it, taking in all that perspiration.

Gurga grunted.

"Are you thirsty?"

"Aye that."

"I'll get you a pitcher."

Gurga glanced at the street. "Water, please."

She nodded then hesitated. "Are you tired?"

"A little."

That meant he was close to exhaustion though he wouldn't admit it.

"I've been thinking," she said, looking him up and down. "Perhaps I'll take on a few extra guards. To help until . . . all this passes over."

Gurga studied her. "Guards?"

"Yes. Just a few. Men we can trust."

To her surprise, he didn't protest.

"What do you think?" she asked.

He went back to watching people walking along. Gurga sighed. "Maybe."

That was as good as a yes.

"How are things thus far today?" she asked.

"Good. Quiet. Hot."

"I'll get you a towel as well."

He nodded at that.

"Thank you for your effort, Gurga," Sindra said and placed a hand upon his upper arm, a cut of meat thick enough that she would need four hands to fully encircle it. "You're a good man. And a dear friend."

He looked back at her, eyes lowered, mouth partially hidden by his beard, and nodded.

"He'll be gone soon," Sindra said.

"All right."

"I know he'll be gone."

Gurga nodded again, met her eyes briefly, and went back to watching the streets.

Sindra left for the towel and drink. She would even visit Telda and check whether she had anything for the big man's afternoon feeding. *Gurga*, she thought and stopped herself again. So many years he'd watched over her, protected her . . .

Only in the last few years or so had she come to recognize his look when it was fixed upon her.

One of quiet affection never spoken of . . . or pursued.

Three buildings back and standing in the captured shade of a narrow alley, Jaro, the Sons' head enforcer, and Paze watched the front of the alehouse. Jaro had pulled on a pair of black pants and a proper shirt this day, a red one that appeared a size too large for him. Sweat stained his back and front, but he didn't care. The bold clothing concealed his inked skin, and he needed to not be recognized. Perspiration soaked Paze as well as he furtively attempted to see everywhere at once, pausing only to check on his fingernails.

They stood at the corner of a store belonging to a merchant selling clay jars and other earthenware. Wooden pillars supported a broad overhang just over the store's main entrance, but Jaro had a relatively unobstructed view of the alehouse entrance. People flowed by in opposing currents, some smelling worse than others. Jaro hoped the more offensive ones would be heading for the public baths, considering the stink coming off them.

The two men faced each other although when he wanted, Jaro could easily see over Paze's head. The two nodded and gestured as if in deep discussion, but Jaro's focus was the big enforcer guarding the alehouse entrance.

"Did he check those?" Paze asked, white teeth flashing, taking care not to stare in the same direction as his master.

Jaro didn't bother answering, his dark eyes fixed upon the enforcer. The man had been checking everyone heading inside.

Paze squinted, waited for a few moments, and looked down the street, getting the message. "He's been checking everyone else going in there," he muttered. "That's all I'm saying. All I meant."

"He's big," Jaro finally allowed.

"Name's Gurga," Paze supplied.

"You said that already."

Paze's nervously cleared his throat. "Apologies." The gang member again checked on his fingernails, searching for a quick nibble.

Jaro casually placed his shoulder against the wall as though taking a rest. He scratched his gray beard.

"There's an alley behind the place," Paze said, rubbing his nose. "Six rooms on the second level."

Second level. Jaro focused on an open window there, above and to the right of the main entrance, situated just over Gurga's head. "You haven't been inside?" he asked with divided attention.

"Not when I saw that brute checking people. Got one of the lads to go in. Young Mero. He doesn't have any ink on him."

"And?"

"He moved about. Got himself a drink and asked to see the rooms. Said he was thinking about staying the night. So they gave him a key for one. Nice place, he said. Said he'd stay on if he—"

Jaro leveled his dark gaze upon his henchman.

Paze swallowed, deciding it best to get to the point. "He asked for a room with a view of the street. He saw the one on the left. The other room there with the open window was locked. He said one of the women went in there with a bit to eat but he didn't see her leave. The brute there, Gurga, started watching him, so he got nervous and left."

Jaro studied Gurga again. He was indeed a brute, but Jaro had killed many brutes in the past. "Any other enforcers?"

"None that I could see or know of. Just him. And I've been watching the place for a day. When the alehouse is open, he's at the door. He just stands there and watches."

Just stands there and watches. Jaro returned to that open window. Sweat slipped down the side of his face, but he didn't wipe it away. Jaro stared, hoping someone would appear. Paze's logic seemed sound. The street snake had followed a woman from a healer's house to this very place. If Borchus had been hurt, and hurt badly, he'd need time to mend, and he might very well be taking up residence in one of those rooms . . . if it was Borchus.

But the enforcer checking people on their way into the alehouse seemed overly vigilant. Gurga was specifically looking for ink. Only gangs and street clans wore ink. No other alehouse bothered with checking wrists and arms. Someone didn't want any street snakes going into their alehouse.

Someone perhaps fearing revenge.

Jaro's stare deepened as he inspected the upper level of the alehouse.

"This way," he finally said.

28

After Goll's victory, the House of Ten remained in their private chamber underneath the Pit, watching the other gladiatorial contests while Muluk and Koba fetched their winnings from both the Domis and the Madea. Koba also handed over a sizeable purse to Clavellus, who dropped it at his feet with a wink and nod at Goll.

Deciding to avoid the crowds, they left their chamber before the final match of the day and headed for Shan's house. The walk back was a quiet one despite Junger being recognized twice. The Perician greeted his admirers with a smile and a kind word. Goll didn't comment on the attention. His thoughts swirled upon another troubling revelation.

Are you surprised Sorban had a wife? Surprised that she wants you dead?

Truth be known, he was.

"You're quiet," Clavellus said at his side. "Something bothers you?"

"No."

"All right. Be that way. I'm willing to listen if you want to talk."

Goll glanced at the older man but didn't say anything more.

"By the way, my thanks," the taskmaster said. "You won me a nice purse of coin this day."

"You wagered on me?" Goll asked.

"Of course. Stupid if I didn't. I do have a fair eye when it comes to judging a fighter's ability. And chances."

Goll grudgingly absorbed the indirect compliment. "You won't be able to spend it here. I want to leave and be back at the villa before midnight."

Clavellus frowned, disappointed at missing another pickled stroll along the infamous Arbin's Row. "Suppose we could be home by that time. If we leave soon enough. The missus will be happy."

"You'll have to do without the taverns and alehouses."

"I've done without them before. They'll be here long after I'm gone."

They walked in silence.

"That man I put down today . . ." Goll finally said.

"What about him?"

"He said . . . he said Sorban had a wife."

"Sorban . . . Ah, the Balgothan. And?"

"He said she was watching the fight."

"And that bothers you?"

Goll didn't answer.

Clavellus checked on the others before stepping a little closer to the Kree. "A man might say anything during a fight, to distract his opponent. You know that. Sorban had a wife. All right, so what if he did? That didn't stop him from fighting. Certainly didn't stop him from fighting you. And she didn't keep him from the games, did she?"

"Zillari said she was watching," Goll said in a low voice, not wanting anyone else to hear. "And that she wanted me dead."

"No doubt she does. That's the risk, Goll. And a terrible risk it is even though we all accept it. Every time you pick up your weapon of choice. Truth be known, no one with a family should partake in the games, but they do, despite the danger. Did Sorban know if you have a wife? Did the Marrnite? I think not, yet they were both looking to take your head. You were looking to take theirs. No one gives a thought about if their opponent has a family or not because most don't want to dwell on such. To think otherwise might twist their intentions. Soften their resolve. It's easier to think of your opponent as one who is trying to kill you. No one wants to think about why their foe is fighting, what drives them to win, because you have your own reasons, and that is all that matters."

Goll trudged on. "So what should I do?" he finally asked.

The question caught the taskmaster off guard as the Kree rarely asked for such guidance. "You do nothing. Nothing has changed. So the woman wants your head. She'll try for it. Or, more to the point, she'll try as long as the Stable of Slavol is willing to try for her. You continue fighting your fight, Goll. Anyone facing you across the sands is still a foe needing to be put down. They are just one more challenge on the way to becoming champion. You cannot let their choices, their history, influence you. Nothing has changed in that sense."

But something had changed in Goll's mind.

And Seddon above, it gnawed on his conscience.

"Muluk," he said and glanced over his shoulder, only to see the shaggy countryman just behind him. The closeness startled Goll.

"Did you . . ." he started, not really wanting to know if the man had overheard the conversation.

Muluk looked as though he'd just been shaken from a daydream. "Quiet, aren't I?"

Goll glared. "Try being that way next time you have a squat. Listen, or have you been listening?"

Muluk smoothed back his tangle of hair, revealing the scarred hole where his ear had once been attached. "Best you repeat it all."

"Daresay, but no. We're leaving. I want to be back at the villa before midnight. Tell the others."

"Might we have a bit to eat first?" Muluk asked. "That's a long trip on an empty stomach."

"We'll eat in the wagons."

"All right. That doesn't bother me. I'll let the others know. And watch for anyone roasting chickens." He left the two men, dropping back to inform the rest of the house members.

"Might be an idea to grab a bottle or two for the trip back," Clavellus said, more to himself than the Kree.

"Lords above, man," Goll said with a scalding eye. "Can't you go without the drink for just a day?"

"Of course I can. Just don't want to, is all."

"You're not going to drink all the way back, are you?"

"Rather not say. We're not aboard the wagons yet."

"You'll anger Nala."

"I will not," Clavellus said dismissively. "She expects me to be somewhat pickled these days. It's who I am."

"I just remember that first day we met. At your villa gates."

"Oh," the taskmaster said. "That again. Well. That was a bad time, and I only remember parts of it. You saw me at my worst."

Goll kept his mouth shut for that one.

They stopped at the first food stall selling roasted chicken, enticed by a delightful smell of garlic and butter, and bought whatever was hanging off the spits. Beef strips were also purchased, and instead of sitting and enjoying their food properly, they stuffed it all into cloth sacks. Clavellus located a merchant selling bottles of Sunjan mead along the way, and he bought enough bottles to give to everyone who could carry them.

Muluk filled his arms, much to Goll's displeasure.

When they entered the lane leading to Shan's house, Goll turned to them all. "We're stopping only long enough to gather the lads and belongings, and then we're off. Understood?"

They understood.

Goll turned back and immediately jumped at the sight of Naulis standing before him.

"Frightening, I am," the spy said. "Good thing it's day. S'all I can say about it."

"What is it?" Goll snapped.

"You have a fight tomorrow."

That silenced the Kree.

"What's that?" Clavellus asked, his hands full of bottles. "Fights, you say?"

"Aye that. A pair of them. Blood match for Goll and one for that one." Naulis gestured toward Junger. "They both face house gladiators. Better you than me."

"We only just left the Pit," Goll said.

"Yes, about that," Naulis said. "I wandered by there and saw one of them robed fellows about to toss the scroll into your room there. We were both surprised to find you already gone. You know I could smell general quarters from—"

"Who're the fighters?" Goll asked.

Naulis stopped at the interruption, then remembered himself. "You'll fight a lad called Aidas, a blood match."

"Aidas," Goll repeated.

"Yes, Aidas."

"What about Junger?" Clavellus asked.

"He'll fight one from the House of Ustda. Called Orzata."

"What do you know about them?"

Naulis shook his head at the taskmaster. "Not much, I'm afraid. I asked the attendant. He said both men are capable. Both have seven fights thus far this season. Same winning records. Five victories and two losses."

"Not to be underestimated," Clavellus said.

"Well, no," Naulis agreed. "I suppose not."

"Anything else?"

"Apologies, no. I'll go back and put my ear to the wall. If I hear of anything, I'll return."

"Well done," Goll told him.

"Do they ever clean general quarters?" Naulis asked.

Not appreciating the hint, Goll glanced over at Koba, who carried part of the house winnings for the day. "Give him an extra three coins."

Naulis brightened at the sum and went straight to the trainer.

Goll turned toward Clavellus. Muluk and Machlann gathered as well.

"They're eager," Clavellus said of the blood matches. "I'll give them that."

"It's because of her," Goll said. "I'd put coin on it."

"She wants you dead," Muluk said with a worried look.

Goll did a double take of the Kree before scowling and looking at the others. "We're not leaving this day."

"As expected," Clavellus said. "Rest all round. A touch surprising, though. Slavol isn't a particularly vengeful sort. Not old Slavol. The one I knew. His son seems eager."

"Or pushed," Muluk added.

That quieted the four.

"All right, then." Goll looked toward Shan's front door. "Tomorrow. Muluk, pass on the word."

As the Kree turned away from the little group, Goll faced Clavellus. "Apologies for this. I know we've been in the city for several days now."

"It's the games," the taskmaster said. "Expect everything. Until the end of the season, at least."

"Your wife won't be happy."

"Don't worry about her," Clavellus said. "She doesn't say much at times, but she can manage the villa. I have no worries there."

With a cup of wine in her hand, Nala sat in her bedroom and stared at a white wall, waiting, listening for a shout that Pirrus had returned. The young guard been gone two days now, and though the weather had cleared, no sign of him yet appeared. That worried her, making her tense. Brozz had settled back somewhat after her attempt at surgery even though the very thought of what she'd done soured her innards. She'd taken a knife to the poor man, perhaps coming close to doing more damage instead of good even though Garl had assured her that the Sarlander seemed better since the cutting. The very thought of the crude operation caused her to shudder. Only just the night before, she'd wakened from a dream where her hands, old and knobby at any time, had been slicked in Brozz's blood.

She looked at the balcony doorway, where vibrant brushstrokes of pink and violet gave color to the evening sky. The house was quiet without Clavellus around—peaceful, yes, but an empty peace, one where something was obviously missing and one's mind was very much aware of it. Her husband should have returned by now as well, and she wondered about what might've happened to delay him. How his long tongue got on her nerves at times, but once he was gone . . . Nala again looked toward the balcony while gripping her cup. She sighed, reflecting that if she had to wait any more she'd probably forgo her preferred wine and sample some of her husband's firewater. They had plenty of the sacred Sunjan Black as well, but she would leave that for him. Upon her request, Clurik had prepared a small meal for her as she couldn't stomach anything more, and she'd only picked at her food then. Even Ananda barely ate, worried as well for the suffering Sarlander.

They should have returned by now, Nala's mind whispered. *Clavellus. Shan. Pirrus.* They *all* should have returned.

It was the games, so any number of reasons could have delayed her husband, and the recent rainstorms would be the most logical. She could calm herself with that bit of logic. He'd been gone for longer times in the past, she knew, leaving her with just the guards and household staff.

Brozz and his suffering were making this time different, making it urgent.

She thought of when they'd been younger and still living in the city. Clavellus trained gladiators for one called Curge then, but that turned rancid, resulting in their leaving the city without goodbyes to any of their friends—any of *her* friends. It had been a difficult time in their lives, when they lived in the fringe villages surrounding Sunja, but they eventually found and bought the villa from an old farmer. The first year had been hard, but they worked, hired servants and guards from Pynn's Brook, and made it work. Nala endured it because even though she missed the city and her friends, Clavellus was away from the games. For a short time, anyway. Until the owners of budding gladiatorial houses discovered where the respected taskmaster had hidden himself. Once that happened, Clavellus began receiving requests to train fighters for the lesser gladiatorial games.

Pynn's Brook, she thought. The name hooked her thoughts.

Pynn's Brook was only a half a day away. Pirrus had left two days before, in the afternoon, during the storm. The weather would've slowed him down, but he still should have arrived there before dark. Other guards were at her disposal—Maro was still here and usually accompanied her when she ventured forth. She wondered if she should send him to Pynn's Brook to investigate what had happened to Pirrus.

Nala fiddled with her cup and turned to see Ananda standing in the bedroom's doorway, watching her pensively. The new woman, Kura, the wife of the once Sujin, Clades, stood beside her. Kura appeared worried as well, perhaps all the more so because she saw Nala and Ananda thus stricken. Ananda was the shorter of the two, with Kura being a few fingers higher. Ananda had brown eyes where Kura had blue, but both women possessed lovely blond hair.

"No word from the gates?" Nala asked though she knew the answer. The guards had been reminded constantly of her wishes to be informed as soon as they spotted anyone approaching.

Ananda shook her head, while Kura stood by, wanting to do something but at a loss as to what.

"Let's take a walk, then," Nala said mostly to herself. "Perhaps check in on our boy."

The two women nodded. Every day since she'd been alerted to his condition, the lady of the house had checked on her "boy," morning, noon, evening, and night.

A ray of light reflected off the silver mug belonging to her husband, catching Nala's attention. Frowning at the reminder, she led the way down the stairs and out the door, grateful that rain cloaks were no longer needed. The evening sky was clear and spotted with clouds, and as her gaze fell, she noticed that the new armorer, the one called Ajik, had stopped whatever he was doing and was looking in her direction. Nala raised a hand, thinking it unfortunate no one spoke the man's language. Moving at a leisurely speed, the three ladies crossed the sands while guards upon the villa's battlements watched them, right up until they disappeared inside the gladiators' barracks.

As Nala entered, she heard old Garl, as she'd come to think of him, and the younger man called Torello swearing at one another.

"He's not going to live through this," Torello said as if delivering the last line in an ongoing argument.

"Not with you standing about," Garl responded.

"There's nothing we can do, I tell you."

The one-legged man didn't reply to that. Nala and her escort moved into the sleeping area of the gladiators, getting a nod from one of the guards standing just inside the doorway.

"Any change?" she asked.

The guard shook his head.

Hearing the lady's voice, Torello turned from where he stood just outside of Brozz's alcove as Garl stuck his head out.

"My Lady," the pair greeted as Nala stopped beside Torello.

"No improvement?" she asked, taking in the unmoving form of the Sarlander lying on the bed. Garl sat near the tall man's legs.

"He's practically a corpse," Torello muttered.

Garl flashed a warning glare at him. "He's running a fever again. Skin's all slick with sweat. When I changed the bandages, another one of those rises was forming. Hard to the touch."

Infection, Nala knew, mentally slumping in defeat though she maintained an outwardly calm demeanor. Clavellus might say she'd learned that from him, but she knew it was the other way around.

"The saywort closed the wound," Garl said, "but it didn't clean up the problem. At best, it . . . it merely *pushed* the infection back a bit. Saywort's only good for sealing up cuts and holes, not battling infections, and this one has deep roots—much deeper than what you were able to cut away."

The dreary news leeched at Nala's strength. Despite having used the ointment sparingly, they'd run out the previous morning.

"Excuse me," she said and moved into the little area, causing Garl to jerk back his leg. Nala went to the head of the bed, where she looked down at the Sarlander. *Stitches. So many stitches.* The man had become a trussed-up slab of meat fit for an oven. She placed a hand in front of his mouth and felt a faint but regular breath upon her skin.

"Show me," she said, nodding at the place she'd cut into before.

Garl leaned over the larger man, picking at the wad of bandages covering the festering wound. He pulled them back, revealing that ugly line of a mouth. Twine sealed the blood-crusted edges, but the mouth looked ready to burst and scream. The area had deflated somewhat, after Nala had cut away the bad bits, but what remained was red and black and glaring, as if it were a blind thing sensing her return.

"No word of your man? The one sent to Pynn's Brook?" Garl asked softly.

Nala shook her head and indicated the wound be covered once again.

"That one could be dead any number of ways," Torello said in a low, snarky voice and earned a warning look from Garl.

"He's not dead," Nala said. "But he is late."

"Could be strung up by—"

"Shadd*up*, Torello," Garl insisted.

That time Torello listened and released a frustrated shot of breath.

"You're right, Torello," Nala said, "Pirrus could indeed be dead. Perhaps I should have sent two riders, but I thought one would be enough. I was wrong. In any case, they're not here, and we are."

She thought about matters then. "Do you think we could cut again?"

"Cut what?" Garl asked.

"The wound. The flesh around it."

"There's nothing left from last time. No skin to stretch and sew. Besides, you'd be cutting only meat, and that can't be good for the lad."

"It might help."

An unsure Garl met her imploring stare and said nothing.

"I could squeeze it," she offered. "Force whatever juice there is to the surface. Drain it and put a hot dagger to the hole. Scorch it."

"I don't know," Garl muttered. "My lady, I just don't know. There's a limit to what he can suffer. And he hasn't been eating or drinking anything. The man's drying out."

The man *was* drying out, as evident by his face and the deepening hollows there.

"Well, we have to do something," Nala said. "Ananda, get a dagger from Marden outside there and heat the edge with a torch."

The woman left immediately.

"Kura," Nala said to the other waiting woman. "We'll need fresh bandages. Return to the house. You know where the extra blankets are. Take the first one you find and bring it back here. Get Marden to slice it into strips."

Nodding, Kura left them all.

"It could be dangerous, my Lady," Garl cautioned. "The lad might be near the end as it is. He might not be strong enough to take another cutting."

Nala gently wiped Brozz's forehead. "And if we do nothing, he'll certainly get worse. There's a saying for a situation like this, about the choices we face, but I can't remember what it is. In any case, we've been hoping for a healer to come to us, but I don't think that's going to happen. Our time's becoming short."

That quieted the one-legged man. Torello remained in the background with a frown and a doubtful eye.

"Don't worry," Nala told them both. "I'll do it. I'll take responsibility."

Ananda returned first with the dagger and then went off in search of water. She came back when Kura appeared with an armful of sliced cloth. Bodies moved around the small alcove, getting into position for the approaching surgery. Garl gripped the Sarlander's legs while, under Nala's direction, the nearby guard called Marden would pin the arms. No one was certain Brozz would awake during the procedure, but they weren't going to take chances.

When all was ready, Nala got to her knees and studied the infected area.

"All right." She motioned for the knife.

Ananda held it out for her lady, and the heated blade shone in the torchlight. Nala took the weapon, studied it, then sized up the uncovered wound. She placed one hand against the side. The man's midsection yielded to the pressure, leaving only that rancid hardness underneath the hateful gash.

"This will be . . . messy," she muttered, remembering the last time, and checked upon Kura with the supply of bandages.

"All right," Nala repeated, knowing she had to do something to keep the man alive and not entirely convinced that what she was about to do would save him.

She placed the knife's edge a finger away from the stitched line, intending to cut through the twine.

All went silent, and upon some unspoken word, Nala glanced over her shoulder.

There, in the doorway, standing next to a surprised Torello, was the blocky armorer called Ajik, dressed in a white tunic and stained gray pants. The man's dark eyes narrowed in noble disdain at the situation.

Then, without apology, he shoved his way through the people-cluttered room.

Ajik dismissed Nala with a wave and then shooed the others back, wanting room to inspect the unconscious man. He dropped to a knee, sniffed at the wound, and shook his head as if he'd gotten a whiff of a fresh cow kiss. His fingers prodded at the sewn hole, shifting it one way then the other, before he released it and applied a thumb to Brozz's right eye. He lifted the lid and peered inside, then repeated the process for the left.

Once done, Ajik leaned back and studied the unmoving man.

Then he turned that intense gaze upon those filling the doorway. He snapped fingers for the dagger, and when he got it, he stabbed the weapon into the wall, the blunt smack startling Torello. Ajik spoke then in a gravelly voice, releasing a line of unknown syllables that seemed to stop in midsentence.

"I'm sorry," Nala said for them all, not understanding a word.

The response earned her a dawning look of frustration. Ajik sighed and smoothed out his trimmed beard as though it helped him to think. He then pointed at the dagger and, with grand effort and a warning glare at his audience, said, "No."

That was met with silence.

"No?" Nala eventually asked.

"No."

"Ask him for a little more detail," Torello said sarcastically.

"Shaddup, you tit," Garl warned.

"No, no, *no*," Ajik repeated, punctuating each word by pointing at the knife, then Brozz, and finally everyone else.

"Well then *what*, you little bastard?" Garl fired back.

In response, Ajik pointed at the nearby supplies and declared, "Yes," with a curt nod.

"Damnation," Torello muttered and placed a palm to his forehead. "I think I'm understanding all this."

"I am too," Nala said, her attention fixed upon the armorer.

Once again, Ajik held up a single finger, a lordly gesture indicating they should wait.

Then he pushed by them all, with the exception of Nala. With her, he carefully moved around, though he did so in a rush.

"Watch yourselves," Torello said, backing away from the man moving with purpose. "I don't trust the little topper."

303

"He probably doesn't trust you," Nala said.

That offended Torello. "Why?" he demanded. "What did I ever do to him?"

They moved into the corridor, watching Ajik hurry away.

"Where's he going?" Kura asked.

But Nala was already following the man, along with Ananda and the guard called Marden. They hurried outside the barracks. Ajik was already at the villa's gate, barking at the guards there to open the barrier.

"Do it!" Nala yelled.

The two men complied, and Ajik marched through and out of sight. Aided by Ananda, Nala climbed a nearby set of stairs to the battlement heights, where she spotted Ajik moving about the grassy sea, just beyond the narrow bridge spanning the villa's defensive trench. The short man squatted at times and crawled through the grass before popping up and searching the ground. He moved a few steps, where he repeated the process again, almost disappearing.

"What's he doing?" Ananda asked.

"Looking for something," Nala said. "I don't know what."

"Looks like a field dog, popping up and down like that."

"He's looking for something. Only he knows what. A herb or weed of some kind."

"Something to help Brozz?"

"I think so. I *hope* so."

"Why didn't he do something earlier?" Ananda asked.

Good question, Nala thought, but then she realized the strange man had devoted himself to transforming the forge into a personal island, from which he only occasionally ventured. She couldn't remember seeing him go anywhere near the gladiator barracks or anywhere else, for that matter, not in the week or so he'd been with them.

"I suppose," she said, puzzling over the matter, "he didn't know. He's been working over there most of the time. And no one's been able to talk with the man."

"Clurik brings him his meals," Ananda said.

"Good for Clurik," Nala said in a distracted tone, watching Ajik continue his search through the depths of the grass. "I suppose he noticed us going back and forth and grew curious enough to see what was happening."

"So he's a healer as well as an armorer?"

Nala didn't answer. She didn't know. Footsteps behind them caused her to look away from the armorer in the grass. Kura joined them on the battlements.

"What's he doing?" she asked.

"Looking for perhaps an herb or a weed," Ananda answered.

"Or something," Nala finished and wondered what the chances were of Ajik being able to find whatever he was searching for in the surrounding plains. Even as she thought it, the short man straightened, swatted at a few bugs buzzing for his blood, and waded through the waist-high grass as he studied the ground.

He certainly *seemed* to think he could find whatever it was he was looking for. Nala took in the vast plains, where a few trees spotted the land for color. *Grass*, she thought. Only grass was out there. And the occasional wild blooms, she supposed, one or two different sorts of flowers struggling to survive.

But they were only weeds, with no worth at all, in her mind.

Ajik squatted amidst the grass, disappearing up to his neck.

Then he vanished from sight entirely as the departing sun turned the grass to the dull hue of spun gold.

"He'll run out of daylight soon," Nala said to herself, seeing the sun halfway beneath the horizon.

"What then?" Kura asked.

"Perhaps he'll search by moonlight," Ananda said.

"Or torchlight."

Nala hoped it didn't come to that. She dared not wager on how much time Brozz had remaining. She looked at the roads and saw nothing. No one approached the villa. They were alone upon a small rise in the land.

The sky continued to darken while Ajik stooped and stood, walked a few steps, and did the same again.

Ananda was right. The man did look like a field dog.

And somewhere out there, upon the plains, under clouds fringed with wide streaks of purple and orange, Ajik crouched one final time and vanished from sight entirely, as if the land had swallowed him whole.

Nala was about to call out his name when the armorer popped back into view once again.

And hurried back toward the villa gates.

29

No breeze blew outside the alehouse, allowing the nighttime sound of chirping crickets to invade the rustic interior. Halm listened, really listened, and heard not much else—no children, no people talking, just a deep, comfortable silence that permeated the whole village.

Shoes clacked across the kitchen floor—Miji moving about the kitchen just out of sight. He shifted upon hearing the noise. He leaned onto the bar's countertop, one leg bent and one backside cheek sticking out, in what his countrymen would call "standing at attention."

"All well in there?" he asked, not needing to raise his voice, not in this place.

"All's well."

"What are you cooking?"

"Just a small roast."

"I can't smell it yet."

"I haven't placed it in the oven yet."

He nodded at the subtle jab, supposing that was the way of things, and rubbed the smooth grain of the countertop. Clean. He'd wiped the surface down earlier that day, among other things, and had done a good job—or so Miji had said. Good clean work. Honest work.

"What're you cooking with the roast?" he asked.

"A handful of vegetables."

"Gravy?"

"Juice."

Halm nodded again and scratched behind an ear. On impulse, he inspected his stitched finger, which the pit fighter called Skulljigger had bit into, the middle one of his left hand. It was healing, though in the lamplight, the rosy pink lines appeared a touch darker. He flexed the hand and felt no pain. He then patted down his chin, feeling the residual ointment there from where Miji had slapped it onto his face earlier that day. The scabs there were receding, as well as his facial swelling.

"You did well this day," Miji said from the kitchen.

"I have a good teacher."

He did. She was quite patient with his reading and writing. He could remember most of the Sunjan characters and put a sound to them with little difficulty.

"I'll have you reading short sentences soon," she said.

"Good," he added, placing a hand to his ribs. His breathing wasn't painful, but he didn't force the matter. He was, however, tempted to take deep breaths and hold them. He returned to inspecting his middle finger.

The chatter of a chopping knife drew his attention. "What are you doing now?"

"Cutting the vegetables."

"May I help?"

"There's not room enough in here for two. We'd only be bumping into each other. You stay out there and keep watch on things."

Halm's head bobbed in understanding. She was protective of her kitchen. His mother had been the same way. His attention drifted to the kegs, particularly the one containing the beer. Then he studied the one holding the mead. A small selection of wine bottles was stored underneath the counter, and he wondered what they tasted like before returning to flexing his finger.

Up. Down. Fist. Up. Down. Fist.

Quiet. Peaceful. That was village life.

"Quiet," he rumbled, glancing around at the empty tables.

"It's like this a lot these days," Miji said, moving about the kitchen.

"Daresay if you had a handful of drinkers in here, the whole village would know."

"Daresay."

"I remember places where, well . . ." He trailed off. "Where every night was . . . much livelier."

She didn't comment, and Halm's mind wandered, lighting up memories of moving, shifting mobs underneath smoky alehouse timbers. Smiles gleamed and sparkled along with burning torches and lamplight. Yells and screams of merriment spiked the air, and one had to almost yell to make oneself heard. Women laughed and hung off his arms, and he let them go, focusing on Pig Knot cavorting about, whisking attractive ladies about the floor. Men staggered into one another and good-naturedly went about their business. Then Muluk came to mind, pouring wine down his throat, laughing, sputtering, and talking. Finally, there was Goll, reserved Goll, sitting back and sipping his one drink, watching them all, studying them with an air of cautious disapproval. Muluk would say a few encouraging words to his fellow Kree, prodding him, and that would get a reluctant smile from Goll, but only for a short time.

The memories were good ones. Halm smiled and inspected his middle finger.

A presence pulled his attention to the main entrance.

There, with the fine netting already settling back into place over the doorway, stood an old man. He held a walking stick that resembled a twisted bone. The old man squinted at the bar, and Halm smiled at the customer before gesturing for him to come closer.

"Enter, good sar, enter," the Zhiberian said, putting his hand away and straightening his back.

That squinty face regarded him for a heartbeat and looked about the empty interior. Deeming all was well, he ambled over. His face was lined, wrinkly, while his high forehead crinkled as if he'd caught a falling weight with his skull. Dull gray hair, perhaps silvery at one point in time, covered the top. His sunken cheeks were concave to the point that the remaining teeth could be noticed. Halm wasn't sure of the old man's eyes because he couldn't see any in that nearsighted, face-squeezing expression. Without error, the man stopped before the counter and inspected the kegs.

"You got firewater there?" the old man asked, his voice low and cranky.

"What keg, good sar?"

"That one. Right there." He indicated the container with a nod.

Halm still wasn't sure, then he remembered Miji didn't have any firewater. He stepped behind the bar and placed a hand against the first keg. "Apologies, good sar. We don't have any firewater. This is beer, and this is mead."

The old man thought about it. "Miji in the kitchen?"

Halm was about to answer when she appeared in the doorway. "Good evening to you, Nurm."

"Miji. You don't have any firewater?"

She shook her head. "Apologies. Not for a while now. I will, however, in the future."

"Beer, then."

"Pour that for him, would you?" she asked Halm.

He did as requested, filling a mug and placing the drink before the old man. Nurm took it, drank a mouthful, drank a second mouthful, and softly gasped.

"Good?" Halm asked.

"Very."

"Ah, that'll be—"

"I'll pay for it later," Nurm muttered.

"He'll pay for it later," Miji repeated and winked. She retreated into the kitchen.

Fine then, Halm thought, just a bit annoyed, and returned to his place at the bar. "Warm evening. Air's thick with heat."

Nurm drank again, showing no signs of having heard.

"Still," Halm carried on, "I prefer this over the city. City's much more different. Much more. Everything's fresher. The stars brighter. The streets not choked with people. This is a fine little village—"

"You killed that brute Neven."

Halm stopped talking.

"Killed him with one chop," Nurm said, smacking lips and clearing his throat harshly, as if attempting to disgorge his evening meal. "Took his head off at the shoulders, I heard. Spun and chopped."

As the droning chatter of crickets filled the silence, Halm thought about the best way to answer. He didn't detect any hostility from the older man, and Miji certainly didn't seem to mind him. "I killed him," he said cautiously.

"Killed the other one, too."

"Thaimondus."

"No, not him, his other boy."

Halm realized Nurm was talking about the second son. "Ah, yes, that one too. I forget his name."

"Both were murderous buckets of shite."

"That they were."

"The whole family of them, damn them to Saimon's hell."

Halm was feeling better with each passing moment.

The old man stared at him, taking in his bruises and his teeth. "Lords above, you're hard to look at."

The words took the Zhiberian off guard, so he took a moment to smile—lips sealed—and study the old man before him with greater thought.

"People said you were a gladiator once," Nurm asked, keeping that sour, nearsighted expression upon him. "In the city."

"I was."

"Kill many up there?"

"A few."

"Good with the blade, I take it?"

"When I need to be, good Nurm."

"Nurmo," the man corrected with a well-timed scowl, not quite yet taken with the Zhiberian. "My name's Nurmo. She can call me Nurm. You call me Nurmo."

Halm didn't need to be warned a second time. "Good Nurmo. I haven't seen you in here before."

"Haven't returned here in a bit," Nurm said. "Evening's nice. My wife cooked a haunch of ham. Salted it too damn much. That's her. Salts every piece of meat too damn much. Beef, pork, rabbit. Even chicken. Salts them all until they look like they're covered in snow. I eat it, mind you. I eat whatever she puts in front of me. What choice do I have? She's the missus. Ate it this evening. Meat was tender, but too much salt. Tongue's burning. Guts all burning. Decided to come here. Why not?"

"Why not?"

"How many men you kill?" Nurm asked, changing subjects.

"I don't remember."

"Don't or won't?"

Halm studied the older man's face. "Don't."

"So you butchered quite a number."

"Killed. Not butchered. I took no pleasure in the deed. I mean, I don't enjoy killing a man unless he deserves killing. I suppose."

"I know what you mean," Nurm said in a tone not to be patronized. "So then. You're good with a sword?"

Miji appeared in the doorway, her eyes going from Nurm to Halm.

"I am," he answered.

"Any other weapons?"

"Nurm," she interrupted them, "how is Jomi? Still salting your hide?"

The older man directed his squinty gaze at her then at Halm. He then checked his mug and lifted it to his lips. In one long drink, during which his throat visibly bobbed, he finished his beer and gasped again. Releasing a burp, he placed the empty mug on the counter. His narrow lips glistened, but he made no attempt to wipe them dry.

"That was good, Miji," he said. "Jomi's good. Weather's going fair again. Back to the heat. Plenty hot."

Miji nodded.

"Remember that one." Nurm indicated the mug. "As before. I'll return another evening. Talk to you more." Then he told Halm, "I wager you have some stories in you. Gladiator stories. Right bloody ones."

"He doesn't really enjoy talking about that time," Miji said.

"Well—" Halm started.

"He doesn't?" Nurm asked. "What's he doing here, then?"

"Right now, he's my enforcer."

"Enforcer?"

"Must have one. Since Neven and Tarcul are dead."

That got Halm's attention.

"Enforcer," Nurm said, trying the word while studying the Zhiberian. "Frightful enough, I suppose. Hear that? I said you're frightful. Damn frightful. You won't have many heads to break around here. Not now."

"I'm hopeful," Miji said with a little smile.

Nurm met her gaze then Halm's. "Next time, then," the old man finally said.

With that, he turned and left the alehouse.

Miji held up a hand, asking for silence, until her most recent customer had long departed.

"I heard him from the kitchen," she explained. "Thought I'd come out and save you."

"Oh, I didn't need saving," Halm said, unoffended. "I don't mind talking—"

"About the arena," she interrupted. "I know. I didn't want him to bring up any unpleasant memories for you."

"No unpleasant memories to—"

"I mean," she interrupted again, "that's a part of your life you're not going to return to. Isn't that right?"

She said it simply, but Halm heard the distinct but delicate note of pleading in her voice. A hint of warning might have been in there as well, but he wasn't sure of that. "Aye that. No reason to return, really. Not really."

That visibly pleased her. "Good. I intend to keep you here, Halm of Zhiberia. In a good way, that is. I mean, I intend to see that you have no desire to ever leave this place, that you . . . are content here."

With me, was left unsaid, but Halm detected it all the same. The notion surprised him, truth be known, but he didn't mind it. He'd thought similar things himself. Karashipa and Miji were good, and he recognized that, knew he'd be a fool to toss them away.

And Halm of Zhiberia was no fool.

"Don't you worry," he said, his heart touched.

He usually had to pay coin to keep women around, and this one was doing it for nothing. The idea pleased him greatly. He reached out and clasped her hand. Miji did one better and embraced him.

They hugged, and he took care not to press his face too hard against her. "Don't you worry in the least," he whispered. "I can talk about the arena. Talk freely, in fact. I don't mind it at all. None of it means I'm going back there. Don't you worry. I've been alive long enough to know when good fortune is shining on my shoulders."

"Life is different here," she whispered.

"I know. I like it."

"I'm just afraid you'll be bored."

"I'm not bored."

He said that earnestly, without realizing he was lying to himself. And that instant of tender forgetfulness convinced her that he was speaking the truth.

30

Heat shimmers rose from the sands as the sun roasted the arena floor. Hunting for blood, flies and other flying pests sped by the chamber's arched window. Just inside, Salwark stooped and peered upward, studying the thousands who'd gathered for the day's events. Very little shade covered those seats. Some of those sitting high in the stands would be shielded by canvas tarpaulins. The rest would cook, right and proper. He tsked at the sight and shook his head, not wanting to imagine that wicked heat.

The sands captured his attention then, and his handsome face became a drawn and pensive thing.

"She'll be here any moment," he said to nearby Thurlo, the taskmaster for the stable. Thurlo was an older man, tall and lean with a collection of scars up and down his right cheek as well as neck. He possessed a rich voice, interestingly enough, pleasant to the point that Salwark thought the man could easily carry a tune if asked.

Salwark wouldn't dare ask, however. Thurlo had once been a Sujin with the lost Fourth Klaw, as shown by four curved talons permanently inked on the meat of his right shoulder. Only one thing was more frightening than one of Sunja's reavers, and that was a *retired* Sujin, who'd survived the countless campaigns in the vast northern wilds and lived to speak of it. Even though the taskmaster was quite cordial toward his employer, Salwark watched both his tone and tongue around the old soldier.

"Keep control of yourself," Thurlo said in a low tone, his eyes hard and sharp and fixed upon the owner's son. "You're already twitching."

"I am?" Salwark asked before looking at the nearby trainers Mal and Irva, who completed the entire stable's training staff.

"You are," Mal said and looked toward the arena.

Irva only nodded.

"Damnation," Salwark said, trying to control himself. He massaged his forehead. "This'll drive a man to the drink, I tell you. Straight to the drink."

"Rarely helps," Mal muttered with an unconcerned air.

"Gives you nerve for all the wrong reasons," Thurlo added. "And drowns the senses."

"A cost I'm damn near willing to pay." Salwark glanced past them all toward the shaded interior of the chamber.

Standing amongst a handful of his fellow gladiators was a battle-ready Aidas, mentally preparing himself. A vest of hardened leather covered his chest, the material gleaming with a fine coat of dust. A small shield rested at his greaves. The pit fighter held onto a spiked hilt from which dangled a length of chain. A spiked ball the size of a fist was at the end of that chain. Aidas nodded as those nearby whispered words of encouragement. One man held the gladiator's helmet. The piece sported overly large eyes resembling an insect's.

Salwark turned away, his thoughts preoccupied. He'd sent a pair of men to gather Zelia and escort her to the arena. The gesture gave him hope that she'd recognize his attempts at contrition.

"She hates me," Salwark muttered, not caring who heard. "She truly hates me."

"She's looking to avenge her husband," Mal remarked, his spine straight while looking out the window. "No more. You just happen to be in a position to grant her that revenge. Aidas puts the Kree down, and it'll be over. She'll look upon you in a different light."

"You think so?"

Mal nodded with sagely assurance.

Salwark wasn't convinced, however. He stroked the brick sill, whisking away the sand gathered there, and longed for a drink. Something with bite. *Could Aidas defeat Goll?* He wasn't sure if the man could. Aidas had straightened his mind into *believing* he could, but that was simply part of a gladiator's regular mental preparation. They all had to believe they were unbeatable, that they owned the sands, and all stepping upon it to face them were little more than troublesome maggots. They all thought that . . . until reality stepped in and smashed them repeatedly about the skull. From then on, rebuilding that unshakable confidence was slow work, patching those cracks with reasons for having been defeated, rebuilding a mindset and placing that defeat behind one . . .

This fight would be Aidas's first since his last loss.

The opening matches had already played themselves out, consisting completely of Free Trained brutes hacking and chopping at each other with a wild, if not enthusiastic, energy. There'd been no prisoners to speak of, but the Orator promised they would return the next day, much to the disappointment of the audience. The prisoners made the Free Trained look damn near professional, which in turn elevated the worth and appreciation of the regular gladiators.

A knocking came at the entrance, turning all heads, and one of Slavol's men pulled the door open. The lad then gestured with a hand, allowing Sorban's grieving widow to enter the room. The gladiators in her way stepped back like well-trained dogs, nodding at her as she passed. Aidas in particular gave her a solemn dip of the head, sending the message that he understood his task this day.

She was indeed a lovely woman, with a light shawl that covered her forehead and shoulders, protecting her from the sun. Zelia didn't greet any of the men as she walked through their ranks. Her face was set, impassive. Those blue eyes, once kind and full of warmth, had become frozen knobs of ice.

"Lady Zelia," Salwark greeted as warmly as he could muster, forcing his anxiety down. He moved forward and stopped not an arm's length away. "Thank you for attending."

"If my husband were still alive, I would not be here," she said, turning that icy gaze upon him.

Salwark's anxiety flared back to life. "And again, I'm truly sorry for what's happened. Truly, truly sorry. For everything. We share your pain. Truly. Ah . . . I hope you had no troubles coming here today."

"I should be back in Balgotha, but I am not. I am not because my husband is dead. Every time I come to this place reminds me of that. My very purpose for being here is because of his death. This is not a trouble, as you say. This is . . . torment."

Salwark had no reply to that, nor did any of his training staff offer any assistance. *The punces*, he grumbled internally, feeling completely and utterly alone. An awkward silence settled in then, and the owner's son was at a rare loss about how to fill it. Cheering erupted from beyond the arched window, breaking his paralysis.

"Well," he said, with what he hoped was a sympathetic smile, and gestured toward the arena. "Shall we watch?"

To his surprise, Zelia went to the window.

After Goll and company had eaten, the night became a quiet one at Shan's house. Most of the men retired early, leaving only those volunteering for the first watch. Goll slept better than he thought he would, but as the morning wore on, he focused more on the next blood match. Muluk tried to encourage him, but Goll held up a hand for silence.

Muluk had grumbled over that.

He wasn't grumbling anymore, however.

Various members of the Ten stood in their private chambers underneath the Pit, watching whatever fights were happening while waiting for Goll to step out onto the sands. Muluk walked nervously about the room, scratching at the various clumps of hair growing upon his person.

"What is it?" Goll asked, stopping the Kree in his pacing.

"Nothing."

"It's something. You're limping around like you're in need of a pisspot."

"I'm not limping. Not like before."

"All right, you're not limping like before. So speak."

"It's nothing."

"Muluk," Goll warned.

Nervous, Muluk looked around the room. Clavellus, Machlann, and Koba stood gazing outside through the chamber's only window, while Junger sat on a bench and Valka guarded the entrance.

"Just that," Muluk said, yellow teeth flashing deep within that nest of facial hair, "I don't feel good about this fight."

"You don't feel good about it?"

"Aye that."

"What's that?" Clavellus said, turning away from the window. "Did I hear him say he doesn't feel good about the fight?"

Muluk glowered, not wanting the discussion to go any further than the two Kree.

"Just . . . mind what's going on outside there," Muluk said.

"There's not much," the taskmaster said.

"Watch it anyway."

Clavellus traded looks with Machlann.

"What's troubling you?" Goll asked. "You've already placed the wagers. Are the odds bad?"

"The odds are fine for you."

And they had been. The odds had been outrageous in favor of Junger winning his fight, however, so much so that Muluk didn't even bother putting coin on the lad's name. Nor did he bother with the side wagering, where some people put down coin on the Perician pulling steel for the first time during a match.

"I've been thinking about this woman," Muluk said, switching over to his native tongue. "The one that wants you dead."

"What about her?" Goll asked in the same language.

"What if you defeat this Aidas lad and this Slavol punce sends another?"

"Didn't I have this conversation with you yesterday?"

That stopped the other Kree.

"Ah, that's right," Goll continued. "It wasn't with you. It was with him." He indicated Clavellus.

Muluk glowered at that as well. "Forget that. I've been thinking. If you continue killing these lads, nothing good's going to come of it."

"Why didn't you say anything about this last night?"

"I didn't think it all through."

"And now you have?"

Muluk's frowning mouth practically disappeared in his beard. "Most of it."

"My thanks for your thoughts, but I'll take care of this. And in the future, when we're among the others, speak plainly. You'll make everyone suspicious speaking Kree when they're around."

Muluk was mildly surprised by that point. "Didn't think of that," he said, switching back. "Apologies. Apologies all."

Only Koba glanced in their direction, a question on his scarred features.

The opening matches consisted of energetic Free Trained hacking away at each other, but when compared to the criminal entertainment, they were practically sword masters. While the fights were happening, Goll readied himself by slapping on his armor.

The first gladiator match of the day was between Gair from the House of Curge and Bratto from the House of Ustda. Though Bratto was no slouch with a blade and clearly possessed some skill, he looked sick and completely controlled by the knife fighter. Gair was a living, shining picture of everything a pit fighter strove to be: skilled and muscular but quick of hand and foot, with an intimidating—even dramatic—selection in armor and weapons. A bundle of white-and-red cloth had been wrapped around most of his head while a red iron faceplate hid the man's features. A jutting silver jaw with short, troll-like tusks hung off the mask, gleaming in the sun.

But the impressive thing that caught both Clavellus's and Machlann's attention was the knives he used and how he used them. Gair held a pair of thick boar choppers, the length of a man's forearms. They shone brightly, matching the gleam of the lower jaw, and distracted the opponent from the danger of Gair's metal gauntlets, which were lethally spiked.

Bratto lasted a short time against the knife fighter, who let the match continue only as long as needed before putting Bratto in the dirt and encouraging him to yield.

The fact that Gair belonged to Curge quieted the Ten's trainers.

The next match was between a pit fighter called Jundal, from the House of Vandu, and Hovo, from the School of Vorish. A pair of Sunjan lads, they provided an entertaining show for the audience—before Jundal tripped his opponent and knocked him senseless with a flurry of pommel strikes to the helmed face.

Then it was Goll's time.

The portcullis cranked upward, the sunlight dappling the sand-speckled threshold as Goll wasted no time stepping into the arena. The usual assortment of cheers and curses salted the air, but he paid little attention to either as he strode forward, cringing at the day's heat. The temperature had risen considerably since they'd arrived at the Pit, only made worse by the humidity. He'd already been sweating when he finished pulling on his armor, but now he felt slick and unfit with perspiration. His own breath sickened him as his helm's visor had poor ventilation.

Emerging from the far side was the man called Aidas.

The Orator rattled off an introduction for the Stable of Slavol man chosen to avenge Sorban, but Goll was aware of only the official's voice, not the words. The Kree stopped at the midway point of the arena, hefted his shield and sword, and winced. The cloth wrapped around his head had already soaked through, and sweat dribbled into his eyes.

"Come on then, you unfit he-bitch," Goll muttered, watching the other man.

Though Aidas could not have heard him, the Slavol man started walking. Goll sized up the selection of light armor, no doubt padded with cloth as well. Aidas shone underneath the blazing sun, and as he strode through the heat of the day, it became apparent the man was in solid physical shape. The insect eyes of the gladiator's helmet drew Goll's attention, but only for a moment.

Not five strides away, the pit fighter stopped, turned side on, and pointed the shaft of a morning star with dramatic flair.

The audience loved him for it.

"I've been tasked with taking your life, Goll of Kree," Aidas announced, straining to be heard over the crowds.

Goll didn't have anything to say to that.

"Know that Sorban's wife, the man you killed, watches us."

Goll rolled his shoulders, expecting no less.

"Anything you wish me to say to her when I walk off these sands?"

That bit of confidence irritated Goll. "No," he said flatly.

The morning star dropped, and Aidas assumed his stance. He brought up his own small shield and started swinging the chained weapon over his head. The air *whoop*ed from that spinning ball of spiked iron, and Goll immediately watched its course. He'd have to be especially wary of that skull cracker. If Aidas snapped out his arm—and he would—the morning star would extend its range by an arm or more, and Goll would have next to no time to react.

He scowled at the thought.

The onlookers favoring Aidas began to cheer and, as expected, he lunged, whipping that killer ball at Goll's head.

TO THUNDEROUS APPLAUSE

The Kree ducked and backed away several steps, gauging the range of the thing and how quickly his opponent moved.

The pit fighter whirled the chained weapon, his arm and shoulder working like some infernal bellows. The morning star became a blur under the sun. Aidas took two halting steps before again whipping that prickly chunk of iron at Goll's head.

The Kree ducked and darted away, hearing the *whoop* overhead, foregoing the offensive as the morning star's blazing arc prevented him from doing so.

Aidas strode forward in that halting fashion, the insect eyes scrutinizing the Ten man's actions. The morning star spun over his head, lethal, mesmerizing, and devastatingly fast, which Aidas promptly demonstrated.

Three quick loops sent Goll scurrying for distance, getting out of the thing's range. Aidas charged, angling that destructive orbit downward at a slant, to dissuade Goll from slipping inside. Goll backed away, taking one parting blow upon the shield that nearly ripped the barrier off his arm. The metallic clatter of the connection lifted a cheer from the crowds.

Goll shook out his arm and circled, quickly changing direction and staying well out of range.

The irregular movement hampered Aidas, who stopped, started again, and stopped, seemingly uncertain about whether to attack or defend.

But then Goll halted, flexed his shoulders, and took a firmer grip on his shield and sword. Shield held high, the Kree advanced.

Aidas tensed, sensing a change.

Without warning, Goll charged.

And he leaped over the morning star's spiked head as Aidas lashed out for his legs. In the split instant that he was in the air, Goll jabbed with his sword, attempting to draw his foe's shield.

Which Aidas did, spinning on the move, parrying the thrusting blade with his shield—only to take the full might of Goll's own shield's edge directly across his insect-eyed helmet.

The unexpected blow rang out across the arena and the spectators, bringing several to their feet.

Aidas staggered and fell back.

Goll rushed in, seeking to stab for the heart.

Aidas recovered quickly. He smashed aside Goll's thrust an instant before driving a straight-armed punch across the Kree's helmet, hard enough to back his head up on his shoulders. Goll retreated while shaking his skull, righted his helmet, and glimpsed the morning star's spiked pommel just before Aidas stepped in close and unleashed a three-strike combination.

The Slavol man smashed Goll's head left and right before an afterthought blow put the Kree on his back.

The arena erupted in cheers.

Wasting no time, Aidas chased. He stomped for an ankle, which Goll jerked away, still very much aware. The Kree spun on his back, sword poised and set like some hateful stinger, while Aidas got his morning star spinning once again.

The spikes crashed into Goll's cocked knee, twisting the greave there and keeping him on his back.

Aidas brought the spiked ball up over his shoulder and down.

Goll tried to roll away . . . and sensed iron tips graze the hard leather on his back.

The crowds screamed both warnings and frustration.

Goll tried to rise, but Aidas darted in and kicked him hard in the midsection, throwing him to the ground in a plume of scalding dust. Goll cringed, staggered to his feet, and glimpsed his foe just as he got stomped on again, powerful enough to be driven back a whole stride, where he landed on the inside of his shield.

Morning star, flashing in the sun, spinning.

Goll flailed, and that hateful nugget of iron wrapped around his sword.

Aidas dug in and yanked, and the blade went flying.

Goll, however, went with it.

TO THUNDEROUS APPLAUSE

With a surge of anger and desperation, the Kree scrambled into a crouch as Aidas was flinging his sword free and far. Goll lunged—glimpsing how Aidas was already bracing himself for the expected impact, readying his shield to crack an iron-sheathed skull.

But Goll was faster.

He hit his opponent's midsection full-on, driving a shoulder into Aidas and taking him off his feet. Both men landed amidst the collective gasp of dismay from the onlookers, but Aidas crashed flat on his back, his arms going wide.

Goll clawed at the man's helm.

Aidas smashed his shield's edge into the side of Goll's head.

The blow stalled the Kree but didn't stop him. Aidas's strike was purely reflexive and without much power. Goll held on to the barrier before wrestling it down onto the man's chest.

There, Goll planted a knee on top of it.

The spiked pommel of the morning star appeared at the edge of his vision . . . an instant before Goll drove his shield's edge into Aidas's head. Three successive blows rained down onto that insect-eyed helmet, the impacts startling, silencing the supporters of the Slavol pit fighter. The third strike stretched out his neck and exposed the man's relatively unprotected throat.

Goll smashed the shield's edge down upon Aida's exposed gullet and didn't stop until he was good and certain the man wasn't getting to his feet.

"Oh no," Salwark whispered, lurching toward the window the very instant the Kree climbed on top of Aidas and started hammering. At first, Aidas's legs weakly kicked out with the first couple of strikes, but then they quickly relaxed.

Salwark gripped the rough sill and watched in horror as Aidas had his life smashed from him.

And when Goll rose, somewhat unsteadily, and walked off the field, the son of Slavol stared at his fallen gladiator.

Damn you, Aidas, he thought, barely shaking his head. *Damn you. You said you could kill him. You said you could.*

Then he remembered the woman beside him.

He turned upon her without a thought in his head, at a loss as to explain what had just happened. Zelia watched the arena attendants hurrying across the sands to reach the dead man in the sun.

"I'm—" *sorry* was what Salwark was going say, but the Balgothan woman cut him off.

"Don't speak to me," she said in a low tone, her mouth becoming an angry, hateful cut. Heat rivaling the Pit's own crematory fires emanated from her, turning the nearby space into an uncomfortable thing. "Don't speak."

Salwark did as told, obeying not only her but the looks from his training staff. No one moved for long moments, and the owner's son became very much aware they were all seized by the loss of Aidas, the growing fear of the one called Goll, and the wrath of the woman called Zelia. Time stretched on, broken by glances outside, where the attendants loaded the dead man covered in blood and grit into a cart.

"He was not your best," Zelia finally spoke, breaking that intimidating silence.

Salwark swallowed as an answer.

"He wasn't even close, was he?"

Old Thurlo thought to step in. "He was more—"

"I'm not speaking to you," Zelia said and did something that both impressed Salwark and terrified him. She shut up the old Sujin with a single look. "I'm speaking to him," she clarified, her eyes as penetrating as hot needles. "When I'm speaking to you, you'll know. Do you hear me?"

With an uncertain yet defeated air, Thurlo backed away.

"He was far from your best, wasn't he?" Zelia asked Salwark.

"He . . ." But words failed him.

"Do you have anyone capable of killing the Kree?" she asked.

"What?"

"I'm growing tired of having to repeat myself."

Salwark scratched the back of his head while glancing around the room. "Lady Zelia—"

"Do you have anyone capable of killing the Kree? Not defeating, but killing him?"

His entire face flooding with embarrassment, Salwark couldn't meet the woman's gaze or answer her. So he stood there, wallowing in a melting pot of shame, humiliation, and a little bit of anger, and waited for this uncomfortable moment in his life to pass.

"You do not," Zelia decided softly, which stabbed him through his heart. "I see it now. You don't have any best men anymore. Sorban was your best, and the Kree killed him. My husband was the best fighter in this place, and he's dead. All that remains is . . . scroff. Nothing more. That's the truth of the matter, isn't it?"

Salwark felt her eyes upon him, but he dared not look into her face. "He is proving to be . . . a challenge."

"A challenge?"

He didn't say any more.

"Send another," she said.

Salwark hesitated. "I don't think . . . that will—"

"Send another."

His shoulders trembled.

"Choose one."

Salwark puckered his lips and finally faced her. "The Kree is exceptional. Truth be known, I fear anyone I send to him will . . ."

Zelia faced the gladiators present in the room.

"Do you hear that?" she addressed them all. "Your owner doesn't have confidence in you. He thinks whoever he sends to challenge the Kree will perish."

Eight pit fighters had assembled in the room, and all were deathly silent. They stood with lowered heads, hoping the woman would not speak to them directly.

"Once again, I ask you," Zelia said and walked away from the window, leaving Salwark with a sense of dawning horror. "Who among you can kill the Kree?"

Silence greeted the question, which might've surprised Salwark a few days before, when he thought there would be no shortage of dogs willing to fight the Kree.

Now, however . . .

"One of you must," Zelia said. "Surely there's one who has the skills needed to avenge my husband. My husband. Your sword brother. Isn't that what you call yourselves? Brothers of the sword? Or something of the like? If you're a brother, you're part of a family. Who in this family will challenge the Kree for killing one of your brothers. Ah, I'm mistaken—who here will avenge the deaths of *three* dead brothers? All killed by the same man. The very same man who walked off the sands not moments ago. This is no longer about Sorban. This is about a man who is killing your family one by one, piece by piece. Who will stop him?"

She walked through the channel of gladiators, raking them with her words.

"What about you?" She stopped before one. "Punder. You're called Punder. I remember my husband speaking about you. He thought highly of you. Thought you had talent. Had skill. Will you challenge the Kree?"

Punder didn't move or appear to breathe under that penetrating gaze.

"The Kree has killed *three* belonging to this family of brothers," Zelia continued. "*Three.*"

Punder raised his head and frowned as if powerless. "It's not my decision, Lady Zelia."

"Whose decision is it?"

He didn't answer, but Salwark hated the man for deflecting the question back at him.

"His?" Zelia asked, nodding in the son's direction. "He seems unable to make a decision, which is why I'm asking you. He doesn't seem to think you can do it. Will you challenge the Kree? Can you kill him?"

Punder squirmed and set his jaw. He finally blinked at the woman before him before looking at his feet. That didn't surprise Salwark—not after Goll had killed the stable's best and then butchered the remaining most promising, most capable. Punder might've been a good choice at one time, but the gladiator's mindset had clearly been shaken by those deaths, especially Sorban's.

"No?" Zelia asked. "Seddon above. One can't make the choice, and another says it's not his choice to make. Whose choice is it, then? Tell me so that I might talk to them directly. Well? Anyone? Seddon above. Such fierce men frightened by my words. Such fierce men. And my husband spoke so highly of you as well. He would be most displeased, I think. Most displeased."

With us all, Salwark glowered in shame, wishing once again he had a bottle with him.

"What about you then?" she asked another. "What's your name?"

The big powerful man fidgeted. "Urson."

"You look fit enough to move a city."

Urson didn't respond to the compliment.

"Will you challenge Goll? The one who's killed three of your brothers?"

He wouldn't look her in the face.

Zelia waited and waited, the only sound coming from the vocal audience waiting for the next match. When the big man would not answer her, she scowled in contempt and moved on toward the door.

"No one," she said in a dead voice. "To think he had such high regard for some of you. And this is how you respect his memory. Not only him but the others as well. Too frightened to move upon the killer. Sword brothers. Family. You know nothing about those words. Nothing. And since you know nothing, you *are* nothing."

Salwark took a sharp breath and studied the sands outside the window.

"My husband was wrong... to join this family," she continued, pouring the hot poison of her disdain over all their heads. "You are not worthy of him or those others who perished. Learn from this day, all of you, for this day is showing me your true worth. Not only me, but each of you. All your talk of family is nothing. You bleed and sweat with each other during training, perhaps making noble-sounding vows to each other. The time has arrived to avenge your family, but no one will risk his hide to do anything. Unfit, I say. Unfit. How... ashamed the dead must be right now, looking upon you all. And you, the living, the remaining? See for yourselves—*know* that the sword brother at your side will not avenge you, that if you die, he won't do anything for you. You are not a family. And you are certainly not gladiators. You are nothing."

That stung, but for the life of him, all Salwark wanted was the woman to walk out that door and never come back.

"Are these all your dogs?" she asked Salwark.

The question startled him. "Ah, no. Not all. The rest are back at my father's private property. Training."

"Training," she repeated.

Salwark nodded.

Zelia scalded them all with one sad look and turned to leave.

"I'll fight him," someone said then, and Salwark's head went up.

All attention centered upon one man, one gladiator, appearing as though he'd just downed an unfit mug of pissy firewater and knew, just knew he was going to perish from it.

The words stopped Zelia in her tracks, and she studied the man, dressed plainly, coolly, so as to not draw the heat. He was not so tall, not so burly, but firmly built, with corded forearms and a brown-bearded jaw. The pit fighter had his dark hair cut down, not to the skin but close, and as most in his profession, had an assortment of cuts and scars covering his face. Some were old, while some were fresh.

Salwark exchanged surprised looks with Taskmaster Thurlo and Trainer Mal.

"Your name?" Zelia asked.

"Harook."

"You are Sunjan?"

The pit fighter nodded.

"Can you kill the Kree?"

"I don't know," he answered with quiet honesty. "But I'll try."

"Promise me."

"Lady Zelia," Salwark started and meant to add more, but the woman's baleful expression stopped him like a plank to the skull.

"I promise," Harook said calmly, while the crowds rumbled and cackled in the background, like the surf of some vast ocean upon a shoreline. "I'll kill the Kree. Or perish in the attempt."

Zelia studied the man and nodded in approval.

Salwark hoped she didn't say anything that might draw the ire of the other gladiators present. Harook was a young man, twenty-three if he remembered correctly, and with a season's record of two wins and four losses. The man showed promise and possessed exceptional fortitude and will, despite having been beaten down at times.

But was he capable of killing Goll of Kree?

No, a voice spoke within his skull. *Far from it.*

"Excellent," Salwark announced and forced a smile, despite the doubt already nailed to his mind. "Excellent. I commend you, Harook. You'll have a task ahead of you, but we all rise to the occasion."

That earned him a look from the Balgothan woman, one that immediately quieted him.

"Make the challenge," she said in a tone not to be questioned.

"I will," Salwark replied and headed to the door, grateful to be free of her for the day. He nodded at Harook as he passed.

The gladiator didn't notice.

31

With a weary groan, Goll sat down on a bench and dropped his sword. He'd left his shield on the sands with Aidas, having no desire to bring the thing back with him. Perspiration coated him as thick and as unpleasant as grease, and his head throbbed with a pulse that informed him all wasn't quite well.

Clavellus stood near the window and heaped praise upon him. Goll didn't hear any of it as he struggled to take off his helm.

It didn't want to come off.

"Wait," Shan said, straightening out the house master. Goll watched the healer through eye slits as the man planted both hands firmly on the sides of the helmet.

Concerned, Muluk loomed in, hovering over the man's left shoulder, intently watching the operation.

"Be still," Shan said, and righted the house master's head.

"Have a care," Goll warned. "That's my skull underneath."

The healer made it a point to get into Goll's face. "You think I don't know that? You think I don't know? I know, Master Goll. I *know*. And by Seddon's holy grace, I'd appreciate it if you'd leave the healing to me. I'm the one who has to *deal* with all of this. You don't hear me tell you how to go about butchering a lad, do you? Do you?"

Glaring, Goll settled down and shook his head.

"Thank you," Shan said. "Now then, keep still."

"The helmet's tight." Goll said.

"He got struck upside the head a few times," Muluk supplied, speaking not that far away from the healer's ear. "Hard strikes. Vicious. You could hear them here, in fact."

"I heard," Shan remarked, unimpressed, and set his jaw. "Get me my bag."

Muluk did so.

"Well done," Clavellus said from the window, pumping his fist. "Very well done. Excellent showing, Goll. Excellent."

Goll licked his lips and tasted blood, feeling the sweat cooling on his skin. The men gave the healer room to work, and Muluk dropped a sack at the man's feet. The air was stifling, and the more the helmet hung off his head, the more he wanted a breath of fresh air.

Shan glared at Muluk. "You can do better than that. Open it, and get those bandages out and at the ready."

Nodding, Muluk did as he was told.

"Your worth just became that much more, Goll," Clavellus carried on. "That much more. That poor bastard must be on the verge of letting slip a monstrous cow kiss. A monstrous one."

"Who?" Goll asked.

"The Stable of Slavol."

"We won good coin," Muluk said eagerly, slipping into the conversation. "Some damn fine coin."

"All right now," Shan said, gripping the sides of the house master's head and getting set. "I'm going to pull your helmet off you. Understand? Try and slip it off."

"I've tried that."

"Yes, and you're a punce," Shan snapped. "Probably made it worse by doing so. Now I'm doing it. All right. Now then, I'll count to three and—"

He pulled upward, forgoing the count.

And Goll, his back against the wall, rose with a piggish squeal of pain. "*Dying Seddon,*" he blurted.

Shan released him, and the gladiator collapsed onto the bench with a clatter.

"I *said* I tried that," Goll said with heat.

"And now I understand the problem."

"The problem is the helm won't come off."

The healer rubbed his chin. "That's only part of it. You're not seeing what we're seeing."

To that, Muluk, still standing over Shan's shoulder, frowned and nodded in agreement.

"What do you mean?"

"He means your helm took a few hard kisses," Clavellus said with a chuckle.

"Right hard-looking kisses," Muluk judged with morbid appreciation.

"Now's not the time for that," Shan said sternly.

"Apologies," Muluk said. "Do what you must."

"Do you feel any pain?" Shan asked.

Goll glared.

"Anything other than what I just tried to do?"

"No. It's all because of you."

Muluk considered the healer's profile with a disapproving look.

Shan rummaged through his bag. "You've been hit. That much is obvious. There's blood—that's something else that's obvious. To us anyway. And your face is probably swollen at the points of contact, making it difficult to get your helm off."

None of that made Goll any happier. "Can you get it off?"

"Oh yes. Most definitely. Just a moment."

Goll dabbed fingers at his throat and held them up. Blood covered their lengths—a surprising amount of blood. Shan immediately pushed his hand down and glared a warning to *not* do that again.

"I'm bleeding," Goll muttered.

"You are."

"A lot."

"Head wound," Shan said. "They bleed."

"Like that?" Muluk asked from the side and earned another glare.

Shan dipped into his cloth sack and rummaged about. He passed unseen items to Muluk while, around them, the other house members gathered, watching with interest.

"All right," Shan announced as he readied materials just out of Goll's vision. "All right. Now then, I'm going to have to stick my fingers in through your eye slots here. I have grease on them. I'm going to try and coat the sides of your face with the grease, to try and loosen the helm off your head."

Goll nodded.

"Excellent," the healer said, a touch out of breath. He got in close to the gladiator, peered into one eye slot and then the other, and then jammed a finger through.

"Dying Seddon," Goll swore. "Be careful."

If he heard, Shan didn't bother responding. His finger wormed along Goll's right eye and the surrounding bone, then past it, where the probing started to hurt. The space was narrow, the grease unpleasant, and the healer's finger squirmed upon his closed eye—and not in a gentle way.

"Be careful, I said."

"Almost done," Shan informed him. "Almost."

He pulled his finger free, dabbed it again into a small jar, and once more attacked the eye slot. The finger slipped inside much more easily that time but completely covered Goll's eyelid. Once finished with that, he prepared the other side.

"Almost done," Shan reported, absorbed in the task. "Almost."

He pulled his finger free, snatched something from Muluk, and hurriedly cleaned his hands. "All right, now then, let's try this again."

The healer stood and rubbed his palms before gripping the helmet. He took a breath. "Ready, Goll?"

"Aye that."

"This should work."

"I'm ready. Get it off."

"All right. On the count of three. One—"

Shan yanked.

And the helm popped off Goll's cringing face—an instant before a sheet of red spurted down his profile and a blood bubble expanded and burst just underneath one nostril.

"All right," Shan said, handing off the helmet to Muluk. The healer pressed his patient's head back and inspected the damage. He applied thick wads of cloth to the Kree's face and kept them there, half blinding the man.

"That was unfit looking." Muluk said in a bewildered tone.

"It's not pleasant."

"How bad?" Goll asked through the cloth.

"It's a good thing you wore your helmet. Your right eye is black and swollen, and the skin's split along the temple there."

"Looks like a newborn's mouth," Muluk said.

Goll sighed.

"Your nose might be broken," Shan suggested.

"Said I had a bad feeling about the fight," Muluk added.

"Does it hurt?" Shan asked. "Your nose?"

"No."

"All right, that's good then."

A scowling Clavellus moved in behind them and studied the mess. "I've seen worse. You can still see from it?"

"Aye that," Goll reported when Shan's hand was out of his face.

"A little twine, some of that piss slop that quickens the healing," Clavellus scoffed. "You're all set for the next one."

"Were you hit anywhere else?" Shan asked.

Goll held up his arm.

"And your knee?"

Goll thought about it and nodded.

"The greave's missing," Muluk said. "Lost some skin there. Not as bad as the face, though."

"His greave's in that cart." Clavellus said. "One of the attendants tossed it there. Saw it myself. You're fortunate to walk away from that one."

TO THUNDEROUS APPLAUSE

Goll was beginning to suspect that he was.

"Clean him up," the taskmaster said and nodded at the house master. "Now, you're officially a gladiator."

That didn't lift Goll's spirits. He'd been one since Baylus the Butcher.

Junger stood nearby, watching the proceedings with a concerned expression.

Goll met the Perician's eyes.

Having perhaps seen enough, Junger looked away.

A short time later, after the sands had been cleared, Junger stood shirtless with the portcullis descending at his back. As usual, he wore no armor, but he had wrapped a bit of cloth around his forehead, knotting the length at the back of his skull. The sun welcomed him with a heat as searing as the crowd's reception, which thundered across the glaring sand. Junger stood, as relaxed as ever, his head lowered, holding his scabbard in his left hand. People screamed at him, flailed arms, punched the air, and did everything possible to catch the gladiator's attention. Women waved and flaunted shoulders, squealing at him as if in need of rescue.

The Perician didn't pay attention to any of that, however. He stood in that burning sunlight and waited, with a solemnness not seen before.

The Orator struggled to be heard over the wild applause, and only snips of his glowing introduction got through. At some point, he waved at the opposing portcullis, but his introduction for Junger's opponent failed entirely to be heard.

On the other side of the arena, Orzata, from the House of Ustda, entered. The house gladiator took in the screaming crowds and realized their welcoming noise was not for him in the least. Determined to change that, he strode forward with confidence, sword and shield swinging as he walked. The dust quickly coated his hardened leather vest and dimmed the flash of his bronze bracers and greaves. His helmet shone like moonlight, with stern eye and mouth slits. Curved spikes sprouted from his shoulders.

He walked forward like a man who'd overheard wondrous stories about the Perician gladiator but was perhaps not yet convinced, determined to see the truth of the matter for himself.

When he was within ten strides of Junger, the Perician brought his sheathed sword to guard.

Orzata did the same, keeping his shield before him, with his sword poised just at its edge, the tip protruding like a stinger. That stern faceplate glowered at Junger, as if not believing any of the tales circulating this year's games. He circled his unprotected opponent, coming closer with each step.

Junger stayed at the center of that shrinking wheel, like a predator poised to leap, watching his foe and keeping his sword at guard.

Orzata circled one way and then the other way, sizing up the gladiator and deciding on where to make the first cut.

Junger matched him, tracking his every movement, presenting his sword like a barrier to be respected. Sweat glistened off his bare upper body, placing a shine on the chiseled cuts of his physique. He kept his feet no wider than his shoulders, legs bent slightly as if ready to leap.

Orzata came within five strides, moving one way a few steps before changing direction in the other. He rolled his wrist, twirling his sword in the air as some might do for show.

Tight-lipped, Junger watched him while the crowds settled in, waiting for the inevitable clash between the two pit fighters.

Orzata edged into striking distance, no longer bothering with sword tricks. He hunkered behind his shield, his moon-silver helmet bent as if in deep concentration. He feinted with a snake's speed, flexing his weapon arm, attempting to draw Junger to strike first.

But the Perician did no such thing, refusing to be baited in such a manner.

The audience waited for that expected first strike, watching the two combatants draw closer together. One hunched over, searching for the opening that would end the fight in a blink, while the other waited with nothing more than a sheathed blade.

Orzata stepped in closer, continuing to move in alternating paths.

Junger matched and faced him the whole time.

Orzata crept to within three strides, his helmet focused upon his adversary, the ready shield and sword easily within striking range.

Junger shone in the sweltering daylight.

Then, as if deeming himself close enough, Orzata leaped, springing forth and driving his sword toward his opponent's guts, setting up a one-two strike and already cocking his shield for the fight-ending bash to the side of the head.

Except Junger became a blur.

The Perician sidestepped and upended the warrior, sending him flying into the sand. Orzata landed hard and rolled over in a squall of grit and dust. He scrambled to his feet and brought up his sword. Junger lashed out, and Orzata did a wondrous thing.

He parried the swordsman's thrust.

That startling clack of metal upon sheathed leather both drew a collective gasp from the onlookers. It surprised even Orzata himself at having managed to stop the attack. And for a brief moment in time, the two gladiators kept their blades crossed, and regarded each other.

"Well done," Junger eventually said with a faint smile.

Orzata actually nodded in return.

But then the Perician attacked again and dropped the Ustda pit fighter with two swift blows to the head. The hard impacts rang across the arena, one after the other, signaling the end of an all-too-brief contest. Orzata crumpled onto his back as if hit by a force unimaginable. He flopped over as if half awake and dreaming, the tip of Junger's leather poised at his throat.

Ustda's gladiator relaxed, and that stern helmet stared at his opponent.

Orzata was no fool.

Still dazed, he managed to raise a wavering hand in surrender.

And the Pit exploded yet again at the anticipated outcome.

"Fight's over?" Goll asked, keeping still while Shan threaded a needle through the edges of his cut.

Clavellus turned and smiled. "Fight's done. The Perician won."

"Won easily," Muluk added.

"As usual, he didn't pull steel, and the other lad actually stopped one of his strikes. That in itself is commendable," Clavellus added. "Ustda should give his lad a few coins for managing even that. Daresay we'll be heading home this evening."

Goll wasn't so sure of that.

The knock on the door confirmed his suspicions.

While word of yet another blood match was being delivered to the House of Ten, a flurry of activity erupted within the numerous private chambers along the edges of the arena. Gladiators crammed into the arched openings and watched the swordsman, watching—*studying*—the wonder called Junger. They studied his every movement, noticing his posture as he waited, the flow of motion, and how he struck.

He was blindingly fast—and possessed stopping, if not killing, power.

The man was a monster.

Some of the gladiators were at a loss as to how to defeat the Perician. Some secretly trembled at the very thought of facing him one day, while others stoically looked forward to such a contest, recognizing the man as a walking trophy. A victory over the Perician would not only be a tremendous feat and confirmation of an individual's skill, but might very well establish the conquering pit fighter in the writings of the games' history.

Perhaps even make the man a legend.

TO THUNDEROUS APPLAUSE

The gladiators weren't the only ones watching the Perician. Professional trainers and taskmasters, with long and storied backgrounds in the games, withdrew from the windows and kept their thoughts to themselves. They gathered just out of the sun's searing reach. Scarred faces, long and pensive, clustered in tight knots to discuss their observations about the Perician even as he ambled off the sands. They'd all scrutinized the fight between the swordsman and his opponent of no consequence. In some conferences, an owner was present, listening to his training staff as they spoke of the Perician, taking a greater interest than usual about the subject. They gauged strengths and weaknesses, debated the swordsman's style and defense, breaking down his stance and combat mannerisms into minute bits of information. They compared him to legends and champions of the Pit—living, retired, and long dead—and spoke of how they'd been finally defeated or if they'd ever met their match. They pondered the Perician's dislike for personal armor. Some thought it was for speed. Some called it a well-calculated tactic to cope with the punishing heat. Others argued it was nothing more than show, a distraction to hide some as-of-yet undetermined weakness. They wondered about the reason he hadn't pulled steel in any of his matches, about his perfectly placed strikes, and about his complete lack of wasted movement. The man clearly possessed speed, but they questioned his endurance, as he'd yet to be engaged in a truly lengthy match upon the sands. The swordsman's confidence was unwavering, his poise perfect. His sense of battle flow and anticipation of his adversary's moves were damn near mystical. The man was a mystery and a riddle that would have to be solved, and solved soon—else the season would be lost . . . to a man belonging to the upstart house called the Ten.

They made lists upon parchment, recording the most significant parts of their talks, and when they finished making their notes, they contemplated potential weaknesses to be exploited, going over them with an intense scrutiny that was remarkable and frightening. Somewhere in those details lay clues to fighting the Perician and defeating him.

Thus, upon the insistence of their owners, the best minds of the sport sat and searched for a means to defeat the one called Junger. Death wasn't a concern, as the swordsman had demonstrated he wasn't a killer. That was good and, in some minds, a potential weakness.

Sooner or later, one by one, their gladiators—their *best* gladiators—would meet the Perician within the Pit.

And the one who could defeat the Perician could very well be the next champion of the games.

32

Zelia returned home that afternoon, dismissing Salwark's offers to have a couple of his lads escort her. She despised the owner's son and didn't want to have anything to do with the man. It wasn't because she held him responsible for Sorban's death, but because of his slights against her husband's memory, his slights against her, and his false eagerness to please. Then there was the cowering weakness underneath it all. She sensed he would betray anyone without a second thought, with a smile on his face, and if confronted, would readily admit his fault—only to betray another in the very same way.

No, she did not approve of Salwark in the least. She wondered how Sorban had ever decided to join the Stable of Slavol. That was a mystery to which she would never learn the answer.

The streets weren't crowded, for most people kept to the shade offered by looming buildings or overhangs. No one bothered her as she walked and thought about the man called Goll and the gladiator called Harook, who would challenge and fight him tomorrow. Salwark had supported the notion, but that was Salwark, and Zelia knew he approved of Harook simply to get her out of the stable's room. She wondered if the gladiator was capable enough to kill Goll. She wondered what might happen if he failed. To this point, she'd managed to pressure Salwark to do her bidding by knowing the rules of the arena and taking advantage of a sense of loyalty to her dead husband's memory. However, Salwark clearly didn't have a pit fighter capable of defeating Goll. Her thoughts returned to Harook and his chances of victory. If he failed, if he *died*, how many more would Salwark be willing to commit to avenging Sorban? Would he even pursue it, for fear of losing more gladiators to the Kree? At this point, Goll appeared capable and willing enough to butcher the entire roster. He was clearly much more skilled than Salwark's group of pit fighters.

Could she keep forcing Salwark to challenge the Kree? But if he didn't have anyone capable of doing so, why even bother? And what might she do then?

Enough, she told herself, walking toward her little house. She would focus all her prayers and hopes upon the one called Harook. Perhaps good fortune would find her.

With that, she stopped and faced her front door. A narrow strip of grass and earth surrounded her home. The little house had always been meant to be temporary while Sorban won them riches in the arena. Now however, it looked dark, desolate and haunting.

Knowing she would have bad dreams later that night, she went to the front door and fumbled for her key.

"Zelia," a man called out, breaking her thoughts.

She turned to see Boh approach her—a weaponsmith specializing in small knives.

"Zelia," Boh said, stopping before her and offering a pleasant smile. Boh was a big, burly individual with blond hair—not fat, but thick with muscle. He was young, perhaps in his thirties, with his own wife and children. Zelia remembered the number being three, in fact.

"Good Boh," she greeted, catching a whiff of his perspiration, clean and not entirely offensive.

The weaponsmith pushed his hair out of his brown eyes and shrugged. "I only just heard about the passing of Sorban."

Zelia nodded and unlocked her door, the mention of Sorban already hurting.

Boh followed her. "I'm not so close to the games, you see. And my work has kept me busy. News of his death was slow to reach me. Ah, apologies again. I've upset you. That's the curse of working with metal, you forget about people and how they have feelings."

Despite the stiffening of her back upon being reminded Sorban was no more, Zelia managed to keep her composure and entered her home.

"If I can be of service," Boh said, following her right up to the threshold, "just ask."

Zelia turned, nodded, and offered a glimmer of an appreciative smile.

He stood there, holding his hands. "I'm very sorry about the death of your man," he said with a frown. "Truly."

"Thank you," she said and began to close the door.

Boh placed a hand against it. "I know these are difficult days for you. There's nothing I can say to help that. But . . . once again, if I can be of help. Any help. Please let me know."

He smiled at her then, warmly and perhaps a touch imploring.

"Thank you," she repeated and attempted to close the door again.

But he firmly kept it open while his smile soured into something lewd. "Any . . . help." His gaze flowed over her body.

That unfit message struck Zelia senseless for a moment, and she couldn't believe what she was hearing, horrified at what she was seeing. Boh towered over her and eyed her from underneath a lowered brow, perhaps thinking it somehow appealing.

Zelia slammed the door in his face. The timbers used for barring the entrance were nearby, so she reached for one and immediately fitted the slab to the door. She then grabbed the second and got that one in place. Once finished, she backed away, eyeing both pieces and hoping her house was secure.

"Zelia?" Boh called from outside. "Zelia?"

"Go away," she warned, heat in her voice.

Silence from the other side.

Zelia placed a hand to her chest, felt the day's sweat there, and shuddered at what had just happened. Did that unfit maggot actually express sympathy for her loss while, practically in the same breath, trying to—

"Zelia," Boh called from the main room.

The sound of his voice startled her into action. She moved to the interior and halted upon seeing the big weaponsmith opening the shutters of the main window, his upper torso perfectly framed. He saw her and smiled.

"Apologies again, Zelia," he said in an unconvincingly shy tone. "I'm not very good at this."

"Go!" she screamed, livid at the invasion.

She rushed to the shutters.

Boh held up meaty palms as if ready to fend her off and smiled. "You *are* a handful. I've heard about you Balgothan honeypots. How you're hot to the touch. Even heard you and Sorban from the streets from time to time. Rutting. Packing. The screams that you let loose, if only you knew what they did to me . . . Well, no matter. Look—"

Zelia slapped him, grazing his chin, pelting his neckline. "Be *gone*!"

Smiling, Boh flinched at the contact and drew back. "Zelia," he cautioned softly, making it clear that she would regret that later.

She slammed the shutters, fastened their hooks, and barred them with a single timber.

Boh's shadow loomed between the cracks. "Listen to what I have to say, will you? Be sensible. I have a wife. I know you're alone. We can come to an agreement . . ."

Sickened, Zelia covered her mouth. "Leave this instant, you lecherous maggot. *Leave*, and I won't report you to the street watch."

That seemed to penetrate the weaponsmith's head. His outline halted, seeming to consider the warning. Then he slapped a fist against the shutters, hard enough to test them and more than enough to make Zelia jump.

"Balgothan bitch," he muttered and moved away.

Zelia put her shoulder against a wall and watched the window. No further blows landed against it. No further sound came from the barred door. *Seddon above.* She stared in horrified wonder, not daring to open anything for the rest of the night. She struggled to see outside and realized she couldn't, not through the cracks. That comforted her to a point.

That meant Boh could not see in.

The unchecked confidence in the lout's tone insulted her, as if he'd thought all along that she somehow would agree to his suggestions, after a period of mourning—a *short* period of mourning. Her thoughts whirled at the upsetting encounter, and she wondered what had brought on such an unwanted advance from the pig bastard. And he had a wife and *children*—three of the brazen little toppers.

Her hand rested against her throat.

She remembered her knife, the one Sorban had given her as a gift. The blade had been fashioned for her hands alone, in case their home was invaded and Sorban wasn't about to defend her. He'd even showed her how to use it. Treacherous Boh had actually made the weapon. He'd even talked with both her and Sorban when they walked past his work area just down the street. While her husband was present, the weaponsmith had been a fine and even courteous soul. He'd even introduced her to his wife and youngsters one evening.

His leering face appeared in her mind.

Zelia went to a wall and grabbed a small scabbard hanging from a peg. She pulled the weapon free, appraised its gleaming length and its straight edge, always kept sharp. Sorban had warned her to maintain the blade. He'd even taken a stone and demonstrated how to keep an edge.

Fearing for herself but not about to show it, she stood with her back against the wall and studied the closed window. The memory of Boh played across her mind. She'd heard of men like him, their nerve every bit as thick as their ignorant skulls. However, she'd always had Sorban around. After one look at her husband, most maggots would quickly look away. Zelia had to admit that such reactions pleased her immensely. No one would challenge her husband. No one had ever challenged him, not outside the arena.

He was gone now, while the likes of Boh remained.

Zelia wondered how bad her life had just become.

33

Back at the healer's house, the members of the Ten retired for the night.

Machlann rose from a table, put his hands to his spine, and regarded the ceiling overhead. Clavellus did the same, having said all that was upon his mind about the morrow's fight. The taskmaster looked forward to it, but a part of Goll suspected he longed to return home. In the dim light given by a single lamp, the two men looked old, the shadows failing to hide the lines of their faces and throats. Koba had already retired for the night, leaving the other three sitting about a table with a single bottle at the center.

Machlann nodded at the Kree and made his way up creaking steps to the second floor.

"Get a good night's sleep," Clavellus said to Goll. "And deal with this Harook lad tomorrow."

Goll nodded and touched his right profile. The stitches bristled there, around a mound of raised black skin. A dewy sheen of ointment coated his fingers, and he scolded himself for feeling it.

"Keep your fingers off that," Clavellus warned. "You'll have poor Shan cursing you in the morning."

"He's already cursing me."

"Then he'll curse you more." The taskmaster glanced toward the door leading to the healer's private chambers. "He's not used to seeing so much blood, I think. He's a good man. Skilled healer. But his nerves are being stretched. If you keep rubbing off that salve, he'll be angry."

Goll knew he would.

"In the morning, then," the taskmaster said.

The Kree lifted his hand. Sitting at a nearby table, Muluk did the same and watched the old man climb the steps until he was out of sight. Only Junger and Pratos remained on the lower level. The guard stood inside the main entrance, his hand on his sword's pommel, while the Perician sat with his feet up, head lowered, and back against a wall. Feet scuffled across the ceiling, and the timbers released soft squeaks. All became quiet after a time, and a comfortable silence overtook the room.

Seeing they were relatively alone, Muluk crept over to Goll. "A word with you."

"Out with it."

Muluk glanced around before fixing his fellow countryman with a critical eye. He stared only for a heartbeat, long enough for Goll to wonder what was troubling him, when a barely contained smile replaced his stern expression.

"We have a problem," Muluk said quietly, switching over to his native tongue.

"Must be a good one," Goll said in Kree. "You can't stop smiling."

"I tried to hide it. Ruined the jest."

"You'll have to practice that."

"I will. Guaranteed. Any case. We have to purchase a few more of those strongboxes."

"More?" Goll asked with a slight frown.

"More."

"We got plenty back at the villa."

Muluk's hairy features contorted and twisted, barely suppressing his delight. He furtively checked on Pratos and Junger before leaning in close. "We were doing well before, Goll, but now . . . with today's victory, we're on our way to bursting."

Goll studied the happy man. "Bursting?"

"Aye that."

"You mean . . . with riches."

Muluk nodded.

"How?"

"The *wagers*, Goll, the wagers. The coin awarded from winning the match is nothing compared to the wagers. The *Domis* is where the coin is. There's a considerable amount of wagering on the side. I mean, we all knew that. Everyone knows that. It's how the houses finance themselves. But *this* . . . I'll have you know that the coin we've won—*you've* won—"

Goll held up a hand. "We've won. It's all ours."

"All right, we've won," Muluk conceded. "It's . . . well, it's more coin than I've even seen. More coin than I've ever imagined seeing. Today alone was a landslide in gold. A *landslide*. You saw the sacks?"

"I did."

"That's what we *couldn't* hide away. Koba knows, as does Valka. And then, well, the Domis handed me this."

Muluk glanced around again before producing a slip of parchment.

"What's this?" Goll asked.

"That's our coin. *Our* coin. The sum waiting for us with the Domis."

"The sum waiting for us?"

Muluk nodded. "What we *couldn't* carry with us. The remainder."

Goll's eyes locked on that hairy face. He then took the parchment and saw the number written there. His face became slack with shock. "Is this right?"

Excited, Muluk nodded again.

"It can't be."

"It is."

"There must be a mistake."

"There *isn't*." Muluk almost squealed before checking on the others in the room.

"How much did you wager?" Goll whispered in disbelief.

That stopped the other Kree. "Well, I won't lie to you. I, ah . . . a little more than usual, but only because I had confidence in you. Confidence."

"How much was a little more?"

"That's not important," Muluk said with a wave of his two-fingered hand. "I won't do it again. I swear. The point is, you won. *We* won. And the house is wealthy. *Considerably* wealthy."

"How *much*?" Goll repeated in a tone not to be challenged.

Muluk licked his lips and looked around the chamber. He squirmed, scratched at his beard then an armpit, and finally gave up. "Everything."

Goll felt his guts go cold. "What?"

"Everything."

"Everything?"

"We had here," Muluk clarified, pointing.

"You wagered everything we had here."

"Aye that."

"And they let you?"

Muluk nodded. "Oh, I had to scrawl my mark on a few things. To swear I had the coin in the city else, you know, they'd . . . well, ah, would discipline me."

"Discipline?" Goll asked dubiously.

Muluk fluttered both hands, dismissing the particulars. "The point is . . . *we* won. And we have *that* waiting for us. Or we can leave it there. They called it a record of credit. It's available to the houses if they wish it."

"We'll take it all back. To the villa. In separate trips if we must."

"Aye that. We should. Yes. Can't be too careful."

"This is all ours?" Goll asked.

"It is."

Goll studied that number, concentrating on it, then a smile crept across his face. In the unbroken silence, Muluk matched it with one of his own.

Then the smile disappeared from Goll's face. "Don't do this again."

Muluk rattled his head. "I won't."

"If you're wagering, do it in small amounts. Understand? Only on us. Never risk our fortune again."

"Never. I understand."

"You got fortunate."

At that, Muluk frowned. "I wagered on you. Nothing fortunate about that. Chances are we won't get another pot like this again. Not ever. Not when the people realize who you are and what you're capable of."

After another pause, Goll studied the parchment and the number upon it, and he smiled again. "This is ours?"

"That's ours."

"All of it?"

Muluk nodded.

"Seddon above."

"We're wealthy, Goll. Wealthy," Muluk said, his eyes momentarily becoming moist. "If only . . . my parents were still alive to see this. Their son holding this much coin. The sight of it alone would drop them to their knees. To think I started this season thinking I'd be content winning a match or two, just enough to perhaps buy a good meal. Something to drink with it. Some clothing for the summer. Warm clothes for the winter. And if there was any coin remaining, well, I'd save that for the winter as well. And then wonder what to do after the snow. Maybe do it all again. Maybe find work somewhere. Find a missus. One who would have me, anyway. And just live. Day to day."

"Wise," Goll said.

"Now, however."

"You'll still be wise," Goll said. "And be careful. Just because we have coin doesn't mean we can throw it away."

Muluk frowned. "We can throw away a little."

A smile accompanied Goll's words. "Maybe a little."

"A few coins."

"Nothing more."

"Aye that."

The two men kept right on smiling, as if a considerable weight had been lifted from their shoulders.

"Is it necessary, Goll?" Muluk asked quietly, his demeanor becoming thoughtful.

"What?"

"Killing the lot of them?"

"It's a warning to the others."

"I suppose it is. But . . . we have so much right now. You have so much. I mean . . . with this coin, do we really even have to continue? We could simply retire to Clavellus's villa and do other things."

"Other things?"

"Start a town, perhaps."

Goll studied the other man's face. "We could. But that's not what I'm here for."

"And what's that again?"

"To win it all."

Muluk nodded understanding. "You could still do all that. You could. And spare those trying to do the same thing. I've been thinking about these gladiators coming after you. Some of them might very well be like me. Just trying to get through the season. Perhaps they have families. Wives. Children."

"So you did hear us speaking," Goll said.

"Perhaps a little," the Kree admitted. "But I'm just saying my mind here. I don't expect my thoughts to change yours, but I'll feel better if I said this. If you . . . continue to put lads into the dirt, you're going to make a lot of enemies. Perhaps more enemies than those who fear you. And even if they do fear you, if they meet you in the Pit, they'll fight for their lives and not for the sport, because they know they're dead otherwise. And every lad you put down, well, the more enemies you'll make. More houses and gladiators will seek revenge. Some might come looking for revenge outside of the games. Until they get it."

"I accept all of that."

Muluk was silenced by that stark response. Then he gestured at the sleeping Junger. "Look at him. He probably wants to win it all, too, but he's not killing anyone. He puts his foes down, but they aren't dead. Aren't crippled. And he has no enemies to challenge him. No one hunting him for revenge. And the crowds, well . . . They love that topper."

Goll's eyes flicked from his countryman to Junger then back again.

"I know you don't care about the crowds' approval," Muluk added. "I'm just saying what's on my mind. He's on the same path as you, but he's . . . cleaner about it. Yes, that's what I'm getting at. He's cleaner."

"You think his opponents aren't trying to kill him?"

"Some are, no doubt. But . . . these are the games. There will always be the games. But . . . they're just games, Goll. You say you're putting them down as a warning. A lesson, even. All right, but I think you could put the same message across without taking a life and still win it all. Your purpose is to win it all, not to kill the most people. Wars do that fine. Just defeat your foes. Cleanly. Do that, and I think you'd be even more respected—and admired—for doing so."

Goll remained quiet.

"A bit of mercy isn't a bad thing," Muluk said. "Even if they do look down on us. If our might or skills won't change their minds, maybe our mercy will?"

"You've been doing some deep thinking, indeed," Goll remarked and handed over the piece of parchment.

"Apologies," Muluk said. "It's the coin. You can't enjoy it if you're dead. And you *will* want to enjoy this. Sleep well, Goll."

Goll nodded, thinking he slept well every night.

Satisfied he'd spoken his mind, Muluk rose, studied the interior, and went to the stairs.

The wooden steps creaked softly as he ascended.

Goll watched him until he was gone from sight.

Then he turned his attention upon Junger.

34

Tall rows of firs surrounded the Zhiberian, splitting the sunlight and casting shadows. The forest air was pleasing and empowering, and he placed a hand against the base of a chosen tree. An energy existed there, a subtle but detectable vibe of life, if one took the time to check for it, and that reminded him of days spent gathering wood with his father. The moment didn't last long, as the sounds of falling axes shattered the peace of the forest, breaking the spell.

Halm straightened and glanced around. Bromull was nearby, studying him quizzically. "Something bothers you, good Zhiberian?"

Halm shook his head. "Your companions are eager."

"Winter's not long away. Best to chop wood now and have enough of it back home before the snows come."

"Are the winters bad out here?"

"Bad enough. Some days, it seems the snow buries the world. No one dies, however, if that's what you're asking. The village is small. We help each other out here. No one goes hungry or cold if we can help it."

"That's a pleasant thought."

"Isn't it?" Bromull smiled or appeared to smile through that heavy shag of chain-mail hair hanging off his chin. Perspiration hung off some of the strands, fallen from the man's brow, lending him an even more brutish look. "Much the same everywhere, I suppose."

Halm didn't comment.

"Now then, you think you're able to swing this?" the bearded man asked and held out a single-bladed axe. "And I'm not challenging you, you understand. If you can, good. If you can't, that's fine as well. Just keep talking while I bring this one down."

Halm took the heavy tool. He felt well enough to try, but after a single test swing, and a light one at that, his ribs grumbled and cursed him for thinking otherwise. His bones weren't completely healed despite bandages and ointment. The axe shaft was old and well cared for, and he hefted it, gauging the weight.

"Remembering your days in the Pit, are you?" Bromull asked with what might've been a smirk.

"Ah, well . . ."

"Do you miss it?"

Halm met the other's eyes, and for a moment, he was reminded of seeing Muluk for the first time. Bromull didn't exactly look like the shaggy Kree, but the wild length of beard triggered the memory. Then he was back in the Pit, reliving years gone by and fights he'd won and lost and lived to speak of—armored fiends wielding battle-axes and broadswords; nightmarish behemoths charging, swinging, and cutting, breaking into combinations of strikes drilled into their muscles until their limbs moved without being slowed by conscious thought.

Bromull waited.

"Apologies," Halm muttered with a smile. "What was it you asked?"

"Do you miss it?"

"No," he said simply and hefted the axe again, smiling fondly at the tool.

"No," Bromull said, believing the other man. "I don't suppose I would either. Blood sport. Having some savage trying to bleed you over a purse of coin. All for the screamers, watching and cheering your name."

"Only if they like you," Halm corrected. "Otherwise, they'll curse you. The likes I daresay you've never heard before."

Bromull thought on that. "Women too?"

"Women can be the worst."

That got a chuckle from the woodsman. "Well, no pressure here, good Halm. Strike that base if you feel well enough to do so."

Halm felt his bandages trussed around his belly and such. They were warm and moist with sweat, for these woods weren't as close as he'd been led to believe. He assumed a chopper's stance, tensed, and touched the tree's base where he would make his first cut. His first deep breath delivered another grumble of discomfort, however, daring him to do more and then see, just see, what would happen. With one swing, he'd tear himself apart, ruining whatever progress he'd made up to this point. He'd probably rip out that chunk of meat stitched back into his middle finger as well. Then there was all that other sewing line keeping him together.

But lords above, he dearly wanted to swing that axe.

"Apologies, Bromull," he finally said. "Maybe best I don't. Not with my ribs the way they are. Or any other of my hurts. I'll just stand back and talk."

"Talk is fine," the bearded man said and stripped off his shirt, revealing strong, sinewy arms and a narrow, muscular back. He took the axe and stepped to the same tree. The steel flashed in the light.

Bromull readied himself and swung the axe.

Wood chips flew.

The six men returned to the village by early afternoon, having eaten a small lunch in the woods. They parted ways, and Halm bade his new friends a good day. Halm decided not to accompany them the next day, however. He would wait until his cuts and ribs healed. Despite that, being included in a group once again was good, working toward a common goal, even if he only stood back and watched and prattled. And the looks he received amused him. The men heaped praise upon his name for ridding them of Thaimondus and his evil sons. The subject then switched to his days as a gladiator. They were greatly interested in the Pit, asking him questions about weapons, good and bad, what his preferred weapon was, and who had been his toughest opponent. They were a friendly enough lot, the village men, and Halm didn't mind answering them.

Replaying the conversation, the Zhiberian meandered down the main road, spying the alehouse in the distance and the broad steel platter that was the lake beyond. Thoughts of the evening meal entered his mind. Miji seemed inclined to prepare small salted roasts of beef, and while that was fine, he was growing a little tired of them—perhaps recalling old Nurmo talking about his wife's cooking. Chicken or some other game would be a welcome change.

A shape charged him from the right. Halm turned to meet it head-on and discovered it was a little dark-haired girl, the same little girl who'd been fighting with her three brothers a day ago.

She stopped before him and looked up, her round, unblemished face screwed up by his assortment of scars and the sun pushing through the clouds.

"Hello," she said and waited, her grimace shifting from one cheek to the other.

"Hello, little one. I'm called Halm, of Zhiberia. What's your name?"

"Nohra."

"I see."

"I'm not little anymore."

"You're not?"

"No. I'm seven," she said and held up six fingers.

Halm didn't correct her. "Apologies, Nohra. I thought you were eight."

"No. I'm seven." She dropped her hands. "You're all cut up."

"I am."

"Does it hurt?"

"No. Not much. Not now."

"You're a gladiator?"

The question surprised him. "I was. Not anymore, I suppose."

"Why?"

Halm smiled and touched his collection of sweaty bandages. "This. And this. And these. And this here." He held up his middle finger.

"You're not a very good gladiator," Nohra decided.

"No. I suppose not."

"Did you win any fights at all?" she asked, her posture fine and straight, her hands at her sides.

"Some." He shrugged. "I won my share."

"But you were still hurt?"

"Aye that."

"I want to be a gladiator when I get bigger," Nohra said plainly, her brown eyes squinty and watchful. "I'm a good fighter. Maybe the best."

"Are you, now?"

"Yes. And I'm fast. Very fast."

"Being fast is important."

She scrutinized him earnestly, perhaps deciding if he was being a punce or not. "Can you teach me?" she finally asked.

"What?"

"How to be a gladiator."

The question left him momentarily speechless. He stood there, staring down at the little girl with her hands at her sides. "Ah . . . I'm not a trainer," he said then.

"What's that?"

"That's who teaches a person how to fight."

"Oh. Well, who taught you?"

"A trainer."

"Where's he?"

"In a place far from here."

That visibly disappointed Nohra, and she lowered her squinty gaze, looking back at her home. "My mother says girls aren't supposed to be gladiators. She says girls are supposed to be cooks or healers or farmers or stitch with the needles or things like that. I think that's all gurry. And boring. I don't want to do any of that."

The bad word caught Halm off guard. "Well, I suppose that's the way for most little girls."

"I'm still going to be a gladiator."

A smile spread across his harsh features. "I'm sure you will."

Nohra scowled once more, deciding if that was a jab. Halm believed that if she detected one, she'd lash out at his bells, seeing she was only waist high, after all. She was well positioned to bring him to his knees with one punch.

"I will," she assured him. "I know it."

"I'll watch for you."

"If you change your mind . . ." she said and left the rest dangling. "I live over there." She pointed.

Halm saw her mother in the doorway of her home. The woman was an older version of her daughter, the resemblance clear. She watched him warily. Halm waved, and the mother hesitantly waved back.

"You best go," he advised. "Your mother looks like she wants to speak with you."

Nohra squinted at him one last time and then bolted. The little girl threw her arms around the woman's waist, who staggered under the embrace.

Halm moved on, knowing he'd speak to Miji about the little girl.

I want to be a gladiator when I get bigger, she repeated in his head.

Seddon above, he didn't see anything wrong with that in the least. Not many of them were in the games. The womenfolk would probably take to a female pit fighter. The men wouldn't care. Oh, some would be right and proper kogs about it, of that he had no doubt, but if the woman won, the majority of men would be swayed.

The houses, however, were a different matter.

They were owned mostly by old men who were once gladiators themselves or had some history with the games. The houses possessed the best trainers and taskmasters in the blood sport, grizzled hellpups who would prepare and sharpen a raw recruit into a professional gladiator, with an eye on becoming a champion of the games.

As far as Halm knew, every champion had been a man.

Truth be known, he couldn't recollect if any of the current houses had ever placed a woman in the games, let alone even considering taking in and training one for the sole purpose of fighting in the arena. He couldn't remember anyone ever talking of such, or ever seeing a woman in general quarters for that matter. Considering the type of individual taking up shelter in the Pit's underbelly, most women were wise enough to stay away from that sour hole. Most *men* should have the sense to avoid general quarters, but if a house hadn't expressed interest in them and they were still determined to fight, then it would be as one of the Free Trained.

It was a man's sport.

That thought interested Halm.

His thinking ended when he rounded the alehouse's corner and saw old Nurmo and Miji standing outside. Miji in particular appeared troubled. Nurmo looked the same as before, as if a troll had pinched the fellow's face.

"Halm of Zhiberia," the old man said, lifting his chin. "I have to speak with you."

"Greetings, good Nurmo," Halm said, taking greater note of Miji. "What about?"

"About the village. And its people. And defending them all."

That stopped Halm, and he glanced from Miji's lovely face to the much older one. "Well, let's speak inside, shall we?"

"Here's good enough."

Miji frowned and watched her man.

"Something bothers you, Miji?" Halm asked.

"Aye that. You best listen to Nurm here. He'll explain it all."

"You don't like it, however."

"No, I don't. But what he has to say is right, and you should consider it."

That interested him. Halm cocked his head. "All right then, good Nurmo. Say what you will. I'm listening."

"You're a gladiator," Nurmo said with his distinctive squint. "You killed Thaimondus and his sons. And the brazen ass lickers who joined him. You killed them all. Easily, if you believe those who saw you do it."

"All right."

"Well, for all their wickedness and the cruelty they inflicted upon the people living here, they also defended us. Say if a pack of bandits or Dezer came riding through. If, for whatever reason, the village was threatened, we would gather behind those palisade walls. Some of the lads would be given bows or spears to reinforce the palisade and fight if needed, alongside the louts under Thaimondus's banner. No more. With them all perished and near bones, we find ourselves without anyone knowing how to use a sword or anything else for that matter. You saved us from Neven and Tarcul and the rest of them unfit pig bastards, but you've also left us damn near defenseless."

The speech was unexpected, which showed on Halm's healing face. "But you said you had bowmen—"

"And spearmen," Nurmo interrupted, "but that's not their profession. They might act like soldiers, but they're not. Certainly not trained. Any topper can stick a spear. Twang a bowstring. Get enough of them together, and they'll produce a rain of sorts, I suppose."

Halm didn't rightly agree that just any topper could stick a spear. That gurry took practice, but he didn't say that. And he didn't think any archer would appreciate their business being thought of as "twanging a bowstring." He kept that to himself as well, but he supposed that was the old man's point.

"We're damn near helpless right now," Nurmo carried on. "That palisade might keep us alive for a few moments more, but it won't save us. Not against true hellions, men looking to butcher the lot of us. The Lancers are too scarce these days, even more than they used to be."

Halm shifted from one foot to the other, becoming impatient.

"I've talked to the older ones here," Nurmo said and gestured to Miji. "Talked to the younger ones. We're in agreement. We need a militia. A trained militia."

"Oh," Halm said.

"Now you understand. We've talked about you. Those who saw you take Neven's head off were damn impressed. They were just as impressed when you put Tarcul into the dirt. We think you should train our lads. Whoever wishes to join the militia. A village guard, if you will. You train them, and train them good, because we'll need trained guards—men trained by a gladiator."

Nurmo stopped then, gathering his wind, collecting his thoughts.

"You want a soldier," Halm said, "not a pit fighter. You want one who knows group tactics. Who can train your lads to fight as one. Like a pack. A unit. A gladiator only knows how to fight alone."

"Our lads need training from someone who knows how to fight," Nurmo said pointedly. *"Anyone* who knows how to fight. Right now, that's *you*. Train them first. Train them well enough so that they won't be butchered, and *then* we'll worry about group tactics."

Uncertain, Halm looked at Miji, who reluctantly nodded.

"Is there any coin to be had?" he finally asked.

"Coin?" Nurmo asked back.

"Aye that, coin."

"There's no *coin*, you unfit bastard. You won't be paid like some mercenary. This is a task to keep the village *safe*. To keep souls alive. Around here, coin is scarce. Most have very little.

Items and skills are traded for instead of bought with coin. There's no coin. Forget about the coin. You'll do it because you see the need for it and because you're here. Living here."

"Suppose that's true enough," Halm muttered, his cheeks flaring scarlet for even asking the question.

Nurmo watched him. "But if you do it, the village will remember. Daresay they'll remember it well. You won't go hungry. Or thirsty. Or have need for anything."

Halm kept his mouth shut that time.

"So will you do it?"

"Give me some time to think about it."

"Think about it? You're here *now*. Living here. You're either staying or you're not."

Miji cleared her throat. "Nurm, give us some time to talk about this. Halm isn't Sunjan. He's Zhiberian. To ask him this, to expect him to agree so soon might drive him off. Give him some time."

That sank into the old man's head. "All right. Some time, then. I'm finished here. Said my thoughts. I'll return later. See what your answer is. What your plans are."

With that, Nurmo looked toward the lake. He continued looking in that direction as he walked away.

Halm waited until the man was gone. "My thanks," he said, drawing close to Miji. "I wasn't certain what to say there."

"I saw that. What are your plans?"

He faltered. "I don't rightly know. I want to stay, but . . . I'm not a trainer, Miji. I'm certainly not a trainer of guards for a village militia. What I do is similar but not what the village needs."

"What the village needs are people willing to protect it in case we're attacked. We need trained sword arms. Or spearmen. Whatever you can teach. Whatever you can share. As Nurm said, show them how to use their weapons first, train them to use those weapons well, and we'll worry about turning them into a force later."

Halm wasn't so sure.

"Don't worry about the coin," she said. "That might change."

"I'm not worried about the coin. I spoke too soon then. It won't bother you if I do this?"

That quieted her. "I see the need for it. So, no, it won't bother me. So will you think about it?"

Halm already was.

"Think on this . . ." she said, taking him by one bare, hairy shoulder. "It'll be another thing for you to do. For the good of the village."

He met her eyes and nodded.

35

On the morning of his next blood match, Goll walked through the city with the rest of the Ten around him. They'd left the healer's house earlier, searching for a replacement helmet for Goll. The bruises coloring his face had fattened just a touch more overnight, resulting in Shan declaring that the house master would need a new helm. The usual assortment of wagons and people filled the streets though Koba strode through them all, parting the masses like a quiet bull. Clavellus and Machlann followed behind, taking advantage of the path the big trainer cut. The rest trailed those three, except Pratos and Clades, who'd remained at the healer's house to guard the coin.

As they walked along, Clavellus glanced back at Goll and gestured for him to come closer. Wondering what was on his mind, the Kree complied.

"I've been thinking," Clavellus said, "if we're permitted to leave the city this day, that perhaps we should purchase more strong boxes."

Goll glanced back at Muluk, who frowned a question.

"He told you," Goll said.

"What's that?"

"Muluk. He told you about our winnings."

"He said nothing to me," Clavellus clarified. "Although I would've had to have been blind to *not* see the lads carrying those sacks back to the house. Regardless, I'm not only speaking about your coin, I'm speaking about myself as well."

Goll shrugged. "It's your house."

"Well, the room can take a few more boxes. But if I continue wagering and winning on the likes of you, I'll need the extra containers. You as well. Don't worry. We'll mark them."

"I'm not worried about that."

"Are you wagering?"

Goll nodded. "But nothing like yesterday. He has orders."

That caused the old man to smile. "If he listens."

"He'd better."

"Wager what you can spare, but never risk your entire fortune. Just remember fortunes are made during the games, Goll. Have no doubt of that."

"I don't."

"At his peak, Old Curge earned enough to start his own kingdom. I never saw where he kept it all, but I saw the huge chests being brought into his home. I counted five, all of them big enough to hold a man if necessary. Who knows what other containers he might've had tucked away inside. And Old Curge was a strict teacher. I imagine Dark Curge has learned well. And that's only Curge. Old Tilo stayed in the business, as did Vandu. They've all done well. What I'm saying is . . . Place your wagers wisely. And build upon your fortune. Never take away."

"Understood," Goll replied.

"If we're permitted to leave the city," Clavellus said, fixing him with a wary eye. "Three of these in a row, now. Salwark's looking for your head."

Goll said nothing to that.

"How is your head, by the way?"

In addition to his swollen features, Goll had woken with a ringing in his ear, which had lessened during the morning. He mentioned it to Shan, who recommended not fighting that day. That wasn't going to happen.

"Settled," Goll reported.

"Excellent. You're going to need something with a little more room—"

Goll, however, didn't hear the last bit, for a familiar figure caught his attention.

"I'll meet you at the arena," he said to the taskmaster and quickly left the group. The crowds swallowed up Clavellus and the others as Goll walked away with purpose. He entered a narrow side street, where broad overhangs on both sides almost created a tunnel. A few empty wagons and people stood around, talking, but he pushed by them all to stop at yet another, even smaller intersection. The backstreets of the city could be a maze at times. Goll looked one way and then the other.

There—a man with a familiar face wandered along with a sack in his hand. The night had been dark and rainy, but Goll still remembered the son who'd accompanied his father to the healer's house, to speak with Junger.

"You there," Goll called out, turning the young fellow in his tracks. He was perhaps in his thirties, with a dark complexion and thinning hair. His face fell when he recognized the house master.

"Usually takes longer for a person to dislike me," Goll said as he closed the distance.

The son studied him, frowning at the mess of his face. "You're one of the gladiators? That House of Ten?"

That actually lifted Goll's spirits. "I am."

"What happened to you?"

"I won a fight."

Oh, the son mouthed. "I barely recognized you."

"It was dark. Raining."

The son nodded with a heavy sigh, his eyes straying.

"I wanted to ask a question," Goll went on. "About your father."

The son's shoulders slumped. "My father's passed on."

The news stopped the house master cold.

"That night, in fact," the son explained. "Just after talking with you and that other one. The one father called Arco."

"Arco?" Goll repeated.

"Aye that. Arco."

A moment of silence passed then as people edged their way around the two men.

"I'm sorry to hear about your father's passing," Goll finally said.

"It was his time. He was seventy-eight. Closing in on nine. Passed on in his sleep, so there's that, I suppose. Although who really knows if that's painful or not. He looked peaceful enough. We found him the next morning, my wife and I, when he wouldn't rise for breakfast. What question did you have?"

The news disarmed Goll. "Just . . . what you talked about. Your father and Junger. I was inside at the time."

"Out of the rain."

Goll nodded. "Out of the rain."

The son thought about that night. "My father asked your pit fighter there, the one called Junger, how old he was. The man said twenty-seven. My father then said that Junger . . . resembled a man he knew a very long time ago. When he was a boy. His village was invaded, you see, by a pack of bandits. This happened to the north and east of the city. Days away. There were no Lancers patrolling the area at the time, I suppose. In any case, the bandits moved in during the night and, by morning, called themselves kings. They killed and raped and killed again. Burned and butchered livestock. Men and women were hanged from trees or . . . well . . . the usual acts of butchery, you understand. The kind whispered about in alehouses. They did unspeakable things to those people. Anyone with a sword was killed. Am I boring you?"

The question brought Goll's wandering thoughts back. "No. Apologies. Please continue."

The son studied him, wondering if he should. Then he decided to carry on with the story. "You don't know my father. He was old, yes, but his mind was sharp. Even after meeting your pit fighter, my father told me that even his *voice* sounded the same. My father remembered that voice—that sound—ever since he was a young boy."

"What are you saying?" Goll asked, a chill sweeping over him despite the humid air.

The son paused, stricken with pain. "I don't know. All I know is . . . when my father was a boy, those bandits turned his life and his village into Saimon's hell. For one week, they suffered under a group numbering about three dozen or so. Killers all. Swaggering brutes who knew they were in control, who knew they could torment anyone living in that place without fear of punishment. Until one day, a swordsman walked into the village and killed the entire pack. Swept through them all like a . . . like a torch burning cobwebs. Fighting a running battle through homes and alehouses, over bridges and in fields. Not just that pack, mind you, for the bandits had sent word to a second group. Perhaps about how they'd found a good place for the winter. The second pack was about the same size, and a day after the swordsman killed the first group, he met and killed the second. Having done all that, he stayed within the village for three days more, and on the morning of the fourth day, he was gone. People saw him retire the night before, no one saw him leave, yet the little room he was given to sleep in had been used."

The son gathered his thoughts.

"Was this Arco a Perician?" Goll asked.

"I don't know where he came from. My father never said . . . but . . ." The son shrugged. "He might've known. He remembered everything else about that time. The weather. The things done. The faces of the bandits. It was a horrible thing for a child—any child—to live through. Seeing people you know being killed, knowing you might perish at any time. He remembered the face and the manners of the man who saved his people from those terrible men. I listened to those stories enough times to remember them all. None of what happened is . . . imagined. My father believed your Junger . . . is the man called Arco, who killed over sixty bandits by himself."

Goll's chill became greater. "What do you believe?"

The son hesitated. "Perhaps my father's approaching death twisted his memory in ways I don't know. I've heard it happening to others. Parents unable to remember their own children, thinking them strangers. Some recognized people who don't know them. I've heard of some old ones speaking to people who aren't present in the room."

"So you believe he was imagining . . . this Arco."

"I don't know," the son admitted. "He seemed well enough to me. Right up until he went to bed. He bade me and my wife a good night, even patted me on the head before retiring. The last time I felt his touch or heard his voice. I ask you, would he know if his nearing death was twisting his memory? To somehow . . . lead him to believe that your man resembled that hero of long ago? I don't know. In any case, he passed quietly in the night. I think . . . he was fortunate that way. May we all pass that way."

"He was fortunate to have you," Goll said quietly, and the words crushed something inside the son. His eyes became red and watered, and he clamped down on a quivering jaw.

Goll reached out and gripped the son's shoulder. "Thank you for speaking. I'm truly sorry for your father's passing."

The son nodded, covering his face with one hand, and looked away.

Goll gripped his shoulder once more before releasing him.

The house master walked away then, heading for the arena.

Harook of the Stable of Slavol stood within the private chamber, already sweating under his armor despite the cloth padding. A scratched but polished vest of leather protected his torso, while beautifully wrought bronze bracers and greaves shaped as intertwining tree roots covered his limbs. A steel helm with the disturbing visor of a screaming man lay on a bench nearby. Men moved about his person. They were fellow gladiators, the training staff, and Salwark himself. The owner's son stood near the window, his profile drawn and pensive in the intense daylight. He played with his upper lip while staring outside, lost in thought.

Harook spared him only a glance. He didn't need to think about the owner's son this day. He thought about the one called Goll and how he was going to defeat and kill the man. The Kree had taken a few lives belonging to the stable, and Aidas and Sorban had been friends. Sorban in particular had helped him with his strike combinations, suggested better follow-up movements, and advised him to reduce attacks that were mostly flash and wasted energy. For a young gladiator, having a senior take an interest in what he was doing meant everything to Harook, and like several around him, he had been stunned when the Kree killed Sorban. He wasn't very surprised when Aidas failed to dispatch the Ten gladiator, not after the deaths of Sorban and Zillari, and he was shocked at the lack of pit fighters willing to pursue Goll for a blood match—especially Punder and Urson. Those two had also benefited from Sorban's quiet aid. Harook held back when the lady Zelia had asked both men about fighting Goll. Punder had shifted the question to Salwark, and Urson wouldn't even answer the woman. So when the lady stood among them, so small and yet so powerful, Harook waited, waited for either Punder or Urson to change his mind and volunteer to fight Goll. Though he was keeping ranks, he was damn near bursting, willing them to accept the challenge.

Then it became obvious they would not.

So Harook volunteered even though he suspected he would perish like the rest. He'd given ample time to the most experienced remaining among them, and when no one stepped forth, he didn't want lady Zelia to walk away thinking them all cowards.

Later that day, however, Harook learned that both men doubted they could defeat the Ten gladiator. They didn't say so, but Harook overheard them speaking to their companions, reasoning that if Goll could kill Sorban, Zillari, and Aidas, they wouldn't have a chance against him either. They added that

Salwark thought the same way since he hadn't chosen either of them to avenge the deaths. They also didn't appreciate Harook making the attempt, their sullen looks making their thoughts clear on the matter. Nor did Harook's other so-called sword brothers believe he could kill the Kree. That was obvious as well in their half-hearted words of encouragement and in how they nodded at him as if fully expecting him to be carried off in a wagon . . . even old Thurlo, Mal, and Irva.

They all expected him to die.

Harook avoided everyone after that, not needing their doubtful looks or their flat words of encouragement.

He possessed enough doubt for all of them.

Near the window, the taskmaster and trainers gathered around the owner for a talk. Harook watched them for a moment before he felt eyes upon himself. He glanced to his right and saw Punder sizing him up.

Harook looked away, focusing on what was to come.

The chamber door opened, and in walked lady Zelia, accompanied by a pair of gladiators. She crossed the floor, her dark robes swishing, a cowl pulled lightly over the top of her head. She stopped before Harook and fixed him with those blue eyes, hard and searching. The sun had darkened her face even more, it seemed, and though he knew she was Sorban's widow, he still thought her lovely.

"Avenge him," she said.

"I will," Harook promised.

Her message delivered, she proceeded to the window, where her presence killed all discussion among Salwark and the others. The owner's son clearly forced out a greeting, followed by a display of enthusiasm so feigned it soured Harook's guts.

Taskmaster Thurlo broke away from the gathering and walked over to the waiting gladiator. He stopped before Harook and inspected him. The once Sujin took his time and, after a nod, locked eyes with the young pit fighter.

"Who are you?" the scarred man asked in a tone not to be questioned.

"Harook of Sunja."

"What are you?"

"A gladiator of the Stable of Salwark."

"What do you do?"

"Punish any that oppose me."

"What are you going to do today?"

"Kill a man."

"How are you going to do it?"

Harook didn't blink. "The bloodiest way possible."

Though Thurlo might have doubted him the day before, he showed no signs of such right then.

Harook appreciated that.

"Dying *Seddon*," Goll barked, losing composure as the helmet slipped over the stitched side of his face. He glared at Koba, who'd been the one pulling on that final bit of armor. "Fit the damn thing over my *head*, not pull it to my shoulders."

The big trainer drew back in quiet annoyance.

"You didn't put enough grease on there," Goll then fired at Shan, who stood nearby with wet fingers poised over a small container.

"I greased it enough," the healer replied defensively.

"He did grease it," Muluk added, stepping into the picture. "It was all glistening and such. Like a honeypot's crack."

Goll dabbed at his neck for blood.

"What are you doing?" Shan asked. "There's no blood."

The house master didn't reply as he studied his fingers.

"Nothing," Shan said. "See? Six stitches and everything is holding. You're sealed up well enough to float."

"We'll see about that after the fight," Goll said.

"I'm not responsible for that. I said float. Not open up another man. I've done all I can, and that cut's sewn. What happens from here on is entirely your responsibility."

Having had enough of the healer, Goll looked toward Clavellus and Machlann, standing at the window. "What's happening out there?"

Machlann craned his head about like some harsh owl, studying the house master, while Clavellus peered outside and frowned at the heat. "Nothing."

Four fights had already been fought and decided, all of them Free Trained. The prisoners remained absent, not that anyone seemed to care. The pit fighters rising from the nest known as general quarters had hacked and chopped at each other with all their unskilled might and vigor.

A knocking came from the door.

"That's you," Clavellus said, turning. "Time for the real show. Do what you've been doing all this time."

To that, Muluk uneasily kept his mouth shut. Goll met the eyes of his countryman and had a good idea of what he was thinking.

Goll rose from his bench and held out his hands. Koba provided him with sword and shield.

"Fortune to you," Clavellus said.

Goll didn't comment. He gripped those battlefield tools and walked to the door, passing Junger. When he'd arrived at the Pit, Goll dressed for battle and ignored the Perician. He didn't have the time to talk about the old man dying in his sleep, and he needed his mind clear and focused on the task ahead.

On the one called Harook.

The men wished him well as he departed. Skarrs lined the white tunnel, perhaps a few more than usual, the shade lending their polished shirts of armor an almost dreamlike quality. Goll marched by them all, feeling that unpleasant coating of grease along the side of his face while fighting down the urge to flex his profile. The helm was bigger, but not by much, and for that he was partly responsible since he'd chosen the unfit thing. The heat trapped in the tunnels added to his annoyance. Sweat soaked his cloth padding, clinging to his skin like a pissy afterthought.

These glorious games, he thought blackly, passing flickering torches.

His eye wasn't affected, not yet anyway, but he knew, just *knew*, that with one good blow to the head, everything would open in a gush. The goal was, now more than ever, to meet his opponent head-on, finish him quickly, and get out of the Pit. The sooner he was done, the sooner Shan could administer whatever foul juices or salves he possessed to quicken the healing. The question that plagued Goll, however, wasn't how fast he could defeat the one called Harook.

It was whether or not to kill him.

As an example to the others.

He remembered what Clavellus had said, what Muluk had said, and even the talks with Junger himself. The Weapon Masters of Kree encouraged the quick dispatching of a foe, but Goll now wondered about the wisdom of such an action. Killing them removed the gladiators from competition, and while it might unease future opponents, it also angered the vengeful ones, perhaps even motivating them, inspiring them, even.

Before long, he stood alongside the gatekeeper, who regarded Goll with a squinty-eyed silence. The old man's chin bobbed as though he was chewing on a piece of meat. The gatekeeper didn't bother with words of encouragement, and that suited Goll just fine.

Above, the portcullis allowed light to spill over the staircase. The crashing murmurs of thousands rolled past Goll's ears, quickening his blood.

The gatekeeper pulled a lever, and the metal at the end of the stairs rose.

Goll jogged forward, climbing the stairs, hearing the Orator's words over the rising excitement of the crowds. The speaker for the Pit had already started his introduction.

"Facing the wrath of an older house," the old man was explaining, his voice carrying across the arena, "and fighting for the third time in as many days, this pit fighter once again rises to the challenge. Kree by birth, trained by masters, and belonging to a house emerging from a tangle of Free Trained warriors, this man has shown that he truly belongs in the Pit. He belongs upon the grandest of spectacles of our time, and perhaps even one day, he'll be remembered along with the Pit's greatest legends. Cutting a bloody path through the gladiatorial ranks and not caring in the least who he butchers next, I give you . . . *Goll*, from the House of *Ten*."

The audience burst into cheers, their greeting only slightly ruined by taunts and insults. Goll emerged from the entrance, the day's heat striking him with terrible force and slowing him in his tracks. He gasped at the sharp rise in temperature, took a moment to adjust to the sun, and eventually realized the cheering continued.

For him.

That surprised Goll.

And it was much stronger than any other time. Goll took a moment to look around, taking in the vocal encouragement and the pumping fists. The thought of winning the Pit's approval had never been in his mind, but he had to admit it was better than being cursed at.

Then he saw the man waiting for him, already introduced and standing before the opposite portcullis—the next challenger sent from the Stable of Slavol.

"Begin!" the Orator shouted.

The man called Harook walked across the glowing sands.

Goll went to meet him.

Standing rigid while nervously snacking on his fingernails, Salwark watched the two gladiators approach each other. A sun-bleached pattern of onlookers raved in the background, their numbers threatening to spill over the arena wall. Salwark didn't think Harook could defeat Goll, much less kill him—not really. He cursed himself for hoping otherwise, however. He cursed himself for allowing Zelia to once again watch the fight from the chamber's windows. If Harook failed, Salwark had already made the decision to send forth Punder, as much as it felt as though he would be condemning the gladiator to death.

If Harook failed, he would have to report it to his dying father, and that troubled him even more.

Very much aware of Mal on his left and Zelia on his right, Salwark dearly wanted a mug of something exceptionally strong. He forced what he hoped was a convincing smile to his face and nodded at his unwanted guest.

Zelia scowled back. Looming just over her head, Thurlo cocked an eyebrow, missing the woman's expression entirely.

Salwark cringed inwardly and turned back to the match, fearful of the verbal lashing and shaming to come.

36

Narrowed eyes lurked just inside the slits of that screaming face of steel. Harook circled, his sword and hand axe held at guard, weapons moving in anticipation. He moved right for a few steps, then left, content to simply study his opponent.

"She wants you dead," the man said in a controlled voice that didn't match the helmet's expression. Goll barely heard the words over the crowds' swelling want for violence.

"And she's sent you," the house master said, his shield raised, his eye twitching at not only the glare off the gladiator's head, but the sweat and grease edging closer to his lid. The sensation could not have happened at a worse possible time.

"I volunteered," said the screaming face.

Harook sprang to the attack, sword and axe chopping in a well-practiced weave. Goll parried two blows, and the connections met with the crowd's approval before he broke off and retreated a few steps—only to charge back in, initiating his own series of strikes, limbs moving without thought. Harook stopped three sword thrusts, deflecting each, before ducking and backpedaling, barely escaping a wide slash meant to take his head from his shoulders.

Goll hunted for an arm with a vicious over-the-top strike and finished the combination with a shield punch.

Harook darted away, kicking up dust in his wake.

Goll didn't pursue, content to let the other gladiator go. Inside his helmet, however—the new one barely large enough to fit his injured head—his eye continued to twitch. He squeezed it shut, dearly wanting to rub at the thing.

Seddon above, he swore.

Sensing a lull, Harook rushed his adversary.

Goll suddenly flared to life, meeting the attack.

The pit fighters stood, not two strides apart, and hammered out a destructive tune upon sword and shield and axe. Each man sought to break the other's defenses, but each also thwarted the other's rhythm. With sunlight flashing off their armor, they both grappled, becoming tangled, before shoving off.

Upon parting, however, Goll stabbed Harook's shoulder.

The quick jab connected, collapsing the man, and pulling a collective gasp from the onlookers. The strike was a blur, barely noticed, but the result was clear. Blood ran freely down Harook's side, passing his waist and the leather strips protecting his lower bits, spreading to his knee. The man swayed, favoring his wound.

Goll pounced, seeking a quick finish.

And he was nearly run through the middle when Harook lunged to meet him, pushing off from the sands in a powerful rush. Goll crashed his shield into the man's head, rocking that screaming face aside, but a sword bounced off the Kree's armored midsection. They fell to the ground in a wave of gold, weapons flashing in the sun. Goll fell onto his back and kicked, planting a solid boot into Harook's leather gut, pushing him off and heaving him into the sand. That bit of space allowed the gladiators to stand and right themselves. Bent over with shoulders heaving, the two pit fighters studied each other. Blood colored the sand in places, thick blots resplendent in the sun.

Harook charged, speeding forward like a battering ram powered by a team of brutes. He struck high then low, his sword jabbing, probing, while his hand axe rose and fell in wicked tandem.

Goll parried everything while giving up ground, almost losing his own sword in a practiced hook meant to disarm him. When he retreated, Harook followed . . . and truly stepped up the pace. The man's speed was surprising, his strength shocking, and the angles he attacked awkward. Hindered by his eye, Goll found himself purely on the defensive, dodging, darting, stopping his opponent's blade from penetrating his guard, taking punishing axe strikes upon his shield.

Then Harook slipped his sword past Goll's guard, the tip hammering into the Kree's hard leather vest. The steel deflected off the midsection and slipped underneath an arm, opening a piece of unarmored flesh.

That shocking burning instant cost Goll the initiative.

Harook hooked and yanked Goll's shield down with his hand axe, creating enough of a breach for the Salwark fighter's sword to streak forward in a ballista shot of motion. All Goll felt was the savage pull of the axe, the forceful pull upon his shield, before he glimpsed that straight blade firing toward his face.

Reflex alone saved him from the sword punching through his visor.

As it was, the blade still cracked into the right side of his skull, twisting his head upon his shoulders.

"Damnation," Clavellus whispered at that frightening impact, his eyes unable to blink.

That metallic clap sent a shiver up the length of his old spine.

"*Damnation!*" Salwark squawked and immediately caught himself.

Zelia hadn't noticed, however.

Stars filling his vision, Goll rolled with that jarring blow, his helm half blinding him. He glimpsed a dark shape moving in and so lashed out with his shield, whirling, before punching out with his sword, knowing full well his life might very well depend on it.

Two things happened in a rush of movement, all within an eye blink.

The shield and hand axe smashed together.

Goll's sword barely missed the back of Harook's head.

The pit fighters found themselves in close quarters once again. Harook stabbed downward, his blade coasting along a greave until it slid across leather binding and calf meat.

An unexpected, paralyzing jolt seized Goll then, and he collapsed in a heap.

"I have you," Harook said just as Goll, on his knees, pulled up his shield and braced for impact. A sword pounded into that buffer, and Harook stepped into the blow. He towered over the stricken Ten man, standing over him, striving to get one decisive stab past the upraised shield.

Goll realized the close quarters, realized he was practically between his adversary's legs. With everything he had remaining, he hammered his sword's pommel into the leather strips protecting Harook's thigh.

That one crippling strike staggered the Slavol pit fighter.

And instead of killing his adversary with a quick stab from above, Harook toppled over Goll in a dangerous sprawl.

"*Get up!*" Clavellus yelled, startling his nearby trainers.

"*Get up.*" Salwark lurched, the words coming out in a wheezy whisper.

The two pit fighters rolled to their knees, creating a space between themselves.

Goll lifted his shield, and Harook smacked it back down with his hand axe. Goll cracked his sword's pommel across that screaming face. That pitched Harook to the left, but he didn't fall. Goll struck him again, clanking that hard knob of steel into the visor. Harook steadied himself and replied with two crushing blows of his own, punching Goll's helm three times in rapid succession. The hits came so quickly, so unexpectedly, that the Kree fell over backward, his knees and legs screaming at being plied so.

Goll released his shield and sword. His legs straightened out like war bows with their strings cut. The arena was screaming. The world was screaming. He saw nothing but darkness and felt the earth's sizzle underneath himself. He stared, blinking, before turning his one good eye to the only source of light.

His own helmet's eye slit.

He could just see through the thing.

And managed to see Harook get to his feet and brandish a sword.

"Seddon above," Salwark cried with excitement as Harook stood over the fallen Kree. "He's won!"

Thurlo watched, his jaw set. Trainers Mal and Irva tensed and held their breaths.

Even Zelia stood and stared.

Harook stepped between Goll's knees, the Sunjan's armored frame rising and falling with every breath. The screaming face looked toward the stable's window while the crowds shouted for action.

Harook pointed his sword at the window.

"Yes, yes, yes, *kill him*," Salwark blurted with a flutter of his hands.

Just then, Goll cocked one leg and pistoned his boot heel deep into Harook's crotch.

The world groaned at that rock-solid connection.

Even though Harook had protected his man bits with an iron cup, one desperate boot to the kog and bells was still enough to drop him to his knees. He released his weapons as if stricken with some foul stomach sickness, and he seemed to ponder what had just happened for a fleeting heartbeat, just before he toppled onto his side.

Goll rolled away from the gladiator drawing in upon himself.

The Kree rose like some bleeding sand hellion most displeased, and he righted his helm. He shook himself and stood panting. Once that was done, he looked about for a sword. Locating one, he picked it up and held it weakly at his side for a moment, as if basking in the sun's heat. It seemed as though half the audience was roaring their displeasure at the unexpected turn of events, while the others were cheering wildly.

Goll didn't care about either group.

He lumbered over to Harook's paralyzed form, avoiding the gladiator's drawn-up legs. He turned the man over with a boot, falling to his knees upon doing so. There, Goll pulled an arm away, and planted a knee into an elbow's crook. With his opponent thus spread apart, Goll gripped that screaming face, righted it, and located the eyes within, which were wincing in pain and shock.

Goll cocked his arm.

Finish your foes, the Weapon Masters of Kree had instructed him. *Leave no one to challenge you in the future.*

Goll gathered his strength, intending to drive the sword through that exposed apple of a throat.

Then Harook's eyes opened, focused weakly on Goll, before flicking to the sky above, as though looking upon it for the very last time.

Only to return to the Kree.

Harook waited for the sword to strike, watching, fully aware of what was about to happen.

That sharpening of the senses, the understanding within, halted the Kree's arm and brought him back to another time, to the very first day, when he had made his entry upon the arena's sands and endured a terrible beating at the hands of Baylus the Butcher. Goll had fought back, even mounting the Balgothan in the end, and watched him look about much like Harook did just then. The memory stayed the killing stroke, and Goll hung there, poised to plunge the sword into his defeated foe.

TO THUNDEROUS APPLAUSE

No one needs to perish here this day, boy, the Butcher whispered from beyond.

Then Muluk spoke in his head, cautioning him about that very thing.

Then Clavellus joined in, telling him to forget about what family the man underneath him might have.

Finally, Junger spoke up, asking him why he did what he did to his opponents.

"What's he doing?" Salwark gawked and asked for them all.

No one answered, but Zelia released a grunt of disbelief.

"He's hesitating," Clavellus said, mortified despite his outward calm. "Saimon's crusty pisspot, why is he hesitating?"

The crowds pleaded for Goll to end the fight, screaming at him with all their vocal might. He ignored them and focused on those pain-paralyzed eyes beneath him.

Then the Kree remembered something else.

"Is she watching?" he demanded.

Harook's eyes narrowed in confusion.

"Is she watching?"

The trapped gladiator slowly blinked, fearful to make any move, knowing if he did, it would mean his life. He nodded, barely.

"Where?"

Harook's eyes rolled. He turned his head in the direction of the Stable of Salwark's window.

"Yield," Goll ordered, grimacing under his helm, his skull hurting from both sustained hits and the pulsating screeching from the audience.

Harook's left hand was perhaps only a stretch away from his axe. A fast gladiator could grab that weapon. A very fast gladiator could grab it and perhaps catch the slower, noticeably wounded one. The Sunjan didn't move at first . . . then, Harook's hand lifted a finger off the sand.

Goll watched him from behind that unwavering sword.

Harook's hand quivered, as though he was considering his chances, before finally being raised into the air.

Part of the audience groaned so loudly that Goll winced. The Kree, however, didn't relent, didn't drop his sword. He leaned over slowly, carefully placing the weapon's edge to Harook's neck.

"Give her a message," he said, making himself heard. "You tell her . . . I'm sorry . . . for killing her husband. You tell her . . . to give up . . . these challenges. If she doesn't, I'll kill the next miserable maggot she sends after me. And anyone after that. I'll kill them all. Every one. Until your house master doesn't have a fighting man left. You tell her."

Goll stopped for a breath then said, "You tell *him*."

Harook's eyes had cleared. He nodded once again.

"Is this fight done?" Goll asked.

Harook hesitated. "It is."

Goll pulled back his blade as if to stab, and someone among the onlookers screamed. He drove the sword into the sands with a puff of grit, not two fingers away from Harook's features.

The Sunjan cringed, still very much in pain, and uncertain as to whether he still lived.

He did, however, and a moment later, Goll rose from the defeated man. Goll turned his back on the gladiator, leaving him in the dust, and took his time turning, studying the spectators.

The Pit thundered in approval.

A few heartbeats later, Goll peered at the window belonging to the Stable of Salwark. He could see people there, but none of them were women.

Placing a steadying hand to his head, the victorious Kree took his time walking off the arena sands.

That slow deliberate strut silenced Salwark, and the elation he'd experienced only moments before withered and died within his chest, leaving only the venomous ache of disappointment.

So close. The man had been so close. Salwark's gullet rose and fell as he lowered his head and glanced fearfully in Zelia's direction.

But the woman wasn't there.

Thurlo met his gaze and pointed at the door.

Where Salwark glimpsed Zelia as she disappeared from sight.

37

A warm welcome momentarily blocked out the little pains Goll had sustained during the match with Harook. Smiling faces greeted him, and he lifted a hand in acknowledgement, but he really wanted to be free of his helmet. Warm moisture slicked his neck, and he suspected most of it wasn't sweat. Clavellus was saying something. Muluk was waving his hands and gushing praise. Even old Machlann nodded in approval. All good.

But Goll couldn't care less at the time.

Passing them all, he walked over to an empty bench and sat down heavily, with an audible grunt made metallic by his visor. Koba stepped in front, and Shan was with him, giving instructions.

"Now," the healer said.

The helmet came off in a stinging black rush, and Goll squeezed his eyes shut against a blast of humid air. Just having that uncomfortable pot removed was a relief. Hands pushed cloth bandages against his face, warm and clean and pleasant to the touch. The firm contact alone was comforting.

"You paddled that lad," Muluk said with excited admiration. "Brutal match, but you pushed through it. You pushed through."

"Give me room," Shan commanded.

"Apologies."

"How bad is it?" Clavellus asked.

Goll opened his good eye, glimpsing the strained concern on the healer's face.

"Four of those stitches burst," Shan muttered in a none-too-pleased tone. He pulled the wad away from Goll's damaged profile. "I'll have to sew that up again. Seddon above. That was some fine stitching I'd done, as well."

"That's the business," the taskmaster said. "Your business is keeping him together as long as possible."

Shan fumed, not caring for the notion in the least.

"What else?" Clavellus asked.

"Nothing serious, as far as I can see," the healer answered. "He walked here. Goll. How are you feeling?"

"Well enough."

"You're dripping with every step," Clavellus said.

"I'm well enough," Goll said a touch more forcefully. "Tired is all. Do what you need to do, and fetch me a water bucket so I can wipe myself down."

Shan fussed over him, hissing at the old badges of battle and wincing at the new. Koba was there to offer fresh bandages and cloth when needed. Goll kept still, and when he opened his eyes, he spotted Junger through a fence of bodies, sitting on a bench. A smile covered the Perician's face, faint but pleasantly pleased.

"You spared him," Clavellus said from behind the healer.

Goll looked to the taskmaster. "I did."

"May I ask why?"

"I felt like it."

"You felt like it?" Clavellus repeated, not angry in the least. "Hear that, Machlann?"

"The he-bitch felt like it," the old trainer rumbled in amusement.

"Surprising," Clavellus continued. "Well, we'll see if Slavol feels like sending someone else after you. Someone better."

Goll didn't answer.

"What if they don't have anyone better?" Muluk asked, looking from one to the other. "What if that Harook fellow was their best?"

"Then you just might have fended off the Stable of Salwark," Clavellus said after a moment's thought. "Three dead. The last one beaten. They might very well have had enough of you."

"We'll wait the night," Goll said as Shan pressed a fresh wad of cloth against his right profile. The pressure sent a dull knife of discomfort through his skull.

"They're usually quick with their challenges," Goll added. "We should know soon enough if they want another go of it. But they might not."

"Why?" Clavellus asked.

"I spared that maggot out there so he could give them a message. That message was . . . if they keep coming, I'll kill each one."

Clavellus traded surprised looks with Machlann. "That just might do it," the taskmaster said.

"We'll soon find out." Goll settled back, too tired to say anything more.

So they waited.

And while they did, Koba helped Goll get to an acceptable state of cleanliness while Shan worked a needle and thread. The others watched the healer work. White bandages stained with deep shades of scarlet fell to the floor.

Every now and again, Goll looked toward the chamber's closed door, expecting a knock.

With two bottles of wine upon a silver tray before him, Salwark sat quietly in his father's study and waited—for Zelia. The Balgothan woman had left the arena before he could talk to her. He was grateful for that, in the beginning, until he had time to think matters through. For the rest of the afternoon, he waited for her to return, *braced* for her return, knowing she would eventually . . . yet she did not. Salwark thought deeply about Goll's message, delivered by a defeated and brutalized

Harook. Salwark thanked the man, thanked him for fighting such a close fight, and then stepped away to allow the healer to tend to the gladiator's injuries.

When Salwark and his stable left for home, he scanned the arena passageways for her, dreading catching even a glimpse. During a distracted walk along the city streets, he mistook several other women for Zelia until he finally believed her to be waiting at his front door. His anxiety grew, the closer he got to home.

She wasn't there, however.

The sense of unfinished business remained with him, ruining his appetite for dinner, so he retreated to his study and sat at the head of the table. A servant brought him a dish full of nuts along with the wine, of which he'd quickly finished a bottle. He would need the mental fortitude because he knew she was coming to see him. He would wager coin on it.

So he sat and waited, at times getting to his feet and opening the shutters to gaze outside. A servant arrived and lit the lamps, so that was fine—Salwark was already pleasantly pickled by that point. He even bade the man to bring two more bottles of wine. Salwark saw no reason to *not* get well and truly armored for the coming confrontation.

At the end of the third bottle, while he slumped in his chair, Zelia magically stood at the other end of the table. No servant had warned him, and no sound indicated her entrance.

"Lady Zelia," he blurted before checking his goblet. The wine had truly worked magic upon him.

The woman said nothing.

Salwark's attention went from her to the closed doors, amazed he hadn't even heard the knock—if there was a knock.

"Well," he said, gathering himself. "Won't you join me for a drink?"

He gestured at a second goblet.

Zelia stared, stern faced, wishing him dead by gaze alone.

"Apologies," he said and made a drunken attempt to straighten his robes. "I felt the need for wine. To settle my nerves. I apologize for how I must look, but truth be known . . . you frighten me at times."

He said those last few words with a smile, which quickly faded when she did not return it. "Apologies again. Poor manners indeed, especially for such a time. You would think my mother and father raised me better."

"One would think," she finally said.

He was grateful for that, thankful he wasn't facing a wine-conjured apparition.

"Will you sit?" he asked.

"No."

A dangerous silence passed.

"I know what you've come to ask," Salwark said with a heavy sigh. "I knew you would return. And the answer is . . . no. I will not send another man against the Kree."

Zelia's expression didn't change. She waited, allowing him to talk.

"After you left—quite unexpectedly, I might add—my man Harook returned. Beaten and bleeding, but he walked back to the chamber doors, which surprised and impressed me to no bounds. I'm obviously not a gladiator, but there was a day I wished I could've been. Not for the damage they could sustain or they could inflict upon a person, but for their inner strength. Their willpower is much greater than their physical strength. I admire that. Willpower was never one of my strengths, despite my best efforts. Ah, I've strayed off subject again. Apologies. Well, as the healer was fussing over him, Harook informed me that Goll issued a warning to the stable. He's a fierce one, that Kree. A killer. He's done in three of our lads this season, and he would have done in Harook as well, but he wanted to send a message. To us. Which is the reason he spared Harook when he could have easily taken his life. And that message is this . . . Goll said to tell you that he's sorry for killing your husband. He's sorry. That's significant, I'll have you know, for a pit fighter to say that, especially one with his growing reputation. Anyway, he said he's sorry. And more. He said that . . . if we pursue him, if we keep challenging him, that he'll kill the next man we send after him. That he'll kill any and all others we send after him until we have no one left to send."

Salwark paused then, his throat tightening. He took a drink and, having taken too much, downed the entire mouthful in a painful swallow. "I am sorry, Lady Zelia, but I cannot afford to send another gladiator after him. Truth be known, I don't have a warrior who might challenge the Kree, let alone kill him. No one. I'm not afraid to admit that, despite what you might say or think. Or do. For that, I'm truly sorry. I've failed you and the man who was, in my mind, a friend. As well as one of the best fighters under my father's roof. I will accept the Kree's offer, and I will not pursue another blood match."

He finished, gripping his goblet as though strangling a neck. He waited upon Zelia, whose appearance wavered then slipped from barely controlled anger to one of weary acceptance. The sudden shift caught Salwark off guard.

"You are right," Zelia said, her low voice easily heard in the study. "You have failed me."

Those words stabbed Salwark to his core despite three bottles of armor.

"You've failed me and Sorban. I saw that in the match with Harook. Thank him for me, please. For facing the Kree. He's a brave man. I appreciate the gesture, and I know Sorban would have as well."

"He almost won," Salwark pointed out.

"If he'd won, the Kree would be dead. No, it's clear to me that Goll is a level above you. He killed my husband, after all. I should have realized then how skilled the Kree is. I could . . . convince you to send more of your gladiators after him, but Goll would kill them. Kill them all. I see that now."

A part of Salwark wanted to protest that, but the defeated part of him slapped the notion down.

The silence became oppressive.

"What will you do?" he finally asked.

"Nothing that concerns you."

Feeling another stab to the heart, Salwark failed to conceal his pain. The woman was cutting him deep.

"Well," he nodded, deciding upon an offer of apology. "The Stable of Slavol owes you and your . . ." He caught himself before saying *family*, mentally cursing the wine. "Patience. With us. If there is anything we can do for you in the future. Anything at all. Please. All you need do is ask."

Zelia appeared to consider the offer, and for a moment, Salwark regretted even making it, for fear of what she might ask. Whatever was on her mind, however, didn't come out as she turned away from the owner's son and left the study.

Salwark watched her go.

The relief he felt was genuine.

If there is anything we can do for you in the future. Anything at all.

Salwark had a habit of speaking at length when he should remain silent. Zelia recognized that, and she realized he hadn't truly meant the offer. They were only words meant to ease their parting from each other. Zelia had no further use for the stable or the men belonging to it. They were useless to her.

When she turned the corner and proceeded down the street toward her home, she realized she didn't remember walking all the way back from the Slavol residence. Night was only a short time away, and the brightest of stars were already visible. Sorban had loved taking her to the hilltops, where the unobstructed beauty of the night sky only deepened as time went by. On those nights, they slept under the stars and returned home in the morning. Those were beautiful times, loving times.

All lost.

Zelia reached her little house with its tall roof and narrow strip of grass. She faced the front door and reached for her key. She paused, looking up and down the street for the likes of Boh. The man hadn't bothered her since their last meeting, but she still planned to go to the street watch in the morning and alert them to her problem. She was not going to live her life wondering if Boh was lurking in the shadows. The street watch would take care of the weaponsmith for her.

She had other plans to make.

And all of them concerned Goll.

When she closed and barred the main door behind her, Zelia went to the house windows and checked them all. Once she was satisfied her home was secured, she lit a candle, the only light she needed for the next part. She went to the fireplace and brushed its stony side until she freed a thread. She pinched its end and pulled, extracting a key from a sliver of a crack. Candlelight flickered as she moved with grim purpose to a corner of the main room. She parted the robes covering her legs, revealing the small scabbard strapped to her right thigh. The knife came out, the very weapon Sorban had given her, which she'd taken to wearing ever since her encounter with Boh. The blade glowed in the meager light. She moved a chair and dropped to her knees. The floorboards were well swept and smooth, and she ran her hand against the grain. She inserted a fingernail into a crack, inserted the knife's tip, and sank the weapon deep. Wood creaked. Fibers scattered. Zelia worked the tip into the floor and forced the plank back with a *squawk*. The floorboard popped up on one side, enough for her to grip and pull.

The plank came away.

She placed it to one side and sank both hands beneath the floor. With a grunt, she extracted a single strongbox, one of five she kept in the hiding place.

In Balgotha, the wife traditionally controlled the family wealth, keeping household finances in order, doling out coin when the husband or children required it. Sorban, being her man, had never asked her about how much coin she'd hidden beneath their floorboards. He trusted her completely, as he should.

A part of Zelia cursed herself for not having revealed just how much coin she had managed to save for their return to Balgotha. Even though she wasn't sure of the exact amount herself, she knew it was an impressive sum—more than enough to allow her and Sorban a comfortable life in their homeland—all taken from the games, his winnings and the winnings from the matches he'd instructed her to wager upon. Sorban wouldn't have left the games early even if he'd known about their amassed riches. He still would've fought to the end. He was like that.

In that respect, Zelia was the same.

She inserted the key and turned it.

The strongbox opened.

And she gazed upon its considerable contents.

38

"Mori," Sindra said, stepping out onto the steps of the alehouse.

The once enforcer turned, a question upon his shaven features. Another man, called Lute, stood beside him. Both had been employed by Sindra in the old days but were dismissed when Gurga took over their duties. Mori and his little gang hadn't liked being replaced by the big man, but they went all the same. Over time, they returned to the alehouse for drinks and food and pleasant conversation. That pleased Sindra, for even though she disliked the man then, she admitted he had changed for the better.

Thus, when she thought of hiring extra enforcers to relieve Gurga, for a short time at least, she thought of Mori and his pack. To her surprise and relief, the man accepted.

"Yes?" He wiped his forehead then cleaned his hand on his trousers.

"In case you've forgotten," Sindra said. "Anything Telda cooks and we don't sell, you're welcome to it."

That put a smile on the man's face. "I'd forgotten."

Lute's expression brightened, indicating he'd forgotten as well.

"Just so you know," she said. "We can't throw it out."

"Lords no," Mori said. "We'll eat it. Whatever's left."

"If there's anything."

"Understood."

Sindra gazed out at the streets, lit up by lamps and torches. Currents of people flowed in opposing directions. She realized that only the time of the day changed but not the volume of people—not until after midnight, at least.

"How are things?"

"Pleasant enough." Mori wiped his face. "Warm, though."

"Unfit warm," Lute added. They were both average-sized men, not terribly imposing, but they knew the work and the alehouse.

"Find anyone?" she asked.

Mori shook his head. "No one."

"Good."

"Do you really think the Sons will bother with this place?"

Sindra hadn't told Mori that Borchus was upstairs. She'd only told him that Gurga needed a rest as a result of overworking his shifts. Mori and his lads would only be needed for a few nights.

"I don't know," she said truthfully. "But I'm not one for taking chances."

"No, I suppose not."

"What's that supposed to mean?"

"Exactly that," Mori said. "You're not one for taking chances. Never were."

"Don't be taking jabs at me, young man, not if you wish to ever work here again."

"I wouldn't think of it," Mori said. "Not after so long. Ah, thank you again for remembering us, Sindra. We very much appreciate the work."

Lute nodded as well.

Sindra looked from one man to the other. "You're welcome. And thank you. Might as well go with who I know rather than strangers off the street."

"We're glad you did."

"I'm starting to like you more, Mori." Sindra smiled. "Keep doing what you're doing. I might change my mind about having extra enforcers about."

"Less work for all, then," he said.

Sindra shook her head, smelling the hope off the man. "We'll see. I'll have Telda bring you towels later on. Can't have you sweating like you are now. You'll keep customers away."

"The warmest night of the summer," Lute said.

"And the summer's not finished," she added and wiped away the perspiration on her throat. The layers under her dress were damp, and she knew the only relief to be had from the humidity would be in her hand fan, and working that only brought on more sweat.

Her thoughts then turned to Borchus and visiting him.

"Carry on, then." She left the two enforcers.

Three buildings back and cloaked in a pocket of darkness, Jaro stood just inside an alley and watched the front of the alehouse. The woman appeared and spoke to the pair of enforcers, who continued checking wrists in the absence of the much larger brute who normally guarded the entrance. The two men were new, but that wasn't important to Jaro's plans.

Who lay above in the locked room of the alehouse was very important to him.

Jaro still wasn't sure who was inside that bedroom, but he decided to stop wasting time trying to catch a glimpse of the man.

People walked by, not noticing the alley or the imposing man standing within it. Jaro watched the open window of the forbidden room, waiting for the night to deepen. He glanced at the sky overhead and decided the evening was late enough, decided the time had come.

Jaro stepped out of the alley and scratched the back of his neck for three heartbeats. Once done, he turned and returned to the darkness.

Across the street and atop one of the closed-up buildings, well above the glow of lamps and torches, a figure stood.

Then two more.

Unseen by the night traffic, the three men moved like ghosts across the roof, to the very edge. There they stopped and fussed until a plank slowly extended across the gulf between their building and the next. Jaro watched that piece of lumber stretch across the space and didn't hear a sound over the din of Sunja's nightlife.

The plank made contact with the next building, and one of the ghosts walked across it. The figure crossed without harm and, once on the other side, steadied the narrow bridge for the others. The two men scuttled across, carrying yet another plank between them. Once all three were across, they crawled across the roof and again extended the second plank to the next building.

Jaro watched those silhouettes make their way toward the alehouse.

Borchus lay atop his bed, stewing in his own juices. He glanced toward the open window and begged Seddon above for a breeze—just a little breeze—something to blow through and cool him off. The day had been murderous, but the night was worse, in a way. He could find no rest. He slept but awoke a short time later for unknown reasons. The blanket had clung to him unpleasantly, and he kicked it off halfway through the day and simply lay there with a thin towel across his private bits, sweltering in the heat. A pitcher lay upon the bedside table nearby, but even the water was warm and brought no relief, no comfort. His bandages, thick and changed for the day, absorbed some of the sweat but left him feeling miserable, as if he were swaddled in filth.

Borchus longed for winter.

The merry sound of drunken socializing seeped through the floorboards, and that didn't do much for his rest either.

Borchus shifted and fixed upon the open window and the haunting glow of firelight just outside.

A key scratched at the lock, distracting him. He heard a rattle and a creak, and the door to the room opened. Sindra entered, her face darkened by shadow. She closed the door and stood there for a moment before crossing the floor.

"Awake, are you?" she asked, stopping at his bedside.

"How did you know?"

"Saw your eyes. They sparkle in the dark."

Borchus frowned.

"That lock on your door needs fixing," Borchus remarked.

"Is it loud?"

"Loud enough."

Sindra half turned, considering it. "It's a wonder you heard it at all with the noise from below."

Borchus said nothing to that, content to study her dreamy outline.

She took a step closer, her dress and leg pressing against the bed's lower framework. "You're sweating a lot."

"It's a hot night."

"It's summer. Would you like something to drink? Other than water?"

"No."

"I can see you from here," Sindra said in a soft tone. "You're practically glistening."

Borchus realized he was practically naked. Before he could do anything, Sindra sat down beside him, her hip touching his. That firm contact rendered him speechless, and his breath caught in his chest. He dared not move.

Sindra watched him, and before he could comment, she leaned forward, reaching below the bed.

"There's some spare hand cloths in this," she muttered, reaching past Borchus's shoulder, toward the floor. Perfumed water reached Borchus then, and its pleasant smell further robbed him of speech.

"Where are they?" she muttered, pawing through a sack. She hooked one cloth across the bedpost, partially covering Borchus wide belt, which had been left hanging there.

"You... might find them if you lit a candle," he suggested.

"I like the dark better."

"So do I."

She studied him then, her face round and radiant. Her eyes were black flickers of rock, but they focused on Borchus well enough, mesmerizing him.

"Borchus," she said, her voice barely a whisper. "I've been thinking."

"You want me gone by the morning," he muttered. "I'll truly try, but I can't guarantee—"

"Be quiet," she interrupted. "You never could listen when you needed to."

"That's true enough. Continue, then. What is it you've been—"

Her hand found his chest.

That shut him up.

"That's better," she said, smoothing over skin and bandages before stopping dead center on his heart. "Just listen for a moment. I've been thinking... What would you say if... if you and I... left the city?"

That silenced Borchus even longer.

"I've given it some thought, over the time you've been here, and I've decided that, truth be known, I don't think I want you to leave. Leave me, that is. Besides this place, you're the last thing I have that reminds me of Hadree... but I know you can't stay here. Not with what's going on. So... what would your thoughts be about, say, leaving the city? And going to, perhaps, Vathia. Or Valencia? We could open an alehouse in a city there. I've coin enough to do so. There's rumors that Sunja might lose the war, and I don't like the idea of being here for a siege. Or living under Nordish rule if we do lose."

Borchus slowly released his breath even though his heart was hammering. "Apologies, what did you say?"

That silenced her until she dug her fingers into his chest—and not in a playful manner.

Borchus grunted, feeling stitches stretch.

"Are you in pain?" she asked. "Good. Now I know you heard me the first time, so don't force me to grab something else of yours and squeeze until there's butter."

"I won't," he whispered.

"And don't insult me by asking for time to think," she warned. "You do too much thinking. Of the wrong kind. It's time to do some of the right thinking. You think about . . . about the place I had to go to, to even ask you such a thing. You think about that."

Borchus would, but in the meantime, he didn't say a word. He was still very much aware of her hip against his and her hand on his chest.

So they sat that way for a while and merely looked at each other. At some point, someone started playing a fiddle. The music flared to life briefly before halting on a half-finished note.

"What was all that about?" Borchus asked.

"What?"

"The music."

"Oh that. Probably Telda. Tell them to stop. Gurga is sleeping at the end of the hall. He's been working hard so he deserves a rest."

"Who's guarding the front door?"

"A couple of enforcers I've known for a while now."

"You trust them?"

Sindra thought about that. "I do."

"I see."

"Well?"

Borchus wouldn't tempt fate by toying with her. "When would we go?"

Sindra watched him, unmoving, long enough that Borchus thought she hadn't heard him, but then that lovely face stretched into a little but very pleased smile.

"When you're well enough."

"And this place?"

"Telda will mind it. Or, if she wishes, she could come along, and we could simply board up the place."

Borchus realized she'd been staring into his eyes for a long time, and her hand softly glided over his bandaged chest.

"We'll have to be careful," he said.

"Of course," Sindra replied. "Be sensible."

"I am."

"Yes. I suppose you are. At times, anyway."

She smiled at him and continued to smile until she patted his chest and rose.

"Where are you going?" Borchus asked.

"Away," she said simply. "You rest now. We'll speak again in the morning."

"In the morning?"

"Aye that, in the morning."

Borchus licked his lips, tasting the nasty residue left by the last treatment of saywort. His frown was one of distaste as well as frustration. Sindra walked to the door, and he swore he saw the flash of a smile before she turned away.

"Sindra."

She stopped, her back to him, her hand on the latch.

"Thank you," he said.

Her head rose then, as if she noticed a blemish upon the door's wood. Without a word, she opened the door and stepped outside. The door closed behind her, and Borchus was left in that not-quite-dark room, where the lamps glowed somewhere outside his window.

With a sigh, he adjusted the towel about his fruits and shook his head. He'd gotten a little too anxious that time, despite his shock and surprise at Sindra. He lay back upon the bed, no longer feeling the heat of the room. He replayed the brief conversation in his head, barely believing it had happened but still smelling her perfumed water, still feeling her hand upon his chest.

TO THUNDEROUS APPLAUSE

Considering her warning to him only a couple of weeks before, what had just happened was a complete shock. It was better than a cool breeze. And he couldn't believe his good fortune.

Borchus settled back and closed his eyes, knowing full well he wasn't going to sleep at all that night.

Wood creaked.

He opened his eyes and glimpsed a nearly naked torso poised in the window, the arm cocked back.

An instant later, something flew across the room and bounced off his head.

Sindra paused at the head of the stairs, looking back toward Borchus's room. She listened, waiting for that muted thump to repeat itself or at least for Borchus to swear a bit. Nothing of either sort happened, however, so she turned her attention to the main floor. She didn't descend right away though, as she eventually gazed upon the closed door to Gurga's room.

Her elation at Borchus's agreeing to leave the city with her fell just a bit. She knew the big enforcer would be hurt by her decision, but perhaps not too badly. She'd ask Telda if she wanted to join them as well. If she did, that was fine; if not, that was also fine, but Sindra would miss her friend. Telda would be taken care of—Sindra had always thought of turning ownership of the alehouse over to her, but she wondered if Gurga would stay and continue working. Again, her feeling dipped toward sadness, expecting a falling of faces once she explained her intentions.

And did she really plan on leaving the city with Borchus? After so long?

That stopped her, and her hand lingered upon the wooden railing that she'd polished for as long as she'd been living under Hadree's roof. Doubt filled her then, and she didn't push it away. Perhaps she'd been too hasty, but the choice felt right at the time.

Sindra went to the main floor, where a good number of people were either sitting or moving about, eating and drinking. She walked to the bar and slipped behind young Barrud as he served a few patrons. Her hand went over a few bottles of wine until she found the one she wanted and pulled it from the wall. A line of goblets waited underneath the bar, so she took one of those as well. A little wine would help her, but she couldn't help thinking it would help Borchus as well.

Without a second thought, she grabbed a second goblet.

Rough hands gripped his head and neck and pinched off his air.

Borchus couldn't breathe.

His eyes opened in a weak bulge as the fingers tightened about his throat. Two shadowy heads loomed over him, their faces hidden in black cloth. The smell of ash filled his nose.

"You Borchus?" one of them asked.

Borchus croaked an answer.

"You're holding him too tight," the other man said.

"Am not."

"You are. Look at his face. The lad's eyes are about to pop."

"Well, I'm not letting the punce go. If it is him, the wet bastard up and killed a dozen of our lads."

"It was eleven."

One head regarded the other. "Well, that's nearly a dozen, isn't it?"

"I'm just saying. Get your numbers straight."

"You'd argue about the color of shite, wouldn't you?"

"Are you going to let him answer?"

One head turned to Borchus.

Air rushed down the agent's throat in a much-needed gulp. Borchus intended to punch his strangler but the man not holding him put a length of edged steel to his throat.

"There now," the man whispered, his voice slightly muted by his mask. "Easy. Easy. You breathe and answer the damn question. Fight . . . and you'll be letting in more air than you care to. And letting out a bit more."

Borchus coughed, cleared his raw, stinging throat, and glared.

"Are you Borchus?"

The agent didn't speak.

The strangler shook his head. "Look, we'll kill you anyway if you keep quiet about it. Just say if you're Borchus or not, and we'll make it quick. That's all. No need to be a punce about it."

"Looks like him," the knifeman said, sizing up Borchus while keeping the blade firmly against his neck.

"Too dark to tell."

"He's a short one. Stocky."

"I could light that candle."

"No lighting candles," a third man, whom Borchus couldn't see, said from near the door.

He could see what appeared to be black markings upon his attacker's forearms.

The Sons of Cholla.

A chill overtook him then.

They'd found him.

Lords above.

"Certainly cut up enough," the strangler observed.

"Certainly is," the knifeman agreed and leaned in to better study Borchus's face. "Blocky, sideburns, bandages covering damn near everything."

"Short, too," the strangler said. "He's short."

"I see that."

"I say it's him."

"What do you think, Mero?" the knifeman asked.

The third man appeared over the shoulders of the pair. The dark head moved this way and that. "Looks like him."

"Just need the name," said the knifeman.

"I say kill him," the strangler said.

While they talked, Borchus swallowed, very much aware of the blade at his throat. Just overhead, however, he glimpsed the curl of his belt, hanging over the bedpost. The buckle's face gleamed in the near darkness, and Borchus realized that his hidden knife was very much within reach.

"What's your *name?*" the knifeman whispered into Borchus's face. "I'm telling you. You're going to die this night. It's the difference between going fast or going slow."

"Very slow," the strangler said.

"Hold on," Mero said and drew back from the discussion.

He went to the door.

The knifeman stared at Borchus, being far more careful than the agent had expected. Borchus looked at the buckled knife, knowing exactly where it was located, seeing the weapon's hilt facing him as if doing everything it could to help its owner.

Borchus looked into the masked face of the knifeman, who didn't waver in the least.

"Someone's coming," Mero said.

Telda came through the main doors leading to the kitchen and immediately saw Sindra with the wine and goblets. The cook's expression shifted into a sly smirk, which Sindra didn't appreciate. Frowning, she climbed the steps to the second floor amidst a dull roar of conversation and laughter. She was only sharing a drink with Borchus and nothing more—not a damn thing more. Perhaps they would talk a little, of course, as one has to talk while having a bit of wine, but that was it.

Still, she had to check herself from hurrying along.

A single lamp lit the second floor, which was more than enough to find one's way. Sindra paused at the top, hearing a great snore rip through the door of Gurga's room. Smiling despite herself, she walked past three doors before arriving at the one where Borchus was staying. She gripped the latch and realized darkly that she'd locked the damn thing upon leaving. Adjusting her items into one arm, she reached into her dress pocket and located the key.

Mero held up a hand, calling for silence.

The strangler relayed that by placing a hand on the back of the knifeman, who leaned into Borchus just a little more to whisper.

"Quiet now," he said. "Quiet. Or I'll open your throat."

Unknown to the knifeman, however, Borchus had already moved his right arm just a finger, enough to shorten the grab for the buckle knife overhead. He would have to be fast—the fastest he'd ever been in his entire life—but it was the only chance left to him.

Then he heard the familiar scratching of a key within a lock, and fear the likes of which he'd never experienced enveloped the whole of his person.

Years earlier

"All right, then," a young Sindra challenged with a smile. "What if I was being held captive by a pack of killers, and you were the only one in the room who could save me?"

"Killers?" an equally young Borchus asked, restraining his own smile. "What kind of killers?"

"What difference does it make what kind of killers? Killers should be enough. Especially if they mean to hurt me."

From the other end of the bar, Hadree sat and smoked a pipe while watching the entrance. Pleasing white curls hung on the air around him and drifted across the floor. He stared at the open doorway, where sunlight was framed in wood.

"I mean," Borchus stressed, "are they armed? Unarmed? Are they merely holding you or do they have a knife to your throat?"

"I still don't see the difference."

"Difference is in the level of threat," Hadree rumbled without looking.

"Exactly," Borchus said. "If they're only holding you, that's much better than, say, one of them having a knife to your throat."

Sindra considered that, her beautiful face thoughtful. Borchus could stare at that face for days.

"All right, they have a knife," she finally said. "And there's, say, three of them."

"Only three?"

"Three's enough."

"You're not a master swordsman, lad," Hadree remarked from the other side of the bar, and scratched the side of his face.

Borchus frowned at the older man and shook his head. He faced Sindra again, and they shared a smile.

"I'd warn them to let you go," Borchus said, resuming their conversation. "And make it clear that if you perished, they'd be next to perish."

"Really?" Sindra asked softly, detecting no untruths, as she shouldn't since Borchus meant every word.

"That and more," he said. "I'd never let anyone hurt you."

In the stillness that followed, where pipe smoke wafted like a dream, Sindra studied Borchus's face for long, considering moments before the prettiest smile seeped through.

"Careful, now," she warned. "Those are marrying words . . ."

The key found the lock much more quickly than before, jolting Borchus into action.

"*Sindra, don't open the door!*" he screamed.

And grabbed for the buckle knife.

The door opened, yanked by the one called Mero.

Borchus's scream startled the knifeman, who actually eased off on the blade poised at the agent's throat. Borchus's hand, so fast, streaked to the belt and clawed at the weapon, pulling it free with just the barest rustle of leather, while his other hand grabbed the knifeman's wrist.

Mero jerked Sindra inside and slammed the door, the darkness returning with a thunderclap.

As the knifeman bore down on his blade, Borchus whipped his buckle knife forward and buried it in the killer's face, plunging it to the hilt into an eye. The knifeman's head snapped back in a whip's arc of blood.

The strangler screamed.

Sindra screamed.

The strangler pushed the knifeman out of the way before lunging at Borchus with a gleaming knife.

Borchus released the buckle knife, leaving it in the dead man's head, only to grab the knifeman's weapon, which Borchus immediately rammed into the strangler's neck. All strength left the attacker then, and a horrible gurgle erupted from the dying man as Borchus pushed him off.

Borchus scrambled to his feet, thankful that the room wasn't spinning in the least, and froze.

The one called Mero had his back to the wall and Sindra in his clutches.

A knife was at her throat.

Weaponless, Borchus held up both hands, calling for a stop.

Mero watched Borchus over Sindra's shoulder, the killer's mouth close to her ear.

"What's his name?" he asked.

The question paralyzed Borchus, but Sindra didn't answer.

"Fair enough," Mero said.

And in that instant, Borchus knew the man meant to kill her. He rushed Mero.

Who pushed Sindra away, to meet Borchus's charge full-on.

Borchus slammed into the killer, feeling the knife stab his forearm repeatedly, slicing it up in a bloody flurry of strikes. Borchus punched the man's face twice before Mero countered, cracking a fist off the agent's temple.

All life left Borchus's legs, and he crumpled to the floor.

Mero grabbed a fistful of hair and yanked Borchus's head up. Far from recovered and rapidly burning through his remaining strength, Borchus powered forward as Mero stabbed him through the back. Things got slippery then. They crashed into a wall and rolled onto the floor. Borchus landed on top, mounting the other man. Mero wrenched the knife free with an ominous jet of ink. Borchus blocked a stab with his left arm again. He got his knee onto Mero's arm and drove a fist into the killer's throat.

That stunned Mero, who choked out a dying hiss, long enough for Borchus to grab the killer's knife and stab him in the face.

Mero's limbs stiffened as if gripped by a seizure, then relaxed just as quickly.

Gasping, Borchus slid off the dead man. Blood covered them both, but he paid scant heed to the mess. He immediately located Sindra.

She sat against the wall, her eyes tracking him, one hand pressed to her neck. A disturbing stream dribbled from between her fingers, and the front of her dress, normally gray and white, was a dire, glossy black.

With a moan, Borchus fumbled to her side. Sindra's face resembled a moon more than ever, and her eyes were deep and sunken. Keeping her hand to her neck, she watched him as he staggered side-on against the wall. Despite wanting to help her, Borchus felt the room begin its familiar yet torturous spin, and he slumped down beside her. The lamplight from the open window seemed to blaze, casting a starry hue across the floor, across a pond widening around their legs and feet.

"Apologies," Borchus sighed, a wind rising in his ears.

"For . . . what?" she whispered.

"Everything," he whispered back, a fire blazing around his core.

She smiled then, gently, tiredly. "Careful . . ." she murmured. "Those are . . . marrying . . ."

Her voice faltered. Borchus's eyes became moist then. He clutched her hand tightly while his head rested upon her shoulder. Her head drooped and softly touched his, and for the briefest of moments, an eternity in another place, they stayed that way, sitting together upon the floor, resting, as if all was quite fine with the world.

Then her other hand fell away from her neck, and the stream became a river.

Borchus held her hand, their fingers entwined . . . until his own grip failed him. Sindra didn't release him, however, and that pleased him immensely.

"Words," he whispered as he drifted off to his final sleep.

TO THUNDEROUS APPLAUSE

The window became a frame of light and stars.

And somewhere, along the edge of darkness, the room exploded in a rattle of wood and a bestial roar.

Jaro leaned against a wall to have an unobstructed view of the upstairs window. He watched as his three street snakes lowered themselves by rope onto the first-floor overhang. They gathered then, on the overhang, the enforcers below oblivious to the three men just above their heads.

Then they entered the room, and Jaro waited . . . waited and watched, his eyes fixed on the open window, willing one of his lads to appear and give the signal of yes or no. The occupant of the room would die either way. All Jaro wanted to know was if it truly was Borchus.

But none of his men appeared in the window. And Jaro, for the life of him, wondered what was going on until he thought he heard a man shout something about a door.

Jaro waited, listening.

There was no mistaking the second roar—that cry of rage and pain straightened Jaro's spine. He remained in the dark alleyway, waiting for a sign that the job was done, that Borchus—if indeed it was him—had been killed.

No sign came forth, however.

And not one of his killers appeared at the alehouse window.

Torchlight flickered to life, filling the upstairs window.

Jaro scowled at the sight. His lads had failed and were either captured or dead. Annoyance swelled within the Sons' enforcer then, and he watched the second floor of the alehouse for a bit. One of the enforcers at the main entrance retreated inside. Figures appeared in the window, both civilians and guards. They stuck their heads outside and found the dangling ropes his killers had used to lower themselves to the overhang.

The sight of all those people disappointed Jaro, and he decided the time had come to leave. He stepped out into the street and kept to the shadows, walking away from the scene at a leisurely pace. He would have others investigate what had happened in that upstairs room tomorrow, perhaps even use a contact with the street patrol to learn the finer details.

In any case, someone had died this night.

Jaro would find out who in the morning.

39

By midmorning, no word of a blood match had reached the Ten. Naulis had failed to make an appearance, and Goll actually looked forward to leaving the city. Clavellus did as well but advised to wait until the afternoon in case word arrived a little late.

No one came to Shan's house, however, so the house masters decided to leave.

They hired a third wagon for their journey, purchased supplies for the villa, and distributed both people and materials evenly across the three transports. The heat of the day made travel within the city a terrible thing, and not even the canvas covering their wagons provided much relief. As it was, the Ten's wagons rolled along the streets and slowed upon reaching the easterly gates. Soldiers checked the departing as well as the arriving wagons, and Goll overheard a conversation between the gate soldiers and a smaller group of four men, all Vathian, as hinted by their accents.

Trussed up in bandages, a recovering Goll only listened as long as it took the wagon driver, Bagrun, to steer through the gates.

The temperature eased off just a little upon their leaving the city, and when the three wagons reached the surrounding plains, a pleasant breeze greeted them. The bump and wiggle of the wagons relaxed the men of the Ten, and they watched Sunja and the plateau the city was built upon recede behind them. Thickets of forest and the odd hill periodically broke the surreal flatness of the prairie. Goll slept at times, near the rear, where the air was freshest. Every now and again, he came close to waking, hearing soft conversations between Muluk and Clavellus, the only other occupants. Other times, the trip was quiet, and the only sounds were the driver's urging of the horses and the jostling of the wagons.

The sky deepened with color, only to grow pink later in the evening.

Goll awoke to greetings and straightened to discover nighttime had come. Muluk rose with a limp, rubbed at his backside, and smiled at his countryman.

"Home again, lads," Clavellus announced and walked to the tailgate, where he lowered himself to the ground.

Home again, Goll thought wearily, wondering if it was indeed his home.

Muluk clapped him on the shoulder, urging him to get out. "Rise and get to bed. You'll have a busy tomorrow."

"I will?" Goll asked.

"I don't know. I only said that because I expected you to say those very words to me."

"You can do what you wish tonight."

Muluk's brow bounced with impish glee at the thought, and Goll knew the man intended to drink. He'd heard both Muluk and Clavellus sharing a bottle of mead on the way back, a sample of several dozen bottles the taskmaster had purchased on the way out of the city.

Muluk offered a hand. Goll took it.

"I haven't said it," the shaggy-looking Kree muttered, "but I think you did a fine thing by sparing that lad."

"We'll see, won't we?" Goll said.

"Suppose we will. Need a hand getting off this thing?"

Goll answered him with a scowl.

"Leave the unloading for the morning, lads," Clavellus ordered and spotted his wife, walking from their home toward him.

"Well, isn't this a surprise?" he said and smiled.

"You were gone a few days longer than I expected," Nala said as he took her hands and gave two quick kisses to her cheeks.

"Everything well?" he asked.

Nala thought about it for a time. "Everything is better. Come inside and leave all this for the morning. I'll tell you everything that's happened here."

"Anything wrong?"

She shook her head. "Only that we lost a horse. Brozz took a turn for the worse, so I had to send Pirrus away to Pynn's Brook to locate a healer. Well, the poor man got lost during the night and unfortunately lost his horse when it snapped a leg. Poor thing stumbled down an unseen rabbit hole."

Clavellus made a face at that.

"I know," Nala sympathized. "I don't like the thought of losing an animal either. In any case, Pirrus eventually made it to Pynn's Brook only to discover their healer had been summoned away, so he had to wait until he returned. Meanwhile, we discovered some hidden talents in our armorer."

That befuddled Clavellus for a moment.

"Ajik?" he asked in mild disbelief.

The Perician got off the wagon, stretched, and nodded at the familiar faces belonging to the villa guard. The country air was clean and warm and good. He took a moment to study the walls and the scattered torches burning before turning toward the gladiator barracks. They were the same as when he'd left, and he passed through the common room and into the sleeping quarters, where snoring greeted him. A low-burning lamp illuminated the hall and the many niches containing bunks for the gladiators.

With thoughts of sleep, Junger looked for his bed.

He stopped at a familiar post, where he stretched out his neck and peered inside.

"Not dead yet?" he asked.

A little smile crossed Brozz's features. "Not yet."

"How goes the mending?"

"It goes, Perician. How goes the fighting?"

"It goes."

A loud rattle of a snore distracted Junger then. "Lords above. Is that Torello? No wonder you're still awake."

"I sleep well enough. When it's time."

"Well," Junger said and leaned against the post, "it's time for me though I doubt I'll be sleeping right away. Not with that windstorm."

"It's not so bad."

"I suppose Shan will be along shortly. See how you're doing."

"I'll be glad to see him."

"You're in a right sociable mood, aren't you?"

Brozz smiled again. "Suppose I am. Are you too tired to talk, Perician?"

"With you, Sarlander? Never too tired. I can spare a moment. You can tell me what's happened these past few days at the villa."

"I'd much rather hear about the games."

"I can do that."

So they talked and listened, speaking softly so as not to disturb the others. Goll and Muluk came by and stopped for a moment, only to later retire for the night. Shan appeared and marveled at the work Ajik had done, sparing Brozz the telling of how the aloof little armorer had saved his life.

And when all the stories had been told and the surprises revealed, sleep finally overtook the three men, and they all left for their beds.

Junger lay back and stared at the dark ceiling, processing the news from the villa.

In time, he closed his eyes.

40

Nordish Front

In his personal darkness, Tubrius drifted, aware of being moved at times, even hearing noises before sinking back into unconsciousness. He felt no pain, no discomfort. Twice, he collided with something but had no idea what before he went under again. Time was meaningless, but at some point, the sensation of rising overcame him, accompanied by an odd sound, a very odd sound. After a moment, he recognized what it was, and when he did, he opened his eyes.

Metal, stained by mud and blood—an iron plate belonging to a Sujin's armor. Rain spattered it. The same rain stung his cheek, and he cringed at the contact—only for a heartbeat, however, as the warm water returned him to his senses. He shook his head, took the ache shooting through his skull, and relaxed. It was daytime, and storm clouds hid the sky. He realized he was lying in a puddle, on his side, and the Sujin with his back to him wasn't moving. His hands were tied tightly behind his back, preventing him from wiping his face. A set of muddy boots lay just above his head, and another man was at his feet, as if they were all standing on each other's shoulders.

Axes, several axes, chopped nearby with no rhythm to the noise.

He heard the sound of pulling then, a clamor of activity interrupted by the odd scream.

And voices muttered amongst themselves in a tongue Tubrius didn't immediately recognize.

Nordish.

"What's happening?" he croaked, needing water. The ache at the back of his head pulsated into a blare. He cringed, ignored the dirty puddle at his cheek, and turned toward the rain. He lapped down what he could and tried to think past the hurt of his head.

"What's happening?" he asked again after wetting his throat.

No reply.

Tubrius drew his knees to his waist, gazing at the back of the Sujin before him. With a little twisting, he rolled onto his belly and managed to get his legs under himself.

His head hurt badly. Bad enough that he took time to compose himself for the next part, which would be difficult, for he still wore his armor.

Grunting, straining, and ignoring the odd pressure buzzing around the back of his skull, he lifted himself from the wet ground. He gasped at the puddle of watery blood he was lying in. The next sight stunned him into silence.

The valley he remembered had changed. Under black curls of smoke that rose and pressed into storm clouds, men worked and strained, pulling bodies toward bright bonfires that burned despite the rain. Fires lit up the valley, and figures moved about them. Tubrius blinked at the nearest blaze, where a pair of armored men strained and heaved a headless corpse into the flames.

"Seddon," Tubrius whispered, realizing what had happened.

The Nordish had been victorious.

Through the smoke and the falling rain, soldiers teemed over the slope, disposing of the dead. Wagons piled high with bodies were pulled toward the pyres. Arms and legs sticking out from those masses flopped with every jarring rut in the land. Horses strained with the loads while wheels and leather squealed and creaked. Hundreds of soldiers worked, piling carcasses high as though stacking stones. A few men walked past the wagons, their hands filled with hairy baubles. Tents had been erected on the Sunjan side in areas cleared of the dead. Grim sentries stood watch, positioned at regular intervals all along the edges of the new encampment. Helmets stared on while spears were raised and ready.

The Nordish Ikull rested upon the far side of the valley, away from the bonfires that dotted the land once occupied by Sunjans. The enemy covered the area like a huge slab of scorched metal. Tubrius still wasn't sure if he was seeing the entire force or just a portion, if this was all that remained or if the Nords had sent on an advance guard. The sight robbed Tubrius of speech as his thoughts blurred into a wall of fog.

"What's happening?" his voice rasped, and he immediately cringed at the pain in his head.

He looked at the men surrounding him and gasped—dead. Some more so than others, with their heads either removed entirely or their bodies mutilated by sword chops or axe blows.

Metal clattered, accompanied by an angry string of Nordish syllables. Tubrius jerked around at the sound. Behind him, approaching with a short spear that possessed a broad, serrated blade, was a figure wearing heavy plate armor. Spikes jutted from the shoulder pauldrons. A conical helm, black eyed with a grinning grill beneath, nodded at the survivor. Similar guards, poised around the patch of corpses, turned and studied the lone Sunjan on his knees. Tubrius ignored them, focusing on the menacing soldier with the evil-looking spear.

Grinder, he realized. He was looking at the heavy infantry of the Ikull. They were all Jackals in eyes of Sunja, but like the military Tubrius was a part of, the Nordish army was comprised of several distinct groups with different names and functions.

The soldier stopped two strides away and whipped the butt of his spear across the Right Koor's face. Tubrius crumpled onto a nearby corpse. Dazed, he squirmed and twitched as the Grinder's shadow fell across him, and the stink of burning meat and metal filled his nose. The tip of the serrated spear appeared over Tubrius's right eye, close enough to reveal scratches along the blade. Beyond that dreadful point, the Nordish visor smiled and stared.

The spear suddenly jerked back for one deep, killing thrust.

An angry line of Nordish words stayed the Grinder's spear. The black eye slots above the grinning grillwork seemed to think for a moment, but eventually, the spear withdrew to a foot away from Tubrius's face. Metal clanked and clattered. A second armored figure approached. As Tubrius's senses returned, he heard a curt but firm exchange between the new arrival and the Grinder. The pair argued for a short time before the second man dismissed the soldier with a wave of his hand.

Helmet shaking, the spear-wielder retreated a few steps away, keeping his helmet's deep black eye holes upon Tubrius. The Grinder motioned for Tubrius to rise.

Doing so took a few tries as Tubrius was still somewhat dazed and had his hands bound behind his back, but he finally managed to stand. The pain of his head subsided, however, replaced by that of having his face whipped by the spear. Casting dour looks at the surrounding dead and then the intimidating living, he settled upon the figure that had momentarily saved his life.

A Jackal waited, wearing a black cloth mask, the kind signifying the lighter, more mobile infantry of the Ikull. Overlapping metal rings covered a light leather cuirass, while bracers and greaves protected the limbs. Filth stained the figure, as if he'd been rolling about in soot. A short sword filled a scabbard set across the man's waist. The Jackal watched him through the mask's narrow cut for the eyes, and Tubrius detected impatience there.

The Jackal started walking, motioning for him to follow.

Tubrius hesitated until three Grinders surrounded him and got him moving. The Nordish soldiers herded him through droves of dead. Tubrius saw Sunjans, both military and civilian, as well as the bloody corpses of Paw Savages. Several groups of living Paws were there as well, working, piling their own dead into fleshy cairns of white. Nordish did not walk amongst the Paws, but wary sentries stood back, letting the tribesmen work, confirming at least an uneasy alliance between the two. Blood found his eyes, turning his vision into a smear. Tubrius stumbled to a knee, grimaced, and rose again with a spear poised at his head.

That he could see.

Blinking hard, he walked on, still unable to see details clearly. In short time, the four Nords delivered him to a small group of survivors, mostly battle-weary, unarmed soldiers still wearing their armor. Tubrius didn't see any Sujin, only a few Lancers, regular horsemen, archers, and spearmen. Perhaps over fifty or more were there, all on their knees. They watched the disposal of the dead. A fence of Grinders, appearing as shadowy statues, surrounded them.

The masked Jackal pointed at a spot nearby. The Right Koor hesitated, unsure what was being asked of him. One of the spearmen cracked him across the back of his legs, driving him to the ground.

Since Tubrius had been delivered, the four moved off, leaving him and the others under the close watch of the heavy infantry and their conical helms.

"What's going on?" he asked those closest.

"Shaddup," one man warned from the side of his mouth. He wore the leather belonging to a Sunjan archer. "They'll kill you. I've seen it done."

"I'm Right Koor—"

"You'll be *meat* if you don't shaddup," the soldier responded tersely.

Tubrius quieted and lowered his head, composing himself and still working on clearing his eyesight.

Prisoner, he thought. *They've taken us prisoner.*

The sounds of chopping continued, and he realized it was much closer now. Tubrius struggled to see through the collection of battered soldiers surrounding him, but then his eyesight cleared. There, just beyond the prisoners, were a dozen or so Nordish men, stripped to the waist, swinging axes downward, except there were no trees. A few captured Sunjans shifted and obscured matters, drawing Tubrius's ire. Blood seeped into his eye again, skewing his vision, and he struggled to blink away the mess.

Through the shifting heads and shoulders, enough space cleared, enough to clearly see the Nordish men wielding heavy axes. Dread rose in Tubrius's gullet as he feared a mass execution. He remembered the Field of Skulls then and wondered if the Nordish were working on a second field. They worked hard, hacking at unseen objects at their feet. Other Nords moved in and out of the scene, as did the prisoners, further frustrating Tubrius.

But then a space cleared again, and he saw.

The Nords were indeed busy, decapitating dead men and gathering the heads, which they then tossed into a waiting wagon. The Nordish soldiers worked over chopping blocks, where they collected their gruesome harvest. Once the heads were removed, workers lugged the bodies away while others brought in more dead men to be processed. Axemen stood in reserve behind the choppers, waiting for their turns when their companions grew weary. It was all very efficient.

Tubrius realized then what his and the other prisoners' fate would be.

But that idea felt untrue. None of the Sunjan prisoners surrounding him were being taken to that grisly work area. They were being guarded but not dragged off to a chopping block, and the souls having their heads removed were already clearly dead. Nords carried them to the axemen without struggle. Some bodies dripped gore to the ground, while others were missing limbs.

The pain at the back of his head returned and reached his eyes. Tubrius winced and bowed, waiting for it to end. When he lifted his head, a pair of Nords stood before the group of prisoners. One wore the cloth mask belonging to the Jackals' light infantry, and while the other did not wear a mask, he still wore their armor. The black mask was addressing the prisoners, his words low, while the unmasked man translated the speech into well-spoken Sunjan, surprising the Right Koor.

"—a mistake your commanders should have foreseen. In any case, that was the end of your mighty . . . Klaws," the translator said without emotion.

The masked man spoke at length then, droning on in his unintelligible tongue, gesturing at times with a quick lift of the chin or a sweep of his hand. When he stopped, the translator resumed.

"You see the work being done around you. It's none of your concern. You few have been selected for a different fate. As I've mentioned, we've allied ourselves with the honorable and noble Paw tribes inhabiting these deep forests. Once we communicated our intent to kill every last Sunjan soldier occupying their land—land that once was theirs—they were quite willing to help us. At a cost, however—one that I will tell you shortly."

Indicating he'd finished, the translator looked at the masked Jackal, who again rattled on at length.

"While the Paw delight in killing Sunjans, we've managed to convince them of having some sport with you. You will be released, shortly, and allowed to run, to run as fast and as hard as you're able. Sunja's walls are that way." The man pointed. "Perhaps three or four weeks travel? You know better than I. You will be released—without armor, without weapons." The unmasked man stopped and listened to the black cloth for a few heartbeats before speaking again. "After you've been released, you will have a short time to escape this place, to run anywhere you wish. When the Paw have decided enough time has passed, they will pursue you."

With that, the unmasked man pointed to his right.

Tubrius and the other prisoners looked upon a large group of Paw Savages assembling just beyond the wagons full of heads. At least a hundred of the war-painted tribesmen, perhaps even two hundred, were carrying their usual weapons: crude spears, war clubs, bows, and hand axes. More than a few possessed weapons fashioned by a civilized hand. As Tubrius eyed the savages with growing horror, their numbers swelled beyond two hundred white-painted warriors, perhaps closer to three. They waited in a quiet, contemplative mob, their blackened eyes gazing upon the Sunjan prisoners.

A powerful vibe emanated from the tribesmen, one of palpable, primal hatred, along with an unspeakable desire to make the Sunjans' deaths as grisly and painful as possible. The mob projected that craving for extreme violence onto the prisoners. The Paw Savages didn't move, didn't break ranks like the pack of primitives of lore. They sat and watched, content to wait, exhibiting a patience Tubrius thought disturbing.

One of those white-painted savages approached the pair of Nordish soldiers. He was a short man, sinewy, and walking with the aid of a short Sunjan spear, his fist clasped just below the blade's head. The black mask turned and bowed to the Paw Savage. The Paw didn't return the gesture, but he did nod, a curt, bestial motion that gave away his feelings about the Nordish proceedings. With an expression of dangerous indifference, the Paw then scrutinized the prisoners.

The masked Jackal spoke in a different tongue then, and the Paw responded. They talked for a short time, and then the masked man gestured to the translator.

"They will hunt you. Out there. The Paws hate you with an intensity that is truly remarkable. And most unsettling. They look forward to hunting you in their forests. Their leader has described all manners of excruciating death for those unfortunate enough to be caught alive. We actually considered giving you some weapons, just to make things more sporting, but we decided against it. You are Sunjans, after all, soldiers taken from the once mighty five Klaws. I'm certain you will adapt to your situation and provide your Paw hunters with some measure of entertainment. Each breath you take now? Enjoy them. Treasure them."

The masked man spoke again.

TO THUNDEROUS APPLAUSE

"If one of you does in fact escape the Paws and reach Sunja," the translator explained, "or a group of patrolling soldiers, tell them what you've seen here this day. Tell them of the Klaws' defeat. Warn them."

At that, the masked man pointed toward a fence of freshly cut poles being planted into the ground by Nordish soldiers. As soon as the first pole was firmly set, a decapitated head was spiked atop it.

Tubrius forgot about his pain. His stomach dropped, and his mouth went dry.

A second pole was worked upon, then a third. More Nords joined in the work, creating a gruesome spectacle upon the valley slope.

The translator carried on stoically. "Tell them this fate awaits all people of Sunja. A pole for every soldier, every citizen, when the Ikull comes for their city."

Silence, then, allowed the prisoners time to fully understand what was about to happen.

"I do not pity your fate. If you die out there in the forest, it will be horrible. If you survive the Paws' hunt, the horror will be even greater when the Ikull arrive before your walls and we finish . . . what we've started here today."

Prisoners glanced over their shoulders. Tubrius looked as well though it hurt him immensely to do so. There, at the corners of the group, Nordish soldiers moved. One was cutting a prisoner's bonds while others stood with weapons ready, in case the freed man decided to flight.

"Do not think of fighting us," the translator droned on coldly. "If you die here, you lessen the chances of alerting your city of our approach. You are honor bound to do that."

Prisoners stood, glaring at their Nordish captors before glancing fearfully at the unmoving force of Paw Savages. The Jackal freeing the Sunjans gestured for them to run. Rubbing their wrists, the prisoners reluctantly did just that, running toward the forest edge, through a channel of assembled Grinders. In twos and threes, the prisoners were released.

"Run," the translator commanded imperiously. "Run. Do not linger. To do so means only a quick capture by your Paw hunters. Do I truly need to describe what will happen to you if that happens?"

The freed men ran.

The Nords releasing the prisoners made their way to where Tubrius waited. One after the other, Sunjans stood and staggered away, gaining speed before disappearing inside the foliage. A sour stink of unwashed bodies enveloped the Right Koor then as the Jackals reached him.

Someone spoke a stream of Nordish words that Tubrius couldn't understand. The Jackals spoke for a short time before finally cutting the rope around his hands. Tubrius pulled his hands to his chest and rubbed his wrists, coaxing blood to flow. Leery of his captors, he slowly got to his feet.

Only to have the world spin and tip.

Tubrius dropped to his knees, his stomach flooding with sickness. He placed his face into the damp earth and breathed, gulping down air, pushing back the nausea crippling him. Figures moved past him, and more prisoners were released. Nordish words cut the air, but the stricken Tubrius couldn't care less. He closed his eyes, hoping that would stop the world's spinning.

A presence fell over him. Tubrius looked up into the face of the translator, who studied him with great interest.

"How is it you're still alive, Sunjan?" the translator asked, wonder in his voice.

"Give me a blade, and I'll show you," Tubrius whispered.

"Ha. No. I don't think so. But you're clearly unwell. I don't think the Paws' game is suited for you. Not in your condition."

"I'll run," Tubrius said and pushed himself to his knees. There he remained, however, as the effort drained him of strength. In between gasps, he realized then that he was the only Sunjan remaining and that all the other prisoners had fled into the forest. A growing audience of spiked heads stared back at him, filling the valley slope, and Tubrius grimaced in return.

"You shouldn't be here," the translator said and stepped closer, inspecting Tubrius's head. "The guards say you were among the dead and decided to move you here. I don't know what they were thinking. They have eyes as well as I do."

Faces, dead faces. Rows of them atop of crude poles. Some faces had their eyes open, some were shut. Tongues protruded. Some heads were cleaved in two, while others had clumps of dark matter dangling from their necks. Tubrius inspected them all until one face drew his attention and held it completely. A disappointed sigh left him.

Though a blade had chopped a meaty wedge through the upper part of the skull, splashing his wispy hair and face in blood, Tubrius could not mistake the wide-eyed stare belonging to Jusek. The Second Klaw Commander's shocked expression jumped out from amongst the growing collection, and Tubrius looked away for fear of recognizing another companion decapitated and spiked nearby.

"Easy, now," the translator said and stepped closer to the kneeling Sunjan. The translator's hand reached out as if to caress Tubrius's face. "Easy. Do not move. Fascinating. I've been a soldier a very long time, much longer than the actual years, in fact. I've seen all manner of battlefield mysteries and oddities, and you, by far, are the most . . . recent."

The hand reached behind Tubrius's ear. The translator shifted, obscuring Jusek's head for a moment before coming into view again, allowing him to see his dead commanding officer once again.

And Jusek was staring back at him.

Against a sky of nightmarish red, the eyes blinked with impossible life, and the mouth worked as if struggling to speak. All the while, fingers picked at the Tubrius's skull, carefully, daintily, as if fearful of blemishing the most delicate of petals. Even more disturbing, he could *feel* things back there. Tiny sections were peeled back, and cold air caressed skin. At times, he felt as if an exceptionally large spider was crawling through his hair.

Tubrius's eyes fluttered.

"Ah," the translator said, his features becoming a powdery white. "He feels it now."

Tubrius's mouth dropped open as the sound of burning wood crackled in his ears. The translator's skin had turned gray and stretched over his skull, tight enough to outline the bone lurking underneath. The translator's lips dissolved into teeth, and the teeth dissolved into black nubs before spilling from the crevice of a disdainful leer. He did not seem to mind, as his attention remained fixed upon Tubrius's skull.

A whooping rose over the noise of crackling wood, and beyond the transforming countenance of the Nordish man, the Paw Savages rushed toward the forest wall. Tubrius gawked as they flashed by the translator's back. The translator paid them no mind, however, still fascinated by whatever he was picking at. The Paws streaked past him while the sky darkened to even greater depths of red. The forest blackened as if scorched. The tribesmen became ghosts.

And during those dreamlike moments of time, Tubrius painfully, hesitantly, reached back, his hand brushing against that belonging to the translator, whose face had become a fleshless skull with empty eye cavities. The Koor stopped breathing as his fingers felt chunky pieces of smashed skull, held in place by a pliable gum of hair and skin and dried blood. He explored further, beyond those shifting bone fragments, discovering a deep concave impression at the back of his head, as if it had been crushed like a hard-boiled egg.

The translator withdrew his hand and smiled, waiting for a reaction.

Tubrius remembered flashes of being captured, of having his hands bound behind his back and being herded into a group of other captured Sunjans. He remembered being pushed from behind by a Nord, a touch too hard, resulting in him springing to his feet.

That was when the Nord struck him, hard enough to drive him to the ground with enough force to break his skull, and all went black. They left him for dead . . . but not quite dead enough.

A battlefield oddity.

The Paw Savages continued to surge past the translator in a blizzard of white. The Nordish man waited with a skeletal smile. Tubrius's hand dropped from his head, his fingers dripping.

"Now you know," the translator said, his words stretching into echoes. The sun dropped from the sky, and the ground became a river of sludge where everything stuck fast.

"Have no fear," spoke the thing before Tubrius. "We'll spare you from the Paw. Though . . . you will share Sunja's fate."

Tubrius gawked.

There was a surreal swish of metal.

Just before an axe swiped his head from his shoulders.

About the Author

Keith C. Blackmore is the author of the Mountain Man, 131 Days, and Breeds series, among other horror, heroic fantasy, and crime novels. He lives on the island of Newfoundland in Canada. Visit his website at www.keithcblackmore.com.

JOIN THE FELLOWSHIP

follow us on our socials

 podiumentertainment.com
 @podiumentertainment
 /podiumentertainment
 @podium_ent
 @podiumentertainment

www.ingramcontent.com/pod-product-compliance
Ingram Content Group UK Ltd.
Pitfield, Milton Keynes, MK11 3LW, UK
UKHW041304180426